New Year Heroes

CARLA CASSIDY

DELORES FOSSEN

MALLORY KANE

Mills & Boon, an imprint of Harlequin (UK) Limited, Eton House, 18-24 Paradise Road, Richmond, Surrey TW9 1SR

NEW YEAR HEROES © Harlequin Books S.A. 2013

The publisher acknowledges the copyright holders of the individual works as follows:

The Sheriff's Secretary © Carla Cassidy 2008
Veiled Intentions © Delores Fossen 2004
Juror No.7 © Mallory Kane 2007

ISBN: 978 0 263 90444 4

009-0113

Harlequin (UK) policy is to use papers that are natural, renewable and recyclable products and made from wood grown in sustainable forests. The logging and manufacturing processes conform to the legal environmental regulations of the country of origin.

Printed and bound in Spain
by Blackprint CPI, Barcelona

The Sheriff's Secretary

CARLA
CASSIDY

Carla Cassidy is an award-winning author who has written more than one hundred books for Mills & Boon.

Carla believes the only thing better than curling up with a good book to read is sitting down at the computer with a good story to write. She's looking forward to writing many more books and bringing hours of pleasure to readers.

Prologue

It had been easier than he'd expected. He drew a deep breath to calm the rush of adrenaline he'd sustained for the past hour and a half.

As the adrenaline eased, a new sense of euphoria flooded his veins. He'd done it. He'd actually managed to pull it off. All the months of planning had finally paid off.

To assure himself of his success, he walked across the shack's wooden floor and opened the slat in the door that offered him a view into the small room.

They were both still out, unconscious on the mat where he'd placed them when he'd carried them in from the boat. Billy had been easy. He probably weighed no more than fifty pounds.

Jenny had been more difficult. He'd struggled beneath her dead weight, not wanting to drop her into the gator-infested water that surrounded the shack.

They were out, but soon the drugs would wear off and they'd wake up and know they were trapped. They wouldn't know who had taken them or why they were here. And then the fear would begin.

Although, on the outside, the shack looked as if a stiff breeze could blow it over and into the murky waters of Conja Creek, that appearance was deceiving.

He'd spent the past month making sure the small interior room was strong and secure, like a fortress, not to keep people out but rather to keep people in. It was the perfect place for, when they woke, when they began to scream for help, there would be nobody to hear them but the gators and the fish.

He checked his watch, then closed the slat with a sigh of satisfaction. They had all the basic necessities they needed to survive until he returned here. But now it was time for him to go.

Minutes later he lowered himself into his boat. It would take him nearly an hour to maneuver through the maze of waterways half-choked with vegetation.

He didn't mind the time it would take. He'd use it to think about Sheriff Lucas Jamison, the golden boy who had it all. He tightened his hands on the boat's steering wheel. Sheriff Lucas Jamison, the confident know-it-all, the town's favorite son, the man who looked at him like he was nothing. Right now Lucas was the town's favorite son, but soon he would know what it was like to be terrified.

Chapter One

Mariah Harrington wasn't worried when she got home from work and found her eight-year-old son and her roommate missing. It was a gorgeous late-summer afternoon, and odds were good that Billy and Jenny had walked to the nearby park to enjoy an hour or so of outdoor fun. Jenny's car was in the driveway, so Mariah knew they couldn't have gone far.

She threw her keys on the kitchen table, stepped out of her navy high heels and opened the refrigerator to look for the can of soda that she'd hidden the night before in the vegetable bin. No chance Billy or Jenny would look in there. They both shared the same abhorrence for anything green and good for them.

Smiling as she carried the cold can into the living room, she thought of her son and her roommate. It was hard to believe how much an eight-year-old and a twenty-five-year-old could have in common. But in many ways Jenny was as much child as adult.

Of course, that came from being raised by an overly protective, domineering brother. Her smile fell away as she thought of Sheriff Lucas Jamison.

As the mayor's secretary, she often found herself acting as a buffer between the hardheaded Lucas and the ineffectual mayor of Conja Creek. But it wasn't her job that made her want to keep her distance from the handsome-as-sin sheriff.

There was a touch of judgment in his dark eyes and a command to his presence that made her think of dark days in her past—a past she'd finally managed to escape.

It had been Lucas who had approached her about renting a room to his younger sister. He'd thought Mariah would be a good influence on flighty, immature Jenny.

She popped the top of her soda and took a long swallow. She'd agreed to the idea of a roommate because financially it made sense and because the house was big enough that they could live together without being in each other's pockets.

Jenny had moved in two months ago. Mariah had found her to be charming but lacking in confidence, thanks to too much older brother and not enough life experience. It was an added benefit that Jenny and Billy had taken so well to each other. There were a lot of young women Jenny's age who wouldn't want to bother with an eight-year-old boy.

Mariah unfastened her hair from the neat ponytail at the nape of her neck and slithered her hands through the thick curls to massage her scalp. Then she leaned her head back against the sofa and released a deep, weary sigh.

It had been a long day. She was not only Mayor Richard Welch's secretary, she was also part therapist, errand runner and mommy to the man. Things were particularly hectic now with the mayoral election coming in less than three months. When Richard had won the election that had made him mayor, he'd run unopposed. This election he was facing two worthy opponents.

Checking her watch, she figured she had twenty minutes or so to sit and relax before she needed to make supper. Billy and Jenny would be back by six. They were never late for a meal.

She must have fallen asleep, for when she opened her eyes again the room held the semidarkness of late twilight. For a moment she was disoriented as to the day and time as she stared around the neat living room.

As sleep fell away, she remembered it was Friday night and she'd been waiting for Billy and Jenny to get home from the park. She checked her watch, the first faint alarm went off in her head. Almost seven. They should have been home an hour ago.

She pulled herself off the sofa and walked to the front door, trying to ignore the small niggle of worry that whispered in the back of her brain.

"They've been late once before," she whispered aloud, as if the audible sound of that thought could ease her concern. The last time, they'd found a stray dog caught in some brambles in the wooded area next to the park. It had taken them hours to calm the frightened mutt and get him untangled.

Mariah opened the door, stepped onto the front porch and looked in the direction of the park, hoping to see them hurrying toward the house with a tale of adventure to share. She saw nobody except Roger Olem, three doors down, watering his flowers.

In another half hour or so it would be full dark.

The humid evening air, redolent with the scent of flowers and sunshine, enveloped her as she left the porch and headed down the sidewalk in the direction of the park. As she made her way, she marveled at the happiness she'd found here.

She'd never meant to make Conja Creek, Louisiana, her home. It had simply been a blip on her road map when she'd left Shreveport on her way to anywhere.

It had taken only a single night spent at a local bed-and-breakfast to make her fall in love with the small, quaint bayou town.

She'd just about given up on happiness before landing here. Eight months ago, life had been about survival, but now she was a respected part of the community, and Billy was happier than she'd ever seen him.

She quickened her pace as the park came into view. If they were here, then she needed to have a talk with Jenny about making sure they got home on time when they decided to leave the house for a little fun.

Her heart dropped a bit when she saw that nobody sat on the swings or climbed on the jungle gym. The only person she saw in the park was one of her neighbors, Rosaline Graham who, since her husband's death, often spent the hours between dinner and bedtime sitting on a park bench.

"Hi, Rosaline," Mariah called to the old woman. "I don't suppose you've seen my son or Jenny Jamison lately, have you?"

She shook her head. "Sorry, honey. I just got here a few minutes ago, but I sure haven't seen them."

The alarm bells that had just been whispering

through Mariah's head suddenly pealed so loudly she could barely hear anything else.

Maybe they'd chosen another way home. Maybe they were there right now wondering where *she* was. She started back toward home. After several steps she broke into a run, telling herself not to panic. It wasn't as if it were the middle of the night. It was only about seven-thirty.

But when she got back to the house, there was still no sign of them. The phone had no messages, and the panic that had tried to take hold of her now grasped her with both hands.

She pulled out her address book and grabbed the phone. The reason Billy had been home today and not at his babysitter's was because he'd awakened with a sore throat. Maybe Jenny had taken him to the doctor's office.

The fact that Jenny's car was in the driveway didn't matter. From Mariah's house it was a short walk to Main Street, where Dr. Ralph Dell had his offices.

Her fingers shook as she punched in the phone number. Normally Mariah was the last to panic, and even though she thought there was surely a logical explanation for Billy and Jenny's absence, she couldn't help the swell of inexplicable fear that filled her chest.

By nine o'clock she had called everyone she knew to call. Friends, neighbors and schoolmates of Billy's. None of Billy's friends had seen him that day, nor had anyone seen Jenny.

She'd been reluctant to call Lucas, knowing that if Jenny and Billy came home and nothing was seriously wrong, Lucas would reprimand Jenny for the next week for worrying her.

But now she had no choice. With each minute that passed, the disquiet she'd felt since waking from her unexpected nap raged into full-blown fear.

She punched in the number for the sheriff's office, unsurprised when Lucas himself answered the call. "Sheriff Jamison." His deep, self-confident voice instantly commanded respect.

"Sheriff, it's Mariah Harrington. Have you by any chance seen Jenny or Billy today?"

"No. Why?" His voice held a sudden intensity and she could see him in her mind. The tight jaw, the disapproving line trekking across his forehead, the thin press of his lips.

"I'm sure there's a logical explanation, but I've been home since five-thirty and they aren't here." Although she tried to maintain her composure, her voice cracked and tears suddenly stung her eyes.

"I'll be right there." He didn't wait for her to reply.

Mariah hung up the receiver then walked back to the front door and stared outside, watching the night shadows as they moved in to steal the last of the day.

Fear clawed up the back of her throat as she realized that within fifteen minutes or so it would be night. Where was Jenny? And, dear God, where was her son?

LUCAS JAMISON climbed into his car and headed for the Harrington home, already forming the words to the lecture he'd deliver to his sister when he saw her.

God bless that girl, he thought. Sometimes she just didn't use the brains that she'd been born with. She'd probably taken Billy for ice cream, or decided to get him a burger at the café and had neglected to leave a note.

He just hoped this little escapade didn't screw up the living arrangement with Mariah. When Jenny's last boyfriend had broken up with her, she'd not only lost the man she'd believed was the love of her life but also her living space. She'd refused to move back to the family home with Lucas and had bunked on a girlfriend's sofa for a couple of weeks.

It had been Lucas who approached Mariah about Jenny renting a room from her. He knew Mariah was a widow, alone with her son, and lived in a big enough house that a renter might not be a problem.

But that wasn't the real reason he'd approached the mayor's secretary.

Despite being only twenty-nine years old, Mariah carried herself like a much older, much more mature woman. No-nonsense and with cold blue eyes that could freeze a man in his path, she could potentially have the steadying effect on Jenny that Lucas had never managed. Or so he hoped.

"Jenny, what have you done this time?" he muttered as he pulled up to the curb in front of the Harrington house. He hadn't even turned off the engine before Mariah flew out of the house.

Her chestnut hair, normally pulled back in a tight ponytail, sprung in wild curls around her petite features, making her look far younger than she appeared when she was at her desk in the mayor's office.

He didn't have to ask if Jenny and Billy had shown up. The answer to the unspoken question shone from Mariah's worried blue eyes.

"I'm glad you're here," she said, her usually cool, composed voice holding a telltale tremble.

"I'm sure there's nothing to worry about," he said as he fell into step with her and headed back toward the house. "If I know my sister, this is all just some crazy misunderstanding, and she and Billy are probably down at the café eating pie or star-watching down at the park."

"I've been to the park. They weren't there." She opened the front door and ushered him into the small entryway. When she turned to face him, her eyes flashed with a touch of impatience. "And I haven't known your sister as long as you have, but I know her well enough to know that she wouldn't just take off with Billy and not let me know where they are. Something's wrong. Something is terribly wrong."

She might think she knew Jenny, but Jenny had obviously been on her best behavior since moving in here. "You mind if I look around?" Lucas asked. In the two months that Jenny had lived here he'd only been as far as the front porch. Jenny had insisted that this was her space and she didn't want him checking up on her. He tightened his jaw. Obviously *somebody* needed to check up on her.

"Please, be my guest," Mariah said. "I've already looked in Jenny's room to see if she might have left a note for me there, but I didn't find one."

"Which room is hers?"

She gestured down the hallway. "Second door on the right."

She didn't follow him, but instead moved back to the front door as if she could make them appear on the doorstep by sheer willpower alone.

Mariah's house was exactly what he'd imagined it would be—slightly old-fashioned and immaculately clean. As he grabbed the doorknob to Jenny's room he steeled himself for the chaos inside.

He adored his baby sister, but Jenny had always seemed most comfortable in the middle of chaos and drama. He hoped like hell she hadn't orchestrated this to get attention. It was one thing to be a drama queen in your own life. It was quite another to involve an eight-year-old boy.

Her room was actually fairly neat, except the bed hadn't been made and a pair of jeans had been thrown across a chair in the corner. He looked on the night-stand, checked the small desk but found no note, no clue as to where she might have gone with a little boy in tow.

Billy's room was next door. Bunk beds stood against one wall, the lower bunk not made. A small toy box sat beneath a window. Lucas walked to the window and checked it out. The screen was in place and nothing seemed to be amiss.

The third bedroom had to be Mariah's. He opened the door and paused in surprise at the sight of the king-size bed covered with a scarlet spread and plump matching pillows. Fat candles stood on the nightstand, their dark wicks letting him know they weren't just for decoration but were burned regularly.

So, the cool and distant Ms. Harrington had a sensual side. Lucas was surprised by the little burst of heat that filled his stomach at the thought of her in the bed, candlelight stroking her features.

He frowned and shut the door behind him. He flipped open his cell phone and called his office.

"Deputy Ellis," a deep voice boomed.

"Hey, Wally, it's me," Lucas said.

"Hi, boss, what's up?"

"I want you to get a couple of the guys and check out the café, the bowling alley, the movie theater, places like that. I'm looking for my sister."

"Problems?"

Lucas hesitated. "Jenny's late getting back to the Harrington house and we don't know where she is. I wouldn't be so worried, but she's got Mariah's little boy with her."

"Sure, no problem. I'll call you back when we find them."

Lucas tucked his cell phone back into his pocket, then walked back down the hallway.

He found Mariah where he'd left her, standing sentry at the front door. She didn't hear his approach, and he paused at the end of the hallway to study her.

Though she'd been in town for almost a year, he knew almost nothing about her. He'd heard through the grapevine that she was a widow, and he knew she was a formidable barrier he often had to bulldoze through to speak with the dolt who called himself mayor. But he had no idea where she'd come from before she'd landed in Conja Creek.

As he watched, she tapped two slender fingers against the glass door, as if sending an SOS message in Morse code. Standing at the door, peering out into the deepening night, she looked smaller, more fragile than he could have imagined.

A protectiveness surged inside him and he reached out and touched her shoulder. She jumped and whirled around, as if she'd forgotten he was there. "Sorry, I didn't mean to startle you," he said.

"No, I just…" Her eyes darkened to a midnight blue. "Where could they be?"

"Why don't we go into the kitchen. Maybe you could make some coffee while we wait."

"Wait? Shouldn't you be rallying the troops? Getting together a search party?" Her chin rose a notch even as a sheen of tears misted her eyes. "You expect me to just sit and drink coffee while my son is someplace out there in the dark?"

"I've already rallied the troops. I've got my men looking now and yeah, there's nothing much to do but have some coffee and wait." He swallowed a sigh. "Look, Mariah, right now all we know is that Billy and Jenny are late getting home. There's no evidence that a crime occurred, no indication that this is anything more than my sister's thoughtlessness. Maybe she took Billy to a movie and lost track of time. I'm sure she's going to waltz in here before long, and she'll be shocked that you were so worried. Now, how about that coffee?"

She held his gaze for a long moment, then nodded and headed for the kitchen. As she began the coffee preparations Lucas sat at the oak table.

"I thought Billy went to a babysitter on the days you worked in the summer," he said.

"Normally he does, but he woke up this morning with a sore throat. Jenny offered to stay home with him."

"I thought she had those job interviews today." Lucas frowned. He'd been the one to set up the two interviews for his sister for that afternoon.

"She called yesterday and canceled. She didn't feel

like either job was what she was looking for," Mariah explained.

Lucas tamped down an edge of familiar frustration. "Did you speak to Jenny at all today?"

As the coffee began to drip into the carafe Mariah walked over to the table but didn't sit. "I spoke to her around ten this morning." Nervous energy rolled off her as her gaze shot to the kitchen window.

"Did she mention any plans for tonight?"

She focused her gaze back on him, and he saw a desperate fear screaming from the depths of her eyes. "No…nothing. Please, you need to do something. Jenny wouldn't do this to me. Something is wrong."

Lucas looked at his watch. Almost ten-thirty. He hadn't realized how late it had become. For the first time since he'd gotten the call from Mariah, a whisper of deep concern swept through him.

Sure, Jenny had pulled some stunts in the past that had made him want to wring her neck, but he couldn't imagine her pulling this kind of disappearing act with eight-year-old Billy in tow.

She turned back to the counter to pour them each a cup of coffee, but Lucas was suddenly in no mood to sit idle. The fact that his phone remained silent indicated that none of his deputies had run across them. Conja Creek was a small town, and it shouldn't take this long for his men to find her…if she was someplace where she could be found.

He drew a breath of relief as his cell phone rang. He grabbed it from his shirt pocket and flipped it open. "Sheriff Jamison," he said. There was a moment of silence. "Hello?"

"Twinkle twinkle little star, only I know where they are. A game of hide-and-seek we'll play. Let's see if you can save the day." The voice was deep, guttural and sent shock waves through Lucas. Before he could reply, the caller clicked off.

Chapter Two

Mariah saw the blood leave Lucas's face as he checked the caller ID box, then slowly closed his phone and placed it on the table. Rich, raw fear invaded her, chilling her to the bone. She sank into the chair opposite him, afraid her legs would no longer hold her up.

"Did they find them?" Her head pounded with nauseating tension. "Please, tell me. Is he…are they…" She couldn't say the word.

"No! No, that wasn't one of my deputies," Lucas said hurriedly. A muscle ticked in his taut jaw, and for the first time since he'd arrived, she saw a touch of something deep and dark in his eyes. That frightened her as much as anything.

"Then who was on the phone?" She didn't want to know, was afraid of what he was going to tell her, and yet she *had* to know. She drew a steadying breath.

"I don't know who was on the phone. The call shows up as private on the ID. The caller indicated that he has Jenny and Billy and that a game of hide-and-seek has commenced."

She stared at him for a moment, unable to make

sense of his words. Hide-and-seek? That was one of Billy's favorite games. But this wasn't a game. This was something awful. As she tried to absorb what he'd just told her, he called the sheriff's office.

"Wally," he said into his phone. "Get all the men together and meet me at Mariah Harrington's house. We have a situation here."

A situation. Is that what this was? She swallowed against the scream that threatened to rip its way out of her throat. Billy. Where was Billy and who had taken him?

Calm. Stay calm, she told herself. It wouldn't do any good to fall to pieces. She had to stay calm and focused for whatever came next.

"What happens now?" She was surprised by the composure of her voice when inside she was quietly shattering apart.

He rose from the table. "I'll take a closer look around. We can talk to neighbors and see if anyone saw anything here today." His dark eyes gave away nothing of his thoughts.

Did he feel the same panic for his sister as she felt for her son? Oh, God. As the full impact sank in, she began to tremble. "What can I do? Shouldn't I be out asking questions? Looking for him?"

Lucas placed a hand on her shoulder as if to steady her rising hysteria, then returned to his chair in front of her. "Can you tell me if Jenny was seeing anyone in particular?"

She frowned and tried to focus on his question. "You mean dating?" She shook her head. "She was still nursing her wounds from when Phil Ribideaux broke up with her a couple of months ago." She twisted her fingers in her lap. "But, I don't know what she did or who she saw while I was at work every day. Do you think somebody she was seeing might be behind this?"

"I'm not sure what to think at this point." He got up once again. "I'm going to go check around again. We'll find them, Mariah. Try not to worry. We'll find them."

He left her there, and she knew he was going back to Jenny's room. Try not to worry? Was the man insane? She got up from the chair, unable to sit still another minute longer.

Why on earth would somebody want to kidnap Billy? As her mind whirled with suppositions, she realized she didn't want to go there. Too many of the answers were too terrifying.

A sob choked up from the depths of her as she moved to the window and peered outside into the black of night. Billy didn't like the dark. Now he was out there somewhere, being held by someone so he couldn't come home.

Cold. She'd never felt so cold. She squeezed her eyes shut and willed herself to remember every moment of that morning. She'd been in a hurry. She'd overslept and had rushed around to get ready for work.

When she'd awakened Billy, and he'd complained of a sore throat, she'd barely taken time to console him. She'd taken his temperature, which had been normal, had given him a brisk pat on the head, then had left for work knowing Jenny would handle things for the day.

All she wanted to do now was turn back the hands on the clock, somehow retrieve the precious morning. This time, when Billy complained of a sore throat, she would call in to work and take the day off. She'd stay home with her son and make him chicken noodle soup for lunch and peanut butter sandwiches with the crust cut off just the way he liked them.

She'd stay home, and he'd be safe. Another sob escaped her and she pressed her fingers against her lips in an attempt to suppress it.

She turned away from the window and headed to his bedroom. As she entered, the first thing that caught her eye was the inhaler on the nightstand, along with the nebulizer that had gotten Billy through a rough attack on many nights.

She whirled out of the bedroom and bumped into Lucas coming out of Jenny's room. "Lucas, Billy has asthma and they didn't take his inhaler. If he gets stressed or scared he'll have an attack and…" Her voice trailed off, the sentence too horrifying to finish.

"Mariah, what I need from you is a recent photo of Billy." His voice was calm, as if he hadn't heard what she'd just told him.

"Billy has asthma," she repeated.

"I heard you." His dark eyes held her gaze intently. "But we can't do anything about that right now. We have to stay focused on the things we can do. Now, I need a picture of Billy."

Somehow his words penetrated through the veil of despair that threatened to consume her. She nodded, grateful for something, anything to do.

She went to the desk in the living room and grabbed the framed photo that sat on top. It was the school portrait taken last year. She stared at it. Until this moment she hadn't realized how much he'd changed in the past several months. His dark hair was longer than it had been when the photo was taken, and his face was thinner. He'd been missing a front tooth then. Imagining his beautiful little face in her mind once again brought the press of tears to her eyes.

She set the photo back on the desk and began to dig through the top drawer. It suddenly seemed important that she find the perfect picture of her son.

In a frenzy she searched, more frantic with each second that passed. Her fingers finally landed on an envelope of photos she'd recently had developed. She opened the envelope and pulled out the photos.

The most recent one she had of Billy was of him and Jenny together. She picked it up and traced a finger over Billy's dark, unruly hair. His smile was filled with mischief as he grinned into the camera while making horns with his fingers behind Jenny's head.

Jenny's pretty face smiled back at Mariah from the photo, and her heart squeezed tighter. In the two months that Jenny had been living with her, Mariah had come to care about the younger woman a great deal.

"Did you find one?" Lucas came to stand behind her. She could smell his scent, a subtle cologne she always noticed when he came in to see the mayor. Funny how the familiar scent calmed her just a bit. She turned to face him with the picture in her hand.

"You can use this one. It's of Billy and Jenny together."

He took it from her, and she watched him study it. Other than a muscle knotting in his jaw, there was no sign of emotion. Before he could say anything, the doorbell rang and the deputies began to arrive.

A total of five deputies took their orders from Lucas.

They all gathered in the living room. Mariah sat on the sofa, numbed by the events swirling around her as Lucas took control.

"Wally, you and Ben start canvassing the neighborhood, see if anyone saw anything here today," Lucas said. "John, we need recording equipment placed on Mariah's phone in case a ransom call comes in."

Mariah sat up straighter. "Ransom?" Her gaze shot around to each of the men in the room. "But, I don't have any money to speak of."

"If this is about a ransom, I reckon the kidnapper figures Lucas can pay big bucks to get his sister back safe and sound," Deputy Ed Maylor said.

Lucas's jaw once again tightened in his lean face. "Let's just hope if this *is* about a ransom, we get a call soon." He looked at Deputy Louis DuBois. "Louis, I need you to see if you can get into Jenny's e-mail, find out if there's anything weird there. I tried to log on earlier, but she has it password protected."

The tall, thin man nodded. "It shouldn't take me too long to find a way around the protection."

"And what about me?" Deputy Maylor asked.

"Check all the windows and doors, see if you find any evidence of tampering," Lucas replied.

As the men all left to begin their jobs, Lucas joined Mariah on the sofa. To her surprise, he took one of her hands in his and gently squeezed. The warmth of his big hands around her ice-cold fingers felt good. "You doing okay?" he asked.

"No. I want to scream. I want to claw somebody's eyes out." She wanted somebody to hold her, somebody to tell her that everything was going to be fine, that Billy would be back in her arms in a matter of minutes. But Mariah had never had anyone to hold her when she was afraid, to calm her when she was upset.

She released Lucas's hands as she suddenly realized she was going to have to tell Lucas the truth about herself, about her past. She was going to have to confess that her life here in Conja Creek was built on lies.

It was possible Frank had found them, and it was equally possible he'd taken Billy. Jenny could have just been at the wrong place at the wrong time. And even though she knew that telling Lucas would destroy the facade of respectability she'd worked so hard to create, she'd do whatever it took to get Billy back.

"I have to tell you something," she said. "I don't know of anyone Jenny was seeing who might be involved in this, but I know somebody from my past who might be."

Lucas sat up straighter. "Who?"

Mariah clasped her hands together. Even thinking about the man whose name she was about to utter created a knot of new fear in her chest. "His name is Frank Landers, and last I knew he lived in Shreveport."

A deep frown etched across Lucas's forehead as he pulled a notepad and pen from his pocket. "What's his relationship to you and why would he want to kidnap Billy?"

She drew a deep breath. "He's my ex-husband and Billy's father."

LUCAS LOOKED AT HER in surprise. Her ex-husband? "I thought you were a widow, that Billy's father was dead."

Her blue eyes refused to meet his as she stared at her hands in her lap. "That's because I wanted everyone to believe I was a widow. Because I wanted to forget Frank Landers and my marriage to him."

"You need to unforget now," he said with an edge of impatience.

She reached up and twisted a strand of her hair between two fingers. "Frank and I were married for five years. We've been divorced for two. We lived in Shreveport." She dropped her hand to her lap and rubbed her left wrist like an arthritis sufferer feeling a weather front moving in.

"If you've been divorced for two years, why would your ex-husband decide to grab Billy now?" Lucas asked.

She looked at Lucas. Her cool blue eyes betrayed nothing of what might be going on inside her head. "I don't know. It's possible it took him all this time to locate us."

"He didn't know where you and Billy were going when you left Shreveport?"

She shook her head. "*I* didn't know where we were going when we left Shreveport, and I haven't been in touch with Frank since before my divorce."

He was less interested in what she was saying and more intrigued by what she wasn't telling him. "You don't have a custody arrangement with him?" he asked.

"I have full custody."

He waited for her to elaborate, but she didn't. The woman definitely had secrets, but he didn't have time to be curious about her past.

All he cared about was finding Jenny and Billy, and if she thought this Frank Landers might be responsible, then he needed to call the Shreveport police and see if they could locate the man.

"You have an address for him?" he asked.

"I imagine he still lives in our old house." She told him the address and he wrote it down.

"I'll contact the Shreveport police and see if they can hunt him down." Lucas looked at his watch. Almost midnight. Hopefully the authorities in Shreveport could go to Frank's home and find out if he was there. It was a five-hour drive from Conja Creek to Shreveport. Even if Frank was home, he could have taken Billy and Jenny and gotten back by now.

He tried not to think about where Jenny might be. If Frank Landers had come to get his kid, then what had he done with Jenny?

Mariah stood, her entire body taut with tension and her eyes haunted. "If he's taken Billy it isn't because he wants his son. It's because he wants to hurt me."

He'd always looked at Mariah as nothing more than a barrier he needed to get through to see the mayor, a respectable widow who might be a good influence on his flighty, dramatic sister. Now he saw her as neither of those things, but rather as a woman who had apparently suffered some sort of heartache in her past. Lucas knew all about heartache.

"Within an hour we should know if Frank is in Shreveport. In the meantime, why don't you make a fresh pot of coffee? My deputies should be checking in anytime and they'd probably appreciate the caffeine since it's getting so late."

He knew the moment those last words left his mouth that they were the wrong thing to say. She lifted her wrist to check her watch, and her features seemed to crumble into themselves as a sheen of tears filled her eyes.

"Billy has never been away from me this long," she said, but before he could reply she left the living room and disappeared into the kitchen.

The next couple of hours passed in agonizingly slow increments. Lucas called the state police, and an Amber Alert went out. He also spoke to the FBI, who indicated they would have a field agent there the next morning. The deputies checked in with the news that nobody had seen anything suspicious at the home during the day.

"I'm not surprised," Mariah said. "All my neighbors work except Sarah Gidrow across the street, and she spends most of her days watching soap operas in the family room in the back of the house."

They couldn't be sure Mariah's house was a crime scene, which was problematic. There was no sign of a struggle, nothing to indicate that anything untold had happened there. It was possible the crime scene was the front yard, or the park, or a sidewalk a block away.

Jenny's e-mail had yielded nothing to raise an eyebrow, and Deputy Maylor had reported that there was no sign of forced entry or tampering at any of the windows or doors, leaving Lucas to suspect that if the crime *had* happened here, Jenny had opened the door to whomever had taken them.

If they'd really been taken.

It was that particular thought that haunted him as the night hours passed. Were Jenny and Billy really in danger from a kidnapper, or had Jenny orchestrated this whole drama? What better way to get the attention of Phillip Ribideaux, the young man who had recently broken her heart?

Although this was certainly beyond the pale of any stunt Jenny had pulled in the past, he had to admit that it was something he thought she might be capable of doing.

It was in her genes. He had plenty of memories of his mother pulling crazy stunts in an effort to hang on to whatever man happened to be in her life at the time.

He shoved away those thoughts, not wanting to remember the woman who had possessed the maternal instincts of a rock. She'd died when Jenny was twelve and Lucas was twenty-two, and for the past thirteen years Lucas had spent his time raising Jenny and trying to make sure she didn't turn out like Elizabeth, their mother.

Despite the late hour, he began calling Jenny's friends to find out if anyone had spoken to her that day or knew where she might have gone.

Mariah sat on the edge of the sofa and listened to him making those calls. With each minute that passed, the tension that rolled off her increased and her eyes gazed at him with the silent demand that he do something, anything, to bring her baby boy back home.

By three he had nobody else to call, nothing else to do but wait until morning or for another phone call to come in.

"You still aren't sure that they've been taken by somebody, are you?" she asked when he hung up the phone after talking to one of Jenny's girlfriends. There was a touch of censure in Mariah's eyes.

"I have to look at all possibilities," he replied non-committally.

"It must be terrible, to always look for the worst in the people around you."

He eyed her in surprise. There was an edge in her voice that made him wonder if she was trying to pick a fight. He stared at her assessingly.

Even though exhaustion showed in the shadows beneath her eyes and her forehead was lined with worry, somehow she looked lovely. He'd never really noticed before how pretty she was. But she also looked achingly fragile, as if the mighty control she'd exhibited over the past hours might snap at any moment.

"I'm just doing my job," he said, refusing to be drawn into an argument with the mother of a missing eight-year-old. "Why don't you try to get some sleep?" he suggested. "We've done everything we can do for now."

She sighed and swept a hand through her cascade of chestnut curls. "So, we just wait." Her voice was flat, without inflection. It wasn't a question, but rather a statement.

Lucas didn't reply. He knew there was nothing he could say that would make things better for her. There was no way he could tell her that, no matter what happened, he didn't see a happy ending.

If Jenny were responsible for this, then he would have to do his duty and arrest her for kidnapping. If Frank Landers had taken Billy, then what had he done with Jenny? The answers that sprang to his mind chilled his blood. And if somebody had taken Jenny for ransom, then Billy was expendable.

No matter what, Lucas had the terrible feeling that a tragedy lay ahead and there was nothing he could do to stop it from happening.

THE FIRST THING Jenny became aware of was a headache the likes of which she'd never had before. She winced and reached up to grab the back of her pounding head. Slowly, other sensations and impressions began to seep through her mind.

The smell of rotting fish and dampness coupled with the faint sound of water lapping against wood. The sound of insects buzzing and clicking. She opened her eyes and was terrified when she saw nothing but blackness.

Where am I? The question screamed through her head, making it pound with more nauseating intensity. Panic surged inside her as she sat up, fighting back a scream of sheer terror.

Before she could release the scream, a faint whimper sounded from someplace beside her. And with that whimper, memory returned.

She and Billy had been sitting on the sofa watching cartoons. Billy had gotten up to the bathroom…and somebody had come into the house.

One minute she'd been laughing at the antics of the Road Runner, and the next her mouth and nose had been covered with something that must have rendered her almost immediately unconscious.

"Billy?" She tentatively moved a hand and encountered his warm little body next to her.

"Jenny?" He scooted closer to her as another whimper escaped him.

"Are you okay, buddy?" She pulled him against her and wrapped him in her arms. "Are you hurt?"

"My head hurts and I want my mommy."

"I know, honey. But you're going to have to be brave for a little while, okay?"

She felt him nod. "Where is this place?" he asked. "Why did that man bring us here?" Billy's body trembled slightly against her and she thought she detected a faint wheeze in his voice.

With each minute that passed, Jenny's mind grew clearer. "Did you see the man, Billy? Did you see what he looked like?" If she knew who had done this, then maybe she could figure out why.

"He had on a black mask. I tried to run, but then he grabbed me and put something over my face and I guess I went to sleep."

A man with a mask. What was going on? Who had drugged them and brought them here…wherever here was? Once again a scream of terror rose up inside her, but she swallowed against it, knowing that she had to maintain control. She needed to be brave, not for herself but for Billy. If she lost it, that would only frighten Billy more than he already was.

"Somebody took us, Jenny, and I'll bet my mom doesn't know where I am." The wheeze in Billy's voice wasn't just a figment of her imagination.

"Don't be scared, Billy." She reached her hand up to touch his sweaty head, then rubbed the back of her hand against his damp cheek. "Even if your mom doesn't know where we are, my brother will help her find us. You know Lucas is the sheriff. He's very smart and he'll find us in no time." She hoped he believed her.

She certainly wanted to believe her own words. Billy seemed to relax a bit.

"I think it's the middle of the night. Maybe we should both go back to sleep, then we can figure out how to get home in the morning," she said. There was nothing that could be done in the utter darkness that surrounded them.

"Okay." Billy cuddled closer to her and she could tell by his breathing that he went back to sleep almost immediately.

Sleep was the last thing on Jenny's mind as she fought against a fear the likes of which she'd never known. She had no idea what kind of place they were in, was afraid to explore in the blackness that prevailed. She had no idea who had taken them and why.

There was only one thing she was fairly certain of and it didn't take a rocket scientist to realize it. The buzz of insects, the smell of fish and the sound of water all led her to believe they were someplace deep in the swamp.

As she thought of all the miles of waterways, the hundreds of miles of tangled, dangerous swampland that surrounded Conja Creek, a new despair gripped her, and she prayed that her brother would be able to find them before it was too late.

Chapter Three

Lucas pulled into his driveway at six the next morning. His intention was to take a fast shower, then go talk to Phillip Ribideaux to see if the young man had any clue as to where Jenny and Billy might be.

When he'd left Mariah's house, she'd been seated in the same chair where she'd sat for most of the night, staring out the window as dawn slowly arrived. He'd left her in the charge of Deputy Ed Maylor, who would hold down the fort there while Lucas did a little field investigation. Maylor was a good man, bright and eager to get ahead.

The Jamison home was a huge two-story antebellum mansion that sat on five acres of lush lawn. Lucas's father had been sixty when he married his young bride, Elizabeth. He'd made a fortune playing the stock market with his old family money. He'd died when Lucas was eleven and Jenny was just a baby.

Lucas didn't have many father-son memories. His father had spent most of his time either in his office at home or in bed with a heart condition that had eventually killed him. Although Lucas would always believe it had been his mother's demands and histrionics that had killed his old man.

"Have you found them?" Marquette Dupre met him at the door, her black eyes radiating with worry.

"No, I'm just here to take a quick shower then go have a chat with Phillip Ribideaux," Lucas said as he headed for the grand staircase. Marquette followed close at his heels as he headed up to his bedroom suite.

"That boy needs less money and more character, that's for sure," Marquette exclaimed. "You think he knows where Jenny and that little boy is?"

"I don't know." He stopped at the top of the stairs and turned to face the woman who had been the house-keeper for first his parents and now him. "Jenny hasn't said anything to you that I should know about, has she?"

Marquette's tiny face wreathed into something that looked like a prune. "You know better than that. That girl quit confiding in me when she was sixteen and I told you that she sneaked out of the house to meet that boy she had a crush on. How's Mariah doing?"

Lucas walked into his bedroom and sat on the edge of the bed to take off his boots. "I'm not sure how, but she's managing to hold it together."

"That don't surprise me. That's one strong woman. You can see it in her eyes. She's got that cold gator stare. Besides, she'd have to be a strong woman to put up with that boob we elected mayor of this fine city."

Lucas offered her a grim smile, then disappeared into the bathroom. Minutes later, standing beneath a hot spray of water, he did what he'd done through most of the nighttime hours: In his head, over and over again, he replayed the phone message he'd received.

There had been something familiar…not about the voice, which had obviously been disguised, but in the inflection, in the cadence of the words spoken. A kidnapper, or a friend of his sister's working with her to orchestrate drama?

He'd heard from the authorities in Shreveport, who had let him know that Frank Landers no longer lived at the address Mariah had given him. They promised to continue to look for him. He'd called Mariah with the news and she'd been bitterly disappointed that Frank hadn't been found.

Aware of minutes ticking off, he finished his shower and left the bathroom to see a clean, freshly pressed uniform laid out on his bed. Marquette was as handy as a pocket in a shirt.

Minutes later, dressed and with a thermos of fresh coffee, courtesy of his housekeeper, he drove toward Phillip Ribideaux's place. The shower had invigorated him, washing away the exhaustion that had weighed him down as he'd driven from Mariah's house to his own.

He hoped that, while he was hunting down leads this morning, Mariah was getting some much-needed sleep. There was nothing she could do at the moment to help bring her son home, and being exhausted would only make things worse.

He thought of what Marquette had said about Mariah. He'd known she was a strong woman, but through the long hours of the night he'd seen flashes of intense vulnerability. If she had an Achilles' heel it was definitely her son.

His hands tightened on the steering wheel as her

strange words to him echoed in his head. *It must be terrible, to always look for the worst in the people around you.* He had the distinct feeling she'd been talking about his relationship with his sister.

But she didn't really know Jenny. She didn't know the fear Lucas lived with every day—the fear that his sister would turn into another version of their mother and come to the same kind of tragic end.

Phillip Ribideaux lived in a large, attractive house on the outskirts of town. The twenty-eight-year-old had never worked a day in his life and lived off the generosity of his father, a wealthy developer in the area.

He was a party guy with no work ethic and a sense of privilege that Lucas had seen too often in men who came from money. In fact, Lucas himself and four of his then closest friends might have come to the same end had they not made a pact in college to use their wealth to give back to the community.

Lucas hadn't been sad to see the relationship between Ribideaux and Jenny end. Jenny deserved better than a man like Ribideaux.

It was just after seven when Lucas knocked on Ribideaux's front door. Phillip's sleek sports car was parked out front, but the knock yielded no reply. He rapped again, harder and longer this time.

"All right, all right." The deep male voice was full of irritation. Phil opened the door and glared at Lucas. It was obvious he'd been awakened by the knocking. His dark hair was mussed, a pillow crease indented his cheek and he wore only a pair of black silk boxers.

"Morning, Phil," Lucas said. "Can I come in?"

The handsome young man frowned. "Why? What's going on?" He scratched the center of his chest, then stifled a yawn with the back of his hand.

"I need to talk to you."

"Couldn't it wait? Jeez, what time is it?"

"No, it can't wait," Lucas replied.

"Talk about what?" He gazed at Lucas belligerently.

"I'd like to come in. Now, you can invite me inside and we can have a nice, friendly chat or I can come back in a little while with a search warrant and the chat won't be quite so friendly." Lucas kept his voice pleasant and calm, but narrowed his eyes to let Phil know he was dead serious.

With reluctance Phil opened the door to allow Lucas to enter. "Now you want to tell me what's going on?" he asked.

Lucas ignored the question and walked through the foyer and into the living room. He stopped in surprise, noting the moving boxes lining the walls and the lack of furniture. He turned back to face Phil. "Going someplace?"

"I'm moving, not that it's any business of yours," Phil replied.

"Where to?"

"To an apartment in town. Dad sold this place." A flash of anger shone from the young man's eyes. It was there only a moment, then gone. "Look, Sheriff, you want to tell me what this is about? I've got a lot of things to do today and I'm not in the mood for you."

Lucas tamped down a touch of rising anger. "When was the last time you spoke to Jenny?"

Phil visibly relaxed. "Is that what this is about? Your

sister? Whatever she told you, it's probably a lie. I haven't seen or talked to her for a couple of weeks."

"So you don't know anything about her disappearance?"

"Disappearance? Is she missing?"

"Yeah, since last night." Lucas studied Phil's features carefully, but it was impossible for him to discern if the man was lying or not. "So, you haven't seen or heard from her in the last couple of days?"

"Look, your sister's a nice girl and all that, but she was way too intense for me. We'd only been dating a couple of months and she starts talking about marriage and having kids and the whole traditional route. There's no way I'm ready for that, especially right now with everything such a mess."

"Everything such a mess?"

Phil averted his gaze from Lucas. "Private stuff. It has nothing to do with Jenny. I haven't had anything to do with Jenny for weeks, so if we're through here, I've got things to do." His gaze still didn't meet Lucas's.

Without a search warrant, there was little else Lucas could do here, and no judge in his right mind would give Lucas a warrant to search these premises on Lucas's hunch that Phil was hiding something.

"Where exactly is the new apartment?" Lucas asked as Phil walked him back to the front door.

"The Lakeside Apartments for the time being. Apartment 211." Phil grinned, the boyish, charming smile that had managed to get him into the beds of half the young women of Conja Creek. "I'm anxious to get out of this place. Owning a house is way too much responsibility for me."

Minutes later, as Lucas drove back to Mariah's place, he made mental notes to himself. It was obvious that Phil Ribideaux's life was in flux at the moment. Could that have anything to do with Jenny and Billy's disappearance?

Phil had seemed genuinely surprised to hear that Jenny was missing, but he was a smooth operator and Lucas knew the kid could lie without blinking an eye. And he'd definitely been hiding something. Something private, he'd said.

Tension twisted Lucas's gut as he drove. It had been almost twenty-four hours since anyone had spoken to Jenny and Billy, and there wasn't a lead in sight... except for a haunting voice on his cell phone that had promised a game of hide-and-seek.

"Jenny, if you've done something stupid, then please have the courage to undo it now," he murmured aloud. He hated suspecting that his sister had somehow orchestrated all this, but the alternative was far more terrifying.

He pulled his cell phone from his pocket and called Wally, his right-hand man. "Wally, I want you to do a little investigation into Phil Ribideaux. Find out from his friends what's going on in his life, and I want a tail put on him. Get Louis to do it. I want to know everyplace he goes and everyone he talks to."

"Got it," Wally replied. "Anything else?"

"Nothing for now." Lucas clicked off. He had no idea if Ribideaux had anything to do with this, but he definitely knew something was out of whack in the man's life.

As he turned the corner that led to Mariah's house he sucked in a breath. The place looked like a circus.

Cars were parked up and down the street, and the local news crew truck was parked in her yard. Mariah definitely hadn't been sleeping while he'd been gone.

Mayor Richard Welch stood in front of a camera with a reporter, his chest puffed up with self-importance. The man never missed a chance to get his mug in front of the voters.

Unwilling to be part of the mayor's photo op, Lucas skirted the house to the back door. Ed Maylor met him as he walked inside. "I told her you wouldn't like this, but she wouldn't listen to me," he said.

Lucas clapped the young deputy on the back. "It's all right. Why don't you go home, get some sleep. I'll take care of things here."

Maylor nodded and left by the back door. As he walked out, Sawyer Bennett entered the kitchen from the living room. Lucas tensed at the sight of his old friend.

"Sawyer." He nodded in greeting. "You heard?"

"The whole town has heard. You have any leads?"

Lucas shook his head, aware of the tension between himself and the man he'd considered a brother. Regret played deep inside him as he thought of the events that had put a strain on their relationship. Sawyer was one of Lucas's college buddies as well as a lifelong friend, but their relationship had been tested when Sawyer's wife had been murdered and Lucas had had to investigate Sawyer for the crime. Thankfully Sawyer had been innocent, but the strain still lingered. "What are you doing here?"

"I'm here to help. I can put up posters, talk to people, do whatever you need me to do," Sawyer said. Mariah entered the room, interrupting the conversation.

The hopeful look she sent Lucas broke his heart, because he had nothing to tell her that would make her feel any better. The momentary shine in her eyes dimmed. "Nothing?"

"Not yet. It looks like you've been busy while I've been gone."

"I've contacted everyone I can think of to get the word out that my son is missing. Somewhere in this town, somebody has to know what happened or at least have a piece of information that can help us find them." She raised her chin as if expecting a fight from him.

"It was a good idea," he said, and watched the breath ease out of her. She reached out and took Sawyer's hand. "Your friend here has been helping me print off posters from the computer. He's promised to see that they go up all over town." She released Sawyer's hand and instead clutched herself around the waist, as if she were physically holding herself together.

"I'm going to head out now." Sawyer turned his attention back to Lucas. "Anything else I can do?"

"Not that I can think of," Lucas replied.

"I'll just get those posters," Sawyer said to Mariah. Lucas watched his friend head for the door. "Sawyer?" Sawyer turned back to face him. "Thanks."

Sawyer flashed him a smile that spoke of old bonds and years of friendship, and Lucas felt himself relax somewhat.

"I thought maybe you'd get some sleep while I was out," Lucas said to Mariah when Sawyer had left.

"I'll sleep when Billy is home safe and sound," she replied.

Although she hadn't slept, it was obvious she'd

showered and changed her clothes. Her shiny hair was neatly pulled back and held with a ponytail holder at the nape of her neck.

In all the time he'd known her, he'd never seen her in anything casual, but she now wore a pair of jeans that hugged her long slender legs and a sleeveless cotton blouse that was the same shade of blue as her eyes.

The casual clothing suited her, made her look less stern and more approachable and stirred a protective urge inside him that he hadn't felt for a woman in a very long time.

"Most of my neighbors have shown up to put out posters and search," she said as she moved to the coffeemaker on the countertop. "I did an interview with the local news, and they're going to show it this evening on the six-o'clock broadcast."

Their conversation was interrupted as Candy Tanner came into the kitchen. "I thought I heard your voice in here," she said to Lucas. "I need to talk to you about something." She shifted from foot to foot and looked as if she'd rather be anywhere else.

"About what?" Lucas looked at the young woman who was one of Jenny's closest friends. Her gaze shifted away from him, and a new tension rose up inside him. "You know something about what's going on, Candy?"

"No, not really, but I thought I should tell you that I know Jenny has been seeing Remy Troulous," she said.

Blood roared in Lucas's ears as he stared at Candy. "Seeing Remy Troulous? What do you mean? As in dating him?"

"No, I'm sure she wasn't dating him," Candy replied as she took a step back from Lucas. "But I know she had a meeting with him about something last week."

"What in the hell was she doing with Remy Troulous?"

"I don't know." Candy took another step backward. "She wouldn't tell me and she made me promise I wouldn't tell anyone, but I thought you should know." She turned and fled the kitchen as if afraid of Lucas's wrath.

"Who is Remy Troulous?" Mariah asked.

Lucas knew his reply would only add to the terror he knew she already felt for her son. "He's the head of a gang called the Voodoo Priests. He's not a good guy, Mariah."

She stared at him for a long moment. "And it's possible he has my son."

FROM THE MOMENT that dawn had broken, Mariah had felt as if she'd entered an alternate universe. But now, as she stared at Lucas, that universe took on a new nightmarish quality.

"The Voodoo Priests?" she repeated faintly. A new horror swept through her. She watched as he pulled his car keys out of his pocket. "Are you going to find this Remy?"

"I'm going to try."

"Wait, I'm coming with you."

Lucas's frown deepened. "I think it would be better if you stayed here."

His tone held the strong, authoritative note that she'd often heard him use with Jenny, and it sent a ripple of irritation through her. She embraced it, finding it so much easier to handle than the fear that gnawed at her with sharp teeth.

"And I think it would be best if I come with you. If

this Remy has Billy, then he's going to need me, and he's probably going to need his inhaler." She heard the anger that scorched her words and she drew a deep breath to gain control. "Billy is just a little boy. He'll need me."

He stared at her for a long moment, as if assessing his options, then gave her a curt nod. "Get what you need and let's get moving."

She hurried out of the kitchen and toward Billy's bedroom, her heart pounding with the anxious rhythm it had been beating all night long.

The house no longer felt like her home. People milled about, people she had called in the early-morning hours for help. But there seemed to be nothing anyone could do. It was as if a hole had opened up in the earth and swallowed Billy and Jenny whole.

Remy Troulous. What would a man like that want with Billy and Jenny? If their kidnapping was about a ransom, then why hadn't she or Lucas received a call demanding money?

She entered Billy's room and tried not to breathe in the little-boy scent of him that lingered there, knowing that if she dwelled on the smell of her son or the feel of his mouth against her cheek when he kissed her or the sound of his laughter, she'd lose it.

His pajamas were tossed on the bed. She didn't even know what he was wearing. She didn't know what he'd picked out to wear on the day he'd been kidnapped. Tears burned in her eyes, but she sucked them back, grabbed his inhaler, then hurried back to find Lucas getting people out of the house.

She pocketed the inhaler as her boss, Richard Welch,

approached her. He took her hands in his, his brown eyes radiating true sympathy. "Don't you worry about anything at the office," he said. "We'll manage without you until Billy is home safe and sound."

Mariah squeezed his hands. The mayor might be a self-absorbed big fish in a little pond most of the time, but the concern that radiated from his eyes at the moment was very real.

"Thank you, Richard. Hopefully he'll be home soon and things will go back to normal." Normal? Would anything ever be normal again? she wondered.

Lucas joined them, and Richard dropped Mariah's hands and turned to face him. "I trust you'll do everything in your power to find Billy and your sister. After the debacle with Sawyer Bennett and his wife's murder we don't need any more bad press." He frowned. "Murder, and now this kidnapping. Before long, Conja Creek will have a reputation for being a crime pit. We don't want that to happen. I want this tied up as soon as possible."

Lucas eyed Richard as if he were a creature from another planet. "Our goals are the same, Mayor." Lucas's voice radiated his tension.

"You'll keep me informed?" Richard asked.

"Of course," Lucas replied.

"If nothing breaks before tomorrow we'll set up a press conference to ease the concerns of our citizens," Richard said.

Lucas nodded, his irritation with the man obvious in his clenched jaw and narrowed gaze. Mariah touched his arm. "We're wasting time. Shouldn't we be going?" All she wanted was to find the man who might have her son.

"Absolutely," Lucas replied.

With Deputy Ben Rankell left at the house to man the phone and encourage people to leave, Lucas and Mariah walked outside. The brilliant sunshine burned her eyes as they headed for his car. The night of worry and no sleep weighed heavily on her shoulders, but she shoved the exhaustion away.

"I'll never understand how that man managed to get elected," Lucas said as he started his engine.

"Because underneath all his posturing and grand-standing is a good heart," she replied. "He cares about Conja Creek." She didn't want to talk about Lucas's issues with the mayor, which as far as she was concerned rose out of the fact that each man attempted to control the other. "Tell me about Remy Troulous," she said.

Her stomach clenched as she saw his hands tighten on the steering wheel.

"He's twenty-eight years old and has been in and out of jail a dozen times on different charges, mostly drugs. I've long suspected that he and his gang run drugs up from Florida, but I haven't been able to prove anything." His frown intensified. "If I wanted to arrange my own kidnapping for one reason or another, Remy or one of his gangbangers is who I would talk to."

She looked at him without hiding a new irritation that swept through her. "You still really believe that Jenny is responsible for this? You might have raised your sister, but you sure don't know anything about her."

"And after two months of living with her, you know it all?"

"I know that the only real problem Jenny has is too much of you." She hadn't meant to start a fight, but her emotions were too close to the surface and she'd watched Lucas mentally browbeat Jenny too many times.

"What are you talking about?" He cast her a sharp glance.

What are you doing, Mariah? a little voice whispered inside her head. She realized it wasn't the time or her place to get into this, that she had enough problems at the moment without berating the very man who was trying to help her find her son. "Never mind. So, where do we find this Remy Troulous?"

He shot her another glance, one that told her he was going to let her words go…for now. "I'm not sure. I know his official address is with his grandmother, but he's rarely there. Still, that's where we'll start."

As he headed down Main Street, she stared out the side window, a thousand thoughts filling her head. She'd done a television interview and hoped that stations around the area picked it up.

But she also knew that if Frank had had nothing to do with Billy's disappearance and he saw the interview on television, then he would know for certain where she and Billy had landed after they'd run from Shreveport.

The idea of facing her ex-husband again sent not only icy chills through her but also years of bad memories. And it was those memories, she knew, that had prompted her to attack Lucas about his treatment of Jenny.

She reached into her pocket and touched the inhaler. *Billy,* her heart cried. *Where are you?* She'd face a million Franks if it meant getting her son back.

Her heart pounded so fast, so painfully in her chest that she wondered if she were on the verge of a heart attack.

"When we get to Georgia's place, it would be best if you stayed in the car," he said, breaking into her despairing thoughts.

There he went again, telling her what was best for her, just like he did his sister all the time. *Lucas knows best.* He knew what Jenny should eat, what she should wear, where she should get a job—it was no wonder Jenny floundered around, trying to figure out who she was. Lucas had never given her the independence to find out.

She bit her bottom lip, wondering why she was thinking about such things. She supposed her mind was seeking anything to puzzle over other than the horror of her missing son. If she allowed herself to think about Billy for too long, her thoughts took her to dark places and she felt as if she'd lose her mind.

She glanced over at Lucas, who was focused on maneuvering the narrow road. She'd always thought he was a handsome man, with his dark hair and dark eyes. He radiated a strength of purpose, a self-confidence that could be irritating. At the moment, she found it comforting.

He was a smart man, a good sheriff, and he had a vested interest in solving the case. Jenny. No matter what issues she had with the way he treated his sister, she'd never doubted that he loved Jenny.

For the first time, she realized that maybe the reason he wanted to believe that Jenny had orchestrated this was he feared for her if she hadn't.

"She's stronger than you think," she said softly.

He looked at her again, and for just a moment she saw naked emotion shining from his eyes. Fear, anger and guilt, they were all there for a mere second, then gone as if shutters had closed to block out the light.

"I just can't imagine what she was doing meeting with a man like Troulous."

"When we find them, you can ask her," she replied as he pulled up in front of a small shanty.

She didn't intend to follow his suggestion that she remain in the car. Mariah figured if Remy's grandmother knew anything about Billy's kidnapping it wouldn't hurt to appeal to her, woman to woman.

She waited until Lucas was halfway up the porch, then she left the car and hurried after him. He showed his displeasure with her only in the tightening of his strong jaw as he knocked on the screen door.

Tension welled up inside Mariah, momentarily shoving away her exhaustion. She fought the impulse to grab hold of Lucas's arm, wondering what even prompted the urge.

A little old woman appeared at the door, her dark eyes suspicious as she saw Lucas. "He ain't here," she said without preamble.

"You don't even know why I'm here, Georgia," Lucas replied.

"I know when the sheriff shows up on my doorstep it's because he's looking for Remy, and Remy ain't here. I haven't seen him for a week." Her words caused Mariah's heart to sink.

"You know where he might be? Is he bunking with a girlfriend?" Lucas asked.

Georgia shook her head. "Who knows. What's he done now? Last time I saw him he told me he was trying to get his life together. Told me he was tired of gangbanging and such." The old woman seemed to shrink in size as misery darkened her eyes. "I should have known not to believe him."

"Please, Mrs. Troulous, can you think of anyplace we might find him? It's important. I have a little boy who is missing."

One of Georgia's gray eyebrows lifted. "You looking for the wrong person. Remy might be guilty of many things, but he'd never harm a child."

"I still need to talk to him," Lucas said. "If you see him before I do, tell him I'm looking for him."

Georgia nodded, and together Mariah and Lucas returned to his car. "What now?" she asked. "Surely you have an idea where this Remy might be. We've got to find him. He's the only lead we have."

Lucas started the car engine and puffed out a deep sigh. "I know dozens of places he might be."

"Then we start at the first place and don't stop until we find him." She couldn't stand the idea of another night passing without Billy being home with her.

The afternoon passed with failure after failure as Lucas checked all the known friends and places where Remy might be. Nobody had seen him—or, at least, nobody would admit to it.

Lucas checked with all his deputies throughout the day, but nobody had anything to report.

At two, Wally called Lucas to tell him that an FBI agent had arrived. Lucas and Mariah drove to the office and met with Michael Kessler, a young, earnest agent who listened to the facts of the case dispassionately, then indicated that he'd be doing his own investigation and would appreciate the support of Lucas and his deputies.

"Only one agent?" Mariah said as they drove away from the sheriff's office. "They only sent one man?"

"He'll have more resources than we have," Lucas replied. "Besides, even if they sent a hundred agents, we won't get any answers without a viable lead."

At seven they grabbed hamburgers at a local drive-through. Even though food was the last thing on her mind, Mariah ate, knowing that if she didn't, she'd make herself sick.

Was somebody feeding Billy? Or was he hungry and scared and crying for her? The last of her burger remained uneaten as haunting thoughts filled her head.

They were still parked in the drive-through when Lucas's cell phone rang. Mariah's hope instantly soared. Maybe Billy and Jenny had been found. He answered and she watched the play of emotion on his face as he listened to the caller.

"We'll be right there," he said, then hung up and turned to look at her.

The hope that had momentarily buoyed her up inside crashed back down to earth as she saw the shadows that darkened his eyes. "We need to get back to your place," he said. "There's been another phone call."

Chapter Four

"I don't know if it's a crank or not," Wally said as Lucas and Mariah walked through her front door. "I've got it taped and I checked the number the call came from with the phone company. It was the pay phone behind Jimbo's gas station. I already called Jimbo to see if he saw anyone using the phone, but no one did. I also sent Maylor over there to check out the phone and try to lift some prints."

Lucas had little hope that the caller had been dumb enough to leave prints, and he wasn't surprised that nobody had seen anyone using the phone. The area behind Jimbo's was filled with old wrecked cars and used tires. It was more a junkyard than anything else, and Lucas figured few people even knew there was a phone back there.

"Let's hear it," he said, and gestured to the recording equipment.

Mariah leaned against one of the kitchen chairs, her face as pale as paper as she stared at the phone. He couldn't believe the strength she'd exhibited so far. Most women would be in the care of a physician, swallowing tranquilizers to get through the ordeal. She'd definitely earned his respect.

Wally punched the Play button and his voice filled the air. "Harrington's residence," his taped greeting said.

"I know the sheriff isn't there, and I have no desire to talk to you, so just give him this message." The voice was low, a guttural whisper. It was the same person who had called Lucas on his cell phone.

"A game isn't fun unless two can play. I'll give you a little clue for the day. They're safe in a place where no one can hear, where the cries of the dead ring loud and clear." The caller paused. "Tell Sheriff Jamison to send his men home, to send everyone home. I don't like extra players in my game. Tell him I'm watching his every move and trust me, he doesn't want to break my rules." There was an ominous tone to the already creepy voice.

"Listen, why don't you—" Wally's reply was cut off by an audible click as the caller hung up.

For a moment the three of them said nothing, but simply continued to stare at the machine, as if answers to their questions were forthcoming.

It was Mariah who broke the silence. She drew in a deep breath and met Lucas's gaze. "He said they were safe and sound." Her voice trembled slightly but also held the hope of a woman grasping at anything.

"That's what he said," Lucas replied. There was no way he was going to tell her that the word of a kidnapper wasn't the most reliable in the world.

Mariah turned her gaze to Wally. "You have to go. You heard what he said, he wants everyone to leave and he's watching us. I don't want anyone here except me and Lucas."

Wally looked at Lucas, his forehead wrinkled into a hundred frown lines. Lucas felt the weight of his next decision in the very pit of his gut where tension burned with hot flames. Although he didn't want to play games with a criminal, he was also aware that he wasn't willing to gamble with Billy's and Jenny's lives.

"Wally, head back to the office and keep all the men away from here. Let Agent Kessler know what's going on. I'll be in touch with each of you on my cell phone."

"Are you sure?" Wally asked.

Lucas nodded. "I can't risk not playing by his rules, at least for the moment."

Dusk was deepening into night as Lucas walked Wally to his patrol car. "I've got Louis checking out Phil Ribideaux. The rest of you try to locate Remy Troulous. If you find him, bring him in and call me. Keep questioning whoever you think might have any information that might help us find Billy and Jenny. It would help if we could find somebody that saw them yesterday. Keep me posted on progress. I'm putting you in charge of coordinating things from the office. Make nice with Agent Kessler. If he needs anything, see that he gets it, but just make sure all the men stay away from here."

Wally nodded. "Anything else?"

"Yeah, see what you can dig up on a Frank Landers, last known address in Shreveport. The authorities there haven't been able to locate him, but I'm not sure how hard they're looking. And check around, see if anyone has noticed any strangers hanging around lately."

"Got it," Wally said.

Lucas watched Wally drive away. He stood for several minutes in the driveway and stared around the area. *Tell him I'm watching his every move and he doesn't want to break my rules.*

The people who lived on this street were good hard-working people who valued family and friends. He knew these people...or did he?

Suddenly every drapery drawn at a window might hide a kidnapper, every closed door implied secrets. Was somebody watching from next door? Across the street?

With a sigh he returned to the kitchen where Mariah was seated at the table, playing the message again. She pushed the Stop button when he came in. "The clue. I've been thinking about it." Even though the timing was completely inappropriate, he couldn't help but notice how pretty she looked with her hair coming loose and springing around her shoulders and her cheeks filled with color that had been lacking for most of the day.

"What about it?"

"He said they're where the cries of the dead ring loud and clear. It's got to be the cemetery, Lucas. Maybe they're in a crypt. We've got to go there and check it out."

"Whoa. We aren't going anywhere. I'll go and take a look around."

"If you think I'm going to stay here, you're crazy," she replied. "I can either ride with you or I can take my own car, but one way or another, I'm going to the cemetery. That's where the clue leads and that's where I need to be."

"It could be dangerous," Lucas protested. "You

know that even under the best of circumstances the cemetery isn't a good place to hang out, especially at night."

She stepped closer to him and placed a hand on his arm. This close he could see that her blue eyes had silver flecks. Those eyes pleaded with him. "Lucas, please. I have to go with you. It's my son. I don't care about any danger. This is the first real clue we've had. Don't make me fight you on this."

He tried to imagine somebody trying to keep him from going to find Jenny. There was nobody on the face of the earth who could stop him—and he wouldn't be the one to stop her.

"All right, then, let's go."

Minutes later they were in his car heading toward the north side of town where the Conja Creek Cemetery was located. His car beams penetrated the deepening darkness, and tension coiled like a snake in the pit of his stomach.

"We could be walking into a setup," he said.

"What kind of a setup? If somebody wanted to kill either you or me, they could have done so without all this drama," she said. "If we're the targets, then why involve Jenny and Billy?"

He tightened his hands on the steering wheel. "I don't know. I can't get a handle on this." The words fell from him involuntarily, and he hit the steering wheel with his palm. "He's obviously playing with us and I don't know why. This is probably nothing more than a wild-goose chase."

"Don't say that," she exclaimed with fervor. "Right now my hope is the only thing holding me together. Please don't take that away from me."

He glanced in her direction. "You're one of the strongest women I think I've ever met. Most women would be basket cases by now."

"I've had to be strong to survive the choices I've made in my life."

Again he realized how little he knew about her, and new interest stirred inside him. "Bad choices?"

"Only one. I married the wrong man. Why aren't you married, Lucas?"

"I was once. I'd just graduated college and gotten married when my mother died. Jenny was twelve, and so I moved back to the family home with my new bride. The marriage lasted for six months, then Kerry told me she hadn't applied for the job of helping to raise a twelve-year-old. She gave me an ultimatum—make other arrangements for Jenny, or she was leaving. I helped her pack."

"I'm sorry it didn't work out for you," she said.

He offered her a tight smile. "I'm not. Oh, it hurt at the time, but I hadn't realized until that moment how selfish Kerry was. She definitely wasn't the kind of woman I wanted to spend the rest of my life with."

"And there hasn't been anyone since?"

He wasn't sure if she was really interested or if she was just making conversation to keep her thoughts off their destination and the high stakes involved.

"Jenny has managed to take up most of my time and energy. There's never been much left for anyone else."

"Jenny has been an adult for a while now. Don't you think it's time you give her less time and attention?"

"I think the reasons we're here now put to rest the idea that Jenny doesn't require my time and attention," he replied dryly.

"You still think Jenny had something to do with all this?" Her voice held an edge of exasperation.

He didn't answer for several long seconds. Mostly because he wasn't sure what was in his heart. He desperately wanted to believe that Jenny was nothing more than an innocent victim, but he just wasn't sure.

"Jenny doesn't always make the best choices in her life," he finally said.

"From what I've seen, Jenny rarely makes *any* choices in her life," she countered. "You make them all for her."

He cast her a sharp, sideways glance. "Are you trying to pick a fight with me?"

She flushed and looked down at her clenched hands. "No. I'm sorry. Your relationship with Jenny is really none of my business."

There was something in her tone, a vague disapproval that made him want to continue the conversation, but at that moment the rusted ironwork of the gates to the cemetery appeared in his high beams.

Conja Creek Cemetery was like dozens of other Louisiana burial grounds. Sun-bleached tombs rose up from the earth, some simple square structures, others like miniature houses complete with fencing around them.

There was no caretaker living on-site, and the cemetery was on the edge of town with no surrounding houses or buildings.

"I'll get the gate," he said as he put his car in Park. He pulled his gun as he got out of the car, his eyes scanning the area and his ears listening for any sound that didn't belong.

The gate screeched in protest as he opened it, announcing to anyone who might be inside that they had arrived. He stared inside the gate to the narrow rows that led between the structures. Cities of the dead, that's what people called the cemeteries in Louisiana. He just hoped this particular city of the dead didn't hold the bodies of Billy and Jenny.

MARIAH DIDN'T THINK her heart could hurt as much as it did as Lucas pulled the car through the cemetery gates and parked in the space provided just inside.

Was Billy here? In one of the tombs? She reached her hand in her pocket and touched his inhaler, as if it were a talisman that would lead her to him.

She was light-headed and sick to her stomach, a combination of too much coffee and too little sleep. She just wanted her baby back home where he belonged.

"You stay in the car. I'll check things out," he said as he turned off the car engine.

"I'm not staying in the car," she replied. "If you find them, and Billy is in a full asthma attack, he's going to need immediate medical attention. I didn't come all this way with you to sit in the car." She opened her car door and ignored his muttered curse.

The night air was thick, hot and steamy, and for a moment she leaned against the car door and tried to imagine Billy in this place of death. The very atmosphere itself would work against him, so thick and sultry. Add fear and stress, and he could be in real physical danger.

Lucas joined her and put an arm around her shoulder. For a moment she leaned into him, drawing from his strength. She might not like the way he treated his sister, but at the moment she couldn't think of anyone else she wanted by her side.

"Stay close to me," he whispered. "We don't know what we're walking into."

She straightened and nodded as he once again pulled his gun. Together they left the car and headed for the first "street" between tombs.

"Billy!" The scream tore from Mariah's throat. She waited to hear an answer, but there was nothing.

The area was lit with small electric lights low to the ground, the illumination creating a contrast of eerie shadows. They walked slowly and checked each tomb to see if one might hold a sign that Billy and Jenny were inside.

"Billy, are you here?" Over and over Mariah cried out, desperate to hear the sound of her son's voice.

Lucas moved slowly, cautiously. He'd take a few steps then stop and cock his head, as if listening. The only thing she heard was the buzz of mosquitoes and the continuous click of insects.

Billy, where are you? Her heart screamed as loud as her mouth.

"Jenny, are you here? Make a sound, give us a clue, do something to show us you're here," Lucas called.

Mariah had never been afraid of places. Scary movies didn't bother her. Spiders, snakes and gators didn't concern her. The only fear she'd ever felt was of the man she had married. Frank.

Was he behind all this? Certainly a sadistic game of hide-and-seek wasn't out of character. One of the deputies had called Lucas earlier to let him know that her news story had been picked up by the wire services.

If Frank wasn't behind this, and if he'd been watching television and had seen her, then he would know that she and Billy were in Conja Creek. She rubbed her left wrist—the wrist that he'd broken on the day she'd left him.

The thought of seeing him again sent a shiver of fear through her and she moved closer to Lucas, as if he could keep all the boogeymen out of her life.

As they continued to search, the hope that had filled her began to waver. Had they perceived the clue incorrectly? *Where the cries of the dead ring loud and clear,* that's what the caller had said. Where else could that be but a cemetery, and this was the only cemetery in the town of Conja Creek.

When they reached the last wide aisle between the tombs, despair quickly usurped hope. And when they reached the last tomb on that aisle, the strength that had been holding her together vanished.

She fell to her knees, unable to take another step as the grief that she'd been shoving away since the moment she'd awakened from her nap and found Billy gone rushed in to consume her.

Tears blinded her, and she was unable to control the deep, wrenching sobs that ripped from her throat. She collapsed to the ground, vaguely aware of Lucas holstering his gun and bending down beside her.

"I know," he whispered as he physically pulled her into his arms. "Shh." He stroked her hair as she continued to sob, unable to stop.

"They were supposed to be here," she cried. "Damn him. Damn whoever has them, for putting us through this." She clung to Lucas, surprised to find his arms provided the comfort she needed.

As she remained in his embrace, she became aware of the frantic beating of his heart against her own. She realized at that moment that his despair was as great as her own, his disappointment was as black as the one that filled her.

She raised her head and looked at him through her veil of tears. His eyes held the same rage that filled her, a rage at the man who had brought them here, the man who had ripped the very fabric of her soul.

"Jenny didn't do this," he said, his voice hoarse with emotion. "She'd never put us through this."

"That's what I've been trying to tell you," Mariah replied. She could tell by the dawning horror in his eyes that the realization that Jenny was in terrible trouble was just now sinking in.

"Come on, let's get out of here," he said, his voice filled with rough emotion. He stood and held out his hand to help her up off the ground.

She had just stood when a crack split the air and Lucas threw himself at her, tumbling her to the ground as he covered her body with his.

Chapter Five

Lucas couldn't tell where the gunshot had come from, but he heard the ping as the bullet hit the tomb behind where they had just been standing.

His first impulse was to protect Mariah, and as he lay on top of her, adrenaline pumped through him. He tightened his hold on his gun as he scanned the area.

Dammit, there were too many shadows where a shooter could hide, too many trees and tombs for him to discern the hint of a person. The shot had caused a cessation to the insect noise, but as the minutes ticked by the cacophony of bugs resumed.

As time passed, in the back of his mind he became more aware of Mariah. Her hand grasped the front of his shirt, as if she was afraid he might jump up and run away. Her heartbeat raced against his own, and despite the circumstances, he couldn't help but notice the softness of her lush curves under his body.

Irritated by his lapse in concentration, he rose to a crouch above her. "Stay here and stay down," he commanded. "I'm going to take a look around."

She tightened her grip on his shirt and in the faint

moonlight her eyes shone more silver than blue. "Be careful. He could still be out there." She reluctantly released her hold on him.

Still in a low crouch, Lucas moved away from her, toward the area where he thought the shot might have come from. He didn't think the shooter was still there.

In fact, he didn't think the shooter was still in the cemetery. It was a gut feeling coupled with the knowledge that if the man had wanted to kill one of them, he could have with that single shot.

He might have missed because he was a terrible shot, but Lucas didn't think so. He thought the bullet had missed them because it was just another game the kidnapper was playing. He was taking pleasure in terrorizing them.

He straightened to his full height, making himself an easy target, but no other shots were fired. He walked back to where Mariah was still lying on the ground.

"I think he's gone." He held out a hand to help her up.

"Are you sure?" She didn't move from her prone position.

"As sure as I can be. If he wanted to hurt us, he could have shot us at any time while we were searching the area." He grimaced. "I think that shot was just a playful reminder that we aren't the ones in charge of this game."

She slipped her small hand in his and he pulled her up. "They aren't here, are they? Billy and Jenny aren't here and that clue was just part of his stupid game."

He nodded. "Let's get the hell out of here."

It was a long walk back to the car. Lucas kept his gun ready and every muscle tense as he watched for danger that didn't come.

They got into the car and he started the engine, immediately turning on the air conditioner to relieve the sweltering heat and humidity.

As he pulled out of the cemetery, neither of them said a word. The adrenaline that had surged inside him eased away, leaving him not only exhausted but also defenseless against the dark thoughts in his mind.

Jenny. Pain seared through him as he thought of his sister. He'd spent all his adult life trying to protect her, both from herself and from others. He'd tried to guide her, to make her better than she was, better than the mother who had given her life.

"Are you okay?" Mariah's soft, weary voice pulled him from his thoughts.

"As okay as you are," he replied.

"Then you aren't okay," she said with a surprising touch of dry humor.

"No, I'm not," he agreed. "I'm frustrated and worried and I don't think this is about a ransom anymore."

"Then what is it about?" she asked.

Lucas frowned and tightened his hands on the steering wheel. "I think it's personal. I think the perpetrator wants one of us to be afraid, to suffer."

She leaned her head back and closed her eyes. "Then he's succeeded."

Those were the last words spoken for the remainder of the drive home. When they arrived at her place, the first thing Lucas did was check the phone messages as Mariah got them each a bottle of water from the fridge.

The first message was from Mayor Richard Welch. "Lucas, I've heard through the grapevine that you've sent your men home, but Billy and Jenny are still missing. I hope you know what you're doing. I need to be updated and maybe we need to put our heads together to see what's the best way to deal with this situation. The public deserves to know what's going on in this community."

Lucas puffed out a sigh. "I wish he'd spend his time governing the town instead of trying to govern me."

Mariah sank into a seat at the table, her weariness evident in the slump of her shoulders and the hollowness of her eyes. "He's just trying to be helpful." She unscrewed the lid on her water and took a long, deep drink.

"It would be helpful if he'd just leave me to the job of upholding the law."

The next three messages were from neighbors, offering to cook, offering to help. Another two were from reporters looking for an interview. The next message shot a new burst of adrenaline through Lucas.

"Touching scene in the cemetery." The familiar voice filled the room. "Is she consoling you, or are you consoling her?" The sound of insects was background noise. "A minute ago I stood so close to you both that I could see the sweat on Lucas's forehead and I could smell that flowery perfume that Mariah wears."

Mariah jumped as the sound of a shot filled the room. The sound was followed by a low laugh. "I could have killed you just now," he said. "I'll be in touch."

The line went dead.

Mariah released a loud gasp. "He was watching us as we searched. He was there all along." Emotion choked her voice and she backhanded her water bottle off the table, unmindful of the water that spilled across the floor. She jumped up, her eyes wild. "What kind of person does something like this? What kind of monster is he?"

"I don't know." But there were things Lucas needed to do, and with that in mind he pulled his cell phone from his pocket and punched in the number at the sheriff's office.

"Ben, first thing in the morning I need you to check out the cemetery for me. Somebody took a shot at Mariah and me out there tonight. I want you to see if you can locate the bullet." He quickly explained to his deputy where they had been standing when the gun had been fired and where he thought Ben would find the bullet. It would at least tell them what kind of gun it came from.

The next call he made was to Ed Maylor. "Ed, did I wake you?"

"Nah, I was just sitting here watching the boob tube. What's up?"

"I was wondering if you could do me a favor. Would you run by my place and tell Marquette to give you my overnight bag and a couple of clean uniforms, then meet me at the station with them?" He looked at Mariah, who stood with her back to him as she stared out the window into the night. "I'm going to be here at Mariah's until this is resolved."

"Sure. When do you want to meet?"

"An hour."

The last call was to Deputy Louis DuBois. "Where are you, Louis?" he asked when the man answered his cell phone.

There was a long pause. "I'm in my car between Magnolia and Main. Uh, I'm looking for Phil Ribideaux."

"What do you mean you're looking for him?" Lucas asked.

"Uh, I seem to have lost him."

Lucas closed his eyes and squeezed the phone more tightly against his ear. "What do you mean you lost him?"

"I'm sorry, Lucas, but he got into that little sports car of his and he must have seen me behind him because he took off around a couple of corners and was gone."

"How long has it been since you had him in visual contact?" Lucas asked.

"At least an hour," Louis confessed. "I'm heading toward his house now to see if he's returned there."

"Keep me posted." Lucas clicked off and muttered a curse.

Mariah turned to face him. "What's happened?"

"I had Louis following Phil Ribideaux, and apparently in the past hour he lost him."

She leaned against the wall and brushed a strand of her unruly curly hair away from her face. "An hour. That means it's possible it was Phil Ribideaux who was in the cemetery."

"It's also possible it was a dozen other people," Lucas replied. "In truth, I can't imagine Phillip Ribideaux having the imagination or the balls to pull something like this off." He pulled his keys from his pocket. "Look, I need to go down to the station. Will you be okay alone for a little while?"

Her gaze went to the telephone. "What if he calls again?"

"I don't think he will, at least not again tonight. I think he's had his fun for now." He frowned. Funny…

all the people who had shown up that morning had been well-meaning neighbors, but there had been no phone calls, no appearance of anyone who seemed to be Mariah's close friend. "Is there somebody I can call to be here with you? Maybe a good friend?"

She shook her head. "Jenny was becoming a good friend, but other than her I have no close friends here," she replied. "Between my job and Billy, there hasn't been time for fostering any real friendships." She rubbed her left wrist. "Besides, I'm a private person. Friends want to know where you come from and where you're going. I didn't want to talk about the first and I don't have answers for the second."

She turned back to face the window. "Go do whatever it is you need to do. I'll be fine here."

She might be fine, but he was an emotional wreck as he drove to his office. Despite the lateness of the hour, he'd called Wally and told him to gather the deputies for a briefing. He also wanted to coordinate with Agent Kessler.

As he drove, his head filled with thoughts of Jenny. He'd clung to the perverse hope that somehow she was behind her own disappearance, that she wasn't in serious danger other than getting a butt-chewing from him when she finally showed up.

But as they'd walked the cemetery, he'd realized Mariah was right. Jenny might not mind making him worry himself sick, but she'd never do something like this to Mariah. She'd never keep Billy away from his mother.

However, it was possible that Jenny's bad choices in friends and relationships had put her in this position. Remy Troulous was one of those bad choices. What the hell had she been doing with him? And where the hell was Remy Troulous now?

Lucas knew it was useless to search for the man. He was like a swamp rat, able to scurry through darkness and hide in any number of holes. He wouldn't be found unless he wanted to be, and there was no way to know when he'd decide to make an appearance.

Did Remy have anything to do with this? Or was it possible Phil Ribideaux was behind it? And what about the mysterious Frank Landers? The questions served no purpose other than to give him a headache and intensify his weariness.

He was going to have to get some sleep. He was running on empty and there was no way he could be sharp and focused, either physically or mentally, without rest.

The sheriff's office was in a building smack-dab in the middle of Main Street. He parked in the space allotted to him, then went inside where his deputies and the FBI agent awaited.

They all looked as tired as he felt. It didn't take long for him to fill them in on what had happened at the cemetery, then listen to each of them report on what they'd been doing in the past few hours. None of them had anything substantial to report.

The Shreveport authorities had still been unable to locate Frank Landers, Remy Troulous was missing in action, as was Phil Ribideaux. Further interrogations of Mariah's neighbors had yielded nothing, and by the time Lucas left the office with his overnight bag and clean clothes in hand, he carried with him an overwhelming sense of frustration.

The first forty-eight hours after a crime was committed were crucial, and Lucas was aware that they knew little more than they had in the first hours after Billy and Jenny had disappeared. He and his men were doing everything they could to find Jenny and Billy, but at the moment the kidnapper was definitely in charge.

Eventually he would make a mistake. Lucas had no doubt about that. The phone calls told Lucas that the kidnapper wanted to brag, needed to connect, and eventually he'd make a mistake. But until that happened Lucas could only react, and he hated not being in control.

He told his deputies that he would stay at Mariah's house, since the kidnapper was calling on her home phone. He would be the only law enforcement agent there. For now, he was playing by the kidnapper's rules. He and his deputies would stay in touch by phone and continue to meet at regular intervals at the office.

Although Conja Creek wasn't a hotbed of criminal activity, they still had to contend with the usual crimes that occurred on a regular basis. He put Ed Maylor in charge of coordinating with the citizens who wanted to help find Jenny and Billy and put Wally in charge of the office while Lucas stayed at Mariah's. Agent Kessler would coordinate with the state police and continue to work with the deputies to interview and assess the situation.

Kessler indicated that he was more than willing to call in several more agents, but Lucas feared the wrath of the kidnapper if too many law enforcement agents appeared in town. He and Kessler agreed that for the short term everything would remain status quo.

When he arrived back at Mariah's, he walked through the front door and was met with silence. He dropped his bag and his clothes on the sofa, then went in search of Mariah.

He found her in Billy's room, curled up in a fetal position on the bed. She clutched her son's yellow-and-navy pajamas to her chest, and his heart clenched at the sight.

Her sleep was obviously deep, for she didn't move as he approached her. She must have showered after he left, and changed her clothes, for she now wore a pair of jogging pants and a different T-shirt.

For a long moment he stood and watched her, his heart clenching once again as he saw the dark shadows beneath her long lashes, the faint crease that rode her brow, as if even sleep hadn't offered her the escape she needed.

He wanted to curl up beside her in the bed, take her into his arms and hold her and fill his head with the sweet scent of her. The desire shocked him. With all that was going on, how was it possible that desire managed to rear its unwelcome head?

Maybe because it was a familiar, known emotion as opposed to the unfamiliar torment of fear that rocked through him as his heart cried his sister's name. But, Mariah Harrington had touched him in places he hadn't been touched in a very long time.

Her strength amazed him, her courage awed him and the secrets he sensed she had from her past intrigued him. She was like no other woman he had encountered in a very long time.

He spied a navy afghan folded over the chair at the desk and he grabbed it and gently laid it over her. The house was cool and he wanted to do something, anything that felt like taking care of her.

He was grateful that she was asleep, glad that he wouldn't have to tell her the instructions he'd given his deputies. He left the bedroom and went into the kitchen, where he stood at the window and stared into the black of night.

This was the second night. Almost forty-eight hours had passed since Jenny and Billy had been taken. What were the odds that somebody had kidnapped them and was keeping them alive in a secret place here in Conja Creek? He figured slim to none.

That's why he was glad Mariah was sleeping. So he wouldn't have to tell her that he suspected they were now looking for Jenny's and Billy's bodies.

NIGHT HAD FALLEN AGAIN, and with it the terror of the darkness, the horror of the unknown. Jenny cradled Billy's head in her lap, worried as she heard the sound of his labored breathing.

He was asleep, but it was a fitful rest, and she could only guess at the bad dreams a frightened eight-year-old little boy might suffer.

His breathing worried her. She knew how bad Billy's asthma could get. Twice in the couple of months she'd lived with Mariah, he'd had to be rushed to the emergency room because his nebulizer hadn't been able to give him the relief he'd needed.

Although it wasn't critical yet, she feared what another day away from his mommy, away from his home might bring. As his stress and fear level rose, so did his breathing issues.

Dawn had brought a new level of understanding to Jenny and a heightened sense of simmering fear.

As light had crept in around the cracks in the boards of the structure where they were being held, she'd been able to see that it was a small room built with new, strong wood. The nails—thick, big spikes—were driven in deep and sound.

Besides the mattress on the floor, in one corner was a portable potty and in the other corner was a wooden shelf filled with nonperishable food. There were boxes of breakfast bars and crackers, beef jerky and canned goods with pop lids. Beneath the shelf were cases of bottled water.

It was the plethora of food that frightened her more than anything. Whoever had them had prepared for them to be here a long time. Why? What in God's name could they want?

She racked her brain, trying to figure out who would want to kidnap them and why. But she had no answers. It might be about money. Certainly Lucas could afford to pay a huge ransom for their release. In fact, Jenny had her own trust fund that contained enough to make a kidnapper happy for the rest of his life.

When Billy had awakened, they'd both screamed for help, hoping somebody would hear and come to rescue them. But it was as if they were yelling at the bottom of the ocean. Nobody replied. Nobody came.

When they'd exhausted themselves screaming, she'd spent most of the rest of the day examining their surroundings, trying to find a weakness she could exploit to get them out of there. But there didn't seem to be any way out.

She'd finally given up and had played games with Billy. They'd played I Spy and an alphabet game, then had played Rock, Paper, Scissors until she thought she'd go mad.

As dusk had approached and Billy's anxiety began to increase, Jenny had tried to entertain him by talking about the animals who lived in the swamps. Billy loved to learn, and Jenny had once thought about being a teacher. But when she'd gone to college, she'd taken business instead of education classes, because Lucas had thought that would be a smarter choice.

Tears now filled her eyes as she thought of her older brother. He could be bossy and a know-it-all, but she adored him. He'd been her hero for most of her life, fixing messes she made and taking care of her.

Lately she'd been angry with him, wanting him to back off and let her live her own life. She wanted to make her own choices and figure things out on her own, but sometimes she felt so stupid.

She leaned her head back against the wooden wall and stroked her fingers through Billy's hair. She'd always loved kids, and Billy had found a special place in her heart.

He coughed and she recognized the tight bark as his asthma cough. She closed her eyes, terror once again filling her.

Billy needed to get out of here before his breathing grew worse. But she couldn't physically break through the wooden walls that kept them prisoner. She couldn't even try to negotiate with their kidnapper because, since the moment they had awakened from whatever had knocked them out, they had been utterly alone.

She'd been on the verge of tears all day, but had refused to allow them to fall because she knew it would upset Billy. But now, in the darkness and with Billy asleep, tears trickled down her cheeks. She must have done something stupid, something to put herself at risk. She wasn't sure what it had been, but somehow this had to be her fault.

She needed her brother to find them. She needed Lucas to be her hero one last time, then she swore to herself that she'd never do anything stupid again.

Chapter Six

Sleep fell away in increments. Mariah became aware of the faint sound of chirping birds drifting through the windowpane, and for just a moment a sense of well-being filled her.

Then she opened her eyes and realized she was in Billy's bed, and reality slammed into her a like a sledge-hammer crushing her heart.

Another dawn, and he was still not home. She squeezed her eyes shut as a rush of emotion filled her. She could only assume that nothing had happened while she slept, for if it had, Lucas would have awak-ened her.

How was she going to get through another day... another minute of the tormenting fear? How was she going to survive her next breath not knowing where her son was or if he were alive or—

She gasped, not wanting to even think that she might never see Billy's smile again, would never hear that silly giggle of his.

Drawing a deep breath, she took in the scent of him that lingered in his room, the faint Billy fragrance that clung to his little pajamas. How long before that Billy smell went away? Would he be gone so long that there would be nothing left of him?

Needing to escape her own thoughts, she hurried into the bathroom where she washed her face, brushed her teeth and pulled her hair back with a ponytail holder at the nape of her neck.

She looked tired despite the sleep she'd gotten. Of course, much of her sleep had been haunted by dreams of Billy crying for her, needing her, and she'd been unable to go to him.

She was living every mother's nightmare. She'd read the tragic news stories of missing children, had seen parents on the television years after the disappearance still seeking answers. She didn't want to be one of those parents. She didn't want to think that Billy might be a statistic.

Shoving away the horrible thoughts, she went in search of Lucas.

She found him stretched out on his back on her sofa. He was sound asleep. He wore a pair of worn jeans and a white T-shirt and she realized it was the first time she'd seen him out of his khaki uniform.

He looked good in jeans, and the T-shirt pulled across the width of his chest. She had always been attracted to Lucas. From the first time he'd strode into the office demanding to speak to the mayor, she'd felt a magnetic spark.

But he scared her more than a little bit. He reminded her of the husband she'd fled. She'd already made one major mistake in her life, and she had the feeling that following through on her attraction to

Lucas Jamison would simply be another monumental mistake.

He must have been exhausted, for the lamp on the end table closest to his head burned bright but didn't seem to bother him.

She moved into the kitchen and quietly began to make a pot of coffee. That was all she seemed to be good for. She couldn't find her son. She couldn't figure out who might have taken him. She didn't like feeling so useless, so utterly powerless. She'd had years of feeling that way with Frank and had sworn she'd never allow herself to feel that way again.

Only the first stir of dawn's light brightened the eastern skies and she turned on the small light over the oven, then poured herself a cup of the freshly brewed coffee.

As she sipped, she realized she was hungry, and that sent a stabbing guilt through her. How could she sleep? How could she even think about food when Billy had been kidnapped? Was he being fed? Was he warm? The questions tormented her.

"Good morning." Lucas's deep voice came from behind her and he flipped on the overhead light.

"It can't be good if Billy and Jenny aren't here," she replied.

She heard him open a cabinet and knew he was getting a cup for coffee. A minute later he joined her at the table. His sleep-tousled hair did nothing to detract from his handsomeness. She waited for him to tell her that he'd get them back, that everything was going to be okay. When he didn't, her heart clenched so tight she felt as if she were suffocating.

"At least we both got some sleep," he finally said.

She set her cup down. "I feel horrible, that I could sleep and not know if my son is being fed or being allowed to sleep. And you know what makes me feel even more guilty? The fact that at the moment I'm thinking about making some scrambled eggs and toast because I'm starving."

He reached across the table and captured her hand in his. "You can't feel guilty about the things your body requires to live. You have to eat and you have to sleep."

His hand was big and strong and warm around hers, and she welcomed the warmth, the touch. Maybe the old adage was true, that misery loved company.

"Are they coming home, Lucas?" The question was a mere whisper and until the words left her lips she hadn't realized she was going to ask it.

His gaze held hers. "I don't know." He squeezed her hand more tightly. "I wish I could tell you otherwise, but I don't think you'd appreciate me lying to you."

"Absolutely not," she agreed. "I want to know every piece of information you know, every feeling you have. I need to know what's going on every minute."

He nodded, released her hand and leaned back in his chair. "Now I have a very important question to ask you."

She sat up straighter, steeling herself for whatever he might need to know. "What?"

The corners of his lips turned up in a smile that momentarily erased the stress lines of his face. "Are you making the eggs or do you want me to? I have to confess I make a mean omelet."

Her burst of laughter surprised her, not only with its

unexpectedness but also in the fact that it eased some of the knot of tension in her stomach. She sobered almost immediately and pointed to the stove. "Knock yourself out. I don't think a man has ever cooked me breakfast before."

"Then sit back and relax and let me do the driving," he replied as he stood.

She watched as he began to pull items out of the refrigerator. "You like that, don't you? Being in the driver's seat."

He frowned thoughtfully as he set a carton of mushrooms on the counter. "I've never thought about whether I like it or not, it's just something I've always had to do."

"Why'd you decide to run for sheriff? It's no secret that you have enough money that if you didn't want to, you wouldn't have to work for the rest of your life."

He grabbed a knife from the drawer and began to cut up a green pepper. "When I was young I didn't know what I wanted to do with my life. There was a group of young men here in town. We were all friends and we spent most of our high school days acting like rich jackasses. We were overindulged, full of ourselves and good for nothing. Then the five of us decided to all go to the same college in Missouri."

He stopped talking long enough to get the skillet from the cabinet and the carton of eggs from the refrigerator, then continued. "Anyway, while we were there we all developed a social conscience. We called ourselves the Brotherhood and we all made a pact that we would choose careers that gave something back to our community. We were not going to be the kind of wealthy young men who got our names in the tabloids."

"So you became sheriff. What about the others in the Brotherhood?" She welcomed the conversation to keep her mind from dark places.

"You know Sawyer. He became an architect. Then there's Jackson Burdeaux, who is a criminal defense attorney, Clay Jefferson, who became a psychiatrist and Beau Reveneau, who joined the army."

"I've met all of them but Beau. Does he still live in Conja Creek?"

Lucas poured the egg concoction into the awaiting skillet before replying. "We don't know where Beau is. His family moved from Conja Creek about eight years ago, and none of us have heard from him for several years."

"So you were all close friends?"

"The best." He took a sip of his coffee, his expression reflective. "We swore that we'd always have each other's backs, that we'd support each other for the rest of our lives." He shook his head ruefully. "We were very young and idealistic."

"Must have been tough on you last month when you thought Sawyer had killed his wife," Mariah replied. The crime had been shocking. Sawyer's wife, Erica Bennett, had been stabbed and pushed off the dock and into the swamp water behind the Bennett home. Erica had been an unfaithful wife who at the time of her death had been pregnant. Sawyer had been the number-one suspect.

"The most difficult part was that I knew in my gut that Sawyer wasn't responsible, but I was pressured by your boss to make the arrest."

It had turned out that Erica had been murdered by

her best friend and next-door neighbor, Lillian Cordell. And despite all the drama, Sawyer had found love with the nanny he'd hired to care for his daughter, Molly.

"I hear Sawyer and Amanda are getting married next month," she said.

"Yeah. I got an invitation. It's going to be a small wedding in Sawyer's backyard. I'm glad he found somebody who makes him happy. He was unhappy with Erica for a very long time. And speaking of weddings and marriages, tell me about yours."

As always, whenever she thought of Frank, her wrist ached as if to remind her of all the pain her marriage had brought to her. "There's nothing much to tell. We got married, it didn't work out and we got a divorce."

"But there's more to it than that, isn't there?" He pushed the button to lower the bread in the toaster, then turned and looked at her expectantly.

"I'm surprised you'd find the minutia of a broken marriage of any interest," she replied.

"I think there's more than the usual minutia in your broken marriage. After all, it was you who told me Frank Landers might be responsible for all this."

As he took the eggs from the skillet and ladled them onto two plates, she turned her attention to the window and stared out, knowing that she was going to have to tell him how bad things had been, how stupid she had been. The toast popped up and she turned her gaze back to him.

"I was twenty-one and Frank was forty when we married. We'd met in a bar, and I thought he was strong and smart. He seemed to adore me."

She released a humorless laugh and wrapped her

hands around her coffee cup. "I guess you could say I was a cliché. My father left us when I was ten and I never had a real relationship with him. My mother worked two jobs to support us and I rarely saw her. When I met Frank I was hungry for somebody to love me, and he fed that hunger. It wasn't until after we were married that I realized his adoration was obsession and he was dictatorial and mean."

Lucas carried the two plates to the table and joined her there. She was grateful that his eyes held no judgment, nor did they hold pity. He just looked at her curiously.

"I was smart, but I fell into the same trap that other abused women fall into," she continued. "You've probably heard this story a million times before. At the beginning things were okay, although Frank had total control over what I did, where I went and who I saw. I wanted to please him so I played right into his game. By the time I got pregnant I'd been isolated from my friends and my mother. And while I knew things weren't right, I wanted my baby to be raised in the kind of complete family that I hadn't had."

"When did the physical abuse start?"

She looked at him in surprise. She hadn't mentioned anything about physical abuse. Unexpectedly, tears burned at her eyes as she thought of those years with Frank, years of fear and pain and broken dreams.

"About the time I got pregnant with Billy. Frank wasn't happy about the pregnancy, although initially I thought he'd come to embrace the idea of a child. The first time he laid a hand on me it was just a push…a shove. I fell into the coffee table and got banged up. He was instantly sorry and we put the incident behind us…until the next time."

"When did he hurt your wrist?"

She flushed and realized she'd been rubbing the ache since she'd begun talking about Frank. "The day I left him. By that time I'd been punched and kicked and slapped enough. I'd already begun to make plans to leave him, but that day he raised his hand to Billy. I stepped between them and he grabbed me by the wrist and twisted. I heard the snap when it broke. He drove me to the hospital, apologizing and telling me how much he loved me. But that snap of my wrist was a defining moment for me and I knew I wasn't leaving the hospital with him."

"You pressed charges?"

She nodded and once again wrapped her hands around her coffee cup, needing the warmth to infuse the chill that had taken up residence with the bad memories. "He spent a week in jail, then got out. Billy and I went into a shelter that night and we stayed at the shelter until the divorce was final. That day I packed up and Billy and I got into my car and left Shreveport and Frank Landers behind."

Lucas picked up his fork and pointed to her plate. "You'd better eat before it gets cold."

Although the hunger pangs that had gnawed at her had fled with the talk of Frank, she picked up her fork and took a bite. Instead of hunger, what gnawed at her now was a fire of simmering anger. She was angry with herself for falling into the trap of a battered woman, angry with Lucas for maintaining such control on his emotions, for fixing her eggs instead of finding her son.

She knew her emotions were irrational, that the anger she felt at the moment was misplaced, but she couldn't get a handle on it, and as she attempted to take another bite of her breakfast, it flared out of control.

"You remind me of him," she said.

He looked at her in surprise. "What are you talking about?"

"You remind me a lot of Frank." Careless abandon filled her. Her pain rose up inside her, so enormous she wanted to strike out and Lucas was a convenient target. "You treat Jenny a lot like Frank used to treat me."

He set his fork down and narrowed his dark eyes. "What does that mean? You're somehow comparing my relationship with my sister to the abusive relationship you had with your husband?"

"Oh, I'm sure you've never laid a hand on Jenny, but emotionally you do to her exactly what Frank used to do to me."

His narrowed eyes flickered with the heat of a burgeoning anger. "I think maybe your own emotional baggage is coloring the way you see things."

"On the contrary, my emotional baggage makes me see things more clearly." She wanted an explosion, needed to release not only the tension that balled so tight inside her, but also to diminish the physical attraction she felt for him.

What she wanted more than anything else was for him to reach out to her, to grab her and hold her tight in his arms as he had done the night before in the cemetery.

As crazy as it sounded, she wanted him to take her to bed, to fill her heart with anything other than the agonizing horror that was in there now. And that scared the hell out of her.

"You undermine her confidence, you belittle the choices she makes." She got up from the table, unable to sit next to him and say the things that threatened to burst from her. "You never let her forget that you have to rescue her, that she isn't smart enough, isn't old enough to do things right. That's abuse, Lucas, whether you recognize it or not, whether you mean it or not, it's abuse."

A muscle ticked in his jaw and his eyes were as dark as the night that had just passed. "You don't know what you're talking about. You don't know anything about me or my sister and the relationship we have."

"I know what I see. Did you know that Jenny wanted to be a teacher? But that's not what you wanted her to be. So she flunked out of college on purpose, because that's what you secretly expected of her, because she'd rather disappoint you than stand up to you." She took a step backward, somewhere in the back of her mind appalled at her audacity, yet unable to stop herself.

"You treat her like she's stupid and worthless and that's what she becomes when she's around you. You've stolen her self-esteem. Believe me, I know all about that." Tears fell down her cheeks and she swiped at them angrily.

"You have no idea what a great woman Jenny is. She would have made an awesome teacher, and my only consolation right now is that Jenny is with Billy wherever he is and I know she'll do everything in her power to keep him safe."

She left the kitchen then, horrified by her own

words and consumed with the emotion she'd tried so hard to control since the moment she'd realized Billy had been kidnapped.

LUCAS STARED AFTER HER, stunned first by her emotional outburst and secondly by what she'd said to him. As his surprise abated, anger welled up inside him.

Who in the hell did she think she was? How could she possibly compare him to an abuser? She knew nothing about him, nothing about Jenny.

Lucas pushed away from the table and stood, his intention to chase after her, but by the time he reached the living room he decided to give himself a few minutes to cool off.

He returned to the kitchen and cleaned up the dishes, his head whirling with his thoughts.

She was under an enormous amount of stress, he told himself. Surely she didn't really believe those things about him. He was not abusive to Jenny, he was just trying to save her from turning into the kind of woman who had given them birth.

Mariah didn't understand him, didn't understand where he was coming from where Jenny was concerned. And in any case he certainly didn't owe her any explanations or apologies for how he conducted himself with his sister.

He grabbed his overnight bag, his cell phone and a clean uniform and headed for the bathroom. Maybe beneath a refreshing cool shower some of his anger would dissipate.

It worked. As he stood beneath the spray of water he couldn't sustain the anger that had momentarily gripped him. Instead, a swell of sorrow filled him for her. He couldn't imagine being a young woman with a small child and having to run away in fear from the man who had promised to honor and cherish her.

He'd suspected secrets were in her past, and now she'd shared them with him. Was it any wonder she saw imagined abuse in others? She'd been through hell and had survived only to have her son ripped away from her by some unknown perpetrator.

Dammit. He wanted to be a hero for her. Her father had left her, her husband had abused her. She needed a hero. He wanted to bring her son home safe and sound. And he wanted to be a hero for Jenny. He leaned weakly against the shower wall as his head filled with thoughts of her.

He'd refused to allow himself to dwell on her, had instead tried to keep his focus on Billy. But now a rush of fear consumed him, clenching his stomach muscles as he broke into a cold sweat.

Jenny. His heart cried her name. From the time she'd been born, he'd taken care of her, seen to her needs and protected her from the world. And now he couldn't do any of those things. She was gone, taken for some reason he couldn't discern by a madman playing a game.

He hadn't cried when his mother died. He hadn't shed a tear when his wife had walked out on him, but the thought of never seeing his sister again pulled a deep sob from the very depths of him.

He sucked in a deep breath and stuffed his emotions deep inside. The only way he'd be able to get through this was to keep emotional distance. He wasn't just one of the victims' brother, he was the sheriff of Conja Creek and had to be strong, if not for himself, then for Mariah.

Getting out of the shower, he grabbed a towel and quickly dried off, then dressed in his clean clothes. He opened the bathroom door and bumped into Mariah, who had apparently been waiting for him.

"I'm sorry," she said, obviously tortured. "I was way out of line and I apologize. It's really none of my business."

"Apology accepted," he replied easily. There was nothing to gain by holding on to a grudge, and she obviously felt terrible about what had happened between them.

"I'm scared and I'm angry and you were convenient to vent to," she continued. She worried a hand through her hair. "I don't know why I said those things."

He held up a hand to halt anything else she might say. "We're under a lot of stress. As far as I'm concerned it's forgotten."

"I guess I'm just finding it difficult to think about facing another day," she said as he stepped out of the bathroom door and into the hallway.

"I know." He couldn't fight the impulse to draw her into his embrace. Despite the things she'd said to him, in spite of the fact that he should be angry with her, he felt her need to be held. Or was it his own need?

He pulled her against him, molding her curves against him as her arms wound around his neck. She was soft and warm and yielding.

She buried her face into the front of his shirt as her body trembled. He tightened his arms around her, wishing he could provide a barrier between her and her heartache.

He rubbed his hand down her back and tried to focus on giving comfort instead of the rising desire that filled him with her intimate nearness.

They stood that way for several long minutes, then she raised her head to look at him. He had no intention of kissing her, but as her full, sensual lips parted, he lowered his head and covered them with his own.

He half expected her to pull away, knew somehow that the kiss was out of line, crossing a boundary that shouldn't be crossed, but she didn't pull away. Instead, she seemed to move closer to him.

Her mouth opened to him and he deepened the kiss with his tongue as full-blown desire crashed through him. She returned the kiss, her tongue battling with his.

Her hands tangled in his hair at the nape of his neck and a slight moan escaped her, only increasing his need to take her.

Yet in the back of his mind he knew this was wrong. He felt as if he were taking advantage of her, exploiting her vulnerability. Reluctantly he broke the kiss.

She stared up at him and swallowed. "Temporary insanity," she said, her voice hoarse as she stepped back.

He was saved from making a reply by the ring of his cell phone. He listened to what his deputy had to tell him, then clicked off.

"That was Wally," he said to Mariah. "He picked up Remy Troulous and has him down at the office for questioning."

Her features lit with hope. "Surely he'll tell us if he knows anything about this. Just let me talk to him. I'm sure I can get him to tell us what he knows."

He didn't have the heart to tell her that Remy Troulous was a man who wouldn't be moved by a mother's pleas. If Remy didn't want to cooperate, there was nothing on this earth or beyond that would make him do so.

Chapter Seven

Mariah was grateful that he didn't mention the kiss as they drove to the sheriff's office. She couldn't imagine what had possessed her. But more, she couldn't imagine what had possessed him.

By all rights he should have been livid with her. She'd said terrible things to him, but her bad behavior certainly hadn't stopped him from kissing her.

Definitely temporary insanity, and it was obviously a state they had both suffered—for just a moment at the exact same time.

She was acutely conscious of him and she couldn't understand it. She wasn't even sure she liked him that well, but all she could think about was the heat of his mouth against hers, the memory of his hard body holding her tight.

How easy it was to focus on these things when the only other emotion she had inside her was wrenching, chilling fear. Her need for Lucas was so much simpler than all the other emotions that filled her at the moment.

"Did Wally say where he picked up Remy?" she

asked, finally breaking the uncomfortable silence that had ballooned between them.

"He didn't say, and with Remy it's hard to tell where Wally might have found him." Lucas turned onto Main Street.

The sun broke over the horizon, painting the buildings with a burst of gold light and dancing on the flowers that bloomed in pots in front of the shops.

Monday morning. She should be getting Billy out of bed and ready to go to the babysitter so she could go to work. She closed her eyes as she thought of sitting on the side of the bed next to her sleeping son. He always slept on his side, curled up in a warm toasty ball, and he always woke up with a smile.

He'd been a sunny child from the moment he'd been born. The only thing that had been able to put a cloud in his eyes had been his father.

She opened her eyes, consciously willing away the painful memories as Lucas pulled up in front of the sheriff's office. Please, she prayed. Please let the answer to where Jenny and Billy are rest with Remy Troulous. And please, let him talk to us.

Wally sat at the desk just inside the door and he rose as they entered. "Morning, Sheriff…Mariah." He nodded to them somberly. "I got him cooling his heels in the interview room. I'll warn you, he's not a happy camper."

Agent Michael Kessler also rose from the desk nearby. He walked over and introduced himself to Mariah. "Nice to meet you, although I'm sorry about the circumstances. I've been trying to run down your ex-husband," he said.

"No luck?"

Michael shook his head. "He hasn't registered a car in his name for the past two years nor can I find an employment record for him. I'll keep hunting, and in the meantime I've been interviewing locals for information." He gestured toward the interview room and looked at Lucas. "I'd like to be present when you interview Remy Troulous."

Lucas nodded, then looked at Mariah. "Initially, I want you to sit and watch outside of the room," Lucas said to her. "Let me and Agent Kessler have a go at him and see what happens."

"Before you do that, Louis got some information about Phillip Ribideaux you might find interesting," Wally said.

"And what's that?"

"It seems that ne'er-do-well Phillip has been cut off. According to his friends, his daddy got fed up with him and stopped the gravy train. Young Phillip now has to get a job and pay his own expenses."

Mariah watched the play of emotions on Lucas's face. He looked slightly dangerous, with a muscle ticking in his jaw and his dark-brown eyes narrowed. It was hard to believe that this was the same man who had minutes earlier held her so tenderly and kissed her with a fire that had momentarily chased away the arctic chill that had possessed her for the past two days.

"Louis is still sitting on him?"

Wally nodded. "But no offense, chief, somebody's going to have to take over for him so Louis can get some sleep."

"When Ed comes in this morning, put him on Ribideaux for the next twenty-four hours." Lucas looked at Mariah. "Maybe this is about a ransom after all.

Maybe Ribideaux got desperate when his father financially cut him off."

"Then why hasn't he made a ransom demand?" Mariah asked.

Lucas's eyes were dark as he held her gaze. "Right now the only answer I have is that whoever is holding Billy and Jenny is enjoying the game. Once the ransom demand is made, the game is over." He took her elbow and nodded to Agent Kessler. "Come on, let's go see what Remy Troulous has to add to this mix."

Lucas led her to a closet-size room with a window that looked into the next room. Inside the bigger area was a long conference table, and seated at the table was a handsome dark-haired young man.

He was sprawled in the chair with the arrogance of youth, legs up on the table and a smirk on his full, sensual lips. He wore a pair of worn jeans and a sleeveless shirt and had a large tattoo on his right shoulder. The tattoo was two letters—VP. Mariah guessed it stood for Voodoo Priests.

"I'll be right back," Lucas said as he gestured her to a chair.

She sat and stared at the young man, wondering if he had entered her home and somehow tricked Billy and Jenny into going with him, or forced them from the house at gunpoint. Or perhaps he'd encountered them in the park and seen an opportunity.

Although he looked like a punk, he didn't look evil. She had to remind herself that evil often wore a benign face. True evil could hide behind an easy smile and laughing eyes.

She drew a deep, tremulous breath and stared at the

man in front of her. Did the answer to Billy and Jenny's whereabouts rest with Remy Troulous?

She moved to the edge of the chair as she saw Lucas and Agent Kessler enter the interview room. "Get your feet off the table," Lucas said to Remy. "You might do that at your house, but you're in my house now."

For a moment Remy didn't move. He stared up at Lucas with insolent challenge, and Mariah could feel the tension between the two even though she wasn't in the same room.

She released a small sigh as Remy pulled his feet from the table and sat up straighter in the chair. "Why is it that whenever anything goes wrong in this town one of your men hauls me down here?" Remy asked.

"Because when things go wrong, you're usually in the middle of them." Lucas remained standing. He looked fierce, like a warrior facing his enemy. "You know my sister is missing?" Kessler stood just inside the door, obviously not intending to be an active participant in the questioning.

Remy laughed. "This is a small town, Sheriff. Somebody coughs in one house and the next-door neighbor calls somebody else to tell about it. Nothing much happens here that everyone doesn't know about."

Mariah studied Remy's face, watching his handsome features for signs of something, anything that would indicate he was behind the kidnapping.

"I don't know why your deputy dragged me down here," Remy continued. "I don't know anything about your sister's disappearance."

"One of her friends told me she'd been seeing you." Lucas took a step closer to where Remy sat.

"That's crazy," Remy exclaimed as he broke eye contact with Lucas. "What would somebody like me be doing with the sheriff's sister? Get real, why don't you?"

"Where were you on Friday between the hours of ten and five?"

Remy laughed once again, the sound deep and pleasant. "I'm not sure where I was last night. I sure as hell don't remember where I was on Friday."

Lucas sat in the chair next to Remy. "I think maybe you need to try harder to remember."

Remy frowned and rubbed a hand across his forehead. "I don't know, I was probably hanging out with my boys, that's what I do most days. You can check with one of them, they'll vouch for me."

"You mean they'll lie for you," Lucas replied. "When was the last time you saw Jenny?"

"I don't know. I might have passed her on the street last week sometime. I got me a girl, Sheriff, I'm not interested in Jenny like that."

"Then why was she seeing you?" Lucas pressed. "What interest did you have in her?"

Remy's eyes narrowed and he blinked several times. "I told you already I wasn't seeing your sister, and that's all I got to say on the matter." He crossed his arms over his chest. "I don't know where your sister and that little boy are. I don't have anything to do with them being missing. And unless you're going to charge me with something, I'm leaving. Are you arresting me?"

Lucas shook his head. "Not at this time."

"Then I'm out of here," Remy replied.

Panic shot through Mariah as Remy stood. He was

their best lead, and if he walked out, who knew if and when they would get the opportunity to question him again.

Remy headed for the door and Lucas followed him with Agent Kessler trailing behind. Mariah jumped up from her chair and met them in the hallway.

"Mr. Troulous," she said. "I'm Mariah Harrington and it's my little boy who is missing with Jenny." She grabbed his hand and tried to ignore the smell that emanated from him, the odors of stale sweat and cheap beer and swamp. "Please, if you know anything that might help us find them, if you had anything to do with it, please tell me."

She held his hand tightly, as if it were a rope that held her dangling over an abyss of grief. If she released him, if he walked away, then she was afraid she'd fall and crash into a million pieces.

Remy looked distinctly uncomfortable as he tried to pull his hand from her grasp, but she held on, refusing to allow him to move away from her.

"Billy, that's my son. He has asthma and if he gets scared or stressed out he'll have an attack. He's a smart boy and he loves school and learning about new things. He loves to play baseball and he doesn't like the dark. He needs his medicine but more than anything he needs to be home with me. I need him home with me." A sob welled up in her throat.

"Look, lady. I'm sorry for your troubles, but I don't know anything about it." Remy looked at Lucas for help.

Lucas stepped closer and placed a hand on Mariah's shoulder. "Let him go, Mariah," he said gently.

She didn't want to let him go. She wanted to hold his hand until he confessed he'd kidnapped Jenny and Billy. She wanted to cling to him until he told them where he had the two stashed and how she and Lucas could bring them home safely. But his dark, heavy-lidded eyes let her know she could squeeze his hand through eternity and he wasn't going to give her the answers she needed.

Reluctantly she let go and dropped her hand to her side. Remy raced for the exit as Lucas took Mariah by the arm and led her out of the hallway and into the inter-view room, Kessler following just behind them.

Lucas pulled out a chair and motioned her to sit, as if aware that her trembling legs threatened to give out beneath her. Once she was seated, he left the room then returned with a bottle of water and set it in front of her.

She smiled at him gratefully and uncapped the bottle and took a drink. "You okay?" he asked as he perched on the table next to her chair.

She shrugged. "I guess I was expecting a Perry Mason moment. You know, you lean on him and he breaks and tells us everything we need to know. Stupid, huh."

"Not stupid," he protested. "Just maybe a bit naïve."

"I'll tell you what was smart on your part. Talking about Billy like you did," Agent Kessler said.

"What do you mean?" She looked at the blond-haired man curiously.

"You said his name, told Remy a little bit about him. You personalized Billy to the man you thought might have him. That's a smart thing to do. It's what hostage negotia-tors do when they're trying to resolve a situation."

She sighed wearily. "I don't understand how two people could seemingly disappear from the face of the earth and nobody knows what happened." She put the cap back on the bottle of water and fought against the wave of overwhelming despair that threatened to consume her.

"Why don't you just hang tight right here," Lucas said. "We need to coordinate with my men." He stood. "You need anything?"

"The only thing I need is the one thing nobody seems to be able to get for me," she replied.

They left her then, alone in the interview room with only her faltering hope to keep her company.

THE MEN WERE ALL THERE except Ed, who had taken over sitting on Phillip Ribideaux for Louis. It took almost an hour for them to exchange pertinent information. Wally had been in touch with the phone company, trying to trace the calls that had gone to both Lucas's cell phone and Mariah's home number. As Lucas had suspected, other than the call that had come from the pay phone, the calls had been made by disposable cell phones that were almost impossible to trace.

He'd given the original copies of the recorded messages to Kessler, who would forward them to specialists in the hopes that they could identify a background noise or a voice pattern that might lead to a suspect.

Louis added that while he'd had Phillip Ribideaux under surveillance, the young man hadn't gone anywhere or done anything suspicious. After losing him, Louis had picked up his trail again at his house, where Phillip and some of his friends had spent most of the night drinking beer and packing a rental moving van.

Ben had searched the cemetery to look for the bullet, but hadn't found it.

There was still no word from Shreveport about Frank Landers and no other potential suspects on the list. Lucas instructed Ben to grab a couple of citizens who'd volunteered their time, and search all the empty buildings and storefronts in the city.

With nothing more to do, Lucas left his men and headed back to the interview room. Before he reached it, on impulse he went into the smaller room, sat in the chair and gazed at Mariah through the one-sided glass.

She sat with her profile to him, staring at the wall with no expression on her face. Her shoulders were rigidly straight and she seemed to scarcely be breathing.

He thought of the things she'd said to him during breakfast. Did he really remind her of her abusive ex-husband? Was he too overbearing with Jenny? In his concern that she not become a woman like their mother, had he stolen his sister's self-esteem?

Jenny had once mentioned that she'd like to be a teacher, but he had been adamant that a business degree was a smarter decision. He had just been trying to steer her in the right direction. Was that abusive?

Irritated with his thoughts and with the small flutter of self-doubt that suddenly assailed him, he stood. Dammit, he had more important things to be concerned with than analyzing his relationship with Jenny. He had to *find* her.

He got up from the chair and went into the interview room. Mariah stood as he entered, looking weary despite it being just noon.

"Let's get you home," he said.

She nodded and together they left the office and headed back to her house. They didn't speak. It was as if the failure to learn anything from Remy sat between them, creating a barrier too big for words to get around.

The minute they were back in her kitchen, they both saw the blinking message light. Lucas checked the information on the recorder. One recorded message, and it had come in three minutes before they'd walked through the front door. Without even playing it, he knew it was from the kidnapper.

Mariah grabbed one of his hands as he punched the button and the now-familiar voice filled the kitchen. "No answers at the office, right? Well, I have a little something for you. By the twisted tree you'll find a clue, where the grass is green and the sky is blue. Where the flowers bloom you'll find something rare. So go there now if you think you dare."

Lucas wanted to punch something. The bastard was watching their every move. He seemed to know what they were doing almost before they did it.

"It's the park," Mariah said, her blue eyes lighting with life. "A twisted tree, I know the tree. It's near the swings in the park."

Lucas frowned. "There must be a hundred twisted trees in Conja Creek."

Her eyes flashed with a touch of impatience. "But he would pick the one we know. Everyone refers to the tree in the park as the twisted tree. It's got to be the one in the park."

Mariah's excitement was contagious, but Lucas tried not to get his hopes up. He hated the bright shine of optimism that shone in her eyes—a shine that could so easily be doused.

"Mariah," he began cautiously. "We thought we were going to get something positive when we went to the cemetery, but the only thing we got was shot at."

"Surely he wouldn't do that again." She headed for the front door. "He says there's a clue there. He didn't say that about the cemetery. This is different. I couldn't live with myself if I didn't check it out." The words bubbled out of her, as if escaping an intense internal pressure. "Maybe this time he'll give us something to go on, or at least something to let us know that Jenny and Billy are still okay."

Lucas hurried after her and a moment later he backed out of her driveway and headed for the nearby neighborhood park. He had a bad feeling about this. It worried him that the caller had known that they'd been at the sheriff's office. It enraged him that the kidnapper was obviously close enough to them to know what they were doing and when they were doing it.

Who in the hell was behind this? It was possible Remy had made the call the moment he'd left the office. He probably possessed more than one cell phone that could be used to make the anonymous calls.

Lucas believed Remy hadn't been completely forthcoming, especially when Lucas had questioned him about why he'd been seeing Jenny. Although Remy had professed that he wasn't seeing Lucas's sister, Lucas hadn't believed him. Remy had avoided his glance when he'd answered and blinked one too many times, like liars usually did.

It bothered him that a ransom demand hadn't been made. That meant this was about something more than money. That meant it was something personal. And with both Jenny and Billy taken, it was impossible to know who was the real target.

The park was empty when they arrived, probably due to the intense heat and humidity of the day. Mariah was out of the car almost before Lucas had brought it to a complete halt. She raced across the parking lot toward the gnarled tree that rose up near the swing set. He ran after her, his hand on the butt of his gun.

"Mariah, wait," he called. Dammit, he didn't know if they were walking into some sort of a trap again or not. She didn't slow down.

He caught up with her when she halted in front of the tree. He grabbed her by the arm and pulled her to the ground. "What are you doing?" she asked.

"Have you forgotten what happened the last time we followed the caller's clue? Just stay down for a minute and let me assess things." He held on to her arm with one hand and kept his other on his gun.

He gazed around the area, not liking that the south side of the park was flanked by a wooded area that provided plenty of cover if somebody wanted to hide there.

"Lucas, if he wanted to kill us, we'd be dead," Mariah said softly. "If we're dead, the game ends and we both know that doesn't seem to be what the kidnapper wants."

As much as he hated to admit it, she made sense. The

kidnapper was obviously getting off on running them
around town, feeding their fear and anxiety. If he killed
one or both of them, his game would be over.

Mariah stood and began to search the tree. She
looked up into the branches, then walked around it,
checking out the trunk. Lucas looked as well, but found
nothing. "'Where the flowers bloom you'll find something rare,'" Mariah said, and her gaze focused on the
flower bed in the distance. "It's not the tree, it's the
flower bed," she exclaimed.

A deep weariness overtook Lucas. "Let's see if he
really left us something or if this is just another step in
his sick game."

Chapter Eight

Mariah raced toward the flower bed, her heart pounding with the rhythm of hope…of fear…and a million other emotions. Surely he wouldn't send them out for nothing again. Nobody could be that cruel.

There had to be something here, something that would feed the small glimmer of hope that still existed in her heart. As each hour passed, in the deepest, darkest places inside her, hope was becoming more and more difficult to sustain.

She'd somehow believed that if Billy were dead she'd know it in her heart, in her soul. But over the past couple of days she'd realized that wasn't true. It was possible Billy and Jenny had been murdered in the first hours of their disappearance, and she hadn't felt the loss.

As she stared at the flower bed, she refused to consider that scenario. They had to still be alive. Any other possibility was too horrific to contemplate.

"It doesn't look like any of the flowers have been disturbed," Lucas said as he stood next to her.

"There's got to be something here," she replied. She

stepped into the flower bed and sank to her hands and knees and began to pull at the flowers to see if any of them had been uprooted, then just set back in the ground.

A note, a piece of fabric, something, there had to be something buried beneath the flowers. That's what the caller had implied. It was a treasure hunt and she was desperate to find the treasure.

She pulled and tugged, more frantic with each minute that passed. It had to be here. Something had to be here. She couldn't come away from here without anything and continue to maintain her sanity.

She scrambled at the dirt, unmindful of the flowers she destroyed in her efforts. Flowers could be replaced, but Billy couldn't. Jenny couldn't.

A clawing, frantic desperation built inside her as she dug in the hard dirt with her fingers. She ignored Lucas, who stood just behind her. He wasn't digging, and she knew it was because he didn't believe anything was here. But she had to believe.

"Mariah, there's nothing here." Lucas's voice was flat, without emotion.

She ignored him, moving to a new place in the flower bed. Her fingers hurt from the contact with the hard earth, but she ignored the pain, scrabbling against the ground, uprooting flowers as her breaths came in frantic gasps. She felt half-demented with her need.

"Mariah, you need to stop." Lucas's voice seemed to come from very far away.

"No. Something's here. I know it is." She continued to dig, tears starting to blur her vision. She needed to find it. The clue. The caller had said there was a clue.

"Mariah." Lucas grabbed one of her arms. She jerked away from him, moving to yet another area and continuing her search. Tears became sobs as she dug.

Lucas grabbed her once again, this time more forcefully. "Mariah, dammit, stop. You have to stop! There's nothing here. He's yanking our chain."

As Lucas pulled her to her feet she fought him, slamming her fists into his chest as deep, wrenching sobs exploded from her.

"Let me go," she cried, mindless with anger, with a new kind of grief. "I have to find it."

"There's nothing here to find," he exclaimed, and he pulled her tight against him, holding her so she couldn't move, couldn't escape.

Somewhere in the back of her mind she knew he was right, that there was nothing to find, no clue that would magically lead to Billy. She quit fighting him and instead leaned weakly against him, sobbing as she broke completely.

He held her tight, rubbing her back as she clung to him. "Shh, I know," he whispered.

She cried harder, tears that had been trapped deep inside her since the first night of the disappearance.

"I'm sorry," he whispered. "Let it out. Just let it all out."

Her tears weren't just for herself and her son, but also for him and his sister. And she knew he understood better than anyone the utter despair she felt. Surely he felt the same bitter disappointment that she did. They were no closer to finding Jenny than they were to finding Billy.

They stood in the embrace for a long time as slowly,

painfully, Mariah cried herself out. When her tears were finally gone, there was nothing left inside her.

She was depleted…of emotion, of life. First the interview with Remy and now this, all for nothing. She was completely empty, numb.

"Come on, let's get you home," Lucas said gently.

Home, she thought. That place wasn't a home. Not with Billy gone.

He led her to his car, and she slid into the passenger seat. She'd never felt so numb, as if she were dead. She closed her eyes and only opened them again when the car stopped in her driveway.

She stared at the house that she'd thought would be the place she and Billy would find happiness. They were finally free of Frank, and she'd been filled with such hope when she'd rented the house.

She'd hoped that Conja Creek would be the place where she could work a decent job and raise Billy with the kind of stability and joy that had been missing in the first years of his life.

She'd believed the biggest threat in her life was Frank, and when she'd finally escaped his grasp she thought it would be smooth sailing. She'd been a fool to expect happiness. She'd been a fool to believe that such a state of being was even possible for her.

"Come on," Lucas said, pulling her from her thoughts. "You need a hot shower, and we need to do something about your hands."

She looked at her hands, surprised to see that her knuckles were cut and bloody and her nails were chipped and torn.

Wearily she got out of the car, the numbness slowly passing as a chill took over. Lucas wrapped an arm around her shoulder as they entered the house, and by the time he led her to the bathroom she was trembling uncontrollably.

He started the water in the shower and laid out a clean towel for her. "After you get out, we'll attend to those hands." He stepped out of the bathroom and closed the door behind him.

She slowly undressed and got beneath the hot spray of water, leaning weakly against the wall. She'd never felt so empty inside, as if everything that made her a living, breathing person had been drained away.

It scared her, the utter void. Even during the worst of times with Frank she'd never felt this way. Billy, her heart cried. Where are you?

She got out of the shower and dried off. She pulled a brush through her hair, then put on the white terry-cloth robe she retrieved from the hook on the back of the bathroom door.

Throwing her dirty clothes into her hamper, she felt lost. When she opened the bathroom door, she saw Lucas leaning against the wall in the hall and she knew in that instant what she needed, what she wanted. She needed some temporary insanity and she knew exactly who could give it to her.

LUCAS SIGHED IN RELIEF as she stepped out of the bathroom. She'd scared him. As she'd frantically dug in the flower bed, she'd been like a demented woman, and he was afraid she'd snapped.

But wrapped in a white robe, smelling like minty soap

and with her hair damp, she appeared to be back in control. The crazy, zealous light in her eyes was gone.

"Better?" he asked.

To his surprise she stepped up directly in front of him, so close he could feel her soft breath on his face. "No, I'm not better." Her blue eyes shimmered as she gazed up at him. "I'm cold inside and empty and I need you to make me warm. I need you to make me feel alive again." She wrapped her arms around his neck.

He stiffened and kept his hands at his sides, fighting the impulse to wrap her in his arms and pull her tightly, intimately against him. "Mariah, you're in a bad place right now. We don't want to do anything we'll regret later."

She pressed closer to him, and the first stir of desire didn't just simmer inside him, it crashed through him.

"No regrets," she replied. "I need you, Lucas. I need you to take me in your arms and make love to me. I need to make myself forget everything for just a little while." Her voice trembled slightly.

"Mariah, I don't want to take advantage of you," he replied. He held himself rigid and tried not to think about her naked beneath the robe.

"You aren't. I'm taking advantage of you." She rose up on tiptoe and placed her lips against the underside of his jaw.

Lucas closed his eyes, fighting to be strong. But her lips were hot and sensual against his neck, and as she moved her hips against his the control he'd fought to maintain the last couple of days snapped.

He took her mouth with his, losing himself in the hunger for her and the momentary respite from the horror that had become her life and his own.

The kiss lasted only a moment, then she broke it, took his hand and led him down the hall to her bedroom. There was no hesitation in her step, and her hand held tight to his, as if she was afraid he might try to break away and run.

When they reached her bedroom, she dropped his hand and began to unbutton his shirt. As she worked the buttons, he unfastened his holster, took it off and set it on the nightstand.

Somewhere in the back of his mind he knew this was crazy, that there was no way making love to Mariah would make anything better, easier. It would probably make things worse. When this was all over she'd probably hate herself. But at the moment her need radiated from her and he also couldn't deny that he wanted her.

When his shirt was unbuttoned, she ripped it from his shoulders and tossed it to the floor, then she walked over to the bed, pulled down the scarlet spread and shrugged out of her robe. She stood before him naked.

His breath caught in his throat. With the sunshine streaming through the window, painting her skin in gold tones, she was achingly beautiful. As he fumbled to get out of his slacks, she slid into bed beneath the sheets.

Crazy. He knew they both had gone stark-raving crazy, but he gave in to it, refusing to allow doubts any room in his head. He placed his wallet on the night-stand, then, as naked as she, he got into the bed and pulled her into his arms.

There was a frantic desperation in the kiss they shared, and her naked skin against his drove him half-mad with desire. She was warm and sweetly scented and it had been a very long time since he'd been with a woman. Work and Jenny had kept him busy, and it had been over a year since he'd taken time for even a superficial personal relationship.

But it wasn't just that he was overdue for sexual release that had him gasping with want. It was Mariah herself.

She'd been nothing more than the mayor's secretary when this all began, but in the past couple of days Lucas had seen her interminable strength, and she'd shared with him her past heartaches. He admired her and he liked her, and that as much as anything fed his desire for her and only her.

Their lips remained locked as his hands cupped her full breasts. Her nipples sprang to attention at his touch, and he grazed his thumb over them as she uttered a soft moan.

He broke the kiss and instead nipped lightly at the side of her slender neck, down across her collarbone, then he captured one of her erect nipples in his mouth.

She wound her fingers into his hair as he licked and sucked. She arched to meet his hardness, but he wasn't ready to take her yet. He wanted her mindless with pleasure, knew that's what she wanted…to be mindless.

He ran his hand down the flat of her stomach, down across her hip bones and touched her intimately. She gasped and at the same time she grabbed him. Her hand was warm around him, and he drew a deep breath to steady himself, not wanting to rush things.

He moved his fingers against her, and her breathing quickened as her entire body tensed. Once again he covered her mouth with his as he felt her getting closer to her release.

She whispered his name and he nearly lost it and at the same time she arched and cried out with complete pleasure.

"Take me," she said with a thrumming urgency that radiated through him. "Please, Lucas. Now, please take me now."

He rolled off her and grabbed his wallet, fumbling for the condom he carried inside. It took him only a moment to get it out and on, then he positioned himself above her and gazed down into her eyes.

"It's not too late to stop," he said, his voice hoarse and ragged. "You can stop this right now if you want to. I won't be mad."

She reached up and placed her hand on his cheek, her eyes filled with a depth of emotion. "Don't stop," she said.

He entered her, sliding into her awaiting warmth with a slow, sure stroke. She moaned her pleasure and wrapped her arms around his back.

Slowly he moved against her, but it didn't take long before his own frantic need moved him faster and faster. She wasn't a passive lover. Her hands raked him as she threw her head back and gave herself completely to the act.

All too quickly he felt the build up, and just before he exploded, she cried his name and his release washed through him with an intensity he'd never known. He kissed her then, a soft, tender kiss.

He rolled to one side of her and she turned to face him. For a long moment her gaze remained locked with his, and in the depth of her eyes he saw her heartbreak once again darkening her eyes.

He stroked her face, a sense of failure sweeping through him. He might have taken her away for a few minutes, but until he brought her son home safe and sound, her pain wouldn't ever let her go.

And with each hour that passed, the possibility of bringing Billy home safe and sound grew dimmer.

BILLY WAS IN TROUBLE.

Jenny stared at the sleeping little boy and feared that he wouldn't make it through another night. The sound of his ragged breaths filled her with a fear she'd never known. He hadn't even had the energy to get off the mattress during the day.

He'd spent most of the time just lying there, the mere act of drawing breath taking every ounce of his strength. He didn't even have the strength to be afraid. He seemed resigned to whatever was going to happen, and Jenny wanted to weep because an eight-year-old boy shouldn't be resigned to his own death.

She walked around the small room and wondered if they both would die here. She didn't care so much about herself, but it wasn't fair that a little boy die in this ugly place without his mommy to hold him, to comfort him.

If she could just find a way out, or some means to summon help. But she'd been over the small room a hundred times and couldn't find a way to do either. She'd pulled at the boards that imprisoned them, seeking a weakness, a flaw in their prison, but there was none.

She'd just sunk to the floor when she heard the

sound. *A boat.* A motorboat. Maybe it was help! A search party. She sprang to her feet, hope raging through her. Maybe Lucas had found them!

Or maybe it was their kidnapper returning. The hope that had momentarily surged through her transformed to fear. She stood perfectly still, frozen as the sound of the boat grew closer…closer…then finally stopped.

There was a moment of complete silence, then heavy footsteps rang against wood. Jenny stifled a scream. If it were help, then somebody would have yelled. Somebody would have shouted their names.

The footsteps drew closer, then a slat in the door opened. Jenny ran to the door. "Hey…hey, you've got to get us out of here! He's sick. Billy has asthma and he's in bad trouble."

Dark eyes peered back at her, then the slat closed.

She slammed her fists against the door as she heard footsteps going away. "Wait, please come back. Did you hear what I said? He's in bad trouble. He needs to get to a hospital." Again and again she slammed her fists against the wood as she began to cry. "Don't go. For God's sake don't leave him here."

It was only when she heard the motor on the boat start up again that she stopped beating the door and sank to the floor in tears.

He was leaving. He was leaving them here. Tears blinded her and she fought against the deep sobs that welled inside her.

She turned and saw Billy watching her. She quickly swiped at her cheeks. She didn't want to cry in front of him. She didn't want to upset him any more than he already was.

"Hey, buddy." She scooted over next to him and pulled him into her arms. His wheezing seemed to intensify. She needed to distract him.

"Have I ever told you that female alligators usually lay about fifty eggs? Can you imagine having fifty kids?" As she told him everything she'd ever known about alligators and crocodiles, she felt him begin to relax against her.

But she couldn't relax for, more than fear of her own safety, her biggest fear was that when morning came, Billy would no longer be breathing.

Chapter Nine

Mariah awoke as the faint purple spill of dusk filtered through the window. The bed next to her was empty, but the pillow still retained the scent of Lucas's cologne.

She didn't feel guilty about making love with him. She didn't feel guilty about seeking warmth and life when her heart had been so dead. Nor did she have any illusions about what their lovemaking had meant. It had meant absolutely nothing.

Rolling over on her back, she stared up at the ceiling and realized that in some way the lovemaking and the sleep afterward had given her a new strength to survive whatever the rest of the evening might bring.

She got out of bed and dressed in a comfortable pair of gray jogging pants and a T-shirt, then went in search of Lucas. As she reached the hallway, she heard the voice of the kidnapper.

"…by the twisted tree you'll find a clue." She froze, heart banging against her rib cage.

The voice stopped, then started again. "…by the twisted tree you'll find a clue."

She relaxed a bit as she realized it wasn't a new call.

She followed the sound to the kitchen, where Lucas sat in front of the recording machine with a legal pad in front of him.

She stood in the doorway and watched as he pushed the Play button again. "Where the grass is green and the sky is blue." He punched the Stop button, then rubbed the center of his forehead with two fingers as he stared down at the legal pad.

"What are you doing?"

He looked up at the sound of her voice, then leaned back in his chair and sighed. "Making notes, listening to the messages, trying to make sense of all this."

She slid into the chair next to him. "And have you managed to make any sense of it?"

He shook his head. "No." He leaned back in the chair and released a weary sigh. "I'll tell you what we know. There was no sign of forced entry, so the odds are good that Jenny knew the kidnapper, that she not only knew him but trusted him enough to open the door to him. If they were taken from here."

She frowned. "What do you mean? Of course they were taken from here."

"We don't know that for sure. We don't really know where the crime scene is located. For all we know they were taken from the front yard or the park."

She frowned. He had mentioned that before, but she couldn't imagine Jenny and Billy being hustled into a car off the street or taken from the park…unless they knew their kidnapper…unless they'd trusted the kidnapper. That thought certainly didn't make her feel any better.

He flipped through his legal pad. "We also know that

the kidnapper is watching us. He was in the cemetery the other night, and he knew that we'd gone to the sheriff's office this morning. Something else that strikes me is that he doesn't seem to want dialogue, but instead wants monologues."

She frowned at him curiously. "What do you mean?"

He leaned forward. "Other than the first call that I got and the one that Wally answered, he hasn't called to talk to us, but rather to leave messages on the machine. He's specifically chosen times when he knows we aren't here. He wants to talk to us, but he doesn't want us talking to him."

"So what would happen if we don't leave here? If we answer every call that comes in instead of letting the machine pick up. Would he stop calling?"

"It would be interesting to see," he replied.

A flash of anger burned inside her. "He might think he's playing a game with us, but he's not. Games have rules and when he says there's a clue, then there should be a clue." She released a bitter laugh. "I know it's ridiculous for me to be mad because a kidnapper doesn't play by the rules I think are fair."

Lucas nodded, his forehead still furrowed with a frown. "Our two main suspects are Remy Troulous and Phillip Ribideaux. I know Phillip has been financially cut off by his father."

"Which might make him desperate enough to kidnap for a ransom," she said. "He certainly doesn't have the tools to make a living the right way."

"But…I keep going back to the same problem. If this is about a ransom, then why take Billy?"

"Because he saw the kidnapper?"

He nodded. "Then we have Frank Landers, whom we can't locate and have no idea if he has a hand in this. And if he took Billy, then why Jenny?"

"For the same reason. Because she saw him and could identify him."

"I feel like we're going in circles," he said in frustration. He swiped a hand through his dark hair, and for a moment she remembered what those dark, rich strands had felt like between her fingers.

"Let's take the suspects one at a time," she said, focusing on the conversation. "We can pinpoint a plausible motive for Phillip. Maybe he's just entertaining himself before making a ransom demand. What about Remy? Same motive? Money?"

Lucas sighed again. "The longer this thing goes on, the less I think it's about money."

"What other motive could Phillip have?" she asked.

"Who knows? I know Jenny was talking a lot of smack about him after they broke up. Maybe he's trying to teach her a lesson."

"And what about Remy? If you take away a money motive, then why would he be involved in something like this?" It helped, talking rationally about all the players. It felt constructive, and that was what she needed at the moment.

"Who knows what drives Remy? Certainly he's always walked a line outside the law. I don't think he was forthcoming in his answers to me about seeing Jenny, but I can't imagine what he hopes to gain by a kidnapping."

"It could be Frank," Mariah said. "The caller is getting off on tormenting us. That's definitely Frank's style."

Lucas reached out and covered her hand with his. "I'm sorry you had to go through what you did with him."

The warmth of his hand was welcome, and she offered him a small smile. "I survived. But, as sheriff of this parish, you should know that if I find out he's responsible for this, I might just kill him."

"I understand the sentiment," he replied, and by the darkness in his eyes she knew he felt the same rage that she did.

She pulled her hand from his and leaned back in her chair. "Any other viable suspects?"

"No, and that's what's so damned frustrating. Not knowing for sure what the motive might be makes pointing a finger at a viable suspect that much more difficult." He tapped the recorder. "And what's driving me crazy is that there's something about the caller's voice that's vaguely familiar, but I can't figure out what it is."

This time it was her turn to place her hand over his. "You're doing everything you can. You've got people searching and watching the suspects. There's only so much you can do with so little to go on."

He smiled, filling her with a welcome warmth. "I'm the one who's supposed to be making you feel better."

"Then who makes *you* feel better? Why have you remained alone?" During the past couple of days she'd seen a side of Lucas she'd never guessed he would have possessed. It was a tender and gentle side that was in direct contrast to the kind of man she'd believed him to be.

He rose from the table and went to the counter,

where the pot of coffee was still warm. He poured himself a cup. "Want one?"

She shook her head, and he returned to the table.

"When my wife left me I decided to devote my life to Jenny. Someplace in the back of my mind, I knew that women would come and go, but that my sister would always need me. She had nobody else. I have my work and I date occasionally, and for the most part that's been enough for me."

"But a sister and work can't be a partner for life," she replied.

He cast her a wry smile. "Jenny could definitely be a job for life."

She bit her tongue, not wanting to begin another contentious discussion about his relationship with his sister.

He seemed to read her mind. "You have to understand where we came from. My old man died when Jenny was just a baby and our mother, who was never real maternal, seemed to forget she was a parent."

He got up from the table as if unable to sit any longer and began to pace the small confines of the room. "Mom was one of those women who thrived on attention and drama. She wasn't happy unless everything was in an uproar, and she definitely wasn't happy if she wasn't with a man." He paused and stared at the wall just over her head, his eyes dark with memories.

He focused back on Mariah. "Maybe I have been too hard on Jenny. I've just been so afraid she'd turn out like our mother. Mom killed herself with drugs. I don't think she meant to die, but she had just broken up with some loser and I think the suicide was an attempt to get him back. She took pills then called him, but he didn't believe her and she died."

"But you've accomplished what you wanted. Jenny is nothing like the woman you've described," Mariah said softly. Certainly what he'd just told her helped in her understanding of his relationship with Jenny.

He stared at her for a long moment. "If I've been the man you described, if I've been emotionally abusive and overbearing to her, my biggest fear now is that I won't get the chance to change things."

His voice broke and Mariah rose from her chair and walked to where he stood. She wrapped her arms tightly around him, knowing the torment that was in his heart.

"You'll get your chance to make things right with Jenny," she said. "And I'm going to get the chance to see my son grow up." She said the words fervently, but what frightened her more than anything was she wasn't sure she believed them anymore.

LUCAS STOOD at the front window, staring into the bright afternoon sunshine. He stretched, attempting to unkink muscles that had been knotted from the moment he'd awakened on the sofa that morning.

He'd spent a miserable night with horrible dreams of Jenny crying out to him and him unable to find her. When Mariah had gotten up, it had been obvious that she'd spent an equally miserable night. Her face had been lined with stress, and exhaustion had placed even darker circles under her eyes.

He wanted to be outside, searching, but he'd determined that the best place for him to be was here, waiting for another phone call. This time the caller wouldn't talk to a machine, but to him.

Mariah had gone back to her bedroom a little while ago, and Lucas had almost been grateful that she had. Their conversation had been empty and strained today, as if the emotional outbursts from the day before had drained all the energy, all the will from them both.

Enough time had passed, now, that most of the concerned citizens who had come out on that first day to help search would have returned to their jobs, their lives.

Even when a young woman and a little boy were missing, life went on. What if they never found Jenny and Billy? People disappeared every day, and when foul play was involved bodies were often never found.

How would Mariah cope if Billy never came home? She'd survive, because she was a survivor, but her life would never be the same. He felt confident that she wouldn't remain in Conja Creek, that the town itself and this house in particular would hold too many bad memories for her to stay.

He would miss her. The thought shocked him. In the course of these past days, he'd grown closer to her than he could ever have imagined, closer than he'd been to anyone for a very long time. He felt he knew her better than anyone, but more than that, he felt she knew him.

Lucas recognized he could fall for her if he allowed himself. But he wouldn't allow it, because even though she'd made love with him, he guessed that the emotions they felt were driven by circumstance.

Sooner or later this case would be resolved one way or another, and with that resolution would come an end to the unusual and intense relationship they'd forged.

As he moved away from the window, he realized it was time for him to build a wall around his emotions where she was concerned. He'd allowed himself to get too close, both in his position as sheriff and as a man.

He returned to the kitchen, where his legal pad awaited him at the table. One thing he and Mariah hadn't discussed the day before when they'd been going over things was the fact that the kidnapper could be almost anyone.

Just because they had Phillip Ribideaux and Remy Troulous in their sights didn't mean either man was responsible. Just because she thought this was something her ex-husband might be capable of didn't mean Frank Landers was responsible.

Who knew what acquaintances Jenny had who might want to do this? Who knew what neighbor or friend might harbor some sick twist in their mind that might have led to this?

The phone rang and Lucas snatched up the receiver, his heart pounding as it had every time the phone rang. "Hello?"

"Hi, this is Miranda Thomas with Channel Four news. I was wondering if I could speak with Mariah?"

His heart slowed once again. "She isn't taking calls."

"Who am I speaking to?" she asked.

"A 'no comment' kind of guy," he replied, and hung up the receiver.

The calls from the press had been constant, as had the calls from Richard Welch wanting updates. There had still been a few other phone messages, also—well-meaning people who wanted to know what they could do, how they could help. But so far the call Lucas most wanted hadn't come.

This time there would be no taped monologue. This time there was going to be a dialogue and maybe, just maybe, in having that dialogue Lucas could figure out what about that voice sounded so familiar.

The doorbell rang and he hurried out of the kitchen to the front door. He met Mariah coming down the hallway. She cast him a tired smile as he peeked out the door and took a step back in surprise.

"It's Remy Troulous," he said to her as he opened the door. What was he doing here?

Mariah stepped in front of Lucas. "Mr. Troulous, please come in," she said as if he were an expected, welcome friend.

Remy looked distinctly uncomfortable as he stepped through the door and into the small entry. "Please, come in and sit," Mariah said, and gestured him into the living room. "Would you like something to drink?"

"No, I'm good," he replied.

Lucas frowned at the young man. "What are you doing here, Remy?"

"I didn't want to talk to you at the office. My business is nobody's business, and I didn't want anyone to hear what I'm going to tell you." Remy's eyes gleamed with a hard edge, and he lifted his chin defensively.

"Do you know where my son is? Where Jenny is?" Mariah asked, her voice filled with urgency as she stepped closer to him.

"No." His gaze softened slightly as he looked at Mariah. "I'm sorry, but I really don't know anything about what happened to them." He looked back at Lucas. "You and I have butted heads a lot of times in the past, but even you should know this isn't my style. I don't mess with kids."

"So, what do you have to tell us?" Lucas asked.

"It's about me and Jenny."

"What about you and Jenny?" Lucas tried to hang on to his emotions.

"We were sort of seeing each other, but it's not what you think." Again Remy's chin lifted. "It wasn't anything romantic or nothing like that."

"Then what was it?" Lucas couldn't imagine what this man and his sister would have in common, why they would be seeing each other at all.

Remy shoved his hands into his pockets and gazed first at Lucas, then at Mariah, then back to Lucas. "Look, this is something I don't want anyone else to know. That's why I came here instead of telling you yesterday. You had that other dude in the room and I wasn't going to talk about it."

"Talk about what?" Lucas asked with more than a touch of impatience.

"Jenny was teaching me to read, okay? I know I can't be a gangbanger forever. I want something better, okay? But I can't do nothing about my life unless I learn how to read."

He eyed them belligerently, as if expecting them to mock or belittle his efforts. "Anyway, that's why I was meeting with her. I just thought you should know so you'll get off my back 'cause I had nothing to do with her being missing." He backed toward the door. "Sorry I can't help. I liked Jenny a lot and she was nice to me even though she didn't have to be." He dug into his pocket and pulled out a crumpled piece of paper. "This is my cell phone number. If I can do anything to help find her, give me a call."

Lucas could feel Mariah's disappointment, as rich and deep as his own. He took the piece of paper from Remy but wasn't finished with his questions. "How did you arrange this with my sister?"

Remy shrugged his narrow shoulders. "I was in the library and looking at books on reading. Jenny was in there, too, and she saw the books I was looking at. We started talking and she offered to help me. I trusted her: I knew she wouldn't tell nobody, so we met a couple of times here during the day."

"And you haven't heard anything on the streets about her disappearance?" Lucas asked.

Remy shook his head. "Nothing. Whoever took them, he ain't talking to nobody. Look, Jenny was helping me. I wouldn't have repaid her by doing something like this. I just wanted you to know." Without another word, Remy shot out of the front door.

Mariah closed the door after him and turned to face Lucas. "Do you believe him?"

"I have absolutely no reason to believe anything that falls out of that man's mouth, but yeah, I believe him."

She nodded. "So do I. It's just the kind of thing Jenny would do. I told you she would have made a great teacher."

A stab of guilt gored him. He'd been so busy worrying about the kind of woman Jenny *might* be that he hadn't taken the time to see what kind of woman she had become.

He sighed. "So, if we believe Remy, then he comes off our list of suspects."

"And since Phillip Ribideaux has done nothing suspicious in the past couple of days and we don't know where Frank is, that leaves us with nothing."

Lucas opened his mouth to protest her assessment, then closed it. Because she was right.

Chapter Ten

It had become a waiting game, and as the afternoon hours crept by, Mariah felt as if she might explode. Why didn't he call? If she and Lucas walked out the front door, would the kidnapper call then? Leave one of his cryptic messages to lead them on yet another wild-goose chase?

Lucas had remained for much of the day at the table, alternately talking on his cell phone and staring at her telephone as if willing it to ring.

Dusk was falling and the panic that night brought with it formed a big, tight lump in her chest. Another night. How many nights could she survive? How long before she lost her mind with grief?

The house had been so quiet. Until his disappearance, Mariah hadn't realized how much Billy filled up the house with sound. He often clomped when he walked, he hummed and whistled while he did his chores. And he laughed. God, what she wouldn't give to hear the sound of his laugher once again.

When the doorbell rang at seven that evening, Mariah hurried to answer it, grateful for the break from the tension, from the monotony of waiting for the kidnapper to call.

She opened the door and froze as she saw the man with a sprinkle of gray in his black hair, the narrow dark eyes that had once haunted her dreams.

"Hello, Mariah. How in the hell did you manage to lose our little boy?"

"Frank." Mariah wouldn't have thought it possible for the cold inside her to intensify, but it did at the sight of the man who had caused her such pain. A fear she thought she'd gotten past filled her.

"Your hair always looked so nice when you wore it short," he said. "Now, aren't you going to invite me in?"

Mariah felt Lucas's presence just behind her. "I don't know if she'll invite you in, but I certainly will."

As Lucas placed a hand on Mariah's shoulder, she was filled with strength. This man, this monster, couldn't hurt her ever again, and she refused to allow him to create fear inside her.

"By all means, come in," she agreed and opened the door to her past. "We've been looking for you."

"Who are you?" Frank asked Lucas as he stepped into the small foyer.

"I'm Sheriff Lucas Jamison and I have some questions for you, Frank."

"I've got questions for you. Where in the hell is my boy? What kind of an investigation is going on that a little boy and some woman have been missing for the past four days and you can't find them?"

Lucas's eyes narrowed. "Why don't we all go in and have a seat. I'll be happy to answer your questions after you've answered mine."

It was obvious Lucas intended to maintain the control in the situation. The three of them moved into the living room where Frank sat on the sofa and patted the cushion next to him with a smile at Mariah.

"When hell freezes over," she muttered under her breath and sat in the chair opposite the sofa. Lucas remained standing next to Mariah's chair.

"Can you tell me where you've been for the past four days?" Lucas asked.

Frank straightened his shoulders, as if affronted by the very question. "Surely you don't think I had anything to do with this." He glared at Mariah. "Ask her what she did to put our boy at risk. She's always been irresponsible. If anyone is at fault here, it's her."

"Right now we're talking about you," Lucas replied, his tone holding an iron edge. "I'm going to ask you again, where have you been for the past four days?"

"Up until this morning I was in my home in Shreveport," Frank said.

"We had the authorities in Shreveport looking for you, but they couldn't find where you lived or worked," Mariah said. Funny, for so many years he'd been a monster in her mind. He'd been big and strong and scary. But now, seated on her floral-patterned sofa, he looked small and petty and nothing like a monster at all.

"I've been living with a friend and I'm between jobs at the moment. It was during breakfast this morning that I saw a newscast about Billy and Mariah and of course I came right here." He cast a sideways look at Mariah. "My new friend knows how to treat a man right."

If Mariah had to guess, his new "friend" was probably a young, impressionable woman who didn't realize the path she'd chosen when she'd hooked up with Frank Landers.

"I'll need your address in Shreveport and the name of your friend," Lucas said.

Frank's square jaw tightened. "You're wasting your time investigating me."

"It's my time to waste," Lucas replied evenly.

For the next few minutes Lucas questioned Mariah's ex-husband, and though she tried to stay focused on the conversation she found herself comparing the two men.

She'd once thought Frank the handsomest man she'd ever known, but now she saw the weakness of his jaw, the furtive cast of his eyes and the voice that radiated belligerence rather than strength.

Handsome was a man who loved his sister to distraction. Handsome was a man who had held her in his arms when she thought she might fracture. The fact that Lucas remained standing next to where she sat, creating a subtle united force to Frank, that was beyond handsome.

Somewhere in the madness of the past four days, her attitude toward Lucas Jamison had changed. As she watched the byplay between the two men, she realized she'd allowed her past to color how she saw Lucas and his actions toward Jenny.

"I demand to know exactly what's being done to find my son," Frank said, his strident tone bringing Mariah out of her thoughts. He stood as if unable to sit still another moment.

"We can discuss all that at my office," Lucas replied. "Tomorrow morning at ten. I'll meet you there and fill you in."

"Fine. I look forward to hearing what's going on." Frank headed for the front door. Mariah started to get up, but Lucas touched her shoulder.

"Stay put," he said. "I'll walk him out."

She remained in the chair and realized seeing Frank again had somehow freed her. She hadn't known until this moment that he'd still owned a part of her, that a little piece of fear still reigned in her heart where he was concerned. Facing him again had evaporated that fear, and she knew he'd never have the power in life or in dreams to scare her again.

Now if she could just get her son back…. She rose from the chair and went to the window that looked over the backyard and stared out into the deepening shadows of the night.

Strange. The wrist Frank had broken didn't ache now. Her worst nightmare had come true. Frank knew where they lived, but she wasn't running this time. He'd chased her from everything she'd known once. He wouldn't do it again. This was Billy's home. He loved it here, had friends and roots here.

She'd gone to court before to ensure that Frank had no visitation with his son. He had no legal right to be here, and this time she wasn't running.

She heard the front door open, then close. She knew when Lucas stood behind her, because she smelled the familiar scent of him. She wasn't surprised when he placed his hands gently on her shoulders and turned her around to face him.

"You okay?" he asked, his features radiating concern.

"I'm fine." She smiled. "He was my boogeyman for

so long, but seeing him now I realized he isn't anymore. He's just a pathetic little man who likes to abuse women."

"I called Agent Kessler while I was outside," Lucas said. "I want your ex-boogeyman checked inside out and upside down. I want to know everything about his movements over the past four days."

She frowned. "So you think he has Billy?"

"I think his concern for his son came off like an orchestrated act," Lucas replied. "I've definitely moved him to the top of my suspect list." He frowned. "He's a nasty piece of work." His frown fell away for a moment and a soft smile curved his lips. "But I will tell you now that you look beautiful with your long hair."

She touched his jaw, the place where a muscle knotted when he was filled with angry emotion. "I owe you an apology."

He covered her hand with his, his expression curious. "An apology for what?"

"For telling you that you remind me of Frank, for allowing you to believe that you have anything in common with that man."

A pained expression chased across his face and he dropped his hand from hers. "I would never, ever willingly hurt Jenny or any woman, but there was some truth in what you said to me." He stepped away from her and raked a hand through his hair. "I have been overbearing with Jenny. I didn't mean it to be that way, but over the past couple of days I've given it a lot of thought." His jaw knotted and his eyes darkened. "I just want a chance to do things differently."

She moved into his arms and leaned her head against

his broad chest. It scared her just a little bit, how comforting the act was, how much she felt as if she belonged in his arms.

What they were experiencing had nothing to do with real life. The connection she felt with him had been forged in circumstances of heightened emotions, of tense drama and fear. It had nothing to do with reality, and she'd be a fool to think otherwise.

Still she remained in his arms and thought of her son and his sister and wondered if there was a happy ending to be found in this mess.

Then the phone rang.

THE RING OF THE PHONE electrified Lucas. He broke their embrace and raced for the kitchen. He hit the record and speaker button, then picked up the receiver.

"Jamison," he answered.

"Ah, the good sheriff. Listen carefully. At the corner of Main and Cotton Street…"

"Wait," Lucas interrupted the kidnapper. "We need to know that Billy and Jenny are still alive. You've got to give us something."

"I reckon you've forgotten who is in charge here. At the corner of Main and Cotton Street you'll find a bench with a big wide seat."

"*Listen* to *me,* what is it you want from us?" Lucas exchanged a look of frustration with Mariah.

"At the corner of Main and Cotton…" the kidnapper began again.

"Why are you doing this? Just tell us what you want," Lucas interjected. He was trying to pull the kidnapper into a discussion, hoping that something the caller said would trigger a clue. But the kidnapper still had no desire to deviate from whatever script was in his head.

"At the corner of Main and Cotton Street, you'll find a bench with a big wide seat. If you look beneath you might find a clue, a little gift from me to you."

Lucas grunted in surprise as Mariah snatched the receiver from his hands. "Listen you, we're not playing your game anymore. You hear me? I'm done chasing around town looking for clues that aren't there." Her voice was shrill with anger and her eyes flamed with emotion. "Play your stupid game without us, because we're done."

The caller hung up.

Mariah stared at Lucas. She clutched the phone receiver so tightly her knuckles turned white. He gently tried to take it away from her.

"What have I done?" she whispered as she released the phone to him.

"You've changed the game, and that's not necessarily a bad thing," he replied.

She sank into a chair at the table and covered her face with her hands. He pulled up a chair in front of her and sat, then reached out for her hands.

"Mariah, maybe you shook him up and maybe that's what we needed to do," he said. "He's been running us all over town for nothing. It was time we told him no more. We take away the pleasure he's gotten in baiting us and maybe he'll get desperate for attention and make a mistake."

"I just hope I didn't make him angry enough to do something awful."

"If he's going to do something awful, then nothing we can do or say will make a difference," Lucas said. It was possible something awful had already been done. He couldn't ignore the possibility that Jenny and Billy had been killed in the hours immediately following the kidnapping and the killer was just amusing himself now.

"Who are you calling?" she asked as he began to punch numbers on his phone.

"The office. Ed," he said into the receiver. "I want you to do me a favor. Go to the corner of Cotton and Main and check a bench that's there. See if there's anything taped to the bottom of it, then call me back." If the kidnapper was watching, seeing the deputy might force him to act and give them something to go on.

He hung up and Mariah stared at him expectantly. "So, what do we do now?" she asked.

He shrugged and stared outside where night had once again fallen. The fourth night, and they were no closer to finding Jenny and Billy than they'd been on the first night.

He looked back at Mariah. "We do what we've been doing. We let the investigation unfold and we wait for a break."

She sighed. "Did you find out any more about Frank's whereabouts the past couple of days when you walked him outside?"

"No, but I did let him know what would happen if he bothered you while he was here in Conja Creek. I told him exactly what we thought of men who abuse women."

Her eyes widened. "You threatened him?"

"Let's just say I gave him a friendly warning."

"Did you get any feeling that he might be behind this?"

"I don't know whether he is or not, but he's the kind

of man capable of such a thing." He leaned back in the chair. "The caller's voice is so distorted it's almost impossible to match it to somebody we've heard."

"Maybe Agent Kessler will be able to tell us something about the calls," she said.

Lucas nodded. But he knew that it could take weeks, even months to get information from Kessler and his men. The FBI lab wouldn't necessarily see the kidnapping of one child and one woman from a small Southern town as a priority given all the other cases they worked.

Lucas still felt the burning need to be doing something, to tear apart the town in an effort to find the missing loved ones, but logically he knew there was nothing more to be done than what was being done.

The kidnapper was still in charge of things, and unless or until he made a mistake, there wasn't much more Lucas and his men could do.

Maylor called to let them know that there was nothing unusual about the bench at Cotton and Main. Lucas checked in with Kessler and the rest of his men, then the night stretched out before them, long and dark.

"Is your mother still alive?" he asked Mariah, seeking conversation to fill the time.

"No. She had cancer and passed away not too long after my wedding. She died happy, believing that I had found a man to love and cherish me. I'm glad she passed before she knew about Frank and about my divorce." She got up from her chair. "Want some coffee?"

"Sure," he agreed. He wished she'd sleep. What little sleep they'd both gotten over the past four days had been in unexpected catnaps, when exhaustion overwhelmed will.

As he watched her making the coffee he was struck by a burst of desire for her, a need to lose himself in her kisses, in the sweet heat her body offered.

He couldn't know if what he felt for her was real or simply emotions flaring out of control because of the situation.

It also occurred to him that, for the past four days, they'd existed like a married couple, sharing quiet conversations in the predawn moments, listening to each other breathe when the conversation ran out.

Lucas had never been a lonely man, but he had a feeling when he returned to his big house with only Marquette as company, he would be lonely. Talking to Mariah, watching her graceful movements and listening to the sound of her voice had become a pleasant habit, one he knew would be hard to break.

When the coffee was finished, she brought it to the table. She wrapped her slender fingers around her mug and eyed him curiously. "Don't you want children?"

He started to give a quick reply, but instead took a sip of coffee and thought about the question. "I haven't really thought about it for a long time. Certainly when I got married I figured eventually there would be kids. But then my marriage fell apart and I was busy raising Jenny. I didn't give it any more thought."

"Jenny is going to eventually get married and start a family of her own. That's important to her, having a husband and kids." She tilted her head a bit, the light overhead glistening in her chestnut hair. "When do you get your chance, Lucas? When is it time for you to build something just for yourself?"

"I have my work. It's always been enough for me," he replied a bit uneasily.

"Work is what I do, but being a mother is who I am." She took a sip of her coffee, then continued. "I bet you'd make an awesome dad."

He laughed, the amusement surprising even himself. "You can't have it both ways, Mariah. You've told me in so many words that I've been screwing it up with Jenny and yet you think I'd make a great dad. That's a little bit contradictory, don't you think?"

She smiled, and it was the first smile he'd seen from her that wasn't tinged with grief, that didn't hold tense lines and jagged edges. "My complaint about your parenting skills has nothing to do with when Jenny was younger. I'll bet you were a loving caretaker for her when she was a kid. My only complaint is that you don't seem to know that it's time to let go."

"Point taken," he replied. "You're different than I thought you were."

"What do you mean?"

"Whenever I saw you at the mayor's office, you seemed hard-edged and uptight. You're softer than I thought."

"I take my job very seriously. Besides, anytime you came in to see Richard, he freaked out just a little bit. I think you scare him. You're always so sure of yourself and what you're doing. Richard cares so much about this town and the people, but he's less sure about his path than you are."

"Did he know about your past? That you weren't really a widow?"

She nodded. "I had no references to give him and so

I told him the truth, that I wanted a fresh start here and was willing to work hard to create a good life. Harrington isn't my real name. I couldn't use Landers nor could I use my maiden name because I was afraid Frank would find me. Harrington is a name I chose, and the shelter where I stayed for a while helped me get identification in my new name. Richard knew all that and hired me anyway. He gave me a chance and kept my secret, and for that I'll always be grateful to him."

Lucas grinned. "Then I guess I'm going to have to ease up on Richard."

The next couple of hours passed in quiet conversation. The tension, the stress and anxiety of the past four days seemed to have momentarily ebbed, as if their minds and bodies could no longer sustain the heightened sense of fear.

She told him a little bit more about her life with Frank, her lonely childhood with her mostly absent mother, and he regaled her with tales of his life in college with the friends he called his band of brothers, the men whom he still called his friends.

It was almost midnight when the coffee was gone and the fear returned. He saw it swimming back into her eyes, in the slight shake of her hands as she removed the cups from the table.

"You should try to get some sleep," he said.

"I know. But I'm afraid to close my eyes." She placed the cups in the dishwasher then turned back to face him. "I'm afraid I'll have bad dreams, but more than that, I'm afraid those dreams might come true."

Then the phone rang again.

Chapter Eleven

Electricity sizzled through Mariah. "You think he's calling back?"

"We won't know unless we answer." He punched the record and the speaker button. "Jamison," he said.

"Lucas, it's me, Jackson." It was obvious from the background noise that Jackson Burdeaux was in his car.

"Yeah, what's up?"

"Listen, I was on my way home from a meeting and heading down Baker's Street south of town when I saw a little boy walking along the street. I've got him in my car now, but he's having trouble breathing so we're on our way to the hospital. I'm just hoping I get him there in time."

"My God. It's Billy," she said. She pushed away from the dishwasher, and a wave of dizziness struck her. She drew a deep, steadying breath. Her heart beat so fast she thought she might be having a heart attack. Billy! He was having trouble breathing, but that meant he was alive!

Lucas ended the call. "Let's go."

He didn't have to tell her twice.

"It's got to be him, right?" she asked a moment later when they were in Lucas's car. "There can't be another little boy walking along a street at midnight who has breathing problems." Hope filled her and brought tears to her eyes, yet she was afraid to believe. She was afraid the hope that now rose inside her would be smashed, and she didn't think she could survive that.

"It sounds like it's him," Lucas replied. He cast her a sideways glance. "You might want to prepare yourself. We don't know what's happened to him, where he's been. We know he's obviously suffering an asthma attack, but we don't know what else he might be suffering from."

"But surely if there's been other injuries Jackson would have mentioned them," she protested. He had to be all right. He just had to be.

"I'm not talking about physical injuries. We don't know what he's been through mentally, emotionally. He may be very fragile."

"But he's alive," she replied. Surely with enough love and time they could heal whatever might be wrong. Her mind raced with possibilities. "You mentioned that one of your college buddies is a psychiatrist."

He nodded. "Clay Jefferson. Why?"

"Does he see children? If Billy needs help, I'd want to take him to see somebody professionally." She was a jittery mess, her brain shooting in a million different directions as she mentally urged him to go faster…faster.

"One step at a time," Lucas replied as he pulled into the hospital parking lot. She was out of the car and running toward the entrance before he'd brought the car to a full halt.

Conja Creek Memorial Hospital was a small facility, mostly used for emergency situations. Most people with real health issues drove to Shreveport or were transported there.

The first person she saw as she flew through the emergency-room door was a tall, dark-haired man with slate-gray eyes. She knew in an instant this was Lucas's friend, Jackson Burdeaux. Although she wanted to thank him, her most urgent need was to see if Billy really existed behind the closed doors just ahead. She started toward the doors.

"Wait! You can't go back there." A nurse stepped in front of her, blocking her forward progress.

"Please, the little boy who was just brought in. He's my son. You have to let me through."

The nurse's implacable expression softened. "If you're his mother then we need you to sign some forms."

"Gina," Lucas's voice rang from behind them. "Let her through. The forms can wait until later."

Nurse Gina stepped aside and Mariah flew through the doors. The first person she saw sitting up on an examining table was her son.

He was being given a breathing treatment, but when he saw her he pulled the nozzle from his mouth. "Mommy," he cried as she rushed to him.

Never again would she feel the way she did at that moment, so filled with joy it nearly brought her to her knees. He was filthy and sweaty, but she wrapped her arms around him and wept with the joy of holding him.

She cried only a moment, then aware of his labored breathing she let him go and guided the nozzle of the nebulizer back to his mouth. "Breathe, honey. Just breathe."

He did as she told him, and Mariah straightened and saw Dr. Ralph Dell standing nearby. Dr. Dell was Billy's regular doctor and she hurried to where he stood.

He placed a hand on her shoulder, his wrinkled face offering her a smile. "He's going to be all right, Mariah. Other than the fact that he was scarcely breathing when Jackson brought him in, I don't see any other physical issues."

"Thank God," she replied.

"I'd like to keep him here overnight for observation. Just to be on the safe side."

"Of course. As long as I can stay with him."

Dr. Dell smiled once again. "I wouldn't have it any other way. We'll finish up his breathing treatment, then get him cleaned up and into a room."

"Did he say anything to you? About who took him?"

"He didn't offer anything and I didn't ask. My main concern was getting him treatment. He was in pretty bad shape when he was brought in. His main concern was that you were going to be mad at him."

"Mad? Why on earth would I be mad?"

"He told me he got into a stranger's car to come here and you'd always warned him never to get into a stranger's car."

Mariah's heart squeezed tight, and she left the doctor's side to return to her son. As he breathed in the medicated air that would ease his suffering, she pulled up a chair and sat next to him, then took his hand in hers.

As she held his hand she was aware of Lucas coming

to stand just behind her. He placed a hand on her shoulder and squeezed lightly. "How's he doing?"

"He's going to be fine." She smiled at her son. "They're going to keep him overnight. Did you hear that, Billy? You and I are going to stay here in the hospital for the night." He nodded.

"I'd like to have a little talk with him," Lucas said in a low voice. "I'll come back once I've spoken with Jackson," he added, as if realizing Billy would need a little time with his mother.

She didn't even notice when he drifted away, so focused was she on the sight of her son, alive and well before her.

The next half hour passed in a haze. Billy was given a second breathing treatment then washed and dressed in a gown and put in a private room.

As they arrived at the room, Mariah was surprised to see Wally seated in a chair just outside. "What are you doing here?" she asked.

"I'll be here until you and Billy get home safe and sound," he replied.

She realized Wally was a guard. Even though Billy was here, it wasn't over yet. Jenny still wasn't home, and it wouldn't be over until the guilty person was behind bars.

Finally Billy was tucked into bed, and mother and son were alone for a moment. She leaned over him and kissed his forehead, savoring the taste of his warm skin, the scent of hospital soap and precious little boy.

"I was so scared when you were gone," she said softly.

Billy gazed at his mother with big eyes. "I was scared, too, but Jenny helped. She told me not to be afraid, that her brother would find us. Has he found Jenny?"

"Not yet," Lucas said from the doorway. "I'm kind of hoping you can help me find her." He approached Billy with a smile. "I'm Lucas, Jenny's brother. Can I ask you some questions, Billy?"

"Okay," he agreed after looking at Mariah. Mariah scooted her chair closer and took his little hand in hers. She had no idea how traumatic Lucas's questioning might be, and if it became too intense she'd stop it. She'd do what was necessary to protect her son.

Lucas grabbed one of the other chairs in the room and pulled it up on the opposite side of the bed. "How are you feeling?"

"Okay now," Billy replied.

Lucas pulled a small notepad and a pen from his pocket. "Can you tell me what happened last Friday, Billy? The day you stayed home from the babysitter's because you had a sore throat?"

Billy tightened his grip on Mariah's hand, and she wanted to grab him in her arms and shield him from the trauma, from the stress of remembering. But she also knew she couldn't do that, for Jenny was still missing and their biggest lead to her now was Billy.

"Mom went to work, and me and Jenny decided to watch a movie." He looked at Mariah. "It was that new Disney movie you got me. Anyway, we'd been watching for a little while and then I had to go to the bathroom. When I came out of the bathroom Jenny was asleep on the sofa and there was a man there."

"A man? What did he look like?" Lucas leaned forward.

"I dunno. He had on a mask. You know, the kind you wear in the wintertime with just the eyes not covered. I tried to run but he caught me and he held something over my nose and mouth and I guess I fell asleep, too."

So, they now knew the kidnapping had taken place at Mariah's house, in her living room. How had he gotten in? Had the front door been unlocked? So many questions.

"And the masked man. Was he tall or short? Thin or heavy?" Lucas continued.

Billy frowned, obviously trying hard to please. "I dunno, kind of medium."

"Did you see his eyes?"

Billy hesitated, then nodded. "I'm pretty sure they were brown."

"Good, Billy. You're doing a terrific job," Lucas said. "What happened next? After you went to sleep."

"I woke up and me and Jenny were in a place." Billy's voice trembled slightly. "It was dark and I was scared, but Jenny told me not to be afraid, that you'd find us."

Lucas looked haunted by the words. "Tell me more about the place where you woke up."

"When the sun came up we could see it. It was all boarded up so we couldn't get out and there was food on a table and bottles of water. We screamed for help, but I guess nobody heard us."

"Was the man there with you?"

"No, it was just us in the little room."

"Was it a room in a house?" Lucas asked.

Billy shook his head. "Not like our house, and we could hear things at night."

"What kind of things?"

"Like big splashes and a noise that Jenny said was alligators calling to each other," Billy replied.

Mariah looked at Lucas. Once again he looked haunted, and she knew exactly what he was thinking. If Jenny was being held someplace deep in the swamp, they might never find her.

BILLY'S WORDS filled Lucas with a new kind of horror, because they confirmed his deepest fear—that Jenny was being held someplace in the swamp.

Conja Creek was nearly surrounded by swampland, with overgrown passages and areas where men hadn't been for years. It would take a hundred men days, or even weeks, to explore every inch of the swamps in search of his sister. And he knew in his gut that she didn't have days or weeks. The fact that the kidnapper had released Billy didn't bode well for Jenny.

"Billy, what happened tonight? How did you get out on the street where Mr. Burdeaux picked you up?" he asked.

"Somebody came." Billy's eyes darkened and he swallowed several times before continuing. "We heard the boat coming. I could hardly breathe, and Jenny screamed that he'd better let me go, that I was going to die if he didn't get me out of there. She told him she'd do whatever he wanted if he let me come home." Tears filled Billy's eyes. "He unlocked the door and came in. He hit Jenny. He hit her in her face, and she fell down on the floor, then he yanked me out of the room."

"And he had the mask on?" Lucas concentrated on the facts and tried to keep his emotions out of things.

But the thought of Jenny being hurt sent shards of pain slicing through him.

"Yeah, and he put me in a boat, then he covered my eyes with a blindfold. We rode for a long time in the boat then he put me into a car and we rode for a little while, then he made me get out of the car on the side of the road."

For the next hour Lucas questioned Billy, trying to get something from the boy that might lead him to his sister. It was only when Billy could no longer keep his eyes open that Lucas called a halt to the questioning.

"I'll be back tomorrow," he told Mariah as she walked him to the door. "When the doctor releases him I'll drive you both back to your place."

She nodded, her exhaustion evident in the bruiselike darkness beneath her eyes. "I'm sorry, Lucas."

He looked at her in surprise. "Sorry for what?"

"I'm sorry he didn't let them both go. I'm sorry that I have my son back and you don't have your sister. I'm sorry he couldn't tell you anything that might help you."

"But he did," Lucas replied. He drew a deep breath as he realized his emotions were precariously close to the surface. For a moment he couldn't speak as his chest filled and his throat closed with the depth of his feelings. "I thought she might already be dead. I feared they both were. What Billy told me was that she was still alive a couple of hours ago."

Mariah moved into his arms, and he grabbed onto her, surprised to find comfort in the embrace. "I'm going to find her, Mariah. I'm going to find her."

She held him for several long moments, then released him. "I know you will. Maybe after a good night's sleep Billy will remember something that will help."

He nodded and touched her cheek, her soft, smooth skin warm beneath his finger. "And now you can get some sleep, knowing that Billy is safe and where he belongs. Don't feel guilty, Mariah. Don't feel bad that Jenny hasn't come home yet. Rejoice in your son's safe return. Please, you have to do that for me."

Without another word he walked out of the hospital room. Wally sat in a chair just outside the door, a magazine in his lap. "Don't let anyone in but the doctor or a nurse," Lucas said. "And I want a list of anyone who tries to get in to see either Billy or Mariah."

Wally nodded. "Did he give you anything?"

"Not enough," Lucas replied, a ball of emotion knotted tight in his chest. "If you need me, I'll be at the office. Agent Kessler and I are going to coordinate." He started to walk away, but paused and returned to Billy's hospital room doorway and looked in.

Mariah was in the bed with her son, her arms around him as they both slept. Thank God. Thank God Billy was okay and back where he belonged. It certainly hadn't been through any efforts on Lucas's part.

What had prompted the kidnapper to let Billy go? If it had been Billy's health issue, then it was obvious the kidnapper didn't want to be responsible for his death. Or maybe it had been Mariah's challenge to the kidnapper, her refusal to play his game any longer.

As Lucas headed out of the hospital, he realized he couldn't remember when he'd last slept. His eyes felt gritty, but there was no way he was going to sleep now. He needed to catch up with Kessler and coordinate some sort of search.

"At least we know we can strike Frank Landers off

our list of suspects," Kessler said two hours later. "Ben has been sitting on him and said he hasn't left his hotel all day. He couldn't have been the man who got Billy and then dropped him off on the side of the road."

"I'd already pretty much written him off anyway," Lucas replied. "He likes to hurt defenseless women, but he doesn't have the nerve to pull off something like this." Lucas cast a weary hand across his eyes.

"Go home, Lucas," Kessler said. "There's nothing more we can do tonight. You need some sleep. Tomorrow we'll get everyone we can out searching."

Although Lucas wanted to protest, he knew Kessler was right. Nothing more could be done without the light of day. The adrenaline that had filled him when he'd known Billy had been found was gone, leaving behind a weariness the likes of which he'd never known.

As he drove home, Billy's words tormented him. *He hit her in the face.* What did that mean? Had he blackened her eye, broken her jaw? Was she now bleeding and in pain? The very idea of somebody laying hands on Jenny created a rage of mammoth proportions inside him.

Who was behind this? Somehow he didn't think the kidnapper was just going to let Jenny go as he had done Billy. The kidnapper wanted something, and the most frightening thing of all was that Lucas had a feeling Jenny's very life depended on him figuring it out.

His house was empty and silent when he arrived. Marquette had gone home hours ago and wouldn't be back until morning. He checked his watch. It was after three; morning would be here soon.

He fell into bed without showering or taking off his clothes. He stretched out on top of the bedspread and was asleep in minutes.

The dream came almost immediately. Jenny, her face black-and-blue, crying out to him. "Lucas, help me. You have to find me before it's too late."

Lucas walked along the edge of dark, murky swamp water. Nearby an alligator bellowed, and gnarled cypress trees rose up like twisted, sun-bleached skeletons. "Where are you, Jenny?" he yelled. He had to find her, before it was too late. He had to save her; he needed to save her.

"I'm sorry, Lucas. I'm sorry I've been such a pain in your life." Her voice was faint, as if she'd given up hope. "I love you, Lucas."

"I love you," he yelled back. "Jenny, I'm the one who is sorry. Do you hear me? I'm sorry." He waited for a reply, for the sound of her voice drifting to him. But there was nothing, no answering cry.

"Jenny!" he screamed. "Jenny, where are you?" The only reply was a second roar from the alligator.

He sat up, his heart banging with ferocity against his ribs. He looked toward the window where dawn had already broken through night clouds. The clock on his nightstand read almost six. He'd slept for three hours, albeit a sleep filled with nightmares.

He exited the shower and sensed Marquette had arrived. The scent of frying bacon and freshly brewed coffee filled the air as he descended the grand staircase and headed for the kitchen.

"Sit. You aren't getting out of this house without a good breakfast," Marquette commanded. "I might be old but I'll wrestle you to the ground before I'll let you leave here without eating." She pointed to the small oak table where a place setting had already been laid. "Lord knows when was the last time you had a decent meal." She poured him coffee, then returned to the stove.

"Billy was found last night wandering along a highway," he said as he sat.

"I heard." Marquette forked the cooked bacon out of the skillet as Lucas looked at her in surprise.

"It didn't happen until late. How did you hear about it?" he asked.

"Got a call this morning from Levina. Her daughter has a friend who knows a nurse over at Memorial." Marquette broke three eggs into the skillet.

"Ah, nice to know the gossip grapevine in Conja Creek is alive and well," he replied dryly.

"That it is," she agreed easily. "I also heard that Billy wasn't much help in letting you know where our little girl is."

"All he could tell me was that they were being held someplace in the swamp."

Marquette's eyes were as dark as he'd ever seen them as she placed his plate in front of him. "If that's the truth, then how will you ever find her?"

"I'll search until I do," he replied, a knot of tension twisting in his stomach. Marquette knew how futile a search might be, how long it would take to explore each and every inch of the swampland, but thankfully she didn't say anything to remind him of that.

"Why would he release Billy and not let Jenny go?" she asked.

Lucas frowned. "That's the million-dollar question

at the moment." He took a sip of his coffee and eyed the morning newspaper that was next to his plate, still rolled with a rubber band.

He took another sip of coffee then removed the band from the paper, opened it and gasped. The headline read, Two Victims at Risk While Sheriff Plays in the Park.

There was a full-size color picture of Lucas and Mariah in the park. The photo told a false tale, implying some sort of romantic liaison.

Mariah was in his arms and it looked as if they were sharing an intimate embrace. In truth, he'd been consoling Mariah after she'd dug up most of the flower bed looking for a clue. And the kidnapper had not only been there, but he'd taken a photo, a photo specifically chosen to imply ineptitude.

It spoke of Lucas's inadequacies as a law enforcement official, reminding the readers that he'd arrested the wrong man in the Bennett murder case and now couldn't even find a little boy and his own sister.

Lucas really wasn't surprised. The Conja Creek newspaper was something of a joke, offering up tabloid-type stories along with the daily news. Owner Sam Rinkin wouldn't have a problem running a story that made Lucas look bad, despite an anonymous source. Lucas had run for sheriff against Sam's brother in the last election and when Lucas won, the Rinkin brothers hadn't hidden their animosity.

It was public humiliation spread across the front page of the *Conja Creek Gazette*. But more than that, it answered a question that had burned in Lucas's heart since the moment he'd realized Billy and Jenny were in trouble.

He'd wondered if the kidnapping had been about Mariah, or if it had been about Jenny. But now he knew the truth. It wasn't about either of them.

It was about him.

Chapter Twelve

Mariah stared at the morning paper in horror. Billy still slept in the hospital bed. She'd awakened surprisingly early considering the time they'd finally gone to sleep.

She'd remained in bed for a long time after opening her eyes, listening to Billy's easy breathing and thanking the stars that he was where he belonged—in her arms. She'd crept out of the bed without awakening him.

As much as she rejoiced that Billy was home safe and sound, her heart was still heavy, since Jenny remained in danger and Lucas was without any real answers.

She sat in the chair next to Billy's bed and sipped the coffee a nurse had been kind enough to bring to her a few minutes earlier. The article that accompanied the photo was scathing, an indictment against Lucas for incompetence. It rehashed the murder of Erica Bennett and reminded the readers that Lucas had arrested the wrong man for the murder. Mariah knew the truth about the arrest of Sawyer for his wife's crime, that Mayor Welch had pressured Lucas to make the arrest.

Of course it was all ridiculous, and she couldn't believe that Samuel Rinkin, the owner of the paper, had run both the photo and the article without even asking for a comment from either her or Lucas.

She tossed the paper on the floor next to her chair and instead watched Billy sleep. The rhythmic rise and fall of his chest was reassuring, as was the absence of any ominous wheeze.

Although he hadn't spoken much about the days he'd been held captive, he didn't appear to be unduly emotionally stressed now that he was home. His main concern appeared to be for his friend, Jenny.

Mariah prayed there were no emotional scars left from this ordeal, and she prayed that Jenny would come home soon. She turned her attention to the window, where the sun was just beginning to peek over the horizon.

Had Lucas seen the paper yet? What was going through his mind? Through his thoughts? It was so unfair for him to be damned by a photo that was twisted and perverted into something other than what it was.

She picked up the paper once again and stared at the photograph, remembering those moments when Lucas had held her together as she broke apart.

Lucas was nothing like the man she'd once thought he was. In Frank's case she'd mistaken dominance for strength, control for love. But in Lucas's case she'd done the exact opposite. She'd damned him with the taint of her past. There was no question she still believed he needed to give Jenny more space, an opportunity to make her own decisions, but there was not an abusive bone in Lucas's body.

She frowned as she spied a small insert at the bottom of the front page, indicating an interview with one of the victims' father on page three. She flipped the pages and found the article. Frank had given an interview as the loving, caring father.

He'd depicted himself as having a close relationship with his son despite his divorce from Mariah. Lies, all lies. It had been obvious that, at the time they had interviewed him, Frank had believed that Billy was already dead. She wadded up the page and threw it in the corner with disgust.

An hour later she was still seated at the window, while Billy remained sleeping, when she heard a commotion in the hallway.

"I said you can't go in there," Wally's voice drifted from the closed door.

"That's my son in there and nobody is going to stop me from seeing him." Frank's voice radiated the kind of simmering rage Mariah knew well. But this time she felt no fear. After all she'd been through in the past week, she knew Frank Landers could never frighten her again.

Checking to make certain that Billy was still asleep, she walked to the door, opened it and stepped out, then pulled it closed behind her.

Frank glared at her. "I want to see my son."

"The sheriff says nobody goes in, so nobody goes in, and that includes you," Wally exclaimed, his meaty fists clenched at his sides.

"Do something," Frank demanded of Mariah. "Tell him I have a right to see my son."

"You have no rights here, Frank, and you particularly

don't have the right to see the son you never wanted."
Memories assailed her, memories of how angry Frank
had been when she'd become pregnant, how during her
pregnancy he'd acted as though the child had nothing
to do with him. "You don't scare me anymore, Frank
and there's nothing for you here. Go back to wherever
you came from and just leave us alone."

"That's not fair. I didn't know where you were, how
to find you. I figured you changed your name and
probably got some illegal identification. How was I
supposed to go about finding you?"

"I did change my name, but you had my social
security number." She stared at the man who had
haunted her dreams, the man she'd been afraid would
hunt her down. "You *figured* I'd changed my name? You
never even looked for us." The truth slammed into her
and was there in the sheepish expression on his face.

She laughed, unable to stop herself. God, she'd been
afraid for so long and she suddenly realized she hadn't
hidden herself at all. She'd been a fool without a real
plan when she'd left him.

She'd been living a mere five hours from Frank,
using her own social security number. If he'd hired a
good private investigator, even if he'd just looked
himself, she would have been found in a matter of
hours. But Frank hadn't cared to look. All this time
she'd been afraid of a ghost.

And she'd hidden not only from Frank, but from the
people of Conja Creek, who had embraced her. There
would be no more lies. No more hiding away. She was
confident that the friends she'd made here would still
be her friends when they learned the truth about her past.

"Go home, Frank," she said. "I'll spend every dime I have, fight you tooth and nail before I'll let you see Billy. We're out of your life, now get out of ours."

"You heard the lady," Wally said. "Get on out of here before I arrest you for being stupid."

Frank glared at them both, then turned on his heels and disappeared down the hallway. Mariah wasn't sure but she had the distinct feeling she'd seen the last of him. Without her fear to feed him, he'd have no further interest in her or Billy. And Billy had expressed time and again that he didn't want to spend time with his father, although when he came of age, it would be up to him.

"Thank you, Wally," she said to the deputy.

"My pleasure, ma'am," he said with a wink.

She turned and went back into the room where Billy still slept. It was after ten when he finally opened his eyes. "Did they find Jenny yet?" he asked.

"Not yet, but I'm sure everyone is looking really hard to find her." Mariah pulled her chair up next to his bed. She was certain if anything had happened overnight Lucas would have let her know.

She wondered when he'd show up here. He'd said he'd be here to take her and Billy home and she was eager to talk to him about the newspaper article.

As Billy ate breakfast she was grateful to see that his appetite was good, and although he talked a little bit about his time in captivity, he seemed more focused on all the things he wanted to do when he got back home. She thought it was a good sign. He was looking toward the future and not to the past.

What little he did say about his time away let Mariah

know that Jenny had worked overtime to try to keep him from being afraid. She'd put her very life on the line to try to bargain Billy's release. They *had* to find her, Mariah thought with a sense of desperation.

It was just after noon when Lucas walked in. The first thing Mariah noticed was that although he was dressed in a neatly pressed uniform, he looked more exhausted than she'd ever seen him. Still, he offered her and Billy a bright smile. "Hey, buddy, how you doing this morning?" he asked Billy.

"Good, but I want to go home. I've missed seeing my friends and stuff."

"The doctor was just in and released him. They're doing the discharge paperwork now," Mariah explained.

Lucas nodded and pulled something from his pocket. "Billy, I brought you something," he said. He held out a small gold badge. "Since you were so much help answering my questions yesterday I've decided to make you my official deputy."

"Wow!" Billy's eyes lit up as he took the badge from Lucas. "Thank you, this is way cool."

Mariah's heart expanded. With everything that Lucas had going on, he'd thought about a badge for Billy, instinctively knowing that an eight-year-old boy would love the idea of being an official deputy.

"Why don't you give it to me and when you're dressed we'll pin it on your shirt," Mariah suggested.

"And I can wear it whenever I want, right?" Billy asked.

Mariah smiled as she placed the badge on the table next to the bed. "You'll have to take it off when you take a bath, but other than that you can wear it all the time."

"Are you up to answering a few more questions, Deputy Billy?" Lucas asked.

"Sure," Billy said as he sat up straighter in the bed.

For the next half hour Lucas asked Billy the same questions he'd asked him the night before. Mariah knew that Lucas was hoping something new would come to light, but Billy couldn't tell him any more than he had the previous night.

Mariah watched the exchange between her son and the sheriff, not surprised by the gentleness Lucas displayed when asking difficult questions. He was good with Billy and Billy responded to him with an eagerness to please.

She could smell Lucas's familiar scent, the cologne and soap scent one she would forever identify with him. What agony he must be going through. The fact that Billy had been released and Jenny had not been seemed so evil, so ominous.

"Why don't you go ahead and get dressed," Mariah suggested after the nurse dropped off the discharge papers. "Sheriff Jamison and I will be just outside the door."

She and Lucas stepped outside the door to let Billy have his privacy. "Where's Wally?" Mariah asked, noting that both Wally and the chair he had sat in were gone.

"I sent him home. He told me you had a little confrontation with Frank. He said you were awesome."

Mariah smiled. "I don't know how awesome I was, but he won't be haunting my dreams anymore."

"Ben called me a little while ago and said Landers checked out of the motel and headed out of town."

"I pity whatever woman he's living with now." She

took one of his hands and pressed it between hers. "How are you doing? You look exhausted."

"I'm tired," he admitted. "Agent Kessler is coordinating a search of the swamp and I'm just hoping they'll find her." For a moment his eyes were dark and tortured. "So, how does it feel to be front-page news?" he asked.

She grimaced and dropped his hand. "That wasn't news, that was tabloid nonsense. I can't believe Sam Rinkin allowed it into his paper."

"I had a chat with Sam a little while ago," Lucas replied. "He told me the photo and the article showed up in a plain brown envelope yesterday afternoon. He didn't see who left it, thinks it might have been left while he was at lunch. And I'll be checking Sam's and his brother's alibis for the day of the kidnapping."

He frowned, the gesture emphasizing the tired lines on his face. "But at least I now know something about this case. I know it was never about you or Jenny, that it's about me. Somebody wants to discredit me as sheriff, somebody hates me enough that they kidnapped my sister." His dark eyes were bleak as he gazed at Mariah. "I just have to hope that they don't hate me enough to kill Jenny," he said softly.

LUCAS HAD HOPED that in questioning Billy again the little boy might remember something that would point to a specific location in the swamp, but he'd gotten no more from Billy today than he had the night before.

As he drove Mariah and Billy home, he realized the weight of his grief was far different now than it had been the day before. While Billy had been missing he'd managed to keep his focus on the little boy. But now that Billy was home safe and sound, Jenny filled Lucas's thoughts, his heart, and there was nothing to mitigate his pain.

As he drove he listened to Billy talking about Jenny and the time they'd shared in the shanty. It was obvious that Jenny had acted the part of hero, setting aside her own fears to soothe Billy's.

Pride filled Lucas's heart. He would have guessed that Jenny would fall apart, that she would be hysterical, but she'd managed to hold it together for the sake of a little boy. Mariah was right, Jenny was much stronger than he'd ever given her credit.

When they reached Mariah's place Ben was waiting for them on the front porch. "What's he doing here?" Mariah asked.

"I think it would be a good idea if I keep a deputy here for the next couple of days," he replied.

"You really think that's necessary?" she asked softly.

He parked the car in the driveway and turned off the engine. "I'm not sure. I know you want to think this is all over for you, but I'd rather be safe than sorry."

"This won't be over for me until Jenny is home safely. This won't be over until the guilty person is rotting in jail," she replied.

They got out of the car and Ben rose from his chair on the porch. "Hi, Sheriff, Mariah." He squatted down to Billy's height. "I understand you're the new deputy in town."

Billy grinned and nodded his head, touching the badge he wore proudly on his shirt. Mariah turned and looked at Lucas. "Are you coming in?"

He hesitated a moment, then nodded. "Maybe for

just a few minutes." He wanted to talk to her about the thoughts whirling in his head.

The minute they entered the house Billy ran to his bedroom, then came back into the kitchen and asked if he could watch a movie. With him happily entertained by his favorite Disney film, Lucas and Mariah sat at the kitchen table.

"I've told you all along that something about those recorded messages sounded familiar to me but I couldn't put my finger on what it was," he said as she poured them each a cup of freshly brewed coffee.

"And you have now?"

He shook his head in frustration. "No, I still can't figure it out, but I know from the newspaper article that the kidnapper is somebody close to me, somebody I know on a personal level, and it's hatred of me that's driving this train."

"So you think Billy was never the intended victim?" she asked.

"On most days when you're at work, Billy is at the babysitter's. I think the kidnapper intended to take Jenny all alone and Billy just happened to be at the wrong place at the wrong time."

"Do you have any idea who might hate you that badly?" she asked. "Maybe somebody you've arrested in the past?"

He shrugged. "Agent Kessler and I spent the morning going over my files, looking for a likely suspect, but nobody popped out." He leaned back in the chair and studied her for a long moment, then leaned forward once again. "You don't think this is something our good mayor might be behind?"

Her eyes radiated her shock at his words. They widened and blinked in surprise. "Richard? Why on earth would Richard want to do something like this?"

He shrugged again. "It's no secret that he and I don't see eye to eye. We butt heads on a regular basis and I'm sure he feels his life would be much easier if he didn't have to contend with me."

"Richard has trouble remembering to pick his shirts up at the cleaners, I can't imagine him being capable of pulling together something like this. According to Billy, that shanty was stocked with food and water. Somebody spent a lot of time planning this. Richard can't plan his own lunch hour, let alone a crime."

This was why Lucas had wanted to talk to her, because of her intelligence, because he trusted her judgment, and at the moment he didn't know who else he could trust.

"It was just a thought." He drank his coffee, then stood. "I've got to get back to the office."

"You need to go to bed," she replied. "You're exhausted and you can't help Jenny if you crash and burn."

"I know, I'll get a couple hours of sleep later." He was afraid to sit too long in the comfort of her kitchen, was afraid that if he stayed inert for too long, he *would* crash and burn.

Somebody close to him.

Somebody close. The words echoed in his head as he drove back to the office. The newspaper article was obviously meant to humiliate him, to make him appear ineffective to the taxpayers he served. Did the kidnapper want him to resign? To lose his position? Who had anything to gain by that?

Although Mariah had been quick to proclaim Richard's innocence, he still considered the mayor as viable a candidate as anyone. Richard might come off as a buffoon, but he'd been smart enough to get himself elected.

The only other person at the office was Louis, who was manning the desk. "Hey, Sheriff," he said. "I figured you were out on one of the search boats."

"I wanted to interview Billy again, so I went to the hospital and picked up him and Mariah to take them home." Lucas moved to his desk and sat.

"Did you get anything more from him?" Louis asked.

"No, nothing more than I got last night." He leaned back in the chair and fought the overwhelming sense that it was too late. For all he knew the kidnapper had already killed Jenny and fed her to the gators that Billy had heard bellowing outside the place they'd been held.

Don't give up, a small voice whispered inside. But with each moment that passed, it was getting more and more difficult to hang on to hope.

"No more calls?" Louis asked, pulling Lucas from his dark thoughts.

"No. I'm making a calculated guess that he won't call at Mariah's place anymore. With Billy home I think she's been taken out of the game. If he calls, he'll call me on my cell phone like he did the very first time he contacted us."

"So, what are you doing here?" Louis asked.

"I was going to go through some more files, see if I can find somebody who pops out at me, somebody who might want to see me punished in some way."

One of Louis's black eyebrows rose. "Is that what you think this is about? Punishment?"

"I didn't before the newspaper article this morning. I assume you saw it."

Louis nodded. "A bunch of crap, if ever I saw crap. You're a good sheriff, Lucas. I can't think of another man I'd rather work for."

Louis's loyalty soothed Lucas somewhat and raised a lump of emotion in his throat. "Thanks, I appreciate it. I've tried to be good for this town."

For the next four hours Lucas pored over his files, compiling a list of names. He asked Deputy Ed Maylor to bring him a burger for dinner, then continued going over lists, taking off names and adding others.

At dusk he headed to the small town dock to wait for the search boats. As he stood at the end of the wooden structure, his heart was heavier than it had ever been. He'd been so focused on Mariah's pain it had been easy to stuff his own away. But now he felt as if he were bleeding from the inside out, bleeding for a sister he recognized he might never see again.

The sun dipped lower, casting the surrounding swamp in deep shadows. Mosquitoes began to swarm, the incessant buzzing enough to drive a sane person mad. He felt half-mad as he waited. Mad with grief for a sister he feared was dead.

The boats began to arrive, the search parties hot and weary from battling the swamp. Most of the men refused to meet Lucas's eyes as they disembarked, and he knew they held little hope of a happy ending.

Sawyer Bennett was on the second boat, and he walked to where Lucas stood. "How you holding up?"

"As well as can be expected," Lucas replied.

"That newspaper article this morning, I just wanted you to know that folks around here trust you, Lucas. They know you're a good man and you're the person they want as their sheriff."

Lucas looked at the man he considered one of his best friends. "I arrested you for Erica's murder, and you weren't guilty."

Sawyer nodded. "You did what you had to do. Despite our friendship, you followed the damning evidence and did what was right. Besides, in the end it all worked out okay. I don't harbor a grudge, Lucas. I respect what you did."

Once again a knot of emotion crawled up into Lucas's throat. "Thanks, Sawyer. I appreciate your support."

Sawyer held out a hand and when Lucas grabbed it, Sawyer pulled him into a bear hug. "You'll get through this," he said, then released Lucas.

It was dark when the last boat pulled in. Nothing more could be done until morning. As Lucas got into his car and headed toward his house, he was suffused with a chill despite the hot mugginess of the night air that blew into his car window.

Flashes of Jenny filled his mind. He saw her as a young girl, putting on a play just for him, heard the ring of her laughter in his head. He'd built his life around taking care of her, and he couldn't imagine life without her.

It wasn't until he parked his car that he realized he hadn't driven home. Instead he had driven to Mariah's house. A light spilled out of the front window, and Ben sat in his car at the curb.

Lucas got out of his car, his weariness making it difficult for him to put one foot in front of the other. He walked to Ben's car and greeted his deputy. "Go home," he said. "I'll get somebody here to take over, but you go home and get some sleep."

Ben didn't wait to be told twice. He started his engine and pulled away from the curb. Lucas watched him go, then turned and stared at Mariah's front door.

Why was he here? Why hadn't he gone home? He pushed himself forward and lightly tapped on her door. She opened it. Her soft curly hair spilled around her shoulders, and her blue eyes radiated gentle concern as she looked at him. She wore the terry-cloth robe she'd had on the night they'd made love. That night seemed as if it was a million years ago.

It was at that moment that Lucas realized he was falling in love with her, and he knew there would be no happy ending here, either. When this was all over, he feared that to her he would be just a bad memory of the worst time in her life.

Chapter Thirteen

He looked like death.

Lucas's eyes held an emptiness that might have been frightening had she not known what put it there, had she not experienced it herself.

"Lucas," she said softly.

He gazed at her in bewilderment. "I was on my way home. I don't know what I'm doing here."

She took him by the hand and pulled him inside the door. She knew where he was. He was in that same place she had been when she'd been digging up the flower bed in the park. He was in a place beyond grief, outside of despair, a place made worse by his obvious physical exhaustion.

She pulled him through the living room and started down the hallway, but he stopped and gazed at her with his dead, dark eyes. "Wha...what are you doing?"

"I'm putting you to bed," she said briskly.

"What about Billy?" he asked.

"He's sleeping and that's exactly what you need." She tugged his hand and he followed. When they reached her bedroom she dropped his hand. "Get undressed," she said briskly.

He hesitated only a moment, then did as she asked. As he took off his clothing, stripping to his briefs, she pulled down the spread.

She tried to keep herself focused on the task at hand and not on his near nakedness. She tried not to notice his long muscled legs and the width of his tanned chest. At the moment, he didn't need her. What he needed more than anything was the healing power of sleep.

He was like a docile child as she motioned him into the bed. He got beneath the covers and closed his eyes, a deep sigh escaping from him. He was asleep before she left the room.

Mariah went into Billy's room and stood at the side of his bed. Her son slept deeply. She often joked with him that a bomb could go off beneath his bed and he wouldn't wake up.

She listened to the reassuring sound of his regular breathing. She'd stopped believing in miracles a long time ago, but it was nothing short of miraculous that Billy was home and sleeping peacefully in his own bed.

She left his room, checked to make sure the doors were all locked, then went to her bedroom and shrugged out of her robe. Lucas was sound asleep, a faint snore coming from him.

Funny that she'd misjudged Frank. She'd just assumed that he would hunt her down like a dog, unable to let her go. Instead he'd simply found another victim.

She'd misjudged Lucas, as well. He was a good man, with a good heart, a heart that at the moment was beating in limbo, someplace between hope and heartbreak.

She gazed at Lucas. A small frown furrowed the skin between his eyes as if even sleep couldn't banish the all-consuming worry his heart carried. His long, dark lashes rested against dark shadows beneath his eyes. When would this end? And at the end of it all, would he be a broken man?

She crawled into the bed next to him and found the sound of his snoring oddly comforting. He lay on his side and she spooned him, hoping the warmth of her body against his would somehow comfort him.

Within minutes she was asleep. She awakened much later, surrounded by warmth and the achingly familiar scent of Lucas. At some point in the night they had shifted positions. He now spooned her and his hand caressed up and down her hip in a slow, delicious stroke as his mouth pressed hotly against her neck.

She leaned against him, letting him know she was awake, and his hand moved up to cup her breast. Her breath caught as his thumb brushed over her nipple, causing rivulets of heat to spiral through her. He kissed and nipped the back of her neck, down to the middle of her shoulders, sparking a need in her.

She turned to face him and, in the predawn light that spilled through the window, she saw the naked hunger, his need for her in his eyes.

There was no way she could deny him, nor did she want to. She wanted him as badly as he wanted her. She placed a hand on his jaw. His whiskers were slightly rough beneath her touch and she ran her hand from there down into the silky hair that darkened his chest.

His mouth moved to capture the tip of one of her breasts, and she tangled her hands in his hair, urging him closer…closer still.

They made love gently, quietly, coming together easily

and fitting as if they belonged. Lucas's mouth tasted every inch of her skin, taking her again and again to the edge of madness but not allowing her complete release.

She did the same with him, using her hands and her mouth to explore his body, enjoying the soft sounds of his moans and sighs.

She had no illusions about the lovemaking, knew that Lucas was reaching for life, rather than reaching for her. She suspected she could have been any woman in the bed next to him and his need would be just as great. But that didn't matter to her. She just wanted to be here for him.

It didn't take long for their movements to become more frantic. She reached her peak first, spinning out of control with the pleasure that washed over her in wave after wave. Almost immediately he stiffened against her and cried out her name as he found his own release.

They remained entwined, hearts slowing with passion spent. He finally looked at her, his eyes dark and unreadable. "That was a major mistake," he said.

The words pierced through her with unexpected pain. He must have seen something in her expression, for he quickly added, "I didn't use any protection."

"Don't worry, I'm on the pill." She'd been on the pill since Billy had been born and hadn't stopped taking it with her divorce.

He studied her features for a long moment and looked as if he wanted to say something. "What?" she asked.

He shook his head. "Nothing." He placed his fingers against her cheek in the familiar gesture she'd come to cherish. "Thank you, not necessarily for the lovemaking, but for being a safe place for me to fall." He glanced to the clock on her nightstand. "I've got to get going. Mind if I use your shower?"

"Help yourself." As he left the room she rolled onto her back and stared at the ceiling.

Despite the beauty of what they had just shared, she had a bad feeling about things. If Lucas was right and all of this had really been about hatred for him, then what incentive did the kidnapper have to let Jenny live?

IT WAS JUST AFTER NINE when Lucas returned to his office. Mariah had insisted he not leave her house without breakfast, so she'd made him and Billy pancakes.

The breakfast had been a glimpse into a home life Lucas had always lacked. A moment of time—first thing in the morning—shared with people you cared about, people who cared about you.

Billy was a charmer, and Lucas could easily understand how Jenny had fallen in love with the kid. His little gold badge had been pinned to his pajamas when he'd come to the table, and during the meal he'd talked about wanting to be a sheriff when he grew up.

But the moment Lucas walked into his office, breakfast became only a vague, pleasant memory as he greeted Wally, who manned the front desk, and Agent Kessler, seated at one of the other desks.

Search teams had gone out once again at daybreak, and for the next hour Kessler and Lucas compared notes, read reports and interviews and tried to come up with something, anything concrete.

At noon Lucas was alone in the office. Kessler and

Wally had walked to the café for lunch, but Lucas wasn't interested in food.

He leaned back in his chair and closed his eyes, working what few facts they knew through his mind. Nothing made sense. He couldn't get a handle on things. He opened his eyes and began to make a list of new people to interview and check out alibis.

Richard Welch went to the top of the list, followed by two local thugs that Lucas had arrested a month before for attempted car theft.

He knew he was grasping at straws, but didn't have anything else to hang on to. Every place they turned seemed to lead to a dead end, but Lucas knew that somebody close to him, perhaps somebody he liked and trusted, was behind the kidnapping.

When his cell phone rang, he practically jumped out of his chair, but the caller ID showed that it was Ed Maylor. "What's up?" he asked.

"Figured I'd check in. I'm sitting on Ribideaux, but I think he's a dead end. He's moved into his new apartment and doesn't seem to be doing anything suspicious."

"I've got another assignment for you," Lucas said. "I want you to check up on Tebo Wales and Junior Tanner, see what they've been doing for the past week." Maylor could follow up on the two thugs. Lucas wanted to question Richard Welch himself.

"I reckon I can take care of a couple of lowlifes," Ed replied.

"Good, check in with me when you're finished."

Lucas hung up and frowned thoughtfully. Something niggled in the back of his brain. He stared at the phone. What was it? Something…something just on the edge of his consciousness.

He needed to hear the tapes again. Something was there…something important. He felt it in his gut.

He moved over to the desk Kessler had been using. Recording equipment was set up for listening to the taped messages the kidnapper had left.

"Touching scene in the cemetery," the kidnapper's voice rang out. Lucas hit the Stop button and fast forwarded.

"…by the twisted tree."

Again he hit Forward, wondering what it was that had a burst of adrenaline soaring through him, a frantic thrum to his heartbeat.

"I reckon you've forgotten who is in charge here. At the corner of Main and Cotton Street you'll find a bench with a big wide seat."

Lucas stopped it and played it again. "I reckon you've forgotten who is in charge here."

He played two words over and over again.

"I reckon…"

"I reckon…"

He stopped the machine, his heart pounding so loudly he could hear it in his head. *I reckon I can take care of a couple of lowlifes. I reckon the kidnapper figures Lucas can pay big bucks to get his sister back safe and sound.*

He released a low gasp as he thought of his deputy. Ed? Ed Maylor? Although he didn't want to believe it, he couldn't deny that the voice on the tape, in speaking those two single words, had a rhythm just like Ed's.

Ed lived a quiet life alone in an apartment in town,

and there was no other reason for Lucas to think he was guilty except that damning tape and a strong gut feeling that had now moved to a shout in his brain.

Jumping up from his desk, he left the office and walked the short distance to the café. The place was jumping with noontime diners, but he easily spied Wally and Kessler in a booth near the back. He slid into the booth next to Kessler and looked at Wally, who had given Ed a personal recommendation at the time he'd been brought on as a deputy.

"Tell me what you know about Ed Maylor," he said without preamble.

Kessler sat up straighter in his seat as Wally stared at Lucas in confusion. "What do you want to know?" he asked curiously.

"Has he ever mentioned having a beef with me?" Lucas asked.

"No, why? Is there a problem?"

"I don't know. And whatever we say stays here. I don't want any of the other men to know what we're talking about here," Lucas said. If he was wrong, he didn't want to taint Ed's reputation, ruin his career with misplaced suspicions.

"What else do you know about him?"

"He's swamp people, like me," Wally said. "From what I know his mama and daddy weren't much good. They lived someplace deep in Black Bay until Ed was a teenager and left the swamp. From what he told me, one day he went to visit them and they were gone. Ed was determined to make something of himself. He's worked hard to put the smell of the swamp behind him."

"Black Bay. You know where in Black Bay?" Lucas

asked. That particular area of the swamp was difficult to travel, with almost impassable channels.

"No, I'm not sure. What's going on, Lucas?"

"We need to get a boat." Lucas pulled his cell phone from his pocket. "And I'm calling Remy Troulous to see if he'll guide us in. That boy knows the swamp better than anyone."

"What about Maylor? You think he's behind this? You want me to pick him up?" Kessler asked.

"No, I want you both with me in the boat in case there's a situation if and when we find this place. We'll worry about Maylor later. I could be wrong about him, but if I'm right, then I want to be the one to bring him in."

"BLACK BAY IS the devil's playground," Remy said an hour later as the four of them took off in a boat Remy had borrowed from a friend. "Gators are bigger and meaner there, and you can feel the evil in the air."

He manned the motor, steering them easily through the murky, dark water. "There's so many channels rumor has it that fishermen don't even come in here for fear of getting lost."

He grinned at Lucas, that charming arrogant grin that was his trademark. "Who would have thought I'd live long enough to have the sheriff call me for help."

"Just get us through Black Bay," Lucas said. He turned to Wally. "Ed ever tell you exactly where in here his parents lived?"

Wally shook his head. "He just told me it was a stinking shanty that he couldn't wait to forget."

It didn't take long before they were traveling those

half-choked channels. The heat was stifling and the humidity made it difficult to draw a full breath.

Lucas's thoughts were as dark as the murky water that surrounded them. *You're too late,* a little voice whispered in the back of his head. When he released Billy, Maylor had probably killed Jenny.

That's why the caller hadn't phoned again. Because the game was over and Lucas was the loser. His heart hurt, and he closed his eyes against the pain and summoned up a picture of Mariah in his head. It was easier to think of Mariah than it was to picture his sister dead.

In his mind's eye he saw Mariah's features, soft with a smile, as they had been at breakfast that morning. He heard the ring of her laughter, remembered how she'd given to him in bed as if feeding a primitive need of his.

He'd like to think that when this was all over, they could continue to see each other, build on the crazy relationship that had sprung up between them, but in his heart he had little hope for that. Aside from her telling him that he reminded her of her abusive ex-husband, he would also always be a reminder of the days she'd lived in fear for her son.

His thoughts went in a new direction as he played and replayed time spent with Ed Maylor. Had he seen a flash of hatred in his deputy's eyes at any time? Had he sensed a dislike radiating from Maylor each time he'd given the man a command? He didn't know. He'd lost all objectivity.

"You okay?" It was Kessler who spoke, pulling Lucas from his thoughts.

"Yeah, I just want to find her," Lucas replied. He

grimaced, then added, "Even if it's just to give her a decent burial."

Those were the last words spoken for the next half hour. The sunshine overhead disappeared as trees choked off the light, casting them in a weird kind of twilight.

They began to check out the shanties they saw, abandoned structures, some of which had once held Cajun and Creole families with their colorful heritage.

In most cases it was evident just by looking that the shanties couldn't hold anyone captive. Roofs had tumbled, walls had rotted and there was little left except a broken-down frame.

Others needed to be checked thoroughly. Lucas and Kessler got out of the boat, guns drawn, to check the interiors of each structure, and each time they came up empty.

By six o'clock Lucas had lost hope. If they were going to make it back by dark they needed to start heading back. Maybe he'd been wrong. Maybe he'd been so desperate he'd only imagined the similarities between Maylor's voice and the tapes. After all, "I reckon," was a fairly common term.

Maybe the kidnapper was right. Maybe he wasn't a good choice for sheriff. Perhaps he did lack the investigative skills that made a good law-enforcement official.

Through the thick brush he spied another shanty and pointed to it. "We'll check this one out, then I guess we'd better head back. I don't want to be like any of those fishermen who got lost in Black Bay."

Remy guided the boat to the end of the rickety dock, and Lucas and Kessler jumped out. Another dead end, Lucas thought as they approached the structure, which looked as if a stiff wind might blow it into the water. Still he pulled his gun and approached.

Although the sound of the boat approaching would have been audible to anyone inside, Lucas and Kessler approached the structure silently, stealthily.

Lucas smelled the new-wood scent before they'd reached the front door. It was a scent that didn't belong, and a burst of adrenaline rocked through him.

There was only one way in…the closed door just ahead. For a moment he was afraid to go in, afraid that inside was the lifeless body of his sister.

Lucas swept through the door and stopped in surprise. A solid new wooden wall was just in front of him. There was a door with a small slat and a huge padlock.

"I'd say we've come to the right place," Kessler whispered from beside him.

The silence was deafening. Not a noise indicated any kind of life except the breathing of Lucas and Kessler. The silence scared him more than anything.

He drew a deep, unsteady breath and moved to the door. "Jenny?" He called her name, but there was no reply and a dull grief resounded inside him. He banged on the door. "Jenny? Jenny, are you in there?"

"Lucas?"

The faint reply dislodged a sob from his chest. "Jenny, honey, we're here. We're going to get you out of there. We're going to take you home."

Kessler looked around the area to try to find something to pry off the lock, but Lucas didn't want to wait. "Jenny, get away from the door. I'm going to shoot off the lock." He waited only a moment, then fired sideways at the lock, blowing it off the door.

He pushed through the now-unlocked door, and Jenny fell into his arms. "Jenny, honey, it's all right. You're safe now." She cried into the front of his shirt, clinging to him as if afraid he might disappear if she released him. And he cried, unable to stanch the tears that burned his eyes as he held his beloved sister in his arms.

"When I heard the boat I thought he was coming back, and when I heard your voice I thought it was a dream," she cried.

She raised her face to gaze up at him and for the first time he got a look at her swollen, black eye. Lucas's rage knew no boundaries. "I'll kill him," he said through clenched teeth. "Come on, let's get you out of here."

Within minutes they were back in the boat and headed in. As they rode, Jenny told them everything that had happened during her time in captivity. She told them of her greatest fear, that Billy would die in that shanty and there was nothing she could do about it. The only thing she could not tell them was who had held her there.

But Lucas knew. He *knew* it was Ed Maylor, and as he held his sister close, he swore that Maylor would spend the rest of his life behind bars.

Just before they reached the shore, Lucas called the office. Louis answered the phone. "Louis, we got her," he said. "We found Jenny and she's okay."

"Praise the Lord," Louis replied.

"You know where Maylor is?" Lucas asked.

"Yeah, I just sent him over to Mariah's place to spell Ben. Is there a problem?"

Lucas didn't reply. He couldn't speak around the lump of horror that filled his chest.

Chapter Fourteen

All day long Mariah had waited for news about Jenny, but none had been forthcoming. As dusk fell, she sent Billy in for a bath, then she sat at the kitchen table, surprised to find herself lonely.

She was beyond thrilled that her son was home where he belonged. The day had been filled with phone calls from well-wishers who had heard the news of his return. She and Billy had played games, baked a batch of cookies and watched movies, just enjoying being in each other's company.

Every time she looked at his little face, she kissed it, until finally he complained that she was kissing him way too much. "I'm trying to make up for all the days I didn't get to kiss you," she'd explained.

It was the usual routine for Billy to take a bath at this time in the evening, but never had Mariah experienced the kind of loneliness she felt at this moment. And she knew exactly what it was from.

She'd gotten used to Lucas's company. She hadn't realized how he'd filled up the house. He'd become a part of her everyday life, and she was surprised by the hole his absence had left behind.

It was crazy to miss him. She knew that the relationship they'd built had come into being in an alternate universe that had nothing to do with reality. It had been raw and intense, filled with enormous emotions.

Still, it had made her realize one thing—she was a young woman who didn't want to spend the rest of her life alone. Sure, Billy filled her life the way an eight-year-old could, but Lucas had awakened a hunger in her for something more, something adult and precious.

She wanted somebody to share her thoughts, somebody who would warm her through a cold, wintry night. She wanted conversation in the middle of the night, a secret smile over morning coffee.

When she'd arrived in Conja Creek, she'd been determined to keep all men at a distance, determined to build her world without any man in it in a meaningful way. Her need to be alone had been a selfish one, built on broken dreams and the pain of her failed marriage and the utter betrayal she'd suffered at Frank's hands.

But now she realized not only did she want a special man in her life, Billy also would thrive with a father figure in his. He deserved a man he could look up to, a man who would play catch with him and talk sports, as well as be a strong, masculine emotional support.

The problem was that, as she sat and tried to think about all the men she had met since coming to Conja Creek, her thoughts kept returning to Lucas.

Billy came into the kitchen clad in his navy-blue-and-yellow pajamas and smelling of soap and toothpaste. "Come here and give me a hug," she said to him.

He moved to her side and wrapped his arms around her neck, allowing her to hold him for a sweet long minute. It wouldn't be too long before he'd think he was too big for mommy hugs. She intended to take advantage before that time happened.

All too quickly he moved out of her arms. "Can I have some cookies and milk before I go to bed?"

Although normally she might have said no and offered him something less sweet, tonight she couldn't deny him. "Okay, four cookies and a glass of milk," she agreed. As he scooted into a chair at the table, she got up, poured his milk and placed the glass and the plate of cookies in front of him.

He took a sip of his milk then sighed. "I wish Jenny was here. She loves these chocolate chip cookies."

"I know you miss her. I miss her, too. Hopefully Lucas will find her real soon."

Billy's face lit up. "Is he coming over again?" He didn't wait for her answer. "I like him. I know all about him. Jenny told me he took care of her when she was little and she said he was the best brother in the world. Am I ever going to have a brother or a sister?"

Mariah laughed at the unexpected question. "I don't know, we'll have to see what the future holds. So you like Lucas?"

Billy nodded and wiped at his milk mustache. "I think maybe you should marry him and give me a little brother or sister."

Mariah's laughter was interrupted by the ring of the doorbell. "We'll talk about brother and sisters later. Finish your cookies," she said to Billy as she got up to answer. Maybe it was Lucas. Maybe he had news, or maybe he'd just come back again broken and grieving.

She opened the front door and was surprised to see

Deputy Ed Maylor standing on the porch. He offered her a friendly smile as she opened the screen door. "Deputy Maylor," she said.

"Hi, sorry to bother you, but I was wondering if I could trouble you for a glass of ice water. I've been sitting out front in my car and it's so hot. I forgot to pack water before I got here."

"Of course, please come in." She ushered him inside and through to the kitchen. "Billy, this is Deputy Maylor," she said to her son.

"Hi," Billy replied. "I'm a deputy, too. Lucas made me his official deputy."

"Oh, yeah, Saint Lucas," Maylor muttered under his breath. "Good with kids and nice to dogs."

Mariah looked at him sharply, unsure if she'd heard him right or not. Surely she had misunderstood. She got a glass from the cabinet, added ice, then filled it with water and placed it on the table in front of the deputy.

"Thanks," he said, then downed half the glass in three large swallows. "Mind if I have a little more?" She once again took the glass and moved back to the sink.

"You and Lucas, you got pretty close while your boy here was gone," Maylor said.

Something felt wrong, both in the question and with the man. A chill of unease walked up Mariah's spine. "Yeah, everybody loves Lucas Jamison," he continued. "The golden boy of Conja Creek. You know his parents were filthy rich, left him with enough money that he'd never have to work a day in his life. Not everybody is as lucky as our good sheriff."

Alarm bells screamed in Mariah's head. "Billy,

would you run to my bedroom and get my blue sweater out of my dresser drawer? I'm a little chilly."

There was no blue sweater in her dresser. She just wanted Billy away from this man, whose eyes flashed with something dark, something twisted. The flash was only there a moment, then gone. But she knew she hadn't just imagined it.

"Poor Lucas," he said. "I reckon he's going to be broken if he can't find his sister. I imagine he'll be too broken to stay here in Conja Creek."

"We still hope he will find her. Would you excuse me for just a moment? Billy must be having trouble finding my sweater." She didn't want for his response, but moved quickly down the hallway into the master bedroom.

Danger.

Danger. The word screamed through her senses. She could smell it in the air, feel it crawling icy fingers up her back, heard it shouting in her brain.

"Mom, I can't find…" Billy began.

"Shh," she told him. She quietly closed the bedroom door and locked it. "Help me move some furniture in front of this door," she said as she moved a chair and propped it beneath the door handle to create a barrier.

"Mom, what are you doing?" Billy asked in a whisper. He moved to the opposite side of the small wooden vanity and began to push as she pulled, wanting to get it in front of the door.

She was aware she might be overreacting, but she was functioning on a gut instinct that couldn't be ignored and that instinct screamed to her that she and Billy were in imminent danger.

"Mariah!" Maylor's heavy fist banged on the door.

The doorknob rattled and Mariah's heart boomed in her chest. "Hey, what are you doing in there? Come on out. I need to talk to you."

Mariah pointed Billy into the bathroom. "Go, close the door and lock it," she instructed. "Don't open it unless I tell you to. No matter what you hear, don't come out of there."

Thankfully he didn't hesitate but instantly obeyed as if he sensed the danger, too. She raced to the phone on the nightstand and picked it up. Dead. Oh God, help them. And her cell phone was in her purse on the kitchen counter.

Maylor banged again on the door, then laughed. "You really think a flimsy little lock is going to keep me out? Open the damn door."

"Just go away. I don't want to talk to you," she cried.

"Well, I want to talk to you. Now open the door." His voice had changed, deepened to a guttural growl.

"Why are you doing this?" she screamed.

"Because I hate him." A fist fell again, vibrating the door on its hinges. "He needs to suffer. I'm going to make him suffer." That voice, a low growl of rage, torched her fear even hotter. She knew that voice. It was the voice of the man who had taken her son, the man who had left messages on her answering machine.

Frantically Mariah looked around for a weapon she could use if he managed to get through the door. "Ed, be reasonable," she said as she searched the room. "You let Billy go. Nobody has been hurt yet. You can get help and everything will be all right." There had to be some humanity left in the man, he'd released Billy when Billy had been so sick.

"That was a mistake," Ed yelled through the door. "I should have left him there. I was weak, but I'm not weak now." Once again he hit the door and it splintered from the frame.

Mariah screamed, knowing that within seconds he'd be in the room. She picked up a heavy candlestick, but in her heart she knew it would do her little good. Deputy Maylor was armed with a gun.

He slammed into the door once again, and more splintering occurred. Mariah braced herself in front of the bathroom door, knowing he'd have to kill her in order to get past her to her son.

She screamed again, as loud as she could, hoping that her cries might alert a neighbor, a passerby, anyone who would come to help.

The door exploded inward and Maylor easily shoved the chair and the vanity aside and stepped into the room. He laughed as he saw her wielding the candlestick. "What are you going to do with that?" He pulled his gun and pointed it at her.

Tears blurred Mariah's vision. "Why do you want to hurt us? Billy and I have never done anything to you."

"Because he cares about you!" The cords in Maylor's neck stuck out as he screamed at her. "And I need to destroy everything he has, everything that's important to him."

"But why?" She needed an answer that made sense, a reason why all of this was happening.

"Maylor." The voice came from the hallway. Lucas's voice, strong and sure and filled with a simmering rage. "It's over. Throw your gun down and back away from her."

Maylor whirled around to face Lucas. "Ah, there he is, the golden boy of Conja Creek, the man born with a silver spoon in his mouth." The hatred dripped from Maylor's voice.

"I said it's over," Lucas said.

Mariah started to move, but Maylor glanced over and swung his gun at her. "Stay where you are," he demanded. "Both of you stay where you are." He swung the gun back in Lucas's direction.

"You think you're better than everyone else, living in that fancy mansion of yours, treating the rest of us like we're nothing but your servants." His voice was a hiss of hatred.

"I'm warning you, Maylor, toss your gun down. I don't want to hurt you, but I will if I have to," Lucas replied. "Throw down your gun and we can talk about this."

"There's nothing to talk about, there's nothing more to say." Spittle flew from Maylor as he screamed the words, obviously out of control as he waved the gun first in Mariah's direction, then at Lucas. "I'm better than your errand boy. Fetch me a burger, Maylor. Pick me up some clothes, Maylor. I crawled out of that swamp to make something of myself, but it's people like you who keep us down."

Mariah's heart thundered as Maylor appeared to spin completely out of control. As she saw him turn to face her once again, his gun hand rising, she screamed and closed her eyes and at the same time the sound of a shot boomed through the air.

She opened her eyes to see Maylor sprawled on the ground. He clutched his bloody shoulder and writhed in pain. Lucas entered the bedroom and kicked Maylor's gun across the room. "It's over," he said once again as Agent Kessler appeared at his side. "And you're lucky there's an FBI agent here to keep me from beating you to death."

Maylor winced, but forced a grotesque grin to his face. "I still win," he said softly. "You'll never find your sister. You'll never see Jenny again."

"Wrong," Lucas replied. "Jenny is right now at the Conja Creek Memorial Hospital. We found her in the place where you were raised, that little shanty in Black Bay. You're the loser in this little game of yours, Maylor."

Lucas reached down and jerked the deputy to his feet, unmindful of Maylor's yelp of pain. "Agent Kessler, would you please take this piece of garbage out?"

"It would be a pleasure," Kessler replied.

The moment they left the room Mariah raced to the bathroom and knocked on the door. "Billy, it's okay now. You can come out."

The bathroom door opened and Billy launched himself into his mother's arms. Mariah hugged him until he protested that she was squeezing the life out of him. Then Lucas hugged them both. Mariah hid her face in his chest, her arms around the two men in her life.

"It's okay now," Lucas said, calming both of them. "It's all over now."

When he released them, Billy looked up at him with tear-filled eyes. "Even though I'm an official deputy, I was scared."

Lucas crouched next to him. "And even though I'm an official sheriff, I was scared, too. But he won't bother us anymore. He's going to go to prison for a very long time."

"Is it true?" Mariah asked. "Is it true that you found Jenny?"

He nodded. "I was listening to the kidnapper tapes and suddenly I realized what was so familiar about that voice. I suspected it was Ed's. I found out that he'd been raised in the swamp, in a shanty in Black Bay, so with Remy Troulous as a guide we went hunting and we found her. I called the office as soon as we hit land, and Louis told me he'd just dispatched Maylor to come over here and sit on you and Billy. Remy and Wally took Jenny to the hospital and I came here." His eyes darkened. "Thank God I got here when I did."

"Is Jenny all right?" Billy asked. "Can we go see her?" He looked at Mariah who in turn looked at Lucas.

"I imagine she'll be in the hospital until at least sometime tomorrow."

Mariah smiled at her son. "We'll go see her in the morning. Tonight I'm sure what she needs more than anything is some time with her brother and some sleep."

"I'll need a report of everything that happened here," Lucas said.

"It can wait until tomorrow." She placed a hand on his arm. "Go see your sister, Lucas. I'm sure that's all she needs right now."

"You'll be safe now. It's really over." He pulled her to him for a quick embrace, then turned and left.

Mariah watched him go and she had a feeling of something important ending that she wished she could hang on to but feared she'd never experience again.

JENNY WAS LYING on her side facing away from the door when Lucas stepped quietly into her room. He'd already spoken to the doctor, who had assured him that other than the blackened eye, Jenny seemed to be fine. They were keeping her overnight for observation, and he expected she'd be released the next day.

A call to Kessler had let Lucas know that Maylor was someplace in the hospital, under guard and being treated for the gunshot wound to his shoulder. Kessler had assured him that once Maylor was fit to leave the hospital, he'd be whisked right into a jail cell.

Lucas approached Jenny's bed softly, his heart filled with an overwhelming whirl of mixed emotions. Love, relief and guilt all mixed inside him and he fought back tears.

"Jenny." He spoke her name softly.

She turned to face him and the shock of her black, swollen eye made him want to weep. "Lucas," she replied with a huge smile that warmed him to his toes. She reached out a hand. "Did you catch the bad guy?"

He nodded and took her hand in his, noticing the cracked and broken nails from where she had tried to pry off the boards in an effort to escape. "It was Ed Maylor."

"*Deputy* Maylor?"

"Yeah, but he's not going to hurt anyone ever again."

"And Billy and Mariah?" Worry deepened the blue of her eyes.

"Are fine," he assured her. The knot of emotion grew thicker, tighter in his chest. "God, Jenny, I thought I'd lost you."

"I'm sorry, Lucas." Tears filled her eyes. "I'm sorry about all this. I must have done something stupid for this to have happened."

"No, don't say that. This wasn't about you, Jenny. It had nothing to do with anything you did. And you aren't stupid. You're smart and funny and if you want to be a teacher that's okay with me. If you want to wear that red dress that I think is way too short, that's okay, too. Your life is yours to live, and I'll support you whatever you decide to do."

She uttered a small laugh through her tears. "Jeez, I should get kidnapped more often."

Lucas released her hand and grabbed a chair so he could sit by the side of her bed. There were so many things he wanted to tell her, so many things he needed to say. "Jenny, over the last couple of days I've had a lot of time to think, and I'm sorry for being too much of a big brother and not enough of a friend."

She rolled over on her side to face him. "Sometimes I don't know how you put up with me," she exclaimed, tears once again filling her eyes. "You should hate me."

He looked at her in surprise. "Hate you for what?"

"For ruining your marriage, for ruining your life," she cried.

"Oh, Jenny," he said softly. He hadn't realized the kind of baggage she'd been carrying for far too long. "You didn't ruin anything for me. You've been the best part of my life. As far as my marriage is concerned, all you did was save me a couple of miserable years and a messy divorce down the line." He took her hand in his again.

"I've been so afraid that somehow, someway you might turn out like Mom, I haven't paid enough atten-tion to what a great woman you've become. Billy said you made him not be afraid. It was because of you that he was released." He reached over and touched the side of her face with the blackened eye. "You're my hero, Jenny. You make me so proud and from now on I'm backing off. You choose your path through life and I know you'll be just fine."

As he saw the love in Jenny's eyes, love coupled with pride, he knew they were going to be okay. She was going to be all right.

They talked for hours, deep into the night. They spoke about their mother, who had been emotionally unavailable to them both. He talked about his fear for her and his need to be both father and mother, a need that had made him too strong, too severe.

Their talk was filled with tears and laughter and healing for both of them. He stayed at her bedside long after she'd drifted to sleep, his mind racing with everything that had happened.

It was almost two in the morning when Agent Kessler motioned to him from the hallway. Lucas rose and joined him.

"How's she doing?" Kessler asked.

"She's going to be just fine," Lucas replied. "How's Maylor?"

"It was just a flesh wound. The doctor stitched him up, and he's already back at the jail. He's crazy, Lucas. For some reason he honed in on you with all his hatred and it pushed him over the edge."

"I just can't believe I didn't see it," Lucas replied. "I worked with him every day and I didn't see it. I keep thinking I missed something that I should have seen."

"You saw it when it counted the most." Kessler released a tired sigh. "I just have some paperwork to take care of, then I'll be out of here. I wanted to tell you that it was a pleasure to work with you and the rest of your men."

"And I appreciate all your help," Lucas replied. The two men shook hands.

Kessler smiled at him. "You're a good sheriff, Lucas. And the loyalty of your men speaks highly of the kind of boss you are. Don't let the ravings of a lunatic make you second-guess yourself." Kessler clapped him on the back then walked away.

As Lucas watched him go, he realized it was all truly over. Billy and Jenny were home safe, the bad guy was in jail and it was time to get back to something resembling a normal life.

He should be feeling euphoric. He should be feeling an immense sense of satisfaction. But any satisfaction he felt was tinged with a faint feeling of sadness. It was over, and that meant it was time for him to let go of Mariah.

She deserved a happy life with her son, a life without a reminder of everything they had been through. He'd held on to Jenny for too long, long after it was time to let go. He cared too much about Mariah to make the same mistake. He had to let her go.

MARIAH WAS VAGUELY disappointed when she and Billy arrived at the hospital to see Jenny, and Lucas wasn't there. She told herself it was for the best, but she'd hoped to see him there with a smile on his face and his eyes no longer burdened with the darkness of despair.

Even though she knew the relationship they'd shared had been forged by mutual fear, shared grief and dire circumstances, she couldn't help that her heart somehow had gotten involved.

"Your eye looks awesome," Billy said to Jenny. He leaned over her hospital bed to get a closer look. "It's kinda turning green."

Jenny laughed. "Only an eight-year-old boy would think a black eye was awesome."

"When are you coming home?" Billy asked. "Mom bought me a new game and I want to play it with you."

"The doctor said I can get out of here as soon as the paperwork is all done," Jenny replied.

"You want us to hang around and drive you home?" Mariah asked.

"Lucas is supposed to be coming to get me. He should be here soon. I don't know exactly what happened in the time that I was gone, but I have a feeling some alien replaced my brother with a pod person," Jenny said.

"What do you mean?" Mariah asked.

"Lucas and I had a long talk last night and he told me he was going to back off, let me make my own choices and be as supportive as he could be. I think things are going to be different between us, different in a good way."

"I'm glad," Mariah said. So, Lucas had taken her words to heart. She was glad for the joy that shone from Jenny's eyes.

Minutes later, as she and Billy drove home, she wondered if maybe somehow that had been her job through this whole ordeal, to give Lucas the strength to let go of his sister, to help them reach an adult relationship. If that were the case, then she'd obviously accomplished her job. So, why did she feel so bereft?

As soon as they got home Billy set up the kitchen

table with his new game in anticipation of Jenny's homecoming, then he went into his room to make a banner that read Welcome Home.

Mariah sat at the table and thought of all the hours she'd shared this space with Lucas. She'd spent years married to Frank, but in the space of a week she'd shared more of herself and learned more about Lucas than she ever had with Frank in her years of marriage.

A half hour later Jenny arrived with Lucas. Billy answered the door and ushered them inside. Mariah tried to slow the quickening beat of her heart as Lucas came into the kitchen.

He filled the space with his presence and that sweet familiar scent of his. He flashed her a smile that appeared slightly strained, and that more than anything else let her know that whatever they had shared had been just a moment in time and nothing else.

"Oh, it's so nice to be back," Jenny exclaimed.

"You want to play a game now?" Billy said eagerly.

"Why don't you two play a game while I have a talk with Mariah," Lucas said.

Loose ends, she thought a moment later as she allowed him to lead her to the front porch. He probably needed to finish up a report of some sort.

They stepped into the bright sunshine, and Mariah looked up at him curiously. He released a deep sigh, then ran his hand through his hair in a gesture she'd seen a hundred times before in the past couple of days.

He stepped to the edge of the porch and looked at the neighborhood, not speaking for several minutes. Tension built between them and Mariah wondered what was going through his head.

She walked up behind him and touched his back. "Lucas? Is something wrong?"

He spun around to face her, and for the first time she couldn't read his emotions, couldn't guess at his thoughts. "We did this all backward, Mariah. I took you to bed before I ever got a chance to take you to dinner. We built this crazy relationship and I don't know about you, but now that everything is over, I can't seem to get rid of the feelings I have for you and I don't know what to do about them."

A swell of emotion filled her chest. She was in love with this man. It didn't matter that the love had come at a time of intense drama. It didn't matter that it had bloomed in the space of only a handful of days.

"I'd think the first thing you should do about them is ask me out to dinner," she replied.

His face lost some of its tension and his eyes lightened. "And you'd go out with me?"

"I would, because those feelings you talk about having for me, I have them for you, too." Her heart had started beating so fast it threatened to beat right out of her chest.

He took three steps to stand directly in front of her, and there was no denying the glimmer of desire that shone from his eyes. "I don't want to be a reminder of the bad time you've just experienced," he said. "If you need me to stay away in order for you to put this all behind you, I'll understand."

She moved closer to him, breathing in the scent of him that smelled like home. "Lucas, you aren't a reminder of everything bad that's happened over the past week. You're my reminder of everything good.

When I was scared, it was your arms that held me. When I was filled with despair, it was your voice that soothed me. And when I thought I was dead inside, you brought me back to life. I'm in love with you, Lucas, and if you don't take me in your arms right now and kiss me I don't know what I'll do."

He didn't hesitate. He wrapped her up in his arms and took her lips with his. The kiss was soft and sweet but with a simmering heat that promised a lifetime of desire.

Reluctantly he pulled his mouth from hers and kissed the skin just beneath her ear. "If we keep this up, we'll never have a dinner out," he whispered.

She gave a shaky laugh and stepped out of his embrace. "At the moment, eating is the last thing on my mind."

His gaze held hers and he sobered. "I can't promise you that all of our time together will be as exciting as what we've already shared."

"Thank goodness for that," she replied, then laughed.

"What?" he asked.

"Poor Richard," she said.

Lucas frowned. "What about him?"

She moved back into his arms, loving the way she fit so perfectly against him, the way his eyes flared hotly at her nearness. "I don't think Richard is going to enjoy the fact that his secretary and his sheriff are an item."

He smiled at her and in his eyes she saw her future. "Then he doesn't have to dance at our wedding," he murmured just before he kissed her again.

Epilogue

"It was a beautiful ceremony," Mariah said as she and Lucas walked toward the white tent where punch and cake were being served.

Nearby, the bride and groom were receiving the best wishes of friends and family. Amanda Rockport made a lovely bride, and the look she exchanged with her new husband, Sawyer, spoke of the love that had brought them together. She'd come into his home as a nanny for Sawyer's daughter and now found herself a bride.

Lucas tugged at his tie. "Yeah, it was nice." He dropped his hand to her back and gently led her toward the table where the punch was located. "Sawyer looks happy, and that's what's important to me. After his last marriage he deserves all the good that comes to him and Amanda."

"And Melanie," Mariah reminded him. She glanced over to where Sawyer's daughter and Mariah's son sat on a nearby bench eating cake.

She and Lucas got their punch, then sat in two of the white chairs that had been provided for the occasion. As she sipped from her cup and looked around, she thought of how quickly the past month had passed by.

There had been a lot of changes. Jenny had moved into her own little apartment. She'd enrolled in college for the fall semester and was looking forward to getting her teaching degree. She wasn't dating anyone, telling Mariah that she wanted to find out what kind of person she was on her own before she added someone else into the mix.

Ed Maylor had pleaded guilty to the charge of kidnapping, saving the taxpayers the expenses of a full-fledged trial. For his own safety he'd been sentenced to spending his time in a prison where hopefully none of the other inmates would know that he was once supposed to be one of the good guys.

Frank had been arrested for domestic violence against his newest girlfriend and was spending the next eight months in jail. Mariah didn't expect to ever hear from him again.

"Well, well, if it isn't the most gossiped-about couple in Conja Creek," Jackson Burdeaux exclaimed as he joined them.

Mariah smiled at the handsome criminal defense attorney. "Hi, Jackson." Several times over the past couple of weeks he'd stopped by to spend a little time with the boy he'd picked up on the side of the road. Billy had taken to calling him Uncle Jackson, and Jackson seemed pleased by the honor.

He sat next to Lucas. "When are you two going to do the wedding thing?" he asked. "Your deputies are taking bets, you know. Half are betting you won't be a single man by Christmas and the other half are betting you won't be single by the end of the month."

Lucas laughed. "We haven't set a date yet." He

looked at Mariah, and as always her heart quickened its pace at the warmth and love that was in his gaze.

Their growing love for each other was the most amazing thing the past month had brought. Each of them had feared that what they'd gone through with the kidnapping had somehow manufactured a false emotion. But in the weeks since, they'd both been assured that what they felt was real and lasting.

"Nice that things have calmed down," Jackson observed and looked at Lucas. "Must be great to just be dealing with the usual crimes and misdemeanors for a change."

"Conja Creek has seen enough murder and mayhem," Lucas agreed. "Between the Bennett case and then Maylor, I'd say we're due for a little quiet time."

Jackson drained his punch cup and stood. "Enjoy it while you can, because there's one thing I've learned as a criminal defense attorney. As long as you have people, you have people who do bad things to each other."

Lucas laughed. "I'll say one thing for you, Jackson. You sure know how to put a damper on a party," he said dryly.

Jackson cast them a sheepish grin. "Sorry about that. I have a bad feeling in my gut, like we're all just holding our breaths until the next shoe falls." He winked at Mariah. "I think I'll feel better if I go chat up that pretty bridesmaid. I heard she's single."

"Go show her some of that Jackson charm," Lucas said to his friend. "Before the party is over she'll be putty in your hands."

Mariah watched as Jackson walked toward the bridesmaid in the reception line, then turned to smile at Lucas. "I would guess that Jackson was the heart-breaker in your group of friends."

"You'd guess right," Lucas replied. "I have a feeling when Jackson falls, he's going to fall hard."

"Speaking of falling hard…" She took his hand in hers. "I've fallen hard for you, Sheriff Jamison."

"And best of all I've fallen just as hard for you," he replied. "How about we blow this place and go back to your house. We'll order in some pizza, play some games with Billy and then when he goes to bed we'll play some different kind of games."

"Why, Sheriff, that's the best idea I've heard all day." Mariah's heart swelled as moments later they walked to Lucas's car. Billy rode piggyback on Lucas, his boyish laughter filling the air.

Over the past month a wonderful relationship had grown between the two most important men in her life. Billy adored Lucas, and the feeling was mutual and their relationship was both loving and healthy.

This was the family she'd always wanted, and she and Lucas had already agreed that another child was someplace in their future.

As she slid into the passenger seat, she smiled at Lucas, the secret, knowing smile of a woman who knew she loved and was loved.

* * * * *

Veiled Intentions

DELORES
FOSSEN

Imagine a family tree that includes Texas cowboys, Choctaw and Cherokee Indians, a Louisiana pirate and a Scottish rebel who battled side by side with William Wallace. With ancestors like that, it's easy to understand why Texas author and former air force captain **Delores Fossen** feels as if she were genetically predisposed to writing romances. Along the way to fulfilling her DNA destiny, Delores married an air force top gun who just happens to be of Viking descent. With all those romantic bases covered, she doesn't have to look too far for inspiration.

Chapter One

San Antonio, Texas

Detective Katelyn O'Malley stood in the entrance hall and studied each of the wedding guests as they trickled into Sacred Heart church.

If she got lucky, very lucky, maybe no one would be murdered today.

Too bad there was the little annoying buzz in the back of her head that said all hell might break loose before the bride and groom managed to say I do.

While she directed the guests to sign the registry—a duty she'd created for her cover—Katelyn continued her surveillance. She mentally dismissed two giggling teenage girls whose dresses were so skintight that they couldn't have been carrying concealed weapons, or much of anything else for that matter. Besides, if her profile of the killer was right, she wasn't looking for a female but a male in his late twenties or early thirties.

A male who'd already killed two people.

"See anything?" she heard her brother, Garrett, ask through her earpiece. He was posted outside the church. Watching their backs. And sides. It'd taken some effort, but she'd managed to get photos of thirty-nine of the forty-one guests. Not bad odds. If someone uninvited showed up, Garrett would know and could relay it to her.

Katelyn kept her voice at a whisper and spoke into the tiny communicator tucked in the neckline of her dress. "So far, so good. How about you?"

"Nothing. Well, nothing other than being hit on by one of the bridesmaids."

That wasn't anything new. Lots of women hit on her brother. "Was she armed?" Katelyn was only partly sarcastic.

"No. Unfortunately, I have firsthand knowledge that she wasn't, since she tripped over her lavender taffeta gown and fell right in my arms." He paused. "I guess this is a good time to remind you that your lieutenant will have our butts if he finds out about this little unauthorized stakeout you arranged?"

"He won't find out," Katelyn said with certainty she didn't feel. The lieutenant in question was her oldest brother and head of Homicide. And he would find out. No doubt about it. Still, if she could stop someone from being killed today, she'd gladly take the flak over her yet-to-be-an-official-part of this investigation.

"Okay, can I add then that this is probably a waste of a really great Saturday afternoon?" Garrett continued. "You're assuming the other two murders weren't just random acts of violence—"

"They weren't."

He grumbled something that Katelyn didn't want to distinguish. "All right, but even if last week's shooting was the start of some grand serial career, it's the first frickin' weekend in June. There are dozens of weddings going on in San Antonio today. Hear that, sis? *Dozens.* If our gunman's really a wacko targeting brides and grooms, he could be at any one of them."

It was true, and they'd already rehashed this subject too many times. Yes, this was a long shot. Yes, this wasn't exactly standard operating procedure. And yes, they could get reprimanded for this. But after studying all the angles, Katelyn knew in her gut that this particular ceremony was their best bet for saving lives. In her mind, this was one of those times where the means would justify the ends.

An odd sound caught her attention. A scrape of metal. Katelyn whipped her gaze to the other side of the narthex where the lanky, twenty-something photographer was adjusting his equipment. He was definitely on her list of people to be concerned about, and she made a mental note to get a look in his bag. Perhaps she'd try the bridesmaid's flirting/falling in his arms approach. She was certainly dressed for the part in the short, snug emerald silk outfit that she'd dragged from the back of her closet.

The way back.

Katelyn had added some too-high heels, heavy concealing makeup and a blond wig to go along with it. All in all, it was a very uncomfortable but hopefully convincing disguise that could work for her if needed.

"Hold on. We might have something," Garrett informed her. "*If* there's something to have in all this. A male. Brown hair, part Latino or maybe Italian. He doesn't match any of the photos. You'll have visual in under a minute because he's headed right for the church."

"Okay. I'll handle it. You stay put in case this one's a decoy."

"Be careful," he warned.

Oh, she definitely would.

More guests strolled in, bringing with them the June heat and humidity from the nearby San Antonio River. A pregnant woman with a toddler. A middle-aged couple holding hands. All innocent, she was sure of that.

And then Katelyn saw him.

That buzz in her head turned to a full roar.

He stepped into the entry. Well, he didn't step, exactly. He stalked in, smooth and slow, like a jungle cat sizing up his hunting area.

Now here was the male who fit her profile to a proverbial tee. Mahogany brown hair, not too long, not too short. Olive skin. Six-one. About a hundred and seventy-five pounds. No distinguishing marks and definitely no pretty boy. He had badass written all over him.

He wore a midnight-blue suit. Nondescript. Ditto for the crisp white dress shirt and his precisely knotted silver-gray tie. But that's where the nondescript and ditto parts ended. Katelyn had been a cop for nearly eight years and had learned to recognize something lethal when she saw it.

This guy was lethal.

His gaze swept around the room, and like his entrance, it was smooth. He made eye contact with her. Just a split second. Then, he looked away to continue his surveillance. And there was no doubt in her mind that this was surveillance for him. He dismissed the teenagers as quickly as Katelyn had, but his attention lingered a bit on the photographer, before it came back to her.

Was he suspicious?

You bet he was.

His instincts weren't lacking in any area. That meant she had to strike first.

Pulling in a hard breath to steady herself, she eased from behind the narrow table when he walked closer. She wanted a better look, among other things, and she got a dose of those *other things* right away. She caught the scent of his aftershave. Something manly and musky. It was better suited for a long night of sex than a wedding.

Or maybe that was just her imagination working overtime.

Whoa.

An imagination with seriously bad timing.

She brushed her arm against his, purposely, and the soft contact garnered her another glance. Not a dismissive one either. There was interest in the depths of those icy blue eyes. Too bad she couldn't quite make out exactly what kind of interest it was, but it was obviously time for that flirting ruse to see if she had to reel in a killer.

Katelyn smiled, making sure she let her nerves show a little. She didn't have to fake that part. She was well past being nervous. But then, this was a situation where lack of nerves would mean she was a complete idiot. Someone, maybe this man, had already killed two people. Nerves were part of the job description.

"I'm Kate." She offered her hand in greeting, and he shook it. Eventually. "Would you like to sign the guest registry?"

"No, thanks."

"Oh, okay." A roadblock. Not too surprising. Katelyn tried a different angle. "It's a keepsake for the bride and groom so they'll know who attended. Maybe I could sign it for you if you'll give me your name?"

He looked at the book, then her again. "Joe."

She almost pushed for a last name but decided it could wait. "This'll sound like a really bad line, but don't I know you from somewhere?" Katelyn asked, letting her voice purr. "You look familiar."

He spared her another glance. "No. I think I'd remember you."

There was a touch of Texas in his voice. An effortless, sliding drawl that matched his attitude.

And his aftershave.

Maybe the accent meant he was local. If so, it fit another piece of her unofficial profile.

Katelyn looked around to make sure they hadn't garnered anyone's attention. They hadn't. The guests were still ambling into the sanctuary, which was exactly where she needed them to amble. She didn't want an audience, or any bystanders, when she confronted him.

"Say, I'm a little light-headed," she lied. "I have this blood sugar thing. Nothing serious. Just makes me a little woozy. I wondered if I could just catch on to your arm before I fall flat on my face?"

He studied her. A long, snail-crawling moment. And then, as if preparing for a root canal, he offered her his arm. She took hold of it before he changed his mind, and she got a peek inside his jacket.

He was packing a .357 Magnum in a shoulder holster.

Katelyn had anticipated a weapon, of course. However, reality caused her heart to slam against her chest. She pushed that slamming aside and got to work. It was time to move on to the next step of her plan. She needed to get him away from the guests so she could rid him of that weapon and ask a few questions.

She stumbled, just enough to make him grip her arm. That stumble was a real leap of faith on her part, since she wasn't overly confident that he would even catch her. Thankfully, there was at least one gentlemanly bone in his body, because he cooperated. After he had a good hold on her, she led him a few steps away into the narrow hallway just off the narthex.

''I can't believe this is happening,'' she mumbled, leaning against him so he wouldn't easily be able to reach for his gun. ''Not the best time to get one of my dizzy spells. The ceremony's about to start, and I doubt you want to miss that.''

She shoved him into the small vacant room that she'd already checked out. Katelyn didn't waste any time, figuring she would rather be embarrassed from a case of mistaken identity than to have a dead bride and groom.

Blocking the doorway so he couldn't leave, she drew her weapon from her holster, hidden beneath her silky jacket. ''Here's how we're going to do this,'' she instructed. ''Keep your hands where I can see them and explain to me why you brought a .357 Magnum to a wedding.''

He lifted his shoulder in a casual shrug. ''I carry my gun everywhere. I guess you do the same?''

If he was scared, or even remotely concerned, he certainly wasn't showing it. Too bad Katelyn couldn't say the same. Her throat was suddenly dry as dust, and she kept a firm grip on her gun to keep her hand from shaking.

''Yes, but for me, it's part of the job. I'm Detective Katelyn O'Malley, S.A.P.D., and this is what we call a stop and frisk.''

He paused. Said one word of profanity under his breath. One rather crude four-letter word. He tipped

his eyes to the ceiling as if seeking divine inter-
vention.

Or something.

"Know what I think?" he asked.

"Not particularly. But I want you to remove your
weapon slowly and carefully from its holster and
place it on the floor. Notice those operative words.
Slowly. Carefully. Floor. Those are major conditions
here, and you're going to do that while using only
two fingers. Make any sudden moves, and I'll take
you down the hard way."

He looked her straight in the eye. "That wasn't
what I was thinking." He disarmed himself, just as
she'd instructed. Slowly, carefully, and he placed his
gun on the floor directly between them.

"Oh, yeah?" Katelyn caught his shoulder and
turned him around. She positioned his hands, palms
flat, against the wall, and kneed his legs apart. "What
exactly were you thinking?" she asked, patting him
down.

The man was certainly solid. And built. Her fingers
skimmed over lots of hard, sinewy muscles. Odd.
She'd never noticed anything like that before when
frisking a suspect. Maybe it had something to do with
his memorable aftershave.

"I'm thinking you'll regret doing this," he let her
know.

"I doubt it, especially since it might just save a
few people from dying."

She located his wallet in his jacket pocket. Except
when she got a good look at it, she realized it wasn't

a wallet. And that caused her stomach to tighten into a hard knot. It also caused Katelyn to use a little profanity of her own. She flipped open the too-familiar leather case and read the name aloud.

"Joseph Rico."

"Sergeant Joe Rico," he clarified. And with that announcement, he turned back around to face her. "Homicide. S.A.P.D."

Her breath landed somewhere around that knot in her stomach.

Katelyn shook her head. The badge had to be a fake. Except it wasn't. She scratched it with her thumbnail, or rather tried to. It was as real as the one in her purse. Still, there was something off here. "Impossible. I work Homicide, and I've never seen you before in my life."

"Because I was just assigned there." He enunciated each word as if she were mentally deficient. "By the chief of police."

Judas Priest. That bit of information cleared the buzz in her head. Katelyn wasn't sure exactly where this was leading, but she knew for a fact that she wouldn't like its final destination.

Joe Rico calmly picked up his gun from the floor and reholstered it. Somehow, he managed to look cocky even while doing that little chore. No hurried moves. No overt display of emotion.

"Well, Detective Katelyn O'Malley, I'd say we have a problem. A problem with you being here because this isn't your case. Why am I so certain of that?'' He aimed his thumb at his chest. ''Because it's mine.''

Katelyn hadn't thought this moment could possibly get more frustrating—or embarrassing—but she was obviously wrong.

''Yours?'' she demanded.

''Mine.'' Sergeant Rico muscled her out of the doorway and turned to leave, delivering the rest of his news from over his shoulder. ''Oh, and by the way, I'm your new boss.''

Chapter Two

Well, it wasn't exactly the smooth start Joe wanted for this particular investigation. While undercover, he'd been made quite easily—by his subordinate, no less. And then that subordinate had frisked him.

He was sorry to say the frisking had been more enjoyable than it should have been.

Far more.

"The chief assigned you this case?" Katelyn O'Malley asked, following him.

Since he'd already made that perfectly clear, and since he detected some resentment in her voice, he surmised that she'd heard him correctly but wasn't in agreement with the chief's decision.

Joe stopped at the edge of the narthex and pressed the transmitter of the communication device hidden in his jacket. "Did anyone come in the church in the past three minutes?" he asked the backup officer who was positioned in an office building directly across the street.

"No."

So they'd been lucky. Katelyn O'Malley's stunt hadn't allowed the sniper to walk in unchallenged. Of course, if the killer followed the method of operation of the last shooting, he or she wouldn't burst into the church until the I do's had been said. There'd be a frenzied battery of gunfire from a ski-mask-wearing shooter who wouldn't actually enter the sanctuary but would stay in the narthex and then make an easy get-away. Just the way it'd happened to the victims, Gail Prescott and Raul Hernandez.

Joe clicked off the transmitter and glanced back at Detective O'Malley.

She was staring at him as if he were a member of the fungus family.

Too bad he couldn't say the same for her.

She was attractive. Damn attractive. Not like a beauty queen either, but in a strong, athletic, kick-butt sort of way. The girl-next-door meets Buffy type.

The type he found attractive.

And no amount of denial would make his body think otherwise. Fortunately, the parts of his body that noticed her attractive looks didn't have any say in the decisions he made.

"There's been some kind of mistake." She jammed her gun back into her holster. "After the initial investigator dropped out because of family illness, I requested this case, and I was told my request was under consideration."

"It was," Joe calmly assured her. "But the considering part is finished now, and I'm the lead investigator. End of discussion."

There was nothing calm about her response. He saw some fire dance through ultraclear, cool green eyes. He'd obviously stepped on her toes, toes encased very nicely in a pair of sex-against-the-wall stilettos.

Something else about her that he truly wished he hadn't noticed.

Joe quickly pushed that, her physical attributes and the remnants of the frisking aside. What the devil was wrong with him anyway? Even if he'd been looking to spice up his love life, he darn sure wouldn't have been looking in Katelyn O'Malley's direction.

"I knew the woman who was killed last week," she added.

As if that would help her cause.

"Gail Prescott," Joe supplied. "You went to high school with her and you've maintained occasional contact with her and her family. You probably would have attended her wedding even if you hadn't been on a stakeout. Your relationship with the victim, however, doesn't give you priority in this investigation. In fact, it does just the opposite. I don't care to work with an officer who comes into a case with a personal chip on his or her shoulder."

She unclenched her teeth before she could speak. "There's no personal chip, *Sergeant.* Just my desire to bring a killer to justice."

"Good. Then, we're in agreement. I have that same desire, but that doesn't mean I'll allow you to be part of this case." But the moment the words left his mouth, Joe remembered a vital point that had come to mind. "By the way, why'd you stake out this particular church?"

The fire in those baby greens dwindled a fraction. She pulled back her shoulders as if preparing to defend herself and met him eye-to-eye. In those heels, she could almost manage it, even though he was just over six feet tall.

"Because the bride and groom met through the Perfect Match Agency, the same matchmaking service that Gail and her fiancé used," she explained. "They both also had the same florist. I thought there might be a connection so I contacted the minister here at the church—"

"You told him about this possible connection?"

"No. Of course not. There's only been one shooting, and I have no proof that there'll be another one. I didn't want the couple to bring a possible lawsuit against the department for disrupting their wedding, so I simply reminded the minister of some recent robberies in the area and offered my services as a temporary security guard. He agreed, and we came up with the idea of using the guest registry as my cover."

So she'd done her homework. He liked that. But this wasn't a time when Brownie points counted. "The florist and Perfect Match could be a coincidence. There are other possible angles."

"Yes. Gail's fiancé was Hispanic, so the shooting could have been racially motivated. Or maybe their deaths are linked to some other aspect of their personal lives." She paused. "But I don't believe that, and apparently neither do you, or you wouldn't have come here today.''

Touché.

Joe fought back an urge to smile. Under different circumstances, he might have enjoyed this verbal sparring, but these weren't different circumstances. Katelyn O'Malley would be in his way, because despite her denial, this case was personal for her. In his experience, when it got personal, people made mistakes.

That wasn't going to happen on his watch.

''I came here to follow up on one particular theory. *One* theory of several,'' he assured her.

Joe checked the entryway. No new guests, and the others had already moved into the church. He could hear the organ start to play, an indication that the bride and groom were about to make their entrance.

Hopefully, it wouldn't be their last.

Katelyn huffed. ''I know those theories as well as you—''

''Caucasian male is approaching the church,'' the backup officer said through Joe's communicator.

That, and the sound of hurried footsteps, interrupted whatever else she was about to say. Frantic footsteps that sent them both reaching for their guns. In the same motion, she stepped into the hallway beside him. However, the threat for which they'd braced themselves didn't materialize.

Judging from the strong family resemblance, the man who came into sight was Sergeant Garrett

O'Malley. His gun was already drawn, but he held it discreetly by his side so it wouldn't easily be seen.

"Katelyn, what's going on?" her brother demanded.

Because Joe was standing arm-to-arm with her, he felt her muscles relax.

"False alarm," she let him know. Once again, she reholstered her gun. "This is Sergeant Joe Rico. Homicide. This is my brother, Sergeant Garrett O'Malley, Special Investigations."

Unlike Katelyn, Garrett didn't appear to relax. Just the opposite. It was obvious he had issues, and Joe didn't have to guess who or what those issues were.

"Rico," Garrett repeated in the same tone that he no doubt reserved for profanity. "According to the rumor mill, the chief sent you in to investigate our brother, Brayden. And possibly Katelyn and me, too."

"The chief did what?" Katelyn asked. Mouth gaping, she stepped in front of Joe and pinned her gaze to his.

This obviously wasn't the way to win friends and influence people. But that didn't matter. He had a job to do, and he'd do it, with or without the O'Malleys' approval.

"Since it appears you can answer your sister's questions," Joe said to Garrett, "I'll leave you to it and see what's happening in the church. I'd prefer that people didn't die while we're standing around chitchatting."

It was a good exit line. The only thing missing was,

well, the good exit. Katelyn didn't get out of his way so he could leave, and the hallway was too narrow to go around her. He really didn't want to play bump and grind just so he could get past her.

Really.

Even if there were various parts of him that thought it might be fun.

Her hands went to her hips. "I don't know what your agenda is—"

"To do my job," Joe insisted.

That earned him a scowl. "My brothers are good cops. Don't judge either of them by the fact that I came here today. This undercover investigation was my idea and mine alone."

Since it was clear this argument wouldn't be resolved in the next couple of minutes, Joe put his gun back into his holster, firmly caught her shoulders and moved her out of his path. "I'll see you both back at headquarters when I'm finished here."

Joe turned to leave. But he still didn't manage that exit. A few steps was as far as he got. The sound stopped him in his tracks. Because it was the last thing he wanted to hear. A sound he'd anticipated, and dreaded.

A shot blasted through the church.

THE EMOTION of her argument with Sergeant Rico evaporated instantly, and in its place, Katelyn felt the barrage of instinct and adrenaline.

Sweet heaven. The gunman had attacked after all, and she hadn't been able to stop it. She prayed the bullet had missed its target and that everyone was safe.

"The shot came from outside," Rico offered, taking the words right out of her mouth. "The west side of the building, maybe. Maybe the rear. Garrett, secure the front doors, and just in case someone else hasn't already done it, call for backup. Katelyn, you're coming with me."

Rico didn't hesitate. Neither did Garrett nor she. Her brother hurried to the front door, kicking it shut and locking it. He kept his weapon ready, secured a spot near one of the sidelight windows and then pulled out his cell phone. Rico went in the direction of the sanctuary, and Katelyn followed.

"Get down!" Rico yelled to the guests.

Most had already done just that, squeezing themselves underneath the pews. There were raw screams. Chaos. The smell of fear. And in the middle of that, Katelyn saw the bride, groom and the minister cowering between the altar and an archway of pale peach roses.

No visible evidence of blood. Thank God. They seemed unharmed.

For now.

"There's an auxiliary building out there. Two story, brown brick," she relayed to Rico. "Our gunman could be using it as a catbird seat."

He nodded and without taking his attention off the partially shot-out stained glass window, he whispered to her over his shoulder. "You don't happen to have another brother stashed in the parking lot, huh?"

''I wish. But no. We're on our own until backup arrives.'' Which wouldn't be for minutes. Long, critical minutes.

Where just about anything could happen.

''Good,'' Rico responded. ''Because I have an officer out there. One who's *officially* on this case, and I didn't want any of your relatives accidentally shooting him while he's trying to do his job.''

Katelyn didn't appreciate the sarcasm but welcomed all the help they could get. Maybe the officer would be able to stop the gunman before any more damage was done.

But at the moment that seemed a lot to hope for.

There'd been damage already. Even if they stopped the shooting here and now, every one of the guests would remember this horrifying ordeal for the rest of their lives. Katelyn blamed herself for that. She'd been in a position to stop this and had failed.

A second shot rang out, quickly followed by another. And another. Two of the three went through a window on the right front side of the church and tore chunks of glass from the frame. No doubt that's what the shooter had intended to do. Now he or she had a direct line of sight into the church.

Yelling and crying out, the bride, groom and minister scurried to the other side of the altar, but it wouldn't give them shelter for long. Bullets could easily eat through that wood.

''I'll make my way over there.'' Rico tipped his head to a set of ornate double doors, which were only a couple of yards away from the shattered window.

"If necessary I'll return fire to draw the shooter's attention. I might be able to get a visual and take him out."

Yes. Or maybe the gunman would get him first. Of course, that was a chance they had to take.

"I can help." Katelyn kicked off her shoes and peeled off the silky jacket so they wouldn't get in her way. "There aren't any guests near that other window next to the doors. I'll knock out the glass and return fire, as well. Don't worry—I'll keep watch for your officer and make sure I don't send any friendly fire his way."

Rico might have disagreed with that impromptu plan, but he didn't get a chance to say anything. More shots came crashing through the building.

Heavy, thick blasts.

Nonstop, this time.

The sounds were deafening. And they drowned out the shouts, screams and prayers that increased with each new round of fire. Just as Katelyn had figured, those shots were aimed right at the wooden altar. It was the same as the first shooting, the one that had killed Gail and her fiancé. Shots and plenty of them. But that knowledge gave Katelyn no comfort whatsoever. She'd already guessed that Gail's murder wasn't some random act of violence.

For all the good it'd done her.

Her guess was right, and yet it'd still been repeated right under her nose.

The bride screamed. Maybe in pain. Maybe just from fear. Katelyn prayed it was fear.

Rico moved. Fast and low. He was almost graceful, surprising for a man his size. With Katelyn following closely behind him, they went toward the door. Along the way, he identified himself and doled out assurances to the terrified guests.

He kept close to the perimeter wall until he got to the row of the stained glass windows, and then he lowered himself to the floor and proceeded to the doors.

The shots stopped for only a couple of seconds. Not for reloading, Katelyn soon learned. And they didn't stop because the gunman was finished for the day. The break was so the person could change out rifles. The sound of the new shots told her that much since it was a different calibration. Whoever was doing this had certainly come prepared to kill but wasn't necessarily an expert marksman. The stray bullets were landing everywhere—which, of course, made the situation all the more dangerous.

Katelyn made her way right along behind Joe Rico. Trying to time it perfectly to coordinate with his efforts, she sheltered her eyes and used the grip of her gun to knock out the glass that formed the image of the archangel, Michael. The glass was solid and held in place by not just strips of lead solder but also a sturdy frame. It took several hard jabs before she managed to dislodge enough of it so she could see into the parking lot.

Pressing her back against the narrow section of wall next to the doors, she rotated her body and did a quick check outside. She had a fairly good view of the building—and the dozen or so windows facing the church. Too many windows, and the reflection of the early afternoon sun didn't make things easier. She quickly scanned them all as best she could.

No shooter in sight.

Yet, he had to be there.

Somewhere.

Because he was still firing.

While still low on the floor, Rico reached up and turned the old-fashioned brass handle on the door. He opened it a fraction and looked out. Katelyn waited for a signal so she could return fire.

And just like that, the shots stopped.

She felt another surge of adrenaline slam through her. A bad-feeling kind of surge. If the gunman wasn't shooting, then he was likely making his getaway.

That couldn't happen.

Because she knew in her heart that he would continue this until someone stopped him.

It was a risk, but Katelyn moved closer to the window so she could check the parking lot and the grounds. Rico did the same to the door. He stood, took position and aimed.

"Think," she whispered to herself. If she were a killer, what would be her escape plan? Not the parking lot. Too visible. Not the side either since it bumped right against a fairly busy street.

No.

He'd go out the rear of the building and slip into the myriad of old shops and businesses that were crammed into this particular part of the down-town area.

Katelyn heard the sound of sirens the moment that Rico opened the door wider. Mumbling something, he peered out. He'd perhaps come to the same conclusion as she had. The gunman was getting away.

"Stay put," Rico ordered.

It was a logical order.

Katelyn needed to stay there to protect the guests. Still, part of her wanted to go after the gunman.

"Hold your positions," Garrett called out from the arched entryway that led into the church. Katelyn glanced at him and saw that he had his phone pressed to his ear. "Backup is in pursuit of a white car that just sped away."

Katelyn released the breath that she didn't even know she'd been holding. She glanced at Rico, but he didn't seem any more eager than she was to let down his guard. So they did the only thing they could do. They waited with their backs literally against the wall and their guns ready.

"Is anyone hurt?" Rico called out to the guests.

The response varied, most still layered with panic, but from what she gathered, no one had actually been shot. Nothing short of a miracle. Katelyn said a quick prayer of thanks for that and then turned to the man who'd given her so much grief about being here.

"Still think I'm the wrong person for this case?" she asked Rico.

"Yes." No hesitation whatsoever.

The analogy of butting her head against a brick

wall came to mind. "But I guessed right about the gunman picking this particular wedding. Even in your book that has to count for something."

He made another check of the parking lot. "It doesn't count for much."

Crouching there among shattered glass and the smell of gunfire, it seemed petty to dislike this man because he was arrogant and hardheaded, but that didn't prevent her scowl. The scowl didn't lessen either when Garrett called out something else.

"It's over already. Backup lost the guy in pursuit," her brother announced.

"It's over," some of the guests repeated. Slowly, they began to come out of hiding. Hugging each other. Crying. Praying. Most still in shock.

Katelyn groaned and scrubbed her hand over her face. Judas. This wasn't over. In fact, that buzz in the back of her head told her it wasn't over by a long shot.

The killer had just gotten started.

Chapter Three

Joe reread the overview of the proposed mission that Lieutenant Brayden O'Malley had handed him just minutes earlier. The overview didn't read any better the second time around, and he didn't hold out hope that a third read would make it any more palatable.

There were quite a few points of contention so Joe chose the first one. "You really think the shooting day before yesterday was a result of a botched burglary of the building next to Sacred Heart church?"

"No," O'Malley readily answered. "But I'd rather have the press report that than link it with the shooting that happened a week earlier."

Joe nodded, but the two shootings wouldn't stay unlinked for long. All it would take was another incident, and unfortunately another incident was probably in the planning stages. That is, if the gunman hadn't already finalized his next hit. But the real question was—was the killer linked to the matchmaking agency or the florist?

Or neither?

The *or neither* was the most troublesome scenario of them all. If the shootings weren't connected through the businesses, then maybe they had a thrill killer or just a plain psycho on their hands.

Not that they didn't have that anyway.

But Joe preferred his psychos to keep to a discernable pattern, because with hard work and some luck, patterns could be identified.

"The shell casings taken from the two crime scenes didn't match," Katelyn said, reading from a copy of the overview. She gave a weary sigh. "So that complicates things."

"It just means our shooter likes to trade off weapons," Joe advised her. "It doesn't mean the crimes aren't related."

Another sigh from her. This one wasn't weary. It had a you-think? tinge to it.

"Arguments? Comments? Objections?" Lieutenant O'Malley asked. "If so, direct them to me and not at each other."

The man was definitely a multitasker. While he tossed out those leading questions and semireprimands, he looked through a report, scrawled his signature on it and tossed it into his out-box before he went onto the next one. But then, no one had ever accused this particular O'Malley of being inefficient. Just the opposite. The only accusation had been in the area of his preferential treatment.

"Concerns," Joe volunteered.

Time to move on to point two. He had a lot of concerns, but the major one was the woman with the short, flame-red hair who was sitting next to him. Now the question was how to voice that concern without thoroughly riling Katelyn's oldest brother, a man he had no desire to rile. Even under a cloud of suspicion, Brayden was formidable. Joe's investigation into departmental favoritism would no doubt irritate the man enough without adding more to the mix.

"Sergeant Rico thinks this case is too personal for me," Katelyn countered. "He believes I should step aside because I knew Gail."

And with that totally accurate observation, she looked across the desk that separated them and met her brother's gaze. In the next few seconds, at least a hundred or more words passed between them, even though neither spoke.

It was an interesting encounter to watch.

The lieutenant stared at her and lifted his eyebrow, just a fraction. That was it. No other change in his otherwise calm, authoritative expression. Yet the simple gesture caused Katelyn's mouth to tighten, and her grip on the chair arm whitened her knuckles. Joe could have sworn the temperature in the room dropped by a full ten degrees. It was the most efficient warning he'd ever witnessed.

"Your sister has renegade tendencies," Joe added, feeling that after what'd just happened, he was probably preaching to the choir. Still, a little choir preaching might go a long way to some changes in this mission proposal. "I'd prefer to work with another detective on this case."

And Joe already had one in mind. Detective Dawn Davidson, a veteran officer who'd worked a serial killer case just the year before. She had the experience and from all accounts was levelheaded.

"Bringing in another detective might be a problem." The lieutenant extracted a manila folder from a stack and slid it Joe's way. "This'll be an undercover assignment, and Katelyn already has her foot in the door."

"What door?" Joe asked.

"At the matchmaking agency that might be connected to the two shootings."

Judging from the soft groan that Katelyn made and the way she sank slightly lower in her chair, this would not please him. From the lieutenant's elevated eyebrow, it didn't please him much, either.

"I must have missed that foot-in-the-door part when reading the overview," Joe commented.

Brayden pointed to the folder. "It's all in there."

Katelyn turned slightly away when he opened it and kept her attention focused on her brother. The top page in the folder was a rather lengthy questionnaire from the Perfect Match Agency, and it was dated a week earlier. It'd been filled out just two days after the first shooting.

And the name at the top?

Kate Kennedy.

Joe felt a groan coming on, as well.

"Is this your handiwork?" he asked her.

"Yes. But no one at Perfect Match has any idea that I'm a cop. *No one.* Kennedy is obviously an alias.'' Katelyn directed the rest of her explanation to her brother. "I wanted to get a look at the people who worked there. I figured this was the fastest way to do it.''

"But not the smartest way," Joe quickly let her know. "You could have jeopardized everything by going in there on your own.''

"But I didn't.'' Moving to the edge of her seat, she repeated it to her brother. "I can do whatever you need me to do to make this undercover assignment work.''

"I'm not the one you need to convince, Katelyn. The chief assigned Sergeant Rico as the lead for this case.'' And the lieutenant sat back and left it at that.

The proverbial ball had just been tossed into Joe's proverbial court.

Unfortunately, he also knew how these next few minutes were about to play out.

Hell.

Katelyn O'Malley had certainly put him in a hard place with her coloring-outside-the-lines attitude. Still, it'd only compound the problem if he let his personal feelings influence the most logical way to approach this. Well, it was the most logical approach considering she'd already tossed a monkey wrench or two into the scenario.

"It wouldn't be smart for me to use another detective at this point," Joe concluded, speaking more to himself than the O'Malleys. He glanced at the questionnaire while he finished up his explanation. It figured. Katelyn had listed chili as her favorite food. "If the killer's part of the Perfect Match Agency, then he or she might be suspicious of anyone registering so soon after the second shooting.''

''Guess that leaves you out then, huh?'' Katelyn all but smirked at him.

Even though it was borderline petty, Joe liked it when people did that, especially when he could smirk right back. He calmly shuffled through the papers in the folder, extracted his own questionnaire and passed it to her.

Her eyes widened and skimmed over the first page. ''You filled this out the same day I did?''

Let the smirking begin. ''Yes.''

She hissed out a breath. ''Need I remind you that you just accused me of jumping the gun by going to the agency?''

''The difference is—I was on this case, and you weren't.'' Joe held out his hands to emphasize the space. ''Big difference. I'm talking huge.''

The temperature went down another notch, and her eyes narrowed to slits.

''Which brings us up-to-date, I believe,'' Brayden interjected. Good timing, Joe thought, since Katelyn looked ready to implode. ''We have to act fast. There are only five days until Saturday. Five days until a whole host of weddings are scheduled to take place all over the city. Five days to stop a killer from striking again.''

Joe was well aware of that. Those five days were already breathing down his neck. ''I've learned the florist in question is doing the flower arrangements for two weddings this weekend, one Saturday, another Sunday night. But neither couple met through the Perfect Match Agency. If fact, I haven't been able to connect any of the upcoming marriages to a matchmaking agency.''

''Neither have I.'' Katelyn pulled out her own set of notes from a leather briefcase that was leaning against her chair. ''And therein lies our problem. Perfect Match doesn't release all the names of their former customers who've made wedding plans. So it becomes a needle-in-a-haystack approach.''

''It's the only approach we have right now,'' Joe fired back. ''We could stake out all the weddings in San Antonio, but it'll eat up a ton of manpower and cause people to ask too many questions and maybe even panic. Plus, there are the other ceremonies, the ones that aren't listed in the paper. We wouldn't be able to cover those. So our best bet is to go back to the source of the connection—the Perfect Match Agency. They require matched couples to meet there first for an icebreaker, and there's one every Tuesday night, including tomorrow night.''

''It starts at seven-thirty,'' Katelyn provided. ''We don't need an invitation. We just need to be computer matched…somehow.''

It didn't surprise Joe that she knew those details. She'd probably already picked out the clothes she was going to wear. And she'd done all of that before even being officially assigned to the team.

His team.

He hoped like the devil that she didn't wear those

sexy stilettos and the little green outfit. He'd have enough distractions as it was.

"Detective O'Malley and I'll do this intro thing tomorrow night at Perfect Match," Joe continued, making sure he sounded like the boss. Because after the minifantasy involving her choice of fashion, he needed the reminder in the worst sort of way. "We'll pretend we were high school sweethearts and that we're surprised but happy to be reunited."

She nodded. "Good idea. And that'll explain a hasty engagement and equally hasty marriage."

"Well, hopefully." It might also make the wrong person suspicious, but he'd deal with that when and if it happened. "While we're there, we'll have a good look around the place. Without breaking the law, of course."

Another *you-think?* huff from Katelyn.

Joe ignored her and continued. "In the meantime, I'll keep going through the background checks I've been doing on the employees and the owners of Perfect Match and the florist."

"I've done backgrounds checks, as well," Katelyn informed him.

Joe bobbed his head. "Of course you have."

The woman had an incredibly effective scalpel-sharp glare. "I'm not an idiot. I did them discretely."

Joe might have questioned her on what she considered discrete, but the lieutenant spoke first. "Sounds as if you have everything under control."

Not even close.

Joe kept that sentiment to himself.

"Good." Brayden stood and reached for the jacket draped over the back of his chair. "Now, if you'll excuse me, I have an appointment with the chief. Feel free to use my office to hash out the rest of the details. Oh, and it goes without saying—keep me informed."

"Wait," Katelyn called out when her brother headed for the door. "You're both missing a key point. Yes, Sergeant Rico and I filled out these questionnaires, but that in itself doesn't give us a computer match. I hate to state the obvious here, but the *computer* does that. In fact, it generates a list of matches so the candidates can meet the people at the icebreaker. What if neither of us has any matches? What then? We can't just show up."

"I'd planned to have one of the techs go into the system and arrange for the questionnaires to be matched," Joe explained.

Katelyn shook her head. "That sounds risky. Someone at the agency might figure out—"

"A match isn't a problem," Brayden assured them. "It's all in the folder."

There was something about the lieutenant's strange, almost self-satisfied expression that sent Joe thumbing through the rest of the papers in the file. Katelyn must have had the same feeling, because she leaned closer so she could see the documents, as well.

It didn't take Joe long to find it. There it was. The dozen or so men listed as "dream date" matches for client 6341B, Kate Kennedy. His own alias, Joe Farrell, was the first name on the list.

He felt as if someone had slugged him in the solar plexus.

"You already had the tech rig the system?" Joe asked. But he didn't think that's what had generated the look on the lieutenant's face.

"No. The two of you matched without any tech interference." Brayden's eyebrows flexed. "For once, Murphy's Law worked in our favor. Let's hope that luck continues."

And with that little scud missile attack, the lieutenant left them sitting there in somewhat stunned silence.

"It had to be the chili," Joe mumbled under his breath.

Or maybe Katelyn just jotted down a whole bunch of lies while filling out the questionnaire. He hadn't, that was for sure. Unnecessary lies were just too hard to keep track of, so with the exception of his name, address and occupation, everything else was true.

Yet, they'd matched.

Even if she'd lied, that was an unsettling coincidence because it meant her lies matched his truths.

Joe quietly pushed that coincidence aside and moved on to the mission at hand.

"I'll see you at the Perfect Match tomorrow night." He stood and tucked the folder beneath his arm. "Until then, we keep doing these background checks and hope we find a smoking gun. Oh, and by the way, I insist the officers on my team follow the rules. *My* rules," he emphasized. "If you jeopardize this assignment again—"

"I won't."

"If you do, I'll have your butt and your badge."

She nodded, after a contemplative moment.

Joe almost decided to leave it at that, but there was something he couldn't leave unsaid. "I hope it's occurred to you that this plan is designed to send a killer after us."

No hesitation this time. "It has."

Good. At least underneath all that wisecracking talk, Katelyn O'Malley was smart enough to know what they were up against.

And what they were up against was a killer.

Even more, the moment they stepped inside Perfect Match, they would become the ultimate bait.

Chapter Four

Katelyn fanned herself with the Perfect Match folder.

Even though the sun was on the verge of setting, the summer heat was still escaping in filmy waves off the asphalt. It was muggy. A Texas-June kind of muggy that even the locals complained about. The air was heavy with exhaust fumes and the steamy smoke from the mesquite grills of a nearby patio restaurant. Not exactly an enticing combination, but the aroma of spicy fajitas was somehow pushing its way through the rest of the less appetizing scents.

She willed herself not to sweat as she hurried across the parking lot toward the sprawling building that housed the Perfect Match Agency. Willing didn't work. A slick bead of perspiration slithered down the center of her back, and for a couple of seconds, she entertained a pipe dream of stopping by the restaurant for a virgin frozen margarita.

This wasn't, however, the time for pipe dreams or sweat-cooling margaritas, even virgin ones. It was time to look for a killer.

Katelyn stepped through the front door of the agency, mumbled a *thank-you!* for the Arctic blast of the A/C and made her way to the reception area.

An empty area, she soon learned.

Empty, no doubt, because she was early. But then, she usually was. Brayden joked that she'd inherited some bizarre fear-of-being-late gene, but her early arrival in this case would allow her time to double-check the few things she could actually double check. Exits. Bullet-accessible windows. Security cameras, like the one mounted on the light fixture in the center of the room. It also gave her some time to take a deep breath and steady her nerves.

Someone had decorated the spacious rectangle-shaped room. Unlike her earlier visit, tonight there were bunches of gold Mylar balloons in the corners, huge bouquets of cream-colored flowers in crystal vases and bottles of champagne angled into gleaming silver ice buckets. Soft, romantic music filled the background. The stage was set for love.

But hopefully not murder.

She was armed with a Glock in her purse. It was her preferred poison when she needed to carry light. And thanks to the flexible, pencil-size device beneath her collar, she had two-way communication with headquarters. However, neither of those two security measures would give her much protection if someone opened fire through the trio of floor-to-ceiling windows. For all practical purposes, she was on her own.

An obvious drawback to being early.

The sudden clicking sound sent her reaching for

her gun, but Katelyn forced herself not to draw. She needed to stay in character. It was a good thing, too. Because the click was a door opening, and the blond-haired man who came in through the side entrance wasn't carrying a weapon but another bottle of champagne.

He immediately made eye contact and smiled, a slightly too-friendly smile, before he proceeded to the table with the champagne. "Kate Kennedy, right?"

"Yes."

Katelyn didn't have to ask his name. He was Bruce Donovan. Age, twenty-nine. A local, but that sun-bleached hair, tropical tan and muscled torso seemed more suited to a California beach than the Alamo City. His official job title was office manager of the Perfect Match Agency.

He was also a prime murder suspect.

Of course, anyone associated with the agency was a suspect, but Donovan was near the top of that list. According to his background check, he'd been hit with not one but two restraining orders for stalking former girlfriends. The last incident had escalated into an assault. Combined with the fact that he was from San Antonio and a white male, it meant he fit their profile to a proverbial tee.

"I'm Bruce Donovan," he greeted. "I run things around here. In fact, I'm the one who processed your application." His face got a contemplative look for several seconds, then he snapped his fingers. "You're a P.E. teacher on break for the summer. You like old Indiana Jones movies, basketball and chili."

He grinned as if pleased with himself for recalling that information. Katelyn didn't return the grin. If he actually memorized details about every client, it was a little unnerving. If he'd only memorized *her* details, then it went well past the unnerving stage.

"I remember because I kept thinking what a great match we'd be," he continued. "But unfortunately since I work here, I'm not allowed to pair up with any of the clients. Well, not officially anyway."

Good grief. As if he hadn't gotten his message across, he aimed another flirtatious grin in her direction.

"So do a lot of people actually find their *perfect match* at these icebreakers?" she asked.

"Depends on your definition of perfect."

"A lifelong partner," Katelyn quickly offered.

"Ah, marriage." He shrugged. "Sure, it happens." But that was as far as he took the thread of conversation.

She pointed to the wall above the table. "You should put photos of the happy couples there. It'd be great publicity."

"I'll pass on your suggestion to my boss." He placed the bottle of champagne on the table, searched through the two dozen or so plastic-encased name tags and picked up one.

Hers, apparently.

He crossed the room and reached out as if to pin it on her jacket, just over her left breast, but Katelyn intervened and took it from him instead. So he was perhaps a groping pervert in addition to being a stalker and a killer.

What a pleasant guy.

His all-American surfer-dude smile faded. He probably wasn't happy with her insistence that she pin on her own name tag.

Katelyn nodded her greeting in lieu of a handshake, and she tried to pick up on any other vibes. There was definitely that little buzz in the back of her head, but it'd been there since she'd first stepped foot in the place. And speaking of stepping, she backtracked a little toward the door so she could take cover in case Donovan was aiming for a third restraining order.

Donovan tipped his head to the glossy gold-and-white Perfect Match folder she'd tucked beneath her arm. "So did you see any immediate prospects on your list?"

"One. But it could be a coincidence." Since it was time to do a little more stage setting, she pinned on her name tag and opened the folder. She pointed to Joe's alias. "I dated a guy by that name in high school."

Something darted through his coffee-brown eyes. Concern, maybe? "Is that good or bad?"

"Definitely good. He's the one who got away, if you know what I mean."

He made a sound of superficial agreement and then quickly excused himself to leave when a man and a woman came in. Not Joe. But from the already friendly chatter and come-and-get-me smiles, these two had already decided they were a good match.

Once the two newcomers had on their name tags, Katelyn whispered their identities so the tech back at headquarters could begin background checks. In case something serious developed between them, she didn't want this couple to become the sniper's next targets.

"Kate Kennedy?" she heard the now-familiar voice say. "Is that really you?"

It was show time. She took a long breath, braced herself and turned toward him to start the charade.

Oh, mercy.

She obviously hadn't braced herself nearly enough.

At the wedding, she'd seen Joe Rico's *GQ* look, and over the past couple of days, his urban cop look of khakis and button-down dress shirts. But this was obviously his cool hot-guy look.

It worked.

Black pants, perfectly tailored. A deep crimson red crewneck pullover that hugged his chest the way men's chests should be hugged. Well, men with great chests, anyway.

Which he had.

The breeze coming in from the still-open door stirred his lightweight jacket. Also black. He'd likely worn it to conceal his .357 Magnum, but it made him look a little mysterious, confident. And dangerous.

Katelyn bet he'd never had to take a deep breath to steady himself. On the other hand, she required several more.

"Joe?" she managed to say, when she remembered how to form words. Sheez, her throat actually clamped up. She added a staged giggle of excitement to unclamp it. "It *is* you. I can't believe this."

As they'd discussed, Joe and she went to each other immediately, and he pulled her into his arms. Yep. He was definitely carrying concealed, and there was a backup in the slide holster on the rear waist of his pants.

"You're early," he whispered.

"You're not," she countered, also in a whisper.

"I was busy. We might have a little problem."

Okay. *Little* didn't sound so bad. Little problems always arose during undercover missions. "What—"

That's as far as Katelyn got.

Joe brushed his mouth over hers. A friendly sort of gesture—which they'd also discussed should happen. In theory, such a gesture was supposed to announce to the people at the agency that they were staking their personal claims on each other. Like his clothes, it worked. Katelyn heard the other couple and Bruce Donovan mention something about an apparent perfect match.

Katelyn also heard her heart pounding in her ears and felt her body turning soft and warm.

And she cursed herself.

Talk about being a hormonal wimp. Somehow, she had to make herself immune to any carnal-related reactions to Joe Rico, and she did that with a simple reminder that he was not only her boss but also the man investigating her brother.

That immediately cooled off her body.

She pulled back, both literally and figuratively.

"Incoming, six o'clock," Joe whispered.

In other words, someone was approaching from directly behind her. While Joe kept her firmly against him, she turned her head, already smiling, and came face-to-face with Addison Merrick, the owner of Perfect Match. He was also one of their suspects.

He seemed younger than Katelyn had expected, and she'd expected young. Merrick was barely twenty-six but could have passed for a teenager. Well, except for the gunmetal-gray eyes. There was something not so youthful about them.

Merrick wasn't alone. A broad-shouldered man came into the reception area with him and took up position near the door. It was Katelyn's guess that he wasn't a client looking for love but was rather a bodyguard. Maybe this was the little problem Joe had mentioned.

"I smell success," Merrick greeted.

No all-American, surfer-dude smile from him. It was on the mechanical side. Probably no perverted, name-tag-pinning intentions, either. He looked more like the Ivy League type. And was. Old money. And from all accounts Perfect Match was a gift from his megasuccessful father. A way of keeping Addison a productive member of society. So far, it'd worked. Despite a fairly recent dip in business, it was the most successful agency of its type in the city.

"Kate Kennedy, Joe Farrell," Merrick continued. "It's a pleasure to meet you. Welcome."

She felt Joe stiffen slightly but couldn't ask him why. It probably had something to do with the guard who was studying them a little too carefully.

Joe extended his hand to Merrick. "Thanks. It looks like joining Perfect Match was the wise thing to do." He smiled lovingly at Katelyn before he slid his attention back to Merrick. "By the way, a friend of mine said he might be here tonight. Chad Benton. Have you seen him?"

Chad Benton? Katelyn had no idea what this was about. There was no one by that name associated with this case.

Merrick shook his head. "We're expecting a big crowd so you might want to check to see if your friend's name tag is on the table."

Merrick's suggestion was just the beginning, however, and not a prelude to a departure. He wasted no time latching on to her hand, and like a good host, he introduced Joe and her to the other couple. By the time he'd finished, more clients had started to trickle in.

Bruce Donovan did his hosting duties, as well. He began pouring the champagne—lots of it. Nothing like alcohol to kick up the libido and lower the defenses. The piped-in music switched to a slow, sultry beat.

"What about that little problem?" she asked Joe the moment Merrick walked away. She looped her arm through his and leaned against him, snuggling, so she could speak as softly as possible.

"Someone's watching the place."

Okay. Maybe it wasn't so little after all. "Any idea who?"

"Yeah."

Again, no explanation since groping-boy, Bruce Donovan, walked up to them with a tray of filled champagne glasses. Even when they both declined, the man didn't move far enough away for them to have a private conversation.

Joe remedied that. Smiling and whispering sweet nothings about how glad he was to see her again, he led Katelyn to the far end of the room and then just inside the hallway that led to the agency's offices. He angled them so they wouldn't be facing the camera in the reception room.

"Fiona Shipley," Joe informed her. When the static crackled in their respective communicators, he turned his off, because the now close proximity was interfering with reception. "She's parked outside watching the building."

Katelyn didn't have to ask who that was. Fiona was a regular client at Perfect Match and a former acquaintance of Raul Hernandez, the murdered groom, and that was *former acquaintance* in a really bad way. After Fiona and Raul had met, dated and then broken up, she had apparently threatened him. The police had been looking for her but hadn't been able to locate her—not since she'd quit her job and moved out of her apartment. Apparently though, she'd come to them.

"No sign of her carrying an assault rifle, huh?" Katelyn asked, only partly joking.

"Not that I could see, but I've got two officers in a surveillance van watching her just in case." Joe glanced over his shoulder and mumbled some profanity. "Play along."

That was it. No other warning. No hint that he was about to launch into a full-contact charade.

Joe pushed her against the wall and kissed her. He pressed his body against her. Snugly against her. Until they were aligned like human puzzle parts.

Katelyn caught a glimpse of Addison Merrick watching them from the reception room. So this was Joe's version of a get-lost tactic.

Joe kept the mouth-to-mouth clinical. Well, as clinical as something like that could be, considering he had a rather hot kissing technique. No tongue involved. Just pressure. The right amount of pressure, glide and moisture to make her wish, at least temporarily, that he'd use his tongue.

He didn't stop there. His kisses traveled from her mouth. To her cheek. To her ear.

Not good.

She bit off a moan of pleasure. It seemed trivial, considering everything else that was going on, but if these forced kissing sessions continued, she would need to set some ground rules so he could go easy on her erogenous zones.

"Any suspicious activity around the perimeter of the building?" Joe murmured.

Not exactly the sensual question her body had expected to hear from the man kissing her, and it took her a moment to realize Joe was speaking to the officer monitoring the communicator under her collar.

"Fiona Shipley's still watching the place," was the response they got.

Obviously unaware of the effect he was having on her, Joe continued his inquiries while pretending to nibble on her earlobe. "Tail her if she leaves."

Normally, whispered official orders wouldn't have been a turn on for her, but Joe's warm, moist breath hit against her neck and ear. Mercy. Not good. She didn't want to add any more hormones to this volatile mix.

Another glance at the reception area. No Addison Merrick in sight. At least their kissing session had sent him on his way.

"Merrick knew our names," Joe informed her. "I wasn't wearing a name tag, and he never looked at yours. Yet, he knew who we were."

Katelyn went back through the events of that particular introduction and realized it was true. She reprimanded herself for not noticing it, as well. "So that's what *Chad* was all about?"

Not a real person but a test. Since Merrick suggested that Joe look through the name tags, it meant he didn't know the names of all the guests. And unlike a few of the others, Joe and she weren't repeat customers. Nor had they met him when they filled out their applications.

So how had he known their names?

''This might not be such a little problem,'' Katelyn mumbled.

Joe quickly agreed.

In fact, it could mean the killer was already on to them.

Chapter Five

Joe should have been thinking about Addison Merrick. Specifically, about the fact the man was obviously suspicious of them.

With reason.

Both Katelyn and he had registered at Perfect Match just days after the murders. That said, only the shooter himself would have likely made the connection at this point. And that meant that Merrick was possibly their wedding sniper.

So why wasn't his attention on Merrick or the ''security guard'' he'd brought with him?

Because Joe was involuntarily sharing that attention with the woman he had plastered against him, that's why.

He was a fool to notice how nicely Katelyn fit in his arms. A fool to notice that she tasted almost as good as she looked. And basically, he was just a fool to have thought he could kiss her and not lust after her. That meant he had to do something about it.

Joe slid his fingers beneath her collar and temporarily turned off the audio feed on her communicator. The surveillance officers would be able to talk to them, to warn them if necessary, but they wouldn't be able to hear what he was about to admit to Detective O'Malley.

"We'd better try to keep the kissing to a minimum from now on," he whispered.

"Sure," she readily agreed.

Too readily.

Which meant all the supposedly for-show making out probably had an effect on her, as well. Joe didn't care much for the fact that it pleased him a little. This wasn't a competition, but sometimes it felt like one.

"Hey, contrary to public opinion, I'm human," Katelyn said, frowning. And probably so she wouldn't have to add more to an already uncomfortable conversation, she reconnected her communicator.

"Any indication that Addison Merrick has been investigating us?" she whispered to the person on the other end of that communicator.

Joe wished he'd thought of the question first, which was only more proof that he needed a serious mental adjustment. This case was critical. People's lives were at stake, including theirs. Heck, even his promotion to lieutenant was probably riding on this. It was no time for lust.

He repeated all of that to himself several times and hoped those reminders stayed reminders for the rest of this assignment.

"He didn't trigger any info markers to indicate an investigation," the other officer answered through the communicator. "But then, with his resources, that's not surprising."

In other words, Merrick could have done a full-scale check on them—or rather on their false identities—and they wouldn't have known.

"Hypothetically, what would Merrick have learned?" Joe asked.

He glanced at the person who stopped at the end of the hallway. Bruce Donovan. Joe didn't think it was his imagination that the man cast a suspicious glance their way. It made sense. If there'd been a computer search, Donovan would have likely been the one to do it. But the real question was—had Donovan instigated that search on his own, or had Merrick ordered it?

"The only thing Merrick could have gotten was what was in the fake files we created for you and Detective O'Malley," the officer explained. "Fake employment and financial records. Phony e-mail accounts. The addresses of the apartments that were rented to support your covers. That sort of thing. If they went after your real backgrounds, we'd know."

Katelyn opened her mouth, probably to respond to that, but she'd obviously not seen Donovan and his spying eyes. Just in case the man was eavesdropping, Joe did a quick maneuver and put his mouth right against her ear.

"Save your questions," he mumbled. "We have company."

She groaned softly.

So with this latest round of surveillance, things

weren't going exactly as planned. Joe had hoped to establish the pretense of the reunited couple, leave Katelyn in the reception area and have a look around while she covered for him. He'd only managed the first of those and would likely have to save that search for another day. They would have to return anyway in two days, on Thursday, to announce their engagement. By then, he'd figure out a way to do the search.

"Fiona Shipley's about to drive away," Joe heard the backup officer announce into the communicator.

"Go after her." And that meant with the heavy scrutinization from Merrick and Donovan, it was a good time for him to get Katelyn out of there, as well. He caught her arm. "Let's say our goodbyes. We'll come back later for your car."

"Wait." She held her ground. "We still haven't looked around the place."

"And it won't happen tonight." Joe had to pull her closer to him so he could whisper. "You heard— things aren't exactly routine around here, and now we're without backup because they have to go after Fiona Shipley."

She wanted to argue. He could see it in the depth of those slightly narrowed eyes. Heck, he wanted to argue, too. And he really wanted to stay and see what he could find. But he wouldn't do that at the expense of further risking her life. There were already enough risks without him bending the rules.

Since there was no way to make this sound better, Joe just came out with it. "It's time to act as if we're ready to drag each other off to bed."

Which wouldn't be much of a stretch for him.

A few mumbled words of profanity from her, but she cooperated by sliding her arm inside his coat and around his waist. She even added a sultry chuckle and nudged him playfully with her hip.

Nope.

The pretense of dragging her off to bed wouldn't be much of a stretch at all.

Bruce Donovan stepped in front of them when they started across the reception area. "Hey, you're not leaving already, huh?" he asked, seemingly shocked.

"Kate and I have some, uh, catching up to do." Joe made sure there were enough undertones in that remark.

Too bad Donovan didn't pick up on those undertones. He placed his hand on Katelyn's arm and gave her an almost intimate rub with his fingers. His fingers even strayed a bit in the direction of Katelyn's breast.

"But you haven't even checked out the other matches on your list," Donovan reminded her. "And here I selected them just for you."

She chuckled again, a low sexy purr, and lifted her equally sexy gaze to Joe. "I've already found all the matches I need. Now it's time to play with a little fire."

With that naughty double entendre, she pushed Donovan's hand aside, tightened her grip on Joe's waist and got them moving toward the door.

"Man, I hope he's the killer," she grumbled under her breath. "Because I would *so* enjoy kicking his ass."

Joe forced himself not to smile, which was easy, since they'd hardly made it a step before Addison Merrick stopped them.

"Bruce tells me you're thinking of leaving?" Merrick asked.

Katelyn did her part with yet another sultry smile and a sensual snuggle against him.

"Yes. Thanks for arranging this," Joe added, hoping that would be the end of it.

It wasn't.

"But you can't go. Not yet. I need the two of you to sign release forms."

Since this was the first he'd heard mentioned of release forms, and since Merrick was a murder suspect, Joe was automatically suspicious. "We're in a bit of a hurry. Can't this wait?"

"Afraid not. It's a legal requirement. Normally, I put out the forms a little later in the evening, but if you'll come with me, I'll have you sign them in my office."

There wasn't a lot of time for Joe to debate the issue, but what a heck of an issue it was. If he declined, it could very well blow the undercover operation when it'd barely gotten started. If he said yes, it would be a meeting away from witnesses, away from the safety of being in a public place. Besides, standard procedure required—

"Let's make this quick," Katelyn insisted.

And then there was that angle. His partner making a decision without even consulting him.

Joe hoped Merrick didn't notice how much his jaw tightened.

Merrick smiled, that too-artificial smile that Joe didn't even try to interpret, and the man motioned for the guard before he turned toward the hall. It didn't surprise Joe when the guard followed. Basically, Merrick was leading them to a location where they'd be out of sight from the others, and he was taking his hired gun along with him.

And they had no backup.

Maybe he wouldn't regret Katelyn's *let's make this quick* in the next couple of minutes.

"Is this guy a friend of yours?" he asked Merrick. Joe tipped his head to the guard stalking along behind them.

"An employee," Merrick answered without even looking back. "I need someone to witness your signatures."

Of course he did.

Well, at least there was one consolation in all of this. If by some long shot Merrick wanted to do them some harm, then it'd almost certainly mean he was their sniper. Katelyn and he could perhaps end this right here, right now. Of course, that would mean a gun battle in a confined space with innocent people nearby. Not his first choice of ways to bring this to a close.

Obviously Katelyn had figured that out, as well. She kept her arm around him as they followed Merrick, but using Joe's coat as cover, she eased her hand into his slide holster located just inside the back waist of his pants. To a casual observer or the guard behind them, it probably appeared that she was copping a feel. But what she was doing was removing his reserve weapon with her left hand. It made sense because she could easily have been spotted if she'd gone after the gun in her purse.

She didn't stop there. While still keeping her left hand beneath his coat, Katelyn inched just enough away from him that things still looked intimate, but it wouldn't hinder him if he had to draw his primary.

"You're still in hot water," Joe mumbled. Good preparation *after the fact* didn't void the brash decision she'd made on her own.

"Promise?" she tossed back in that same mock purr.

He simply kept his attention on Merrick. Not easy to do, either. Why did it always feel as if he'd been smacked with a two-by-four whenever he was around Katelyn O'Malley?

Just as Joe suspected, Merrick's office was practically at the end of the hall. And also as he'd expected, the guard posted himself in the doorway behind them after they'd entered.

Other than the guard, the rest of the office looked normal. A slick thin-screen computer. Assorted files and papers. Tasteful watercolor paintings on the walls. There was also a rather large Rolodex on the corner of the glossy executive-size desk. Merrick had obviously made a lot of contacts in his line of work.

"This is a formality," Merrick explained. He rifled through his desk, presumably looking for that *for-*

mality. Joe angled Katelyn so if necessary they could return fire in either direction, at Merrick or the guard.

But it wasn't a gun that Merrick pulled out from the drawer but two very official-looking forms.

That didn't cause Joe, however, to relax.

Keeping a grip on his weapon, Katelyn picked up a pen off Merrick's desk and scrawled her alias signature. She passed the pen to Joe, but he waited until he was certain she had good visual and position before he risked occupying his shooting hand with the pen.

"All done," she announced.

Joe agreed, and he didn't give Merrick time to say otherwise. He turned and met the guard's gaze head-on. Joe made sure that the guy understood that one way or another, they would get past him.

The guard stepped aside.

Joe didn't have to tell Katelyn to watch their backs. She did it on her own. So that she could look over his shoulder, she automatically slid herself against him under the pretense of whispering in his ear. The pretense continued to a nip of his earlobe.

"Are you purposely trying to rile me by not following regulations?" he mumbled as they went out the front door.

"Not really. It just comes natural after being a kid sister to two brothers."

Her gaze darted around the area, as well. Joe had gotten lucky with the parking space. He was almost directly in front of the building, and he got her to the car. Fast. He didn't want anyone taking shots at them, and the bullet-resistant windows gave them at least some safety.

"Sorry about that impromptu decision I made back there," she continued. "But I didn't want to tip Merrick—"

"I know what you were doing." Joe couldn't help it, he huffed. God knows why. Huffing only made him sound like an idiot, and it obviously wouldn't change his partner's approach to this case. Still, he tried. "Should I go back over the rules of chain of command?"

Now it was her time to huff. "Don't give me that. You were about to decide the same thing. There's no way you would have blown this because of the slight additional risk of going into that office."

"Maybe. But we'll never know, will we?" And so that Katelyn wouldn't continue to argue, he leaned slightly closer to her neck. "Situation report?" Joe snarled into the communicator.

"We're still following Fiona Shipley. She appears to be just driving around but in the opposite direction of her last known residence."

Bloody hell. He hated unpredictable people and their unpredictable patterns. "Don't lose her."

The moment Joe got his assurance that they wouldn't, Katelyn turned off the audio feed function of the communicator.

"You know what you said back there about keeping the kissing to a minimum?" She didn't wait for him to answer. "Well, I know we can't avoid it, but when we're doing these phony make-out sessions, steer clear of that little place just below my ear. It's a big-time erogenous zone for me.''

Joe eyed the spot and was in such an ornery mood, he considered kissing it just so he could prove that he was the one in charge here. Unfortunately, kissing any of her erogenous zones at this point would be just plain unprofessional and would likely end up giving him an erection.

Hardly a bargaining tool in this game of jockeying for control.

''Any place in particular I should avoid kissing you?'' she asked.

And she was serious.

''Let's just say I'd be attentive to just about anything and leave it at that.'' He glanced back at the doorway of Perfect Match. Not an empty doorway, either. Addison Merrick was there, and he was staring at them.

Cursing, Joe latched on to a handful of that flamered hair and hauled her to him. He kissed her all right, but he kept an eye on their voyeuristic host. When he was satisfied that he'd done all he could to preserve their cover, Joe started the car and drove away.

The next step was to go to Katelyn's fake apartment so they could begin the next phase of the pretense. That meant spending the next four days, and nights, together.

Alone.

''I thought you said unnecessary kissing wasn't a good idea?'' she complained.

''Trust me, it was necessary.''

Besides, it was too late to undo it. And it sure as heck was too late to stop what they'd put into motion. They'd either succeed together.

Or maybe die trying.

Either was possible.

Chapter Six

"I think I might have found something," she heard Joe announce from the other room.

Katelyn leaned back a little so she could glance at him through the bedroom door. For security reasons they had turned off most of the lights, but it wasn't difficult to see Joe working on his laptop at the tiny kitchen table in the equally tiny kitchen. There were no windows in that particular area so he was using the dim light over the stove to read through the latest background info on their suspects.

"Addison Merrick's longtime fiancée broke up with him last month. A bad break, too. Very messy," Joe went on. He positioned one of the other kitchen chairs in front of him and propped up his feet. "And according to his very chatty personal trainer, he's been under psychiatric care since he was a teenager. He suffers from manic-depression coupled with something called radical impulsive tendencies."

"What the heck is that last part?" She opened the suitcase that Garrett had packed for her and plundered

through it for something she could wear to bed. Hopefully, it'd be something that covered a lot of skin
because the apartment only had one small bedroom.
The sleeping bag in the corner let her know that she'd
be sharing that limited space with Joe.

Katelyn took a deep, steadying breath.

"Beats me. Maybe it means Merrick's just an irrational ticked-off killer, as opposed to all those other
nonticked-off rational killers we deal with every
day."

"Yeah, that'd be a nice change, huh?" she joked.

Katelyn studied the garments and realized she'd
gotten her *something to cover a lot of skin* wish.
There was an enormous pair of cartoon superhero
pj's, no makeup whatsoever, only a toothbrush for
toiletries, jeans and a T-shirt. Her underwear choices
were limited to cotton and were the worst ones possible Garrett could have found in her lingerie drawer.
If that's where he indeed got them. They looked like
Salvation Army rejects.

She frowned.

Garrett was either trying to establish a new fashion
look for her or else he wanted to make sure there was
nothing alluring about her appearance. Perhaps the
contents of the suitcase were her brother's version of
a modern-day chastity belt.

With her limited choices, she opted for the pj's that
were dotted with caped and winged crusaders. Katelyn stepped deeper into the dark bedroom, keeping
the door open a crack between them so she could still
hear Joe's ongoing summary of the new reports.

"I think some of the dots are starting to connect," he continued. "Get this—Merrick's shrink is a guy by the name of Dr. Allen Kent. Ring any bells?"

The moment the name registered, Katelyn hurriedly put on the pj's and walked back to the doorway. "He's Gail's ex-husband. Their divorce became final just a couple of weeks before her wedding to Raul."

Now that was an interesting connection. Their prime suspect, Addison Merrick, was in therapy with the ex-husband of their first murder victim.

"Coincidence?" she suggested.

"Maybe." Joe tossed her a glance. And did a double take before he shook his head. "But because he's an ex, he's a suspect. I'll have someone question Dr. Kent tomorrow. Too bad I can't do it myself, but I can't risk blowing our cover."

"It might be a risk no matter who does the questioning, especially since he'll just roadblock us with doctor-patient confidentiality. He might even lawyer up. Wouldn't it be a better idea just to have him followed?"

"Then I wouldn't be able to get his reaction when he's asked about his connection to Merrick."

True. And maybe it was worth the risk just to shake things up a little. It might make the sniper think twice about launching another attack over the weekend.

"What exactly are you wearing?" Joe asked.

She glanced down at the pajamas and shrugged. "I think it belongs in the sleepwear category of garments. Garrett packed for me."

That seemed to be the only explanation Joe required. He mumbled something under his breath about brotherly love, minimized Merrick's file on the computer screen and clicked on to the next one.

While she waited for it to load, she glanced at Joe's attire. He still wore the clothes he'd had on for the icebreaker. Well, minus the jacket. His hair was no longer perfect, however. Probably because he had a habit of scratching his head and running his hand through it while in deep thought.

And then there was the stubble.

No ordinary five o'clock shadow for this guy. Nope. It fell into the category of the desperado look. Very fashionable. Equally sexy. But what made it even more so was that he wore it as naturally as that contemplative cop's look, which sadly for her was the greatest turn-on of all.

"Fiona Shipley," Joe read aloud.

Good. Back to business. It was exactly where her mind needed to be. "Anything new on her?"

"You mean other than the fact that she managed to shake the backup officers who were following her, and now no one knows where she is?"

"Yes, other than that," Katelyn grumbled.

She made her way around him to get to the fridge. Ah, she had much better luck there than her suitcase. It was stocked with fruit and other snacks, but what immediately caught her eye was the six-pack of her favorite Irish beer. It must have been Garrett's peace offering for the botched fashion choices.

"Other than a knack for disappearing," Joe said glancing over the report, "we don't really have much.

We already knew she was a frequent customer at Perfect Match and that the dead groom had been one of her fairly recent dream matches.''

Katelyn opened a bottle of beer and took a long sip. ''Which means nothing, of course. I had over a dozen dream matches so heaven knows how many she's had over the past year.''

There. She'd been trying to figure out a way to dismiss the fact that Joe had been her number one match. Not that it was important, but it'd been one of those little nagging thoughts in the back of her mind.

When he didn't respond, Katelyn glanced at him. No double take this time. Joe was staring at her. Well, he was staring at her beer, anyway.

''Want one?'' she asked, lifting the bottle. ''It's the good stuff. My favorite. I'll have to thank Garrett for buying it.''

''Actually, I asked him to pick it up when he wanted to know what to bring over.''

Katelyn had already reached for the fridge, but that brought her hand to a stop. She forced herself not to stop for too long so it wouldn't appear she was shocked by that revelation.

''Well, then. I owe you the thanks instead.'' She took out a beer from the fridge, handed it to him and left it at that.

Joe closed down the files and started in on his beer. It was obviously his favorite, as well.

''Agreeing to go into that back office with Merrick wasn't a safe idea,'' he let her know.

Oh, that.

She hadn't thought for a minute that he'd forget it. "No. But it was a smart one. Come on, you were on the verge of following him, but I just got around to saying it first."

He didn't agree, or disagree. Joe sat there, staring into space while slowly sliding his fingers through the moisture on the longneck bottle.

Judas.

Even that made her body think of erotic things that it shouldn't be thinking about.

"Talk to me about Brayden," she said to give her body something else to contemplate. "About this so-called investigation that the chief ordered regarding preferential treatment."

That got Joe's attention off blank space. He looked at her again. "Is this the part where you tell me to back off and leave your brother alone?"

"Something like that. He's had a rough time recently."

He nodded. "Yeah, I heard. I'm sorry about his wife's death."

"His wife's *murder*," Katelyn quickly corrected. "She was murdered last year, and the case is practically cold. There are no arrests and no leads. Brayden has to live with that every single moment of his life. Any idea what that does to a good cop, to know he can't solve his own wife's murder?"

Another nod.

"By nodding, I guess you mean to imply that you understand, but there's no way you could," Katelyn went on. There was a lot more emotion in her voice than she wanted. But then, she'd never thought to discuss this objectively. "Brayden loved her, and it rips his heart to shreds to know that her killer is still out there somewhere."

"I'm sorry." It probably would have been easier for him to turn his attention back to the condensation on his beer bottle, or anywhere else for that matter, but he didn't. Joe kept his gaze firmly on her. "Do you honestly think that I'd believe there's preferential treatment just because it's an allegation?"

She opened her mouth. Closed it. Frowned. And silently cursed him. It was a dirty-pool kind of question, one that diffused the indignation she'd planned to hang on to a little longer. It was a good barrier against the effects of that desperado stubble.

"Brayden is lucky to have Garrett and you," Joe said, getting up from his chair. "And you're lucky to have them." He spared her pj's another glance. "I guess."

She couldn't help it. She smiled. But she suppressed it as quickly as possible. "Does that mean Garrett had this same chat with you?"

"Twice."

Katelyn had to suppress a smile again. "I'll bet those were interesting conversations, especially considering you two are the same rank."

Joe appeared to suppress a smile of his own. "And am I supposed to believe you held something back because I outrank you?"

"Busted." She finished off her beer, tossed the bottle into a recycling bin and unstrapped the slide holster from around her waist. "Present levity and warm fuzzy feelings aside, if you hurt Brayden, I'll make you pay."

"Like I said, he's lucky to have you." He tipped his head toward the windows in the living room. "Don't stand in here too long."

Because someone might already be watching them. If the killer hadn't already scoped them out, then he or she would be doing it very soon. It was best not to be in his direct line of fire when that happened.

He glanced at his watch. "It's almost midnight. We've got an early morning ahead of us."

"Should we turn off all the lights?" she asked, going into the bedroom ahead of him. She placed her slide holster on the nightstand next to her badge, primary weapon and the communicator that she'd already turned off. Then Katelyn stepped into the bathroom to brush her teeth.

"No. We should look…active," Joe responded. "That way, it'll convince a killer that we're on our way to becoming a bride and groom."

"Too bad I don't have a pair of those blow-up dolls we could parade past the window every now and then." She paused, and was thankful she wasn't in the same room with him so he could see the blush rise on her cheeks. "I'm *so* sorry I said that."

He chuckled softly. An incredibly sexy male sound that made her want to pound her head against the wall.

This was going to be such a long week.

From the mirror, she watched Joe add his two guns

and his badge to the nightstand, making the rather small piece of furniture look even smaller under the arsenal. He had his shirt halfway stripped off before he stopped and snagged her gaze. "I don't have pajamas. If you're the blushing sort, you might want to look away."

Yeah, right. She was about a hundred percent certain her eyes had no intention of cooperating with that suggestion. She didn't even fight it. Katelyn watched his reflection. A not-so-cheap thrill. And had the privilege of seeing him toss that shirt aside. At least a dozen muscles flexed in his arms and chest as they responded to the simple gesture.

A simple gesture that caused her mouth to go dry. Mercy.

She forced herself to finish brushing her teeth and even looked away when his pants came off. Well, briefly looked away. She thanked her lucky stars that he kept on a pair of dark blue boxers.

"Will this temporary housekeeping arrangement cause any personal problems for you?" he asked.

"If that's a subtle way of asking me if I'm involved with anyone, the answer's no." It made her sound like a social leper. Which wasn't really that far off the mark. Rather than remind him that most men weren't turned on by a woman packing a badge and a couple of Glocks, Katelyn went for levity. "My last boyfriend was a sex therapist who broke up with me because he said I was too aggressive in bed."

She paused a heartbeat before she let their gazes

connect again. Yep. The startled look on his face had been worth it. "It's a joke," she let him know.

Other than a slight sound of amusement, that was his only other reaction. So much for levity. When she went into the bedroom, he strolled into the bathroom to brush his teeth.

"Actually, my last boyfriend was an accountant who broke up with me because he said I was too wrapped up in my job," she confessed and climbed into bed. "Hard to make someone feel even remotely important when you're never around. He got fed up and left me for a kindergarten teacher."

Still no response.

"How about you?" she asked.

"No one current." He came out of the bathroom, and she made a point of looking away. She'd already overdosed on his great bod. No need for more. "The last woman in my life was a kindergarten teacher who left me for an accountant."

Okay. So that broke the ice that had already been thawing between them. She laughed. Then bit her lip so she wouldn't laugh again.

She aimed her finger at him. "Let's get something straight. I don't want to like you, Rico."

He leaned over as if to kiss her good-night, letting his mouth come very close to hers. Breath met breath. And then he turned off the light. "I agree completely."

She lay there silently cursing him. But not for long. His head had hardly hit the pillow on the floor before the phone rang. Since it was supposed to be her apartment, Katelyn rolled to the side of the bed and answered it.

"It's me," she heard her brother say.

"Garrett, just the man I wanted to talk to."

Joe must have felt the same because he pressed the speaker function on the phone. Probably because he wanted to hear anything official. But the official part would have to wait.

"Thanks for the expert packing job," she tossed out at Garrett. "You do know this'll cost you in slow painful ways you can't even imagine?"

"I'm trembling in my Doc Martens." But the sarcasm wasn't nearly strong enough, and it didn't come close to masking his concern. "I'll drop by in the morning, pretending to deliver breakfast. Anything I can bring you?"

"You mean other than Starbucks and some real clothes?" Katelyn inquired cautiously, feeling him out.

"Yeah. Other than that."

Heck. He was placating her.

Never a good sign.

"What about you, Rico? You need anything?" Garrett asked.

Mercy. He'd moved from placating to being nice.

"No, thanks," Joe let him know. "I've got some things in the trunk of my car."

Garrett paused. Never a good sign, either. "So the plan is for you two to pick up Katelyn's car in the morning and then not come up for air again until it's time to announce your engagement at Perfect Match on Thursday?''

"Great summary." But Katelyn had reached her threshold for beating around the bush. "Spill it, Garrett. What's wrong?"

"I'm not sure, exactly." Yet another hesitation. "Someone's digging through the fake files we created for your covers."

"We expected that," Joe pointed out. He sat up in his sleeping bag, leaning back against the side of the mattress.

"Yeah, but I didn't expect them to go at it this way. It's sloppy. Damn sloppy. And that slop leads right to Merrick. It makes me uncomfortable."

Katelyn knew exactly how he felt. Merrick might be a killer, but from all accounts he was smart. If the cyber trail led to him, then it was probably because someone wanted them to think Merrick had done it.

Bruce Donovan, maybe?

Of course, there was also the angle that by being sloppy, Merrick was giving himself a very convincing out.

"If he's that smart," Katelyn mumbled. "We're in serious trouble."

"Yeah," Garrett agreed.

Joe glanced at her. He had that did-I-miss-something? look. At least she thought that's what that glance was about until he shrugged. "I don't care how smart Merrick is. If he's making these sloppy searches to cover the fact he's the sniper, we'll still stop him."

Well, they were all on the same page. Interesting. Most outsiders, including fellow cops, had trouble following Garrett's and her thought processes.

"There's more," Garrett continued. "It sucks, so brace yourself. I got a call from an editor friend at the *Express News*. There'll be a story about the two shootings in the morning paper. They're linking them."

"We knew this was coming," Katelyn offered.

"An article, yeah. But there'll be photos. Some apparently taken at the icebreaker tonight. There'll be one with Rico and you kissing."

Okay. So they hadn't known about this.

Judas.

A photo.

"Supposedly, it's a grainy shot, and you're in a lip lock, but still…" Garrett's explanation trailed off, leaving them with the general idea that this was not a good thing.

"How'd they get the photo?" Joe asked.

"Addison Merrick. He takes stills from the security feed. For some reason, he gave the press a couple of them when they came around sniffing for a story about two hours ago."

And because she and Joe had signed those consent forms, it was all perfectly legal.

"He's suspicious," Katelyn mumbled.

"It could be a ploy to get you to back off," Garrett suggested. "Because something like this darn sure wouldn't be good for business."

"Or maybe he's going for another sloppy tactic so

he can cover his butt,'' Joe contributed. ''The real killer probably wouldn't give up photos of potential victims, but a ruthless businessman trying to get some free publicity might.'' He cursed. ''Or a killer who wanted to appear to be an honest businessman might.''

Neither Garrett nor she disagreed with him.

''This changes nothing,'' Joe insisted a moment later. ''We'll stick with the plan and lay low here until Thursday afternoon when we'll make a return visit to Perfect Match. If the photo's clearer than expected, or if it causes any unwanted press, then I'll deal with it.''

''You do that,'' Garrett fired back.

Katelyn huffed because she understood that tone. It was his brotherly warning for her to be careful.

''I'm not stupid,'' she responded. Katelyn reached over and hung up.

Joe gave her another of those looks, except this time she was fairly sure he was puzzled. ''He's worried about us,'' she interpreted.

And apparently, with reason.

The game had just escalated from dangerous to deadly. But then, Katelyn had known from day one that it was an inevitable escalation. Playing the killer's deadly game was the only way to stop him.

A LOUD RINGING sound jarred Joe from the dream to beat all dreams. He snapped to a sitting position and groped for the phone, the alarm or whatever the hell was making the noise so he could stop it.

Katelyn cursed, a couple of phrases worthy of the awful racket. However, her profanity clipped off unexpectedly about a split second after she latched on to her gun and fell off the bed.

She landed right on him.

His hands were suddenly filled with her. A warm, firm, armed woman who smelled like a strange mixture of sex and gunmetal. Her eyes were still ripe with sleep, and she blinked several times, staring at him as if trying to figure out how she'd gotten in his lap.

Katelyn obviously wasn't a morning person, either.

Thankfully, the noise stopped so Joe could get his bearings. It didn't take long, especially when he realized her fall had aligned their bodies in the best, and worst, possible ways. She was straddling him, her long athletic legs resting against the sides of his hips.

And he had an erection.

It was a product of the dream he'd been having. About her. She noticed it. But then, it would have been impossible not to notice.

"One of the advantages of being a woman," she mumbled, her gaze drifting in the direction of where he was certainly testing the limits of his boxers. "We don't wear our…hearts on our sleeves."

"Smart-ass," he tossed back, because frankly he couldn't think of anything else to say.

Laughing lazily, she climbed off him. Staggered. And would have probably landed in his lap again if he hadn't caught her. Specifically, her left butt cheek. Not the particular part of her anatomy he'd wanted to grab, but it was either that or risk having accidental sex with her.

Joe was certain he didn't want that to happen.

Well, almost certain, anyway.

"I think it was the doorbell." Katelyn glanced at the clock. "Seven forty-five. It has to be Garrett. If he doesn't have coffee with him, he's a dead man."

Joe got to his feet, somehow, and fought through the haze still in his head. When the buzzing sound started again, he realized she was right. It was the doorbell. And yep, it was probably Garrett. Still, Joe wasn't about to take any chances. He pulled on his pants, grabbed his gun and headed into the living room.

"Be careful," she whispered unnecessarily.

He would. No amount of fatigue or dream remnants would cause him to do away with standard procedures. Joe eased against the wall, moving slowly. Quietly. Keeping away from the door, he lifted the blinds a fraction and peeked out.

Not Garrett.

"It's Bruce Donovan," Joe let her know.

She already had her gun, but that caused her to assume a defensive position. No more ripe sleepy blinks or lazy laughter. She morphed into the cop.

Joe took another look outside. Donovan appeared to be holding some papers and wasn't visibly armed.

Which didn't mean anything.

Donovan was the type to carry concealed.

"Back me up," Joe reminded her.

Using the door to hide his gun, Joe opened it. Not

a fraction, either. He might need the extra space if he had to fire.

"Yeah?" he greeted Donovan. Not nicely, either.

Surprise went through Donovan's eyes, and when he tried to speak, he fumbled his words. Definitely not the slick player he'd portrayed the night before at the icebreaker.

"I wanted to drop these off for Kate," Donovan said, offering the papers to Joe. "It's a copy of the release form she signed and the questionnaire she originally filled out. I thought she'd like them for her personal records. Oh, and here's the newspaper. It was on this side of the stairs so I figured it was hers."

Joe took the items with his left hand so he could still hold on to his gun. "This couldn't wait until later?"

Donovan shrugged. "I was headed to work to get an early start and decided to drop it off on my way."

"Right." The apartment wasn't on the way to Perfect Match. Donovan was checking on them. Now, the real question was why. Was it because he was the killer, or because he'd planned to hit on Katelyn again?

If it was the latter, the man had a death wish.

One more attempt by Donovan to grope her breasts, and Katelyn would almost certainly go after him. And Joe would stand back and let her.

"So are you off from work today or what?" Donovan asked.

"I decided to take a little vacation time."

"From your freelance journalism job?" Donovan

paused as if waiting for Joe to confirm that. Joe didn't. "I'm the one who ran your computer matches. Personally, I figured you'd go for the blond speech therapist, but then I didn't know about your past history with Kate."

It seemed like a good idea just to nod. For a man on a delivery mission, Donovan was asking a lot of questions and providing a lot of unnecessary information.

Joe heard Katelyn move around behind him, but he had no idea what she was up to until she ducked under his arm and snuggled against him. She'd stripped off her pajama bottoms, tousled her hair around her face, and with the top that hit her at mid-thigh, she looked as if she'd just finished up a thoroughly satisfying round of sex. And was ready for round two.

"Kate." Donovan attempted a smile and failed.

"Morning, Mr. Donovan. It's early." She slid her left arm around Joe's waist, and with her right hand, she pressed her gun directly against the back side of the door. She aimed it at Donovan. With that Glock, she'd easily be able to shoot through the thick wood if necessary.

Donovan tipped his head to the forms he'd just given to Joe. "I decided to drop off those."

"I heard."

Her tone conveyed no interest whatsoever, and she eased her left hand slightly lower. From Joe's waist and just into his pants—which he hadn't gotten around to zipping fully. She rubbed her fingers gently over the muscles that led directly to his groin. It wasn't just an intimate gesture. It was a sexually charged one.

"Thanks," she added to Donovan.

There was a definite "get lost" at the end of it. For extra measure, she put her mouth against Joe's ear, mumbled a seriously raunchy suggestion that involved them naked on the kitchen table. She issued a goodbye, shut the door in their visitor's face and locked it.

"If Donovan had any doubts about us being lovers," Katelyn whispered as she took her hand from his pants, "he doesn't now."

No. The charade was about good as it could get. Maybe even a little too good.

Man.

Joe stood there for a moment and tried to get his lungs to work.

How the devil was he supposed to handle three and a half more days of this?

While he was staving off another erection, she took the newspaper from him, tore off the plastic wrapper and sank onto the sofa.

"Good news. We didn't make the front page." A moment later, she groaned. "But we made the second."

Katelyn held it up for him. There were three small black and white photos accompanying the article entitled Dying For Love? Theirs was in the center, and even though they were practically wrapped around each other, Katelyn's face was visible.

And clear.

Too clear.

"No," she snarled, looking directly at him. She tossed the paper aside and practically charged at him. "You're not taking me off this case."

"Your cover might have been compromised," Joe pointed out.

"*Might* is the operative word there. But if you pull me now, it'll take weeks to create another cover—if that's even possible at this point. I won't let innocent people die because there's a possibility that someone could identify me from that photo."

In addition to her hand, the woman certainly knew where to aim her arguments. Joe didn't want anyone else dying, either—including her.

"Please," she added.

That cost her. No doubt about it. It was as close to begging as Katelyn O'Malley probably ever got, and it had to have stung her pride for him to be the recipient of that request.

Joe groaned, knowing how this would play out. "I would attach a condition or two—something along the lines of insisting you follow orders and don't improvise—but I won't bother."

"Does that mean you won't cut me from the case?"

He nodded, after making her wait a couple of seconds. "Not unless I have definite proof that your cover's been blown. And don't you dare smile, O'Malley, because you know I just handed you a gift."

No smile. Not even close. But he did see a lot of relief on her face. "Thank you. You won't regret it."

Wrong.

He already did. A lot. But for better or worse, Katelyn was his best shot at stopping another murder.

God help them.

Chapter Seven

"Dr. Kent's interview is about to start," Joe called out. "You were right. He lawyered up."

Katelyn hurriedly applied a slathering of some pale raspberry lipstick that her mother had packed and gave her skirt-suit a quick adjustment. The short mocha outfit wouldn't have been her first choice for a return visit to Perfect Match to announce her "engagement," but it was either that or a cherry-red slip dress she hadn't worn since college.

Heaven knows what Garrett had told their mother about this particular assignment, but it was obvious the woman believed Katelyn needed to show some leg. Maybe she'd seen the photo of Joe in the paper. That meant at their regular family Sunday brunch, Katelyn would have to do some damage control before her folks started planning a real wedding.

When she joined him in the kitchen, Joe already had the laptop opened on the table, and even though he had his attention fixed on the screen, he was also putting on his shoes. Unlike her semi-sex-kitten attire, he'd gone for the brooding businessman look. Dark blue pants and a matching button-down shirt. Since his coat was draped over the chair, that likely meant he'd be using it again to camouflage his shoulder holster.

"Did you ever meet Dr. Kent?" he asked.

"No. Never had the honor. Gail and he weren't married that long."

While she poured them both cups of coffee, she studied the video feed of the man who'd once been her friend's husband. Kent's expensive Italian suit was perfect. Ditto for his bronze-colored hair. But those eyes were all barracuda.

"Gail's mom and I use the same hairdresser," Katelyn continued. The coffee was hours old, bitter and way too strong, but she gulped it down anyway so she could have her caffeine fix. "According to her, Kent liked to play mind games, and he was always ragging on Gail, always taking shots at her self-esteem. He fought the divorce for months before finally giving in."

"Maybe he didn't give in after all," Joe commented with a shrug.

Yes. And because of that bitter divorce they'd added Dr. Allen Kent to the top of their list of murder suspects and had spent much of the previous day going through his background check.

Well, doing that and trying to avoid each other.

The close quarters weren't exactly conducive to avoidance, especially since they had to share the same computer, same reports, same bedroom and same bathroom. But they'd both done their best to keep the other at arm's length. In between that arm's length, however, the air kept crackling between them.

Katelyn sipped her coffee and tried to push that uncomfortable realization aside.

"Did Kent say why he wasn't available for an interview yesterday?" she asked.

"He claimed he couldn't rearrange his schedule."

Claimed was right. He likely wanted to discuss strategy with his lawyer before *voluntarily* coming to police headquarters for questioning. In fact, it was her guess that the lawyer by Kent's side had used a good portion of that extra twenty-four hours to coach his client as to exactly what to say.

And what not to say.

After all, Kent wasn't just linked to Merrick. He was linked to the murdered bride. That would have caused a tense moment or two for an attorney.

Detective Dawn Davidson was the officer doing the interview. Under different circumstances, Katelyn would have asked that Garrett do it, but since he'd been at the apartment twice in the past twenty-four hours, Joe decided it was an unnecessary risk to take. Even though her brother had worn a delivery man's disguise, if someone had been carefully watching the place—like Dr. Kent, for example—he might have been able to make the connection.

Davidson started with the basics and just as Joe suggested, she mentioned the *remote possibility* that the shootings were somehow *loosely associated* with clients from the Perfect Match Agency. For good measure, she even hinted at the article that had appeared in the newspaper the day before. Then, Dawn went in for the bull's-eye and asked Kent about his relationship with Addison Merrick.

"I'm afraid I can't discuss anything regarding a patient," he crisply assured her. "If that's why I'm here, then you're wasting my time."

"As slick as slime," Katelyn mumbled. "No wonder Gail divorced him."

"So Mr. Merrick is your patient?" Dawn commented. But she didn't wait for him to verify it. "He was vague about that yesterday when we questioned him."

Ah, now there was a reaction. Kent's aristocratic mouth tightened for a fraction of a second. Now the trick was to decide if that gesture meant he was riled about the detective's *got-ya* comment or Merrick's vagueness during questioning. A vagueness that would obviously make the police wonder why Merrick felt a reason to hold back information.

"It's good to see him squirm," Joe said, glancing at her. The glance turned into a double take, just as he'd done with her pj's that first night. Katelyn resisted the urge to adjust her skirt again. No matter how much she tugged and pulled, the fabric wasn't going to stretch.

Thankfully, Dawn got his attention off the skirt when she continued the interrogation. The detective went through the other questions, but they were window dressing, since it wasn't Kent's actual responses they were interested in but the way he reacted. Dawn played her part to a tee. And she made just enough eye contact and kept the right inflection in her voice to let Kent know that he was indeed a suspect. When she finished, Kent didn't waste any time getting out of there.

Joe didn't waste any time, either. He grabbed his phone and pressed a few buttons. A moment later, Katelyn heard Dawn's own phone ring on the audio feed of the computer. "Have him followed," Joe ordered when Dawn answered. "Not closely though. And I don't want him approached so he can claim harassment."

He ended the call, clipped the tiny cell phone to his belt and got up. "After I shave, we'll leave for the Perfect Match."

Katelyn almost told him that she'd prefer if he skipped that particular grooming step, but then she'd have to explain why. There was already enough male-female stuff going on between them without her letting him know that she'd liked his stubbled look.

While she put on her slide holster and checked the communicator she'd threaded under her collar, her gaze landed on the papers Joe had left on the table. Specifically, her questionnaire, which Donovan had dropped off the previous morning. It was opened to page three, the section that dealt with her preferences for leisure activities.

Had Joe been reading it?

If so, did he have any idea that the answers were true?

Katelyn didn't allow her ridiculous, hormone-induced speculations to go beyond that. After all, there were probably dozens of legitimate reasons why Joe would be reading her file.

Too bad none of those dozens of legitimate reasons readily came to mind.

Curious now, she sat at the computer and did a search to find his file. Within a couple of seconds, she'd pulled up the bogus information the department had created for him. She went one step beyond that, and with her password, she located his official record.

She glanced over her shoulder in the direction of the bedroom, to make sure he wasn't watching. He wasn't. From the sound of his electric razor, he was in the bathroom still ridding himself of his sexy stubble.

His official photo loaded, as did the rest of the info. Joseph Luis Rico. He was thirty-two. A military brat. Two brothers, a sister. He'd lived all over the world until his eighteenth birthday, when he'd left for college and then the police academy.

''Wow,'' Katelyn mumbled when she glanced through the list of his awards and recognitions. He had a slew of them, including one from the governor. Those accolades accounted for not just one early promotion but two. He was a supercop by anyone's standards.

But she hadn't needed a file to tell her that.

A notation near the bottom caught her eye. Just a month before his transfer to S.A.P.D., he'd taken leave, and the code beside it was one she recognized. Whatever had generated that time off required a clean psych evaluation before he could return to the job. Interesting. He'd either killed someone in the line of duty or else the leave was of a particularly stressful, personal nature.

"Find anything?" she heard him ask.

Busted.

Katelyn didn't even try to hide it. Not that she could have anyway since his picture was right there on the screen. Instead, she pushed her questionnaire, still opened to page three, to the side so he'd know this was a tit for tat kind of invasion of privacy.

As opposed to just a plain ordinary invasion.

"You lived in England for three years," she commented. "When your father was stationed there."

"You run a six-minute mile," he countered. "While listening to Axl Rose."

Not to be outdone, she continued with, "Your brothers are both Air Force Combat Rescue Officers."

"Your mother and father were both cops."

Frowning, she swiveled around in the chair. "That wasn't on the questionnaire."

"No, but it was in your personnel file." His gaze drifted to her clothes, and her legs. "Nice skirt."

Katelyn was sure her frown deepened. "Is that a ploy to get me to forget you were in my file?"

"No. It's a ploy to let you off the hook for snooping in mine." He set a small black velvet box in her lap, right on her skirt. "If you want to know something about me, Katelyn, just ask."

She would have questioned him about that personal

leave, but the box suddenly captured her complete attention. It was the right size and the right shape. Well, depending on one's perspective, it was right. It was not so right from her perspective. "Is that what I think it is?"

"It is if you think it's an engagement ring." He proceeded to fix his communicator under his collar. "We need it for the announcement."

Okay. So those two simple words, engagement ring, shouldn't have sent her stomach into a tailspin, but they did. Jeez, it was such a *girl* reaction. And for nothing, since it was all show anyway.

Katelyn opened the box as if it were live explosives and came face-to-face not with some gaudy lifestyle statement but rather a tastefully delicate diamond set in beautifully etched gold. Definitely a *wow*.

"It looks real," she mumbled.

"It is. It belonged to my grandmother."

"Oh, sheez." His grandmother's? Could this possibly get any more uncomfortable? "I can't wear something like that."

"Sure you can. Well, provided it fits." He took it from the box and slipped it onto her finger. No fanfare. No awkward pause to ponder the moment. Certainly no romantic words or gazes.

It fit.

"Okay, let's go," he ordered.

He would have probably been out the door if his phone hadn't rung. Katelyn grabbed her purse while he answered it. As she moved the meager sunlight slanting through the windows caught the facets of the diamond and sent a rainbow dancing around the room. She turned the ring around so it wouldn't happen again.

She needed rainbows about as much as she needed a real engagement to Joe Rico.

"Did he?" Joe asked.

But it wasn't a casual inquiry. Like the ring box, it snared Katelyn's attention and caused her to tune in to his conversation.

"No. No change in plans," he continued. He hung up and looked at her. "Guess where Dr. Kent's headed?"

"Perfect Match?" Katelyn repeated the words and took out the questioning inflection. Of course, that's where Kent would go. He wanted answers as to why Merrick had brought him into this investigation. And that meant if they hurried, they had the opportunity to hear what Merrick was saying to his shrink. A way to kill two birds with one stone.

Joe paused and combed his gaze over her. "You're sure Kent won't recognize you?"

"Positive."

Well, not positive, exactly. She had no idea if Gail had ever shown Kent her photo, but she couldn't let a mere possibility hold her back now. If Donovan was at work, it would be the first time they'd have their three primary suspects under the same roof. It was perhaps the break they'd been looking for.

Or maybe it would be the very confrontation to make a killer snap.

Katelyn checked her primary and backup weapons to make sure she was ready.

AS THEY'D PLANNED on the trip over, Katelyn lured the receptionist from her desk with a bogus emergency request for her to show her the location of the ladies' room. Joe used the ploy to walk past the other clients who were filling out questionnaires so he could slip unannounced into the hall that led to Merrick's office. Since Dr. Kent wasn't around, that meant he was probably already in there with Merrick.

Along the way, Joe looked for the security guard and cameras to make sure he hadn't missed one. No guard today, and the only camera he spotted was the one in the reception area. It had obviously supplied the photo for the newspaper article and could still possibly be monitoring the hall. So he plastered a silly grin on his face while he was trying to eavesdrop. Best to keep up the facade of the happily engaged man.

Unlike Kent. Who didn't sound happy at all. The man was practically shouting. Joe heard him when he was still several yards from Merrick's office door. Not very shrinklike behavior. Rather, Kent seemed to be in the middle of a Prozac-required moment.

"But why even mention my name?" Kent snarled.

Thankfully they'd left the door slightly ajar. Joe saw Merrick shake his head. "I'm not sure I did."

"But you must have. Jesus H. Christ, Addison, these people think you might know something about those two shootings. Why would you purposely let them believe you're unstable by telling them you were in therapy?''

Another head shake. This one more frantic than the first. ''I swear, I don't think your name even came up in conversation. And they don't suspect me. They can't. They said their visit was just routine.''

Katelyn emerged from the other end of the hall, which meant she'd found a way to the office without going back past the receptionist. She puckered her lips in a *shh* gesture and quietly walked to him. One glance at the camera in the reception room, and she stepped into Joe's arms. But she didn't just step. She immediately launched into her lover's pose. She pressed her body against Joe's and brushed a kiss on his jaw.

''Routine?'' Kent repeated. ''There's nothing routine about a police interrogation. Please tell me your lawyer was here when you spoke to them.''

''No.'' Merrick paled a little. ''I didn't think it was necessary.''

''Well, from now on, it is. I can't afford to have my name dragged through the mud again.''

Again? Since Joe had spent hours pouring through Kent's file, he thought that reference might be for his messy divorce from Gail. It appeared to have cost Kent a client or two. And a small fortune.

After delivering a terse goodbye, Kent turned and stormed out. He paused when he spotted Joe and gave him only a dismissive glance. Kent might have done the same to Katelyn if she hadn't buried her face against Joe's neck.

Definitely not good.

"I thought you said he wouldn't recognize you?" Joe whispered when Kent was out of earshot.

She shook her head. "He didn't."

Which, of course, didn't answer his question at all.

"Why are you here?" Merrick asked. He was staring at them through the now fully opened door.

"We'd like to talk to you." Joe made sure he grinned. Katelyn did her part by sliding her body against his. Well, it was a little more than just a slide. She hooked her fingers onto his belt—and into the waist of his pants. "We have great news."

Merrick mumbled something indistinguishable, sighed and shoved both his hands through his hair. "Give me a couple of minutes." And to make sure he had that time to himself, he shut the door.

Joe clicked off his communicator, checked to make sure hers was off as well and looked down at her. "Put your hands in my pants this time, and I'll take you where you stand."

Katelyn didn't look quite as shocked as he'd hoped. In fact, she didn't look shocked at all. She looked, well, interested. And disgusted with herself for showing that interest.

Joe knew exactly how she felt.

"We're in trouble here, Rico." She added a shake of her head to his disgusted expression. "Because I swear that sounded more like foreplay than a threat."

He fought, hard, to hold on to what little composure he had left. "I really didn't need to hear that, okay?"

"You're right." Another headshake. She huffed and glanced at Merrick's closed door. Like Joe, she was probably hoping the man would open it. Soon. It might save Katelyn and him both from doing something he'd almost certainly regret.

"Besides, it's just all this forced intimacy that's making us think like this," she mumbled. She even repeated a slightly different variation of it as if trying to convince herself.

Again, Joe knew exactly how she felt.

"We just have to remember that the kissing and touching are fake," she concluded.

But Joe wasn't ready to conclude things just yet. He had one point of contention left. "Including the part where you put your hand in my pants?"

"Would I do something like that just for amusement?" But she waved him off. "Don't answer that. For our own sanity, let's just say everything, and I mean *everything,* we've done for the past couple of days has been an act."

It was the right thing to say. The right thing, period. She'd given them both a much-needed out. That's why Joe couldn't understand why he didn't take that out.

Instead, he slid his hand around the back of her neck and dragged her to him. Not that he had to drag her far.

She was already so close he could almost taste her.

So that's exactly what he decided to do. He lowered his head and took her mouth as if it were his for the taking.

THE JOLT WAS INSTANT.

No cool, gentle touch of lips. Not this. This was all fire. All pleasure. All silk and heat. Not that Katelyn expected anything less from Joe, and that made it all the more dangerous.

Did it stop her?

No.

One jolt from his mouth and she was beyond a place where reason and stopping made sense. Instead, she took. She let him claim. Ravage. And just when she thought it couldn't possibly get any better, or worse, he upped the ante with the mating of their tongues. The intimate joining of their mouths. The warmth of their bodies sliding against each other, practically fighting to get closer, to touch more.

To feel more.

It was as close to sex as they could get without clothing removal.

He made a sound. A groan of breath that was male through and through. And possibly the most erotic sound she'd ever heard.

Katelyn felt the world tilt on its axis.

This was wrong. So wrong. But everything about it seemed right.

She forced herself to back off. And she almost lost that battle. Somehow though, she got her mouth to move from his. It took another moment before she got it to speak.

"That wasn't for show," she informed him. A really dumb thing to say, but what the heck? It was hard to beat the mother of all dumb things—that kiss.

"I figured that out by myself." He ran his tongue over his bottom lip. "We can't do it again though because it…felt better than it should have."

You bet it did. And not only that. It felt better than it should have while they were standing only yards away from a murder suspect.

A suspect who opened the door.

Chapter Eight

Katelyn put on the best fake smile she could manage, and while easing her right hand to her slide holster, she flashed her engagement ring at Merrick.

"Joe and I are getting married." She added some excitement to her tone, as well, and she didn't totally have to fake that part. There was excitement racing through her all right, and it wasn't all related to that kiss Joe had just laid on her. There was something downright spooky about the way Merrick was acting.

Was the man about to go psycho on them?

Joe must have considered that as well because he too adjusted his position so it would be easier for him to get to his weapon.

"Congratulations are in order," Merrick finally said after a silence that was too long and much too uncomfortable. "Come this way. We'll celebrate."

Katelyn didn't relax yet. Hopefully, celebrating was all he had in mind. She stayed side by side with Joe as they started down the hall toward the reception area.

"Say, wasn't that Dr. Allen Kent who just left your office?" Joe asked, sounding remarkably casual.

There was nothing casual, however, about Merrick's response. From over his shoulder, he gave Joe a chilly, "Yes."

Katelyn ignored the frosty tone since they needed more info from him than that solo affirmative. "Wow. He's practically a local celebrity. I'm in therapy, you know. In fact, my therapist thinks I've gone off the deep end by getting engaged to Joe. But I know it's the right thing to do. That's why we don't want to wait." She paused only long enough to draw breath. "Wonder what Dr. Kent would have to say about that?"

It was a weak attempt to get Merrick to open up. And an unsuccessful one. He didn't say a word about therapy or Dr. Kent. But his silence told her loads. That shouting session with Kent had upset him, no doubt about it, but he was keeping it inside for the most part. No fists through walls. No profanity. A still-waters-run-deep kind of person.

So how would a man like that kill?

Would he gun down happy brides and grooms because his own fiancée had crushed his hopes of having an equally happy life? If so, how could Joe and she stop him from trying to kill again?

As those questions ran through her head, Merrick paused at one of the doors. Knocked once. And opened it. Bruce Donovan was seated at a desk littered with computers and other equipment.

"We need champagne," Merrick advised him. "Meet us in reception."

Katelyn's gaze connected with Donovan's. His *disapproving* gaze. Definitely not a still-waters kind of guy. She made a mental note not to sample the champagne in case he decided to poison it.

"Something tells me they've done this before," Joe muttered to her as they watched Merrick assemble an impromptu celebration.

Their host motioned for the four other clients and the receptionist to join them. They did. The clients put their questionnaires aside. Donovan appeared with the champagne and a stack of plastic fluted glasses. Merrick popped the cork and began to pour.

"So a lot of your matched couples get engaged?" Joe asked Merrick.

He lifted a shoulder. "Some."

Katelyn pressed for more. "I'll bet you keep press releases and such of your success stories."

"Not really." And with that, Merrick stepped away to pour more champagne.

"Okay, what's wrong with this picture?" Joe whispered to her. He slipped his arm around her and launched into a mock cuddling session so they could continue their discussion without being overheard.

"The clients," Katelyn immediately offered. "I was alone in here the day I did my questionnaire. How about you?"

"Me and one very old guy."

These people weren't old or even socially desperate-looking. They were young and practically buzzing with energy.

Katelyn bit off a groan. "They don't appear to be drunk or high so that probably means they read the article in the newspaper."

"Adrenaline junkies," Joe added.

A moment later, one of the female clients confirmed that. Katelyn heard her talking almost breathlessly about the possible link to the sniper. *Isn't it soooo scary?*

Great. Sickos. Just what they didn't need to blend with the rifle-firing sicko they already had. However, it did give Katelyn something else to consider. The shootings had perhaps boosted business. A business that had recently been sagging. Merrick couldn't have been unhappy about that particular side effect, but was he smart enough, calculating enough, to have known it would happen?

Because Katelyn had her attention on the group, she didn't miss the nudge Donovan gave his boss. Merrick turned, aiming his gaze in the direction of the reception doorway.

The still waters became a little turbulent.

Katelyn followed his narrowed gaze to a tall, attractive brunette. A woman she recognized because she'd studied her file and accompanying photos.

Fiona Shipley.

"I see her," Joe whispered.

"Just the person we've been looking for."

From the look on Merrick's face, he didn't feel the same. He handed off the champagne bottle to Dono-

van, whispered something terse and then stormed
straight for the woman. Fortunately, one of the other
clients stopped him, but that diversion wouldn't last
long. Katelyn could tell from the look in Merrick's
eyes that one way or another, he intended to get Fiona
out of here.

"We'll intervene and talk to her," Joe insisted.

"Something tells me she won't go for the let's-be-
gal-pals ploy. You need to put some moves on her
before Merrick whisks her away."

Joe's eyebrow lifted. "Moves?"

She nodded. "Trust me, you've got some good
ones." Great ones, in fact. The kiss had proven that.

He didn't seem flattered. "I don't guess Fiona will
consider those *moves* bottom-feeding gestures since I
just announced my engagement to you?"

"Let's hope not. You occupy Fiona, and I'll take
care of Merrick. Maybe I can put him in a more talk-
ative mood and learn the names of any recently engaged Perfect Match couples."

Joe caught her arm when she tried to step away.
"Please tell me you're not going to try to rile him
enough so he'll come after you."

Katelyn tried to look offended. "You think I'd do
that?"

"Yeah, I do," he said without hesitation.

If it wouldn't have blown the lovebird facade, she
would have scowled at him. "Are you saying divide
and conquer's not a good idea?"

Several muscles stirred in his jaw, a definite sign
he agreed with her plan but probably wouldn't ap-

prove of her methods. "You've got ten minutes max," he finally said. "Get everything you can from him. I'll do the same to Fiona. Just don't shake things up too much, okay?"

This time, it was Katelyn who stopped. "I'll say the same to you. Fiona's the one with a hostile history, not Merrick."

In fact, this divide and conquer investigative approach suddenly didn't seem like a good idea. Even more, Katelyn didn't want to explore why it occurred to her that it wasn't good.

Judas.

She was worried about Joe.

A man who could clearly take care of himself.

"Are you about to quote regulations about approaching a potentially violent suspect without proper backup?" Joe asked.

"You wish."

He stared at her several long seconds, and cursed. "It's about that kiss?"

She nodded. "Probably."

But when she repeated that to herself, it didn't seem so much like a probably as a definitely.

Praying she was wrong, Katelyn turned to head Merrick off at the pass.

JOE MADE IT to Fiona before Merrick did. Thanks to Katelyn. She latched on to Merrick and somehow brought him to a stop. God knows what she was saying to him, but she seemed to have captured his attention.

Fiona offered him a tentative smile when Joe approached her. The smile vanished when she glanced in Katelyn and Merrick's direction.

"Joe Farrell." He extended his hand, and she shook it. Not a delicate grip, either. She could probably hold her own in an arm wrestling competition.

"Fiona Shipley." She slid her gaze over him and up. "I haven't seen you in here before."

It was almost certainly a lie. She'd been watching the place the night of the icebreaker.

She moved slightly to the side, probably so she could keep her eye on Merrick. He did the same, angling his body so he could watch Katelyn. Since she was the only redhead in the room, she made a great visual target. The skirt helped, too. She had the best pair of legs in the room.

Maybe the world.

And maybe he was still recovering from the effects of that kiss, because everything about her suddenly seemed damn incredible. Thankfully, she'd probably do something to rile him before the night was over. That would get his mind back where it belonged.

"So you know everyone here?" Joe asked Fiona. Not exactly chitchat, either. It was an opening to bring the subject around to Merrick, the man who was glancing in her direction as much as she was glancing in his.

"No. Just Bruce and Addison."

Joe skipped right past the Bruce part and went for the jugular. "Merrick's a friend of yours?"

She gave an unnecessary adjustment to her gold hoop earring. ''Something like that.''

In other words, *nothing* like that. She was either Merrick's former, present or even wannabe lover. With the way she kept eyeing Katelyn, it was highly likely that it wasn't the latter.

Interesting.

''How about you?'' she asked. ''Are you a new client, or are you with someone?''

''I'm with my fiancée, Kate.'' He pointed to Katelyn but made sure he only showed minimal interest in the woman whom he'd supposedly asked to be his wife. ''Old flames reunited thanks to Perfect Match. Things happened pretty fast between us.''

And he let Fiona fill in the blanks. Maybe she'd think he was having second thoughts. Or maybe she'd just think he was a bottom-feeder. Either way, she didn't seem turned off with the idea of an engaged man chatting her up. But then, maybe she was trying to make Merrick jealous. Or something. There were a lot of dynamics going on in the room, and not all of them were limited to Merrick and Fiona. Some of them were obviously happening between Katelyn and him.

Since Joe could feel his self-imposed time limit ticking away, he took a pen from the receptionist's desk and passed it to Fiona. He discreetly put out his hand, palm up. ''In case things don't work out with Addison, or Kate, why don't you give me a number where I can reach you? I'd like to give you a call sometime.''

That got Fiona's attention. Man, did it. She gave him several more once-overs, not exactly carnal ones, either. There was some disgust. Some loathing. Even a hot flash of anger in her eyes. That's why it surprised Joe when she scribbled some numbers on his hand.

That was it. No sultry invitations, no warm goodbyes. No explanations as to why she'd give a man her number when she obviously disliked him.

"If you'll excuse me, I need to speak with Addison." Fiona tossed the pen back on the desk and stepped away.

Merrick moved toward Fiona at the same time he left Katelyn and walked toward her. Merrick said something. Something harsh, judging from the way she reacted. She looked as if the man had slapped her. Then, she angled her eyes in Katelyn and Joe's direction. Merrick's gaze followed.

Oh, yeah. Merrick was definitely suspicious of them, and their latest round of unofficial questioning had probably made it worse.

Fiona gave Merrick a not-so-friendly glower, turned on her heel and headed for the door. Merrick aimed a similar facial expression at them and went in the opposite direction toward his office.

"Should we follow one of them?" Katelyn asked in a whisper.

"Not with that camera looming over us. We've already peaked their interest too much for one night." Way too much. "Did you learn anything new?"

"No. He's not flirtatious or chatty like Donovan."

Katelyn glanced around the room. "Speaking of the devil, where is he?"

"He left not long after you started talking to Merrick."

She made a sound to indicate she didn't care for that. Neither did Joe.

"Maybe we should follow him instead?" she suggested.

"He went in the same direction as Merrick. Besides, we have this." Making sure he was out of camera angle, Joe flashed the number that Fiona had given him.

She blinked. "You got her number that fast?"

"Maybe. It could be a fake."

"Yeah, right. It's not a fake."

Joe wasn't sure if he should be complimented by that, but unfortunately it felt like a compliment.

"So what's the deal between Merrick and her?" Katelyn asked. "Are they involved?"

"That'd be my guess. It's also my guess that one or both isn't too happy about that."

"Merrick, maybe. It might explain why he had the guard here the night of the icebreaker. Maybe he wanted to keep her away from the place."

"It's possible. Merrick certainly wasn't happy to see her. I'll call her tomorrow and see if I can arrange to meet her somewhere."

"With proper backup, correct?" Katelyn whispered.

Since it didn't sound even remotely sarcastic, he

stared at her. "Why this sudden fixation with backup?"

She dismissed it with a wave of her hand. "I don't know. There's this little buzz in the back of my head. It's making me antsy."

"Then obviously it's a good time for us to get out of here. We'll come back tomorrow and invite them to the wedding."

After he called Fiona, of course. If he got lucky, that number would be real so he could continue their discussion.

They went out the door. Not alone, either. Two other clients were right behind them, and the woman was still chattering about Perfect Match's possible connection to the sniper. If the sniper had indeed been inside that reception room and heard her, it would have no doubt made him or her nervous.

Or maybe not.

Maybe that's exactly what the nutcase wanted. Publicity. Recognition. A moment in the spotlight, even if that moment meant people dying.

All four of them headed toward the parking lot. Unlike the night of the mixer, Joe hadn't managed to get a decent parking spot. They were almost a full block away. In the dark.

"So did you learn anything new when you talked to Fiona?" Katelyn whispered, presumably so that the couple behind them wouldn't hear. "Like maybe how many eyelashes she had? You probably had a chance to count them when she was fluttering them at you."

Joe geared up to give her a smart-ass comeback.

The glint of movement stopped him. The glint he caught out of the corner of his eye.

But it was too late.

The shot rang out before he could get Katelyn out of the way.

KATELYN FELT the searing hot pain slice across her arm.

She ignored it and drew her weapon while she yelled for the couple to get down. They did, diving for cover behind a parked car. She latched on to Joe at the same moment he latched on to her, and they dragged each other to the ground.

It wasn't a second too soon.

Another bullet smashed into the building, into the exact spot where they'd been.

Katelyn couldn't take the time to berate herself, but she would sure as heck do it later. She should have paid more attention to that buzz in her head instead of dismissing it. And she darn sure shouldn't have been playing twenty questions with Joe about his encounter with Fiona Shipley.

Now that mistake might cost both of them their lives.

She checked the other couple. They were cowering, their hands protectively over their heads. All in all, it wasn't a bad position. The car would give them some measure of protection, but it wasn't the same for Joe and her. For all practical purposes, they were still out in the open.

''Let's move,'' Joe ordered.

Katelyn didn't waste any time. She got to her feet, and they scrambled for the narrow alley between the two buildings. He maneuvered them to the far side of an overflowing Dumpster, but it wasn't an ideal position either since bullets could go through the metal.

"Rico here," Joe said into his communicator. "We've got a shooter. Send backup to the outside perimeter of the area and await further orders."

The outside perimeter so that it wouldn't blow their cover. Not that it wouldn't anyway. But Joe was obviously hoping to salvage this mission and keep them alive.

Katelyn pulled in a few steadying breaths and glanced down at her arm. She saw the gashed fabric, and the blood. Nothing serious, she decided, but she angled her body so that Joe wouldn't notice it. He didn't need that kind of distraction now.

Another shot.

It slammed into the exterior wall and tore off a chunk of brick, sending mortar and dust flying through the air. Two more shots quickly followed, both of them gashing into the Dumpster and the wall just above their heads.

The bullets came close.

Too close. And the thought of them coming any closer set Katelyn's heart pounding.

She leaned forward slightly, trying to see if she could pinpoint the origin of those bullets so she could get off a shot.

"Don't even think about it," Joe snarled.

Katelyn started to argue, to remind him that she

could return fire as well as he could, but that probably wasn't a good option anyway. The gunman clearly had an advantage, and if she moved away from cover to get a better shot, it would also leave her vulnerable. They were already too exposed as it was.

Still, that didn't stop Joe.

He aimed. And she knew that he was about to do something she'd already dismissed.

But then the shots stopped.

The waiting began.

Katelyn counted off the seconds, the quiet seconds, until she got to sixty. Joe grabbed her shoulder when she started to move and he put her right back against the wall. "Not yet." He took the end of his communicator and put it against his mouth. "Situation report."

"Additional officers are on the way," the backup officer responded.

Which meant the sniper was getting away.

Again!

Worse, it didn't exclude any of their suspects. Fiona, Merrick or Donovan could have left Perfect Match and sneaked into any of the multistory buildings across the street. For that matter, Kent could have done the same thing. He could have been lying in wait for them.

"Pick up Bruce Donovan, Dr. Kent, Addison Merrick and Fiona Shipley," Joe snarled into his communicator. "Bring them in. I want them all interrogated. And by God, they'd better have answers."

Chapter Nine

Katelyn shut the bathroom door and peeled off her top. Somehow, she'd managed to keep the streak of blood from Joe, but if she didn't get rid of the evidence, she wouldn't be able to keep it from him for long. Thankfully, he'd planted himself in the living room and was still immersed in the necessary calls and reports to headquarters.

''Judas,'' she mumbled looking down at the shallow but angry gash that the sniper's bullet had left on her arm.

The bleeding had already stopped, and it wasn't especially painful—okay, it did hurt—but what hurt even more was the realization that it could have been worse. Much worse. The gunman could have killed Joe, the other couple and her. It was a miracle that all she had to show for the encounter was a minor two-inch abrasion, some dried blood and a pair of shredded panty hose that she'd damaged when she dove down on the sidewalk.

She stuffed the top in the cabinet beneath the sink

and while she was at it, she took off her panty hose to add them to the stash. She located a first aid kit in the medicine cabinet and got to work cleaning the wound. When she finished, Katelyn covered it with a bandage and slipped on a white cotton shirt, the only other long-sleeve garment her mother had included in the bag. Maybe the quick change in clothes wouldn't make Joe suspicious.

Or maybe it would.

He was standing right in front of her when she opened the door. He had his hands bracketed on each side of the frame, essentially blocking her path.

"Everything okay?" he asked. But it wasn't a simple question. There were some dangerous undercurrents in it.

"I'm fine."

Those now infamous jaw muscles went to work against each other. "Take off your shirt, or I'll take it off for you."

Oh.

"Does this mean you want to have sex?" Katelyn tried. But it was a lousy try. Anyone with half a brain would have known it wasn't sex on his mind. Not with that warlike expression.

He waited only a second or two before he reached out, grabbed the sides of her shirt and ripped it open. A few of the buttons merely gave way and slipped through the buttonholes. Others didn't. They landed with tiny bouncing pings on the tile floor.

His gaze raced over her body, and it obviously

wasn't her lacy bra or her breasts that captured his interest. His attention quickly landed on the bandage.

Katelyn braced herself for him to rip the shirt right off her. But he didn't. His touch gentled and Joe eased it off her shoulder to expose her arm.

"It's not bad," she insisted.

He didn't take her word for it. Not surprising since he'd just caught her in a lie. With that same gentle touch, those same careful movements, he lifted the bandage.

And cursed.

The jaw muscles started again.

"How did you know I was hurt?" Katelyn asked. God, her voice actually cracked.

"There was blood on the sleeve of my jacket. It's not mine. I figured it had to be yours."

She shrugged. "And here I thought I'd contained my bodily fluids."

"This isn't funny!"

Because he looked ready to lose it, she ran her hand down the length of his arm. "It's nothing. I've gotten worse from shaving my legs."

He pressed the bandage back in place, gently, and skimmed his fingertips from it, across the top of her left breast and then to her heart. "Six inches in this direction, and the bullet wouldn't have grazed you. It would have killed you."

His gaze came to hers.

Unlike his touch, there was still no gentleness in those glacier-blue eyes, but Katelyn knew without a doubt if gentleness was what she needed, he could have easily provided it.

And he did.

Without moving his hand from her heart, Joe pulled her to him. Where she felt incredibly safe and warm.

Katelyn went with it, against her better judgment. Full-blown sex would have been far less of an intimate risk than this. But her better judgment and her resolve went south. Unable to hold back a shudder of breath, she rested her head against his shoulder and took things from him that she hadn't known she needed.

They stood there for heaven knows how long. Minutes, maybe. Perhaps longer. The rhythm of her heart seemed to fall into cadence with the pulse that throbbed in his wrist. And the world seemed to just melt away.

Until the doorbell rang.

Joe immediately stepped back, drawing his gun, and their tender moment ended.

"Wait here," he ordered.

"Right, and leave you without backup. Like I'm really going to do that."

Knowing she couldn't do much to fix the shirt, she shucked it off and put on one that Joe had left in the bedroom. Katelyn had her weapon drawn before he even made it to the door.

"It's your brother," Joe let her know.

Great. She didn't want to face Garrett now. "Don't say a word about the scratch," she warned in a whisper.

But she soon learned it wasn't Garrett when Joe opened the door and let him in.

It was Brayden.

Even worse.

He was part bloodhound and all cop, and he could sniff out problems a mile away. She made sure Joe's shirt covered the bandage before she joined the two men in the living room.

"I came by to check on you," Brayden greeted. He was dressed like a delivery man, but the disguise wasn't limited to just his clothes. He was carrying a white bag. "Dad sent some chili."

"Thanks." Katelyn took the bag, knowing she should dig in right away to prove all was right with the world, but her stomach wasn't quite ready for food. She set it on the table instead.

"You can do your initial reports on the computer," Brayden instructed. "But I'll still need you to do a face-to-face at headquarters. No way around that. We'll send a cruiser for you tomorrow so it'll look as if you're being brought in for questioning. In fact, we'll bring in all the people who were at Perfect Match tonight."

Brayden gave them both a considering glance and sat on the sofa. "Did either of you fire your weapons?"

"No," she quickly volunteered.

Joe stared at her.

Brayden paused, as if waiting to see what had caused that stare. "Any reason to think your cover's been compromised?'' he asked, and Brayden directed that question at Joe.

Joe leaned against the narrow snack bar that divided the kitchen from the living room. ''Hard to tell. Just about everyone in Perfect Match was talking about the shootings. And that other couple was walking right behind us. Maybe the sniper just wanted to make his or her presence known.''

Brayden didn't say anything for several seconds. ''Well, we're rounding up Bruce Donovan and hopefully Fiona Shipley for an interrogation, so maybe we'll know something soon. Fiona checked herself into a residential mental health clinic about an hour ago. Lots of freedom for her to go from one place to the other, but it doesn't give us a lot of access to her unless she's willing to grant us that access. Oh, and we learned that Donovan owns several hunting rifles so I went ahead and requested a search warrant.''

''Good,'' Joe said.

Katelyn muttered an agreement as well, even though Donovan probably wasn't stupid enough to leave murder weapons lying around for the cops to find. Still, it'd prevent him from getting a good night's sleep—which would apparently be her fate, as well. Joe probably wouldn't drop that *six inches over and you could have been killed* discussion.

''You intend to continue with the present mission plan?'' Brayden asked Joe.

Joe stared at her again. Katelyn stared back and tried to put the words in his mouth. Or rather the word. And that word was *yes.*

He didn't say yes.

But then he didn't say no, either.

"I'll have to get back to you on that," Joe told her brother.

Brayden nodded. Made a sound of contemplation. Then looked at Joe. "Would you mind if I spoke to Katelyn in private?"

Another glare from Joe aimed in her direction, but this one had a *tell him the truth* warning in it. It was a warning she'd definitely ignore. Joe would thank her for it later, after they'd collared the sniper.

Her brother motioned for her to sit down the moment Joe left the room. "What's wrong?" Brayden asked.

She didn't sit, but put on her best butter-wouldn't-melt-in-my-mouth expression. "Why would you think anything's wrong?"

Brayden's eyebrow lifted.

So much for the nonmelting butter routine. That eyebrow was a very effective BS monitor. Still, it didn't stop her from going on the offensive. "What— being shot at isn't reason enough to make me cranky?"

His eyebrow stayed up. "You're wearing Sergeant Rico's shirt," he pointed out.

"Oh, that." Not that she'd thought for minute Brayden would miss something like that. However, since he'd broached the subject, Katelyn went with it. It might get him off the undercover assignment. "I'm not allowed to have a lover? Garrett is the wild child of the family, and you don't lecture him about it."

"Garrett doesn't sleep with his boss."

"My *temporary* boss," Katelyn corrected.

Brayden shook his head. Nothing overt. Just a simple gesture. "You know something I don't? Joe Rico's a sergeant in Homicide. You're a detective in the same department."

"For now, yes. But I figure he'll get promoted, and then he'll be moved." If not, then it might come down to her asking for a transfer, a thought that had her feeling a little nauseous. She'd worked hard to get into Homicide, damn hard, and she wouldn't just give that up. Well, unless there was no other way. Then she'd consider it.

Heaven help her.

"And I haven't actually slept with him," she said more to herself than her brother. "I've just been flirting with the idea. *Lightly* flirting with it. And even if something happened between us, it's not against the regs per se. It's just frowned upon because it could cause, well, morale problems." She added an indignant huff just because she'd delivered Brayden's lecture for him. "Is this why you came over? To grill me about my love life?"

He caught her wrist and sat her on the coffee table in front of him. "Quit being so defensive. I came to see if you were all right."

Katelyn leaned closer into his personal space. "I. Am."

"Yes. I can see that."

She didn't want to know if he was being sarcastic, mainly because she was certain that he was. After all, his eyebrow was still cocked and locked, ready to fire, and she'd delivered her *I. Am.* comment through clenched teeth.

"I also wanted to talk to you about Sergeant Rico," he calmly went on. "And about this mission."

Since she was already on the defensive, she just stayed there. "Oh, no. Don't even think about pulling the plug on it." Katelyn held up her thumb and index finger to indicate a miniscule space. "We're this close to getting the sniper, Brayden."

"I don't doubt it." And there wasn't anything defensive-sounding about that. He eased down her hand. "Sergeant Rico and you make a good team."

That improved her posture. But she wouldn't let a compliment, if that's indeed what it was, blindside her. "What the heck is that supposed to mean?"

"It means you each have talents that balance the other's." He leaned back against the sofa and tucked his hands behind his head. "For Rico, procedure is rote, so deeply engrained he doesn't have to think about it. The vast majority of the time, following procedure's the right thing to do. So that practically ensures a successful mission. You, on the other hand, think outside the box, and that gives you the edge when you're in an evade and escape mode."

"Thanks. I think." Suspicious, she squinted one eye. "Is this some kind of law enforcement version of a hunters versus gatherers theory?"

He smiled. "Well, sort of." His mouth quivered as if he might smile, but then he lowered his hands and continued. "Rico's never missed a shot during firearms qualification."

Another posture improving remark. *"Never?"*

"Never."

"Sheez." She let that sink in. "Even Robocop misses every now and then."

"Rico's also never blown a case. He's batting a thousand in that department."

She frowned, realizing all the blindsiding was probably leading somewhere after all. "And your point would be?"

"No point. You're smart, and that means you know if it comes down to a tight situation, then Rico can handle it. No matter how good of a shot you are— and you're good—he's better."

"And he'll be even better if I'm backing him up," she promptly added.

"Absolutely." He stood, kissed her cheek and headed for the door. "Be careful, okay?"

Katelyn nodded, and even though she wasn't pleased with the minilecture, she went to him and returned the kiss.

She locked the door after she let him out. "One down, one to go," she grumbled. She'd probably convinced Brayden to keep this case alive, but now she had to do the same with Joe.

"Want some chili?" she called out.

She took the two plastic containers from the bag. They were still warm so she grabbed a couple of spoons and prepared herself for a feast—which she really didn't want yet—but that was beside the point.

Wolfing down some chili might go a long way toward proving to Joe that she was fit for duty.

He came out of the bedroom and started that staring thing again, so Katelyn shoved both the container of chili and a spoon into his hands. "Eat," she ordered.

She did. Katelyn sat back on the coffee table and dug in. "Practically orgasmic, huh?" she asked after he'd had his first taste.

"Close." Joe sampled another heaping spoonful. "Speaking of orgasmic, you'd rather let your brother think you have the hots for me than just tell him you're hurt?"

It was a good thing she'd just swallowed that mouthful of chili, or she might have choked on it. "You eavesdropped?"

"Thin walls," he countered. "Hard not to eavesdrop."

True. But that didn't let him off the hook completely. "I didn't want him to take me off the case, all right? Sometimes, he weirds out a little when he starts to think hard about what I do for a living. It's that you're-my-kid-sister routine. It brings out his protective instincts."

"If he'd known you were wounded in the line of duty, he would have pulled you off the case. It's not protective instincts. It's procedure."

She stabbed at the chili with her spoon. "I was *scratched* in the line of duty. Big difference."

"Why do you feel the rules don't apply to you, huh? And before you start defending yourself, just hear me out. Officers who are wounded, even when it's a scratch, take time off to recoup.''

''I don't have time to recoup.''

He smacked his chili onto the snack bar and stared down at her. ''Am I supposed to understand that?''

No. And no explanation would probably help, either. Still, that didn't stop her. ''I want to be promoted to sergeant, okay? And I wish there were a stronger word than *want,* because it'd definitely apply here. In six months, I'll be too old for that promotion.''

''Too old?'' he repeated. ''You'll be what—the ripe old age of twenty-nine?''

''Both Brayden and Garrett made sergeant by the time they were twenty-nine.''

He looked at her as if she'd sprouted wings. ''This is about competing with your brothers?''

She was right. He didn't get it. He couldn't. ''It'd be simple if it were a competition,'' she muttered, frustrated. ''But it's more than that. The job is who I am. If I come up short, then I'm not the person I thought I was, and I don't think I could handle that.''

Katelyn glanced at him, sorry that she'd just blurted out what was probably the only deep, dark secret she had.

''And, no, I don't really expect you to understand,'' she added. She poked at the chili again, glad that she had something to prod. Maybe the fake violence would rid her of the alley-cat war going on inside her body.

He dragged a chair closer and sat down right in

front of her so they were eye-to-eye. And only inches apart. "I understand."

Of all the things that Katelyn thought he might say, that wasn't one of them. "Which part?"

"All of it."

She hadn't expected that, either. The skeptical look she gave him no doubt prompted him to continue.

"You know how everyone in your family are either cops or former cops? Well, in my family, they're all military officers. All successful. My dad is a retired one-star general, and he never forgave me for breaking ranks to become a police officer. As much as he was sure I'd fail, that's how determined I was to succeed. Every promotion, every citation, every award is to prove to him—and me—that I made the right decision."

"Wow." That's all she could manage for a couple of seconds. Talk about revealing deep, dark secrets.

Somehow, this conversation had taken a very unsettling turn. And more. He was so close that she took in his scent—and that mixed with the understanding look on his face was a dangerous combination.

"Okay, so maybe you do get it," she managed to say. And there was way too much breath in her voice.

"Yeah. But that doesn't mean I think it's a good idea to toss out the regs and procedures. Sometimes, you just have to step back and look at the bigger picture. Like this…" He reached for her bandaged arm.

Katelyn snagged his wrist, a variation of cutting him off at the pass. Or something like that. All she knew was it wouldn't be a good time for him to touch her. ''Put your hands in my shirt again, and I'll take you where you sit.''

She waited for him to laugh or give her a wiseguy comeback for using his words against him.

He didn't do either.

Joe sat there staring at her. Just staring. With those intense blue eyes that seemed to make her melt.

Mercy, where did the air suddenly go?

But it was too late for her to care about such things as air, or breathing. Katelyn let go of his wrist so she could reach for him.

Joe beat her to it.

Chapter Ten

The timing sucked.

Joe forced himself to remember that. Katelyn was injured and coming down from a terrifying ordeal. However, the reminder lasted for only a couple of seconds, for just the short period of time that it took him to haul her off that coffee table and onto his lap.

Her mouth came to his. Man, did it. Her moist, sweet, hot mouth. The kiss was hard and hungry, and in that moment, Joe knew he was sunk. There wasn't enough willpower in the universe to make him back away from her.

He slid an arm around her waist, another around the back of her neck and pulled her against him. To him. Until they were pressed to each other.

She wasn't a passive participant. Not that Joe had ever thought she would be. It was a battle. Her kiss was an assault. A sweet one, but still an assault. Her fingers dug into his shoulders, fighting to bring him even closer—not really possible since he'd have to be inside her to achieve that. The way things were going though, that just might happen.

Soon.

He decided not to think about why that wouldn't be a good idea.

Joe reached for her shirt, or rather *his* shirt that she was wearing, and would have ripped it off her if he hadn't tried to be considerate of her injury. Katelyn gave it no such consideration. She stripped it off and sent it flying across the room. Joe went for her bra instead but changed his mind when she shifted her legs to straddle him.

Oh, man.

There was no chance he'd talk his body or hers into slowing down so they wouldn't kill each other. So without breaking their kiss, he went with it, embracing that dangerous energy that was already on the verge of erupting.

He gripped her thigh and just kept going. Up. Not slowly, either. And not gently.

There was a lot of bare skin thanks to her short skirt, and she'd apparently removed her panty hose. The only thing he encountered along the way was the woman going after his zipper—something he preferred not to have happen anytime soon. She'd have managed it, too, if Joe hadn't maneuvered his own seeking hand around hers.

Since there wasn't time for finesse, he went for impact instead. He succeeded. Joe shoved his hand into her panties, into the fragile swatch of lace and silk. His fingers found her. Wet and hot. He made his way through the slick moisture.

One touch, and he heard her breath shudder.

She stopped her quest for his zipper and instead anchored her hands, one on his stomach. The other slipped into her own hair. Meeting his gaze head-on, she rocked shamelessly against his hand. One stroke. Two. Three. A long, lingering caress that brought on another shudder, another erotic hitch of her breath. And he was sure he had her close to release.

He was wrong.

Katelyn located his mouth again, kissing him as if she'd escalated the war. And maybe she had. She skipped the zipper part she'd started earlier and moved her hand from his stomach. Down.

Inside his pants.

No fumbling. She got it right the first time. Those agile fingers bypassed his boxers and slid right over his erection. One stroke. Two. A rather skillful swipe of her thumb, and she had him close to begging for mercy. Or close to begging for something else.

Joe gritted his teeth and launched them forward. Her back landed on the coffee table, and he landed on her. Between her legs. All in all, it wasn't a bad place to be. For a moment, anyway. And then there was another round of jockeying for position. She rolled. Until his back landed on the table.

Katelyn went after his shirt. He went after her skirt. It was out-and-out warfare, and for some reason speed counted. They battled the clothes and won. She even got her way with his zipper and managed to shove it down.

"Now," she demanded, already aligning the parts of them that would have made *now* happen once he rid them of their underwear.

Maybe it was the sound of her voice, or maybe there was a thread of common sense that hadn't been smothered in all that fire, but Joe remembered something he almost wished he hadn't remembered.

"I don't have a condom," he let her know.

Katelyn stopped instantly and stared at him. "Neither do I."

Her eyes were wild, unfocused, and her breaths came out in short, hot spurts. She looked on the verge of cursing, but since she didn't, Joe cursed for both of them. What he didn't do was move away from her. It would take more than a lack of a condom for that to happen.

In one swipe with his forearm, he cleared the coffee table. Chili, magazines and papers went in every direction. He didn't stop there. Because she'd already started reaching for him, specifically for his erection, Joe latched on to her panties and pulled them off her. They tore. And neither he nor Katelyn obviously cared.

Now.

It had to be now.

With the blood raging, and his heartbeat hammering, he went straight for that hot, sweet part of her that he'd already touched. But this time, he used his mouth and tongue instead of his fingers.

The taste of her went straight through him like a double shot of whiskey. And more. It was a taste he wouldn't forget, and somewhere in the back of his mind he knew he'd never be with another woman without thinking of this.

Of her.

She mumbled something and sounded as if she were on the verge of protesting, but a well-placed stroke of his tongue stopped her.

"Okay," was all she said.

She arched her back, moaned and began to move to the rhythm of his mouth. It didn't seem possible, but he'd actually found a way to get Katelyn O'Malley to cooperate. And he pleasured them both in the process.

For a couple more seconds, anyway.

"Maybe there's a condom in the bathroom," she decided, her tone more desperate than hopeful.

Her hands were suddenly everywhere. Touching as much of him as she could possibly touch, she slid lower and caught on to his hips, dragging him to the bathroom with her.

Still, the war didn't stop.

She did though.

But only so she could take her mouth to his bare stomach. No simple kiss. No, not her. She had him seeing double when she circled his navel with her tongue and sucked not-so-tenderly. Before he could muster enough strength to stop her, she kissed his erection as intimately as he'd kissed her. She pleasured him, and from the way she moved against him, she pleasured herself, as well.

Somehow, he stood upright so he could maneuver her and hopefully reciprocate. She caught on to his shoulders and pushed him against the wall. Normally, that wouldn't have been an enjoyable experience, but he was in the zone where anything she did would have been enjoyable in this erotic battle they were waging on each other.

Joe dragged her up with him. And turned so that she was the one against the wall. He was careful not to hurt her arm, but he wasn't so gentle with the rest of her. He kissed her. Hard.

She tasted of him.

Smelled of him.

Yet, somehow her own unique scent and taste were there, as well. Lingering around him and making him crazy.

Turning as if in some bizarre dance, they made it into the bathroom. He couldn't have told anyone how, but it qualified as a miracle.

His shoulder slammed against the jamb when she looped her arms behind his neck and leaped up to wrap her legs around his waist. With one hand he fumbled through the medicine cabinet while he used his other hand to keep her fingers out of his boxers.

She searched for a condom as well, tossing things from the glass shelves. Throughout her quest, she kept up the kisses, the touches. Until Joe was absolutely sure he couldn't take any more.

But somehow, he took more.

She made him take more.

"Truce," Katelyn mumbled. With her breath thin, her voice had hardly any sound. "There's not a condom in here."

Fighting with his own breath, he nodded. "It was a long shot anyway."

And it no longer mattered.

He'd already prepared himself for the final battle, and he didn't need a condom for what he had in mind. Joe turned and pinned her against the sink. Without her panties in the way, he wedged his knee between her legs and eased his fingers inside her.

A long, deliberate sigh left her mouth. A moan. And a gasp of pleasure. Once again she moved into the strokes. And she moved against him. Deeper this time, though. Against his fingers, and against his body. A slow, sensual slide that brought out every basic, every carnal instinct inside him.

"Not without you," she insisted.

"Yes, without me."

But he might as well have been talking to the air because she clamped her leg along the outside of his. Holding him in place. And she got her way by sliding her hand back into his boxers.

Since it was obvious she wouldn't give up, Joe just gave in.

"Move with me, Katelyn. Move with me."

She did. She moved with him as if her very life depended on it. And with their blood raging, that wasn't too far from the truth.

Face-to-face. Body-to-body. Wet skin whispering

against wet skin. His fingers, in her. Moving. Hers, on him. Clutching. Gripping. Sliding. To a frantic, feverish pace.

"Take me where I stand," she offered.

And he accepted that offer.

He snagged her gaze, because he wanted to watch her go over. Joe fought through the clawing primal need to claim and possess so he could see exactly what this did to her. It didn't matter that he felt his own body going over, as well.

Nothing mattered.

Except this.

Except her.

They took that last climb together with strokes. Touches. Caresses. And they were right there to catch each other when the fire tore free and released them both.

KATELYN SO HOPED the ringing in her ears was a post-orgasmic response.

No such luck.

When she heard Joe curse, she realized it was the phone. A phone she should probably answer since this was supposedly her apartment and since they were in the middle of an undercover murder investigation.

Somehow, Joe got their bodies untangled so she could make it to the bedroom. To prevent herself from having to stand around naked, she grabbed a towel and her pajama top along the way. Naked was great during the throes of passion, but now that the passion had been sated, she was already starting to feel as if she'd done the ultimate no-no.

Which in a way she had.

She'd just had sex with her boss, and even though it wasn't full-blown sex, it qualified in every possible way that counted.

Katelyn pushed that disturbing thought aside and grabbed the phone. After a couple of tries, she even managed a meager hello.

"We have a problem," Brayden immediately informed her.

Okay. So that rid her of any lust-induced cobwebs. "What's wrong?"

She tried to brace herself, but the bracing failed when she heard her brother's response.

"The sniper struck again. There's been another shooting."

Chapter Eleven

"It takes thirteen average-size steps to go from one side to the other," Garrett commented from the doorway of the headquarters' conference room. "But then you probably already figured that out since all you've done is pace for the past fifteen minutes."

"I beg to differ." Katelyn held up the foam cup. "I've had coffee with my pacing."

"How very multitasked of you. Try it with gum, and you'll really impress me."

Too bad their attempts at levity failed.

Mercy. Another shooting.

She tried to choke back a sigh, failed, and dropped down into one of the burgundy leather chairs that encircled a massive oval table.

Garrett glanced at Joe, who was in the adjoining room. He'd kept the door open, and the glass panel allowed them both to see that Joe was still talking on the phone. Too bad she couldn't hear what he was saying.

"You have an update on the wounded couple yet?" Garrett asked her.

"That's what Joe's getting now." She set her empty cup aside. "Their names are Melissa and Brad Garcia. They're alive. At least, they were when they arrived at the hospital a couple of hours ago, but they're both in surgery."

"I heard the shooting happened not too far from the Municipal Auditorium?"

She nodded. "They were getting married in a late night ceremony on one of those tour boats. Just the couple, a minister and two others who were witnessing the wedding."

That in itself posed some serious questions as to how the sniper had learned about the ceremony. It wasn't exactly a well-publicized event. If she could somehow pick up the information trail, it might lead her to the person responsible. And in this case, the person responsible had shot the bride and groom within seconds after they said I do.

Just the thought of that made her stomach churn. What was supposed to be the happiest night of their life had turned into a nightmare.

Katelyn shook her head, and her fingers curled into a fist. "I should have stopped him, Garrett. This shouldn't have happened."

"You know, in some cultures that remark would be considered heresy. You're not God. Heck, you're not even in the angel category." And though it was a typical cocky Garrett response, he gave her a brotherly pat on the back. ''Are you close to collaring this shooter?''

''He struck twice in the same night so at least we know we're pushing the right buttons.'' She glanced in Joe's direction, but he was still on the phone. ''Or in light of the wounded couple, maybe it was the wrong buttons.''

''It's not wrong. You'll get him.'' Garrett unwrapped two mints that he took from his pocket, popped one in his mouth and uncurled her fist so he could put the other one in her hand. ''I heard the owner of Perfect Match might be closing down the place for a couple of days. Will that affect your follow-up plans?''

''I don't know yet.'' She stared at the mint because it gave her some place to focus her attention. ''Joe just got the news before the hospital called.''

But it would definitely have an effect. After all, they were supposed to go to Perfect Match that very afternoon and invite Merrick to the wedding. Since that was a critical step in the plan, it meant they'd have to make other arrangements to see him.

Not an ideal contingency.

If they met Merrick elsewhere, it only increased problems for securing yet another location. But then, calling the man and asking him to meet them at Perfect Match might make him even more suspicious than he already was.

Garrett took a chair, turned it backward and sat across from her so they were face-to-face. When she didn't make eye contact with him, he put his finger beneath her chin, lifted and forced the eye contact. He tipped his head toward Joe. "So how hard are you falling for that jerk?"

Katelyn frowned and tossed the mint into her mouth. She cracked it with her teeth. "He's not a jerk."

"How hard are you falling for him?" Garrett flatly repeated.

The mint crunching didn't last nearly as long as Garrett's inquisitive, in-her-face expression. "As hard as a massive crate of concrete," she admitted.

Garrett made a sound of disappointment, lifted her hand and studied the ring for her fake engagement to Joe. "I thought I taught you better than that. The badge first. Family second. Lust and laundry last."

"I'm scared it's more than just lust," Katelyn whispered.

"Hell."

"Yes." She considered some profanity of her own.

"What about all the other stuff going on?" Garrett asked. "You just plan to forget that Rico's investigation could ultimately hurt Brayden?"

"Don't give me that." Katelyn managed to keep her voice at a whisper. An angry whisper. But it was still hopefully low enough that Joe wouldn't hear her. "The chief ordered that investigation, not Joe. And it could only ultimately hurt Brayden if there were some truth to it. There isn't."

"You think Rico knows that?"

"I think I'll trust him to figure it out. Judas Priest, Garrett, he's not the bad guy in all of this. Heck, maybe the chief isn't, either. Maybe he just wants to make sure he doesn't have a potential problem in the department that could affect morale.'' But Katelyn groaned when she heard herself. "Good grief, I sound like Brayden. And Joe.''

"Scary, huh?'' He took her empty coffee cup, crushed it and launched it into the trash can. "Wanna know what else sounds scary? According to the rumor mill, Rico will probably be promoted to lieutenant. If that happens, he'll almost certainly be put in charge of Special Investigations since Brodell's retiring. That means Rico will be *my* boss.''

Katelyn gave him a weary smile. "You've got nothing to worry about. Joe's a good boss.''

"Yeah, but there's no lust factor in this for me, just the concern that I might have to beat him to a pulp if he doesn't do right by Brayden.''

"He'll do right by Brayden.'' And Katelyn was surprised to realize that she believed that with all her heart.

She was *so* in trouble.

One fantastic orgasm, and she was falling head over heels for a man she certainly shouldn't be falling for.

Because she couldn't sit still and because she noted a renewed concern on Joe's face, she got up and continued her pacing. Mercy, how long did it take to get a status report on patients?

"So the rumor mill is saying he'll be promoted?'' Katelyn asked just to get her mind off that phone call.

"Apparently.''

"And what about my promotion?"

It was a gutsy question because she knew Garrett wouldn't lie to her. But there was a good chance he might try to sugarcoat it.

He lifted a shoulder. "It's just a rumor mill. What the heck does it matter?"

She groaned. Definitely sugarcoating. In other words, the odds were against her. However, it seemed a trivial worry with people's lives in limbo. Later, when this was over, she'd spend some time worrying about that particular aspect of her life.

Joe finally put down the phone and came out into the conference room. He nodded a greeting at Garrett before his gaze came to hers.

"The Garcias are out of the woods," he let her know. "Both required surgery, but they're stable. The doctors are hopeful they'll make a full recovery. Not only that, we should be able to get an officer in there by evening to ask them some questions."

Katelyn took a deep breath and said a prayer of thanks. Finally, a break. Now if they'd just get one with stopping this sniper before he could do any more damage.

"That's my cue to get out of here," Garrett insisted. "Remember what I just told you, Sis."

"No, thanks," she tossed back.

He smiled in that secretive way that only Garrett and Mona Lisa could have managed, lifted a hand in farewell and headed out the door.

"A problem?" Joe asked, watching Garrett leave.

"No." She glared at Garrett until he was out of

sight and then turned back to Joe. "Is this one connected to Perfect Match?"

"Afraid so. According to the minister, the couple met there at an icebreaker about three months ago."

Katelyn had known he would say that. The sniper was back to the pattern. "Did anyone see the shooter?"

Joe shook his head. "No one's come forward, but it's early. We have an evidence response team checking the scene now. Brayden is still rounding up Bruce Donovan and Fiona Shipley. We might have answers soon."

"What about Dr. Kent and Addison Merrick?" she asked.

"Supposedly they were at their residences, asleep. But three of the four suspects live alone so any of them could have sneaked out to commit the crime. Fiona could have left the mental health facility, as well."

"Wait a minute—they weren't being watched?"

"They were, but it would have been easy enough to get out without being seen."

True. So no breaks in that particular area. "This time the shots were fairly accurate?"

"Accurate enough to wound two people, but there were strays. At least a dozen. And the minister's leg was grazed with a bullet." Joe scrubbed his fingers over his chin. "You're thinking about Donovan and those two rifles he owns?"

"Yes. Maybe he's a lousy shot despite being a gun owner? Or maybe he just wants to make people believe the sniper has a bad aim so it'll take suspicion off him?''

''Or maybe he's not the sniper.'' Joe stopped, apparently gave that some thought, and then looked at her. ''What's going on in your head?''

''I was just thinking about how the sniper broke his own rules when he fired shots at us. We weren't a newlywed couple. Now with this latest shooting maybe he, or she, wants to remind everyone that he's really only after brides and grooms who meet at the agency. And if so, then it's obviously an important message to get across.''

''That brings us back to motive.'' He flexed his eyebrows. ''All four of our suspects have that in spades.''

Katelyn might have dwelled on that a little longer if she hadn't noticed the paper in Joe's hand.

''It's the details for tomorrow,'' he said, obviously aware of what had caught her attention.

With everything else going on, she hadn't even thought that far in advance. She did now.

A wedding.

A fake one. With Joe. Tomorrow. Maybe what'd happened in the bathroom was coloring her opinion, but that suddenly sounded as nerve-wracking as facing a gunman.

''The ceremony's scheduled for noon,'' Joe explained, handing her the paper. ''The plan is for us to have officers and the SWAT team stake out every building around the church. We're hoping to catch the sniper before either of us get near anything resembling an aisle.''

''That's something worth hoping for,'' she mumbled, going over the mission summary.

''Of course, we'll be armed and wearing bullet-proof vests just in case he manages to get through.''

Of course. ''Sounds like you've covered the primary bases. Well, except for maybe clothes. Do we need anything special to wear?''

A wedding dress, for example?

''Brayden's taking care of that. He knew your size,'' Joe clarified when she stared at him.

''Better him than Garrett, I guess. I'd end up wearing pajamas to the church if you put him in charge of wardrobe.''

He reached out and touched her cheek. A quick, nonsexual tap. ''Are you okay?''

''Of course.'' She rubbed her arm in a *see?* gesture. ''It really is just a scratch.''

''I wasn't talking about your arm.''

''Oh. That.'' It seemed a good time to stare at the floor. The ceiling. Or anything other than Joe. ''That's the problem with the morning after. Things seem, well, awkward.''

''Which is why I should have backed away.''

Heck. She hadn't meant to put this all on his shoulders. ''I heard recently that in some cultures a comment like that could be considered heresy. You're not a supreme being, Joe, and don't worry—what happened between us won't affect the job.''

She hoped.

But she kept that inkling of doubt to herself.

"We're both consenting adults," Katelyn continued. "Besides, we didn't even fully sleep together. It was just…lust." There, that was the word she was looking for. "And now that we've taken the edge off, so to speak, everything should be fine."

Mercy, she was babbling.

And lying.

Really lying.

That episode hadn't taken the edge off anything. It'd just made her aware of how hot Joe could get her and how masterfully he could satisfy that heat—all without fully having sex with her.

"Are you finished?" he asked.

She nodded.

And Joe stole her breath by leaning forward and kissing her.

It was nothing like the frenzied lip lock at the apartment. It was gentle. Comforting. Easy.

So easy.

It seemed as if her bones turned to liquid. But that only made it more memorable.

"Sergeant Rico?" she heard someone say. "Sorry to interrupt."

Katelyn glanced at the door, fearing who might be there. It was Detective Dawn Davidson, who'd done the initial interrogation with Dr. Kent. Thankfully, the woman looked away while Katelyn broke the kiss. Not that it would diffuse much of anything. By afternoon, the rumor mill would have something savory to nibble on.

"Here's that info you requested. And the chief wants to see you right away." Dawn handed Joe the folder and quickly excused herself.

The chief's request would have been alarming enough news without the "right away" part. It was probably about the investigation into the favoritism allegations.

Oh, to be a fly on the wall.

Despite the command from the highest ranking man in the building, Joe didn't leave. He did, however, let her fully slip out of his embrace so he could open the folder.

"I asked the techs to tap into Perfect Match's files and give me a list of all of Fiona Shipley's dream matches, plus the matches of the murdered couple." He handed her half the pages. "Look through those."

It was a good task to eliminate any residual effects of that kiss, and the events of the night before. They were Fiona's files, and they were sizable. Twelve of twenty-three pages. Of course, she was a frequent customer so the high volume wasn't that surprising.

Katelyn skimmed through the names to see if anything popped out at her. One did. "Raul Hernandez," she read aloud. "But we already knew about him."

And he was very much dead.

"Kirk Masterson," Joe announced. "The second groom. Fiona's high on his list. Third, in fact."

Pleased that the pieces might be falling into place, Katelyn turned another page, and her attention immediately landed on a name near the middle. "Bingo. She was a match with Brad Garcia, our latest victim."

Finally!

But her *finally* wasn't much of a celebration. Joe checked his watch. "There was no answer when I called that number Fiona gave me so I passed it on to the tech guys so they could check it out. If it holds, I'll try to set up a meeting with her this afternoon. Maybe we can finish this today so we won't even need the ceremony."

"Yes, maybe." And then she remembered Joe's *other* appointment. "After your meeting with the chief, of course."

"Of course."

As if it were the most natural thing in the world, he gave her hand a gentle squeeze and walked out, leaving her with a thousands questions and not many answers. Too bad a lot of those questions centered around Joe and the fact that he was setting a scenario to put himself in danger.

Which was his job, she reminded herself.

And hers.

A job she needed to focus on if she wanted them both to walk away from this alive. Suddenly, that focus seemed a lot more critical than it ever had.

Katelyn sat down, cleared her mind and began to study Fiona Shipley's file. Maybe somewhere in all those names and information, there would be clues to bring down a killer.

Chapter Twelve

Apparently, right away meant something different to the chief than it did to Joe. He checked his watch—he'd been waiting in the hallway for the man for nearly a half hour. Either something unexpected had come up or else this was some sort of power play to remind Joe who was in charge.

As if he could forget that.

He owed a lot to Chief Mark Ryland. After all, the man had made Joe's transfer to Homicide possible. Ryland had also put tremendous trust in him by asking him to look into allegations regarding a fellow officer.

Well, maybe it was trust.

And maybe it was just something as simple as Ryland not wanting to make the investigation official unless he knew for certain there were improprieties. Or maybe he thought Joe would be relentless in getting to the truth. In doing so, however, Ryland had pitted him against not just Brayden but the entire O'Malley clan—including Katelyn.

Yet, it hadn't kept them apart.

Of course, probably nothing short of critical injury or death could have done that. There were times, like now, when Joe felt as if he were in the path of a speeding train, and there was nothing he could do to stop it.

Nothing he *wanted* to do to stop it.

Talk about confusing. They had a killer to catch, and his every other thought was of the redhead he'd left in the conference room. She deserved better than that and so did the victims.

"Bad morning?" he heard someone ask.

Not the chief. Brayden. He was coming down the hall directly toward Joe. And he wasn't alone. He had a big white box in one arm and a little boy squirming under the other. An O'Malley clone. He looked to be two or three and was a miniature version of Brayden.

"I've had easier," Joe answered. Something told him this one wasn't going to get much better. "Is this your son?"

"Yes. My mother came by to drop off something for Katelyn so she brought him with her. Colton, this is Sergeant Rico."

The child gave a little wave, but he was obviously far more interested in the fake police badge he was playing with than meeting Joe.

"I just heard the latest victims pulled through," Brayden commented, putting the boy down. Colton didn't waste any time exploring the fake moss in an equally fake plant. "Good news."

"Definitely. Maybe we'll be able to get something from them when they're out of recovery."

"Too bad though we haven't been able to locate Fiona Shipley. She hasn't returned to her apartment or the mental health facility, and that number she gave you was a fake. It's for some shop down on Commerce Street."

Well, so much for the woman hitting on him. Katelyn had been wrong about that. Fiona had probably been trying to make Merrick jealous. Or else maybe she was suspicious and had just wanted to get Joe off her back.

"We'll keep looking for her," Brayden continued. "But if you're still able to meet with Merrick this afternoon, maybe you can talk him into giving you info about where to contact her."

Joe nodded, not really hopeful about that. "We're definitely meeting with Merrick. In fact, we'll leave just as soon as I'm done here." Merrick probably wouldn't give up the information voluntarily, but maybe they could get it some other way. His mind kept going back to that Rolodex he'd spotted on Merrick's desk. If Merrick and Fiona had had an affair, then her number was probably in there.

It seemed more than a little awkward standing outside the chief's office and having such a civil conversation with the man he was supposed to be investigating. Brayden had to know why Joe was waiting to see Chief Ryland, but he didn't show it. No dark emotion simmering just below the surface. No pon-

dering look. Just shop talk and an occasional fatherly
glance in his son's direction.

"How badly was Katelyn hurt in the shooting?"
Brayden asked.

Okay. So maybe not totally shop talk. That question threw Joe off balance. "Hardly more than a
scratch on her arm. She's fine. How'd you know?"

The corner of his mouth lifted. "Lucky guess."

Right. The man had probably never relied on luck
or guesses in his entire life.

Brayden did a no-no motion with his index finger
when his son started to remove a flyer from the bul-
letin board. The child promptly obeyed and moved on
to a hands-on examination of the carpet.

"If you're waiting for my permission to discipline
Katelyn for not following procedure about an injury,"
Brayden told him, "the wait's unnecessary. You're
her boss."

"Believe me, I haven't forgotten that." Well,
maybe he had while they were in that bathroom. Joe
shook his head. "No disciplinary action will be required. Not unless you want to aim it at me. I didn't
report her injury even after she...informed me of it."

"Then you must have believed it wouldn't have an
impact on this assignment."

"She convinced me that it wouldn't," Joe said,
rather than lie to the man.

Brayden grunted. Not an ordinary grunt. But one
to indicate he was deep in thought about something.
"That day in my office, you said something about
Katelyn coloring outside the lines."

Joe winced, recalling the words in perfect detail. "I meant—"

"She does. So does Garrett. It drives me nuts, but I swear they can sort through things that look like a junk pile to me. Like zooming in on Perfect Match after only one shooting. You managed to do that, too, but you used department resources. Katelyn didn't, because she worked on it while off-duty. Added to that, she was also dealing with the grief from her friend's murder. Yet, I believe she got to the right place about the same time you did?"

"She did." Joe smiled, but he made sure it didn't stay on his face too long. In this case being proud of her probably wasn't a good thing to display. "Is there advice somewhere in that?"

"There is. If it comes down to a situation where someone negates the rules, trust Katelyn."

Joe met him eye-to-eye and nodded. "With my life."

And it wasn't something he had to think about.

Nor was it a question.

Brayden gave him a pat on the back and turned to leave.

"What—no veiled threats about not hurting her?" Joe asked, certain that he deserved such threats. Heck, they might even make him feel less guilty.

Joe felt Colton tugging on his pant leg, looked down, and the boy flashed the fake badge at him. "Know what a frisk is?" Except instead of frisk, it was *fisk*. Joe winked at the kid, ruffled his hair and assured him that he did.

"That's something my brother taught him," Brayden explained, obviously not too pleased about it. He passed the box to Joe so he could scoop up his son in his arms. "And as for your relationship with my sister, Katelyn can take care of herself. I'm more concerned about you than her."

"Me?"

"Katelyn feels she has to work twice as hard and twice as long to prove herself. Added to that, she's not just married to the badge, she's in love with it. And she won't give that up for you or any other man."

Not exactly a newsflash. Joe had known and admired that about her from day one. "I wouldn't even think of asking her to give it up."

Brayden stared at him a moment, and Joe felt as if the man were sizing him up. Probably was. "It'll be interesting to watch."

"Know what interrogation is?" That from Colton. Except it was *terrogation*.

"I know." In fact, Joe thought he might be in the middle of one. A subtle one, where the lieutenant was getting him to ask the questions and then provide the answers, as well.

"What'll be interesting to watch?" Joe directed at Brayden.

"How Katelyn deals with you."

Joe got the feeling Brayden left off a portion of that observation. The flip side to that coin was how the heck was he going to deal with her?

"Wait," Joe said when Brayden started to walk away. "You forgot your box."

"It's for Katelyn. Make sure she gets it."

There it was again. That almost smug look that Brayden aimed his way. Or maybe it was a look of sympathy. If so, Joe needed it.

The door to the chief's office swung open. "Come in, Rico."

Definitely not a polite suggestion, and judging from the way the man gruffly gestured for him to sit down, this wouldn't be a long meeting.

"You're closing in on this sniper case?" Ryland asked, which was probably the only semblance of a greeting Joe would get.

"I hope. Detective O'Malley and I have been undercover on it all week."

"I heard. I'm not sure why Brayden paired you with her for this."

"She was the right person for the assignment," Joe calmly insisted.

Best to leave out the part of *how* she'd become the right person. Besides, it no longer mattered. She was the right person, and that had nothing to do with all the sexual stuff going on between them.

The chief put his elbows on the desk and steepled his fingers. "So what about these allegations?"

Now this was the part where Joe wouldn't leave anything out. "I haven't seen a single incident of favoritism, and I've been in contact with all three of the O'Malleys on this sniper case."

The fingers unsteepled, and the man made a huffing

sound. "Did Katelyn O'Malley have anything to do with helping you out with that conclusion?"

Joe pondered that a moment. Not because he needed time to think about it, but he wanted to put a chokehold on the anger he felt over that question. "No," he said honestly.

"No," the chief repeated. "You sure you're not thinking below the belt on this, Rico?"

Joe tightened that chokehold a little more. "If you're questioning my objectivity—"

"I am. And don't look so damn riled about it. It wouldn't be the first time."

"It would be for me." If that didn't thoroughly tick off the chief, the next thing he had to say probably would. "I'm attracted to Katelyn O'Malley, but I wouldn't lie about allegations because of my feelings for her. And if you think I'm the kind of man who'd do that, then you need to get someone else to do this investigation."

The chief studied him. Scowled. "I don't want anyone else. You've got a fresh eye since you haven't been here that long. Keep looking. If there's something to find, I want to know about it."

Ryland gave him a dismissal wave, which Joe ignored. Joe got to his feet, but instead of leaving, he stared down at the chief. "Have there even been any legitimate complaints against Lieutenant O'Malley?"

Ryland had already reached for his brown-bag lunch, but that stopped him. "A rumor or two."

"Rumors?" Joe couldn't help it. He cursed, and he

didn't keep it under his breath. "And you're willing to put his career at risk for rumors?"

With his scowl tightening, Ryland snatched his lunch bag and dumped out the contents. He rifled through, found a Snickers bar, and ripped off the wrapper. "I'm willing to do whatever it takes to make sure morale stays high."

"That's the wrong way to go about it, sir." Joe's hands went on his hips. "I'll give you my final report when I'm finished with the sniper case, but there won't be anything in it that I haven't already said to you right here, right now."

And with that, Joe walked out, no doubt leaving any chance of his promotion behind in the chief's office.

Chapter Thirteen

Katelyn had braced herself for just about anything to happen during their meeting with Addison Merrick. But what she hadn't anticipated was that things would get *interesting* before they even reached Perfect Match.

She stared in the side mirror, her heart rate automatically kicking up a few notches.

"You see it?" she asked Joe.

"Yes." He continued to drive, but like her, he was keeping an eye on the rearview mirror. "A black BMW."

"That's the one." At the moment it was three cars back, but it'd stayed close enough behind them since they left the parking lot of the apartment. "Did you happen to notice it when we got back from headquarters?"

"No. You?"

She shook her head. And if it'd been there, Katelyn almost certainly would have seen it. That's exactly the sort of flag that she'd been looking for. If the sniper was truly suspicious, then in all likelihood he or she would try to follow them.

And perhaps even try to kill them again.

"I can't read the license," Katelyn informed him. "How about you."

"Not yet, but it's Texas plates." Joe took the last turn toward Perfect Match.

So did the other car.

"Maybe it's Merrick?" she suggested.

"It's possible."

After all, Joe had called the man an hour ago and had asked him to meet them at Perfect Match, so it wasn't so much of a coincidence that they'd arrive at the same time.

But this just didn't feel like a coincidence.

She squinted against the sun and tried to get a glimpse of the driver of the BMW. However, in this case, the late morning sun was a serious hindrance. It glinted off the other car's windshield, making it impossible for Katelyn to see who was following them.

"The windows are bullet resistant," Joe reminded her. "We'll park and stay put to see what our visitor does."

It was a good plan, if the sit and wait didn't take too long. They still needed to work on contacting Fiona Shipley, and that wouldn't happen if they had to play games with the driver of that BMW.

Joe pulled into a parking space directly in front of the agency. The spots normally filled with cars were practically empty. The closed sign on the door likely had a lot to do with that, and the fact that there'd been a recent shooting in the area.

The BMW passed them and parked behind one of the few vehicles at the far end of the block.

Katelyn tried to see through the sunny glare, but she could only make out a shadowy figure. She slid her hand over her weapon. And waited.

Mercy, the waiting was the hardest part.

A stir of movement to her right caused her to glance in that direction. Merrick opened the front door and motioned for them to come in.

"Well, whoever's watching us, it's not Merrick," she mumbled. That left Fiona, Donovan or even Dr. Kent. Of course, it also left any other sicko they might not have considered. Some other client or rejected lover with an attitude problem. Still, Katelyn didn't think they were off the mark with their short list of suspects. It was more than likely one of those four. She just didn't know how to go about proving which one.

Merrick motioned again. This time, it wasn't so friendly. It was definitely a hurry-up signal. But Katelyn was fairly sure that no matter how frantic the man's signals got, Joe wouldn't let either of them step out of the car with that BMW still lurking about.

With a squeal of tires, the BMW backed up just enough so it could circle around to a side street, and it sped away.

"Should we pursue?" she asked Joe.

"No. Let's stick with the plan. If it follows us

when we come out, we'll try to run the plates to see who's interested in what we're doing.''

She smiled at Merrick and held up her index finger in a one-minute gesture. The man ducked back inside. That didn't mean, however, that he wouldn't be spying on them from the window.

''This'll be a quick in and out,'' Joe said, going over the rules. ''We tell Merrick about the wedding being set for tomorrow and see if he'll give us Fiona's number under the guise of us inviting her to the ceremony. And that's it. Those two things, and we get out of there.''

While he checked his weapon, Katelyn stared at the building that housed Perfect Match. But not just the building. The alley up the street where someone had tried to gun them down. Yes. She definitely understood Joe's insistence of a quick in and out. Looking at that spot made her arm ache, and it didn't do much for the rest of her, either.

''What if Merrick won't tell us how to get in touch with Fiona?'' she asked.

He shrugged. ''The rules still apply here.''

Not exactly the answer she wanted to hear. ''I swear I'm going to needlepoint that on a pillow.''

''No detours, Katelyn. No shortcuts.'' That was as much of an order as it was a warning, and void of sarcasm or humor. ''This isn't the time to try to bring down a killer. We've got a plan set in motion to do that.''

''Okay, okay. It just makes me crazy to think of this piece of slime walking around free while we've got two people dead and two more seriously wounded.''

''I know, and we'll get the person responsible.''

That soothed her a little, but not nearly enough. Even though her brain told her the shootings weren't her fault, there was still the sickening feeling that she should have been able to stop it. People were hurt because she'd failed. No words, even those coming from Joe, could ease that.

Worse, that dread had spread to other areas.

She caught his arm when he started to open the door. Unfortunately, she hadn't really thought beyond that. Well, she had, but Katelyn hadn't quite figured out how to convey the things she was feeling. ''Let me just blurt this out because I don't think I can make it sound palatable. You won't take any unnecessary risks, right?''

He angled his head to stare at her. ''What's this all about?''

''I've already said it won't make sense. There's just this…fear. There, I've said it. I'm afraid. Not for me, but for you. And that's so stupid because you're a cop.''

Joe did something with his mouth. Not really a gape but his version of it. ''You're worried about me?''

Disgusted with herself, she nodded. She would never believe anyone who told her that sex didn't change things between a man and a woman. Except she'd had sex with other men, and it *hadn't* changed things. Not like this, anyway.

Nothing had ever changed things like this.

He slid his arm around her and pulled her to him. "I can take care of myself, Katelyn. You can take care of yourself. And when all else fails, we both make great backups."

"It's that fail part that's giving me some trouble here. It can't happen, okay?"

He nodded. "Anything else before we go in there?"

Oh, she knew what he was getting at. His meeting with the chief. It was a bit of unfinished business that would have to remain unfinished a little longer. "Nothing else." Katelyn took a deep breath. "Let's do this."

She made yet another mental check of her weapons and communicator as they stepped from the car. Joe had parked close enough so they only had a few steps before they made it to the door. Moving straight into their lovers' pose, they latched on to each other.

"Kate, Joe," Merrick greeted, opening the door and motioning for them to come in. "I was surprised to get your call. I figured all our clients had been scared off by the latest shooting."

"Oh?" And that was all Joe said. All in all, it was a good leading question.

"You haven't heard?" Merrick shook his head. "It's been all over the news. There was another couple injured last night by this so-called Veiled Sniper. Unfortunately, they were former clients."

Joe nodded. Katelyn mumbled something about

how horrible it all was. She certainly didn't have to fake that part.

Merrick went to the cooler tucked away in the corner and helped himself to not one but two cups of water. While he was there, he pressed some buttons on a wall pad, and music began to play. A heavy, sensual sax that didn't exactly mesh with the adrenaline surging through her.

"If you don't mind, I'd like to make this visit quick," Merrick continued. "The security guard that I hired part-time couldn't come in today. He's sick. So I'd rather not stay around here too long."

"We won't keep you. We just wanted to invite you to the wedding." Joe produced a mock invitation from his pocket. "It's tomorrow. That's short notice, we know, but we'd love for you to be there to celebrate with us."

"And not just you," Katelyn added, making sure she sounded happy and not suspicious. "We want Bruce Donovan and all the other nice people we've met here to come, as well." She snapped her fingers. "Including Fiona Shipley. I'm not sure if you know her, but Joe and she chatted."

Merrick's smile faded, and he gripped the invitation with far more force than necessary.

"Fiona was so friendly," Joe added when Merrick didn't say anything. "But I don't know how to get in touch with her. I thought maybe you'd have her number so we could call her?"

"Sorry. I'm not allowed to give out that kind of information. Tell you what though—if I see Fiona,

I'll tell her. And I'll make sure Bruce gets the word, too. This might be just what we need to lighten the mood around here.'' He studied the invitation. ''You're not worried though? I mean, because of these other shootings.''

It was on the tip of Katelyn's tongue to lie, but the door behind them flew open. Only because she saw Joe reach for his gun, she forced herself not to go for hers. Not immediately anyway. That way, if it were some legitimate visitor, it wouldn't totally blow their cover for both of them to draw. One gun they could justify. Maybe.

Instead, Katelyn kept her attention firmly on Merrick in case he planned to use this as some kind of diversion to try to kill them. Merrick's eyes widened when he caught sight of Joe's weapon.

Dr. Allen Kent stepped in.

No widening of his eyes. But he did stop. He glanced at the gun. Joe. Her. And then at Merrick.

''What's going on here?'' Kent demanded. ''Is this some kind of robbery?''

Joe didn't exactly relax. Nor did he lower his gun. ''No robbery.''

It was obviously time for damage control. ''We're a little shaken.'' Katelyn's voice quivered slightly, which although unplanned contributed to the proof that the *shaken* part wasn't all facade. She caught Joe's wrist and lowered his hand, and his weapon, to his side. ''It's the shootings.''

Kent nodded. ''I heard. In fact, the cops came by to see me this morning.'' He fired a glare at Merrick.

"They asked for an alibi. Can you believe that? They wanted me to provide an alibi. I live alone for Christ's sake. Am I supposed to have friends sleep over just so I won't be accused of some crime?"

"I think they're questioning anyone associated with Perfect Match," Katelyn provided. "Joe and I had to go in this morning, as well."

Kent glanced at her again, but this time it didn't stay a glance. He combed his gaze over her from head to toe. "Don't I know you?"

Oh, mercy.

That was not what she wanted to hear right now. Beside her, she felt Joe's arm stiffen. He was no doubt thinking the same thing she was. That maybe Kent had somehow connected her to Gail after all. If so, they were in trouble.

Forcing herself to remain calm, Katelyn pretended to study his face. "Maybe we've met. I've been here a couple of times. In fact, my fiancé and I met right here at Perfect Match." For good measure she thrust out her hand so he could see the engagement ring.

"Very nice," he said without even looking at it.

"We're here to invite Addison to the wedding," Joe explained. "And Fiona Shipley."

At first, she was surprised that Joe had included the woman's name, but she soon realized it was a smart thing to do.

Kent's mouth eased into a sarcastic smile. "Trust me, you don't want to invite Fiona. She's not exactly wedding guest material."

"You know her?" Joe asked.

But the answer didn't come from Kent, but from Merrick after he had shared a glance with Kent. "We both know her. I'm afraid Fiona sometimes has trouble distinguishing reality from fantasy. She's no longer a client here. That's the main reason I had security here the night of the icebreaker. Fiona has a tendency to show up uninvited."

"She seemed nice enough when I spoke to her," Joe insisted. "And I told her I'd invite her to the wedding. I'd really like to get in touch with her."

There was a long silence, and Katelyn didn't even try to fill it in with useless chitchat. Something unspoken passed between Kent and Merrick.

"I'll get the number for you," Merrick announced.

He turned and went down the hall, presumably to his office. Katelyn didn't take any chances. She positioned herself so that Joe would be able to return fire if the man came back not with an address but with a gun.

Kent picked up a pen and a sheet of note paper from the receptionist's desk. He wrote something down and then handed the paper to Joe. "That's Fiona's cell phone number. I doubt Addison has it. And don't worry. I'm not violating any doctor-patient confidentiality since I've never seen Fiona professionally. The truth is, we met here one evening and exchanged numbers. It didn't work out between us, but she continues to call dozens of times each day."

Joe stuffed the piece of paper into his pocket. "Thanks."

"I'm not doing you any favors," Kent insisted.

"The truth is I'm hoping that if the two of you offer Fiona friendship, it'll be a more positive direction for her."

"And maybe she'll stop calling you?" Joe tossed back.

A little flash of anger danced through Kent's eyes before he smiled. "That, too."

Merrick returned and handed Joe a piece of paper as well, but when Katelyn glanced at the number, she realized it wasn't the same one Kent had given them. Maybe one of them would pan out.

"Now, if you'll excuse us," Kent said, taking Merrick's arm. "Addison and I have some things to discuss in private. Good luck with your wedding plans."

Joe and Katelyn started for the door, but he stopped as soon as the two men disappeared into the hall.

"You think Kent drives a black BMW?" Katelyn whispered over the music.

"We'll know soon enough."

He glanced at the corridor on the other side of the room, and she knew what he was thinking. On the pretense of going to the ladies' room, she'd used that corridor to circle around the back of the building so she could get to Merrick's office.

"I can pretend to go to the bathroom," Katelyn suggested. "I might be able to hear what they're discussing."

Joe obviously thought about it but then shook his head. "It's too risky."

"Not if you wander over toward that hall so you could keep an eye on Merrick's office. That way, you can alert me if they come out. And if they're suspicious, you can just say you're waiting for me to get out of the ladies' room. In the meantime, you can call Fiona and check on vehicles registered to Dr. Kent.''

''It's still risky.''

''So is waiting for the sniper to strike again. I'm betting those two know something.''

''Yeah.'' And he repeated it before he angled his eyes in her direction. ''Tell me you can take care of yourself.''

Katelyn smiled. Not from joy, exactly. But from the weirdness of the moment. She'd succeeded in winning him over to her impromptu plan, but it didn't exactly leave her feeling victorious. ''I'll be careful. You do the same. I'll keep my communicator on in case you need me.''

Katelyn gave him one last look, one that she hoped calmed his concerns. But there was nothing calm about what she was feeling.

She drew her weapon, shielding it against her leg and started down the corridor past offices on both sides, the restrooms and then into the back bend of the U-shaped network of hallways. Thankfully, there weren't any employees or clients lingering around.

But had someone turned up the music? The sensual sound of the sax no longer seemed so sensual. It just seemed loud. Overpowering, actually. Or maybe it was because the beat now matched the heartbeat drumming in her ears.

''Everything okay?'' Katelyn whispered into her communicator.

"They haven't come out," Joe let her know.

She paused at the final section of the hall that was only about ten yards from Merrick's office and took a quick look around the corner. She caught a glimpse of Joe at the end of the hall before she ducked back.

"Great," she mumbled under her breath.

Even with the music, she should have heard shouting or even a normal conversation between Merrick and Kent. Kent had certainly done some shouting the last time he was there. It was Murphy's Law that he wouldn't cooperate in the volume department today. That meant she needed to get closer.

It wasn't an actual sound that alerted her, but something did. Something that sent her spinning to the side.

Everything happened fast.

Too fast for her to go on the offensive. The man came out from one of the rooms and rammed his body against hers, slamming her against the wall. Her injured arm hit first, and the pain was immediate and searing. Katelyn saw stars.

Another body slam. He threw the full force of his weight right into her. The impact knocked the breath out of her, and while she was fighting to pull air into her lungs, Katelyn got a good look at her attacker's face.

It was Bruce Donovan.

He clamped his hand around the front of her throat. But not to try to choke her, she soon learned. He ripped the communicator from beneath her collar.

"I knew there was something wrong about you," he snarled. "Who the hell are you?"

Katelyn knew she had to act fast. Joe was no doubt already on his way, and she didn't want him walking in on this, especially since he'd have to go past Merrick and Kent first. This was not the time for a gun battle.

Ignoring the pain in her arm and lungs, Katelyn brought up her leg, and using as much force as she could marshal, she kneed Donovan in the groin. He howled in pain and immediately released the grip he had on her.

She didn't stop there.

Katelyn grabbed his forearm and slung him forward so that he was the one against the wall. Face-first. A quick pat down, and she discovered he wasn't armed.

"Kate?" she heard Joe call out.

But that wasn't all she heard. She heard footsteps coming from the other direction, as well. They were all converging toward her.

She kept her forearm pressed against Donovan's back and snatched up her gun. That couple of moments must have given him his second wind because he tried to come at her again. He whirled around, his fist ready to bash her right in the face.

"Kate!" Joe yelled.

She was vaguely aware of Joe rounding the corner. But just vaguely. Thankfully, he didn't dive in and pull a knight-in-shining-armor maneuver. He stayed back and let her do her job.

Katelyn ducked.

Donovan's attempted jab breezed past her head, and in the same motion, she delivered a snap kick to his stomach. She didn't give him a chance to get a second wind. Recoiling, she pivoted and landed another kicking blow to the back of his legs. Donovan went down to the floor, hard, gasping for breath.

It took everything inside her not to slam him right back against that wall and read him his rights. But that wasn't a smart thing to do. There was still a chance that Joe and she could keep their cover intact. If not, then they were in trouble because they were in the same building with three of their four murder suspects.

Doing some light gasping of her own, Katelyn glanced around to get her bearings. Joe was on one side, his weapon drawn. On the other side were Dr. Kent and Merrick. They stood there in stunned silence.

"Are you okay?" Joe asked. The muscles in his jaw had turned to iron. He looked ready to rip Donovan limb from limb.

Katelyn nodded. "He tried to assault me. He wasn't successful." And after delivering that news to Joe, she made certain she added a stern look that hopefully would convince him to stay in cover. "Guess all that self-defense training finally came in handy."

"She's got a gun," Donovan managed to say. He struggled to get to his feet. Staggered. And dropped back to his knees.

Katelyn angled her body so she could deliver another snap kick if necessary. "Good thing too, huh? A woman never knows when she'll need a gun."

Merrick came closer. "What's going on here?" Maybe the adrenaline was clouding her senses, but Katelyn couldn't tell if he was concerned for her, or for Donovan.

"I think she's the sniper," Donovan snarled.

Oh, great.

It was either fast thinking on his part to save his butt, or else he genuinely believed that. If it was the latter, it would explain why he'd come after her in the first place. But Katelyn wasn't about to stake her life on anything that Donovan said. Even if he wasn't the sniper, the man was slime.

"She's wearing some kind of wire." Donovan leaned into the wall so he could stand. Not easily. However, he eventually got to his feet.

"This?" Katelyn made a point of showing both Merrick and Kent her communicator when she picked it up from the floor. "It's not a wire. It's a walkie-talkie, a way for Joe and me to stay in touch when we can't be together. Call me overly devoted, but I like being able to talk with the man I love 24/7."

Joe gave a confirming nod, and turned back his collar so they could see his communicator, as well.

There were several tense seconds, several uncomfortable glances between Kent and Merrick before Merrick finally moved and took Bruce's arm. "Let's discuss this in my office."

"Wait," Donovan said, holding his ground. He

fired a nasty glare at her. "If she's not the sniper, then what the hell was she doing sneaking around back here?"

"I was looking for the bathroom," Katelyn quickly provided. No glare for her. She made sure she looked upset, which wasn't that difficult considering what had just gone down. Her heart was still racing from the fight.

More tense moments. Joe walked closer to stand right by her side. Maybe for comfort. Or maybe he just wanted to be in a better position to fire if it came down to that.

"I'm sorry this happened, Kate," Merrick finally said. "I hope you'll accept my apology." And he didn't just say it, either. He *appeared* to be sorry. Of course, that sincerity could have been for all the wrong reasons. "Now, if you'll excuse me, I need to talk with Bruce in private. I trust the two of you can see yourselves out."

Yes, they could do that, but it meant turning their backs on at least one potential killer. Still, leaving was about the only way to maintain their cover. Joe obviously felt the same. He didn't reholster his gun, nor did he take her arm—a move that would have hampered her ability to return fire. However, he did gesture with his head for them to get moving.

Katelyn complied. But she glanced over her shoulder. And neither of them stopped glancing until they were out of the building and in the car.

Joe started the engine and drove away. He made it a full block before he slid his arm around her and pulled her to him. The muscles in his body were still rock-hard, and that jaw told her that he was far from winning the battle with adrenaline.

"Thanks for not jumping in fists first back there when you saw me with Donovan."

It seemed as if several times he changed his mind about what to say. "You didn't appear to need me to jump in."

Oh, that cost him. The words were right. So was the sentiment. However, he'd not said it easily. "I didn't, but Garrett forgets that sometimes."

"I can see why." That was all he said for the next couple of seconds. "Just don't expect me to forget it again if Donovan comes near you."

Chapter Fourteen

Katelyn O'Malley slept the same way she did everything else in life—thoroughly.

At first, she'd balked at his idea of resting while they waited for Fiona to return his call, but once Joe had coaxed her into lying down on the sofa, she'd fallen asleep within minutes. He even managed to take a nap in the adjacent chair. Since they'd gotten virtually no sleep the night before, it was a necessity. He wanted to be as alert as possible for the meeting with Fiona.

And for anything else they might face today.

A lot of things had gone wrong at Perfect Match, and that was an understatement. It could have been much worse. When Donovan came after Katelyn, she'd fought him off, subdued him—all without blowing her cover.

That pissed Joe off.

Katelyn can take care of herself, Brayden had told him. It was true. She could. That didn't mean, however, that she couldn't be hurt. It sure as heck didn't mean she was invincible.

Rather than identify herself to Donovan as a police officer, read the scum his rights and/or take him down the hard way, she'd risked everything. Part of him, the cop part, greatly admired her devotion to duty. But the rest of him just wanted to grab her by the shoulders, give her a hard shake and yell at her for taking chances like that with her life.

Not that yelling would do any good, but at least then she'd know...

...what?

Joe stopped and brooded over that for a moment.

And he decided it wouldn't be a good idea to finish that thought.

He stood, brushed a loose strand of hair from her face and forced his attention away from her mouth—which somehow managed to look both innocent and sensual at the same time. He went into the bathroom so he could call headquarters.

He reached Detective Davidson who in turn transferred his call to Garrett, who'd apparently been doing the trace on the vehicle that'd followed them. Not exactly a duty in Garrett's job description. Well, not unless the case had strayed over into Special Investigations.

"Please tell me you volunteered for this extra work, Sergeant O'Malley," Joe commented.

"What can I say? I'm a glutton for cyber searches," he said sarcastically, but the sarcastic tone quickly faded. "Davidson's working on the wedding details so I figured I'd pitch in and do my part."

In this case, his part was over and above. "Thanks."

"Let's just say you owe me and leave it at that." He didn't give Joe a chance to ask him to elaborate. "Okay, here goes. There are hundreds of black BMWs registered to owners who live in the area. Guess that's not a surprise. So I did some cross-referencing with your suspects and got lucky. One of them has a late model black BMW."

"Bruce Donovan," Joe provided.

"You got it. I guess that's not a surprise either?"

"Not really. He came after Katelyn while we were visiting Merrick."

There was a short pause. "Define *came after Katelyn*."

Joe hoped this sounded better aloud, but he wasn't counting on it. "Donovan claimed he thought she was the sniper so he tried to *apprehend* her."

Another pause, a long one, and Joe didn't need to see the man's expression to know that Garrett was not happy with this latest development. "She wasn't hurt?"

"No." But the images of her pulverizing Donovan didn't do much to ease that tight fist around his heart. If she hadn't ducked, if she'd been just an inch or two out of position to deliver those snap kicks, if the man had been a fraction faster, then...

There it was again.

Those running commentaries in his head that he

really didn't want to finish. But these wouldn't back off. The truth was, even if all those other things had happened, she would have no doubt found a way to kick Donovan's butt. Katelyn wouldn't have given up.

That last part didn't exactly make him feel better, either.

"She handled Donovan on her own?" Garrett asked.

"Yeah." Joe braced himself for Garrett's lecture that would no doubt contain a lot of profanity and a thorough dressing down for not protecting his sister.

A lecture that didn't come.

"She wouldn't have *appreciated* the help anyway," Garrett grumbled.

"That was my guess, too."

Now there was some profanity, but it wasn't aimed at Joe. "It doesn't make it any easier to watch."

Joe settled for a "No."

The conversation might have lacked quantity, but at the end of the next pause, Joe felt as if he'd reached some sort of truce with Katelyn's brother. It was a truce he hadn't even realized he wanted until it happened.

"So the next step is to speak to Fiona Shipley?" Garrett asked, getting them back into a comfort zone they both understood—the job.

"I'm waiting for her to return my call now." He checked his watch. That wait was now on its third hour. "I got her cell number from Dr. Kent and left her a message."

"Kent, huh? That's an interesting source for that particular bit of info."

Yes, Joe thought so, as well. "Sometimes, Garrett, I wonder if all four of them aren't in on it. Like some conspiracy to cover up something that got botched either at Perfect Match or Kent's office. They just keep coiling and winding around each other like a nest of vipers."

If he thought for one minute it would stop the sniper, Joe would haul all of them in and lock them up for as long as possible. Without physical evidence to connect them to the crimes, however, that lockup wouldn't last long. They'd lawyer up and be out before the ink dried on the paperwork.

There was a tap at the door, and he opened it to find Katelyn standing there. "Hello, Garrett," she said, leaning closer to the phone. "Thin walls," she added when Joe just looked at her.

"Thanks for the BMW info," he told Garrett. "I'll let you know how it goes with Fiona."

"*If* it goes," Katelyn corrected when he hung up.

"It'll go." But Joe was beginning to doubt it himself. If she didn't call soon, they'd have to look for her. Fiona was the one player in all of this that they hadn't had a real chance to question. Joe had absolutely no proof, but the feeling in his gut told him that she had information that could help them get a handle on this case.

Or else she was the killer.

But either way, he needed to talk to her. With the wedding only a day away, that talk had to come soon.

Joe watched as Katelyn peeled off her jacket, and in the process he felt his body rev up for all sorts of carnal possibilities. A glimpse of her lacy bra egged those possibilities on even more. But they came to a quick crash and burn when she reached for the first aid kit.

"Another *scratch?*" he asked. Joe tried to keep emotion out of his voice, but the battle was lost before he opened his mouth.

Katelyn shook her head. "Same one."

She quickly tossed the old bandage in the trash. It wasn't so fast that Joe didn't see the fresh blood.

"That fight with Donovan," he mumbled.

Hell.

"It's no big deal." She wiped the wound with antiseptic, hissed out a breath at the inevitable sting and put on a fresh bandage. "I just didn't want to get any blood on the wedding dress when I try it on to make sure it fits."

He was glad Garrett wasn't around to hear that one. Heck, he didn't even want to hear it, so he focused on the second part of her oh-so-casual comment that wasn't anywhere in the realm of being casual. "What wedding dress?"

She turned and went into the bedroom. "It was in that box Brayden gave you."

And now it was on the bed. The corner of the large rectangular box was lifted slightly, and Joe caught a glimpse of ivory silk.

"Look the other way," she instructed. "I'm about to strip down to my underwear."

His body revved up again. "Modest?" Hard to be-lieve, especially since they had a go at each other in the bathroom the night before.

"No. Considering you've already seen me naked, modesty would be pointless. I just don't want you looking for any bruises that Donovan might have left on me."

Another immediate halt on the revving. With lots of effort, he could ignore the blood comment but not that one. "Damn it, Katelyn, did he hurt you?"

"No, but he likely bruised me when he slammed me against the wall." She discarded her top on the bed and unzipped her skirt. "Don't worry, I'm posi-tive his bumps and bruises outnumber mine, and I seriously doubt he'll be able to sit for a while."

That didn't help one bit. "This isn't a contest. Or a joking matter."

Huffing, she sat down on the edge of the bed and pulled the dress from the box. But her attention wasn't on the heap of silk, lace and seed pearls. Her eyes lifted to connect with his. "Don't you think I know that? Care to guess what was going through my mind while I was ramming my knee into Donovan's reproductive organs? I was thinking, no, *worrying* about you. I was afraid if you came in with guns blazing and fists flying, you'd get hurt."

"Guns blazing and fists flying?" Joe was on the verge of telling her that those things would have never happened. *Never.* But it was too uncomfortably close to a lie. The truth was he'd considered blazing guns, flying fists and any other extreme force when he saw Donovan swing that punch at Katelyn.

"Great," she mumbled. "Brayden didn't pick this out. This is my mother's dress."

It took Joe a moment to pound down the anger he was still feeling over those possible bruises, but from the groan that Katelyn made, it was obvious they had another problem to deal with first.

"It's a message," she went on. "Like the one in that scene from *The Godfather* when they sent the fish wrapped up in the newspaper."

Joe shook his head, sure he'd missed something. "I don't make the connection."

"It's my mother's way of saying 'I know you won't do anything that'll result in bullet holes or bloodstains on this wedding dress since it's practically a family heirloom." Katelyn gave a heavy sigh. "She's worried about me.'"

"Well, that makes two of us."

Except he knew it wasn't limited to such a small number. There was Brayden, Garrett and probably a whole multitude of other O'Malleys. Joe would have loved to say that their concern wasn't warranted. But it was. In less than twenty-four hours, the undercover assignment would take them in the direction of the church—and the sniper.

He was still in knots about that when he felt her fingertip skim over his stomach. His bare stomach. "Your button's undone," she said, remedying that for him. Well, she remedied it after another brush of her fingertip.

"You're trying to distract me from those possible bruises," he let her know.

"Yes, I am." She smiled, undid the button again and planted a kiss on his stomach. "Is it working?"

He fought to hang on to the anger a little longer, but it slipped away. "Like a charm." And because the distraction felt so damn good, he slid his finger over the lacy edge of her bra. White lace. Against her cream-colored skin. Talk about erotic. Of course, it was highly possible it was erotic simply because it was Katelyn's bra, Katelyn's breast. "What can I say—I'm easy."

"You're a lot of things, Sergeant Joseph Luis Rico, but easy isn't one of them. In fact, I'd say you're the hardest thing in my life right now. And no, there are no raunchy hidden meanings in that."

Joe smiled anyway and pushed the thoughts of bruises and snipers aside when she grabbed a handful of his shirt and hauled him onto the bed with her. He landed on top of her, but like the previous night, she quickly did something about that. Katelyn shifted, rolling them both over the soft mattress, and when she'd finished the rolling she was on top, straddling him.

"Control issues?" he asked.

But her mouth was already swooping down on his. Fast. A hungry kiss that left no doubt that she wasn't after conversation. It was next to impossible to argue with that, even though he should be arguing. Instead, he was just thankful he'd picked up some condoms when he'd filled up the car with gas at the nearby convenience store.

Joe reached up, opened the front closure on her bra and had the satisfaction of her breasts spilling out into his hands. She was small. Firm.

Perfect.

He cupped one, then the other and ran his thumbs over her nipples. It was obvious she enjoyed it from the way her mouth opened, and the soft sound of pleasure she made.

Katelyn didn't take the time to savor that pleasure, however. She pulled off her skirt, dragging it up and over her head and flinging it aside. No pause. No hesitation. She went after his belt and zipper. And Joe surprised her, and himself, by catching on to her wrist to stop her.

"Control issues?" he repeated. "Claustrophobia? Is that why you like to be on top?"

She gave him an *all right, here goes* huff. "The missionary stuff is just a little scary for me, okay? It's that whole being passive part."

"Passive?" Sex with Katelyn was anything but passive.

Another flustered huff. And a hesitation. "It just doesn't feel right. Or fair. It's almost no work being on the bottom, but yet I'd still get all the...benefits."

Interesting. She carried her belief in the bedroom that she had to work twice as hard and twice as long to get what she wanted.

As her cue that the conversation was over, she leaned down and went after his neck with a kiss. She didn't stop there. Katelyn slid her hand over the front of his pants, a move that had Joe going from seriously aroused to rock-hard. "But if it's something you want—"

Joe ended that with a kiss of his own. "The only thing I want is you, Katelyn."

That slowed her down. She lifted her head, and her gaze met his. In the depth of those green eyes, there was concern that he was sure was mirrored in his. Concern they might have actually discussed.

If his cell phone hadn't rung.

Cursing, she rolled off him so he could snatch the ringing annoyance that was still clipped to his belt. "Hello," he barked. And this had better be important. Critical, even.

"Joe?" the woman said.

Even with the untimely interruption and his reaction to it, it only took him a split second to realize it was Fiona Shipley. He said the woman's name aloud so that Katelyn would know, as well. She moved closer to him so she could hear the conversation.

There wasn't much to hear.

"I'll meet you at the coffee shop at the intersection of Highway 1604 and San Pedro," Fiona instructed. "You know the place?"

"I'll find it."

"Good. I'll see you in one hour. And Joe? My advice is to watch your back. Someone's been following me. I think it might be this sniper."

And with that, Fiona hung up.

"I GUESS IT WON'T DO any good to remind you this could be a trap?" Katelyn asked.

Joe shook his head, his attention not on her but on driving through the massive parking lot that serviced not just the coffee shop but at least a half dozen other businesses. "What would you do if Merrick, Kent or even, heaven forbid, Donovan called and asked you to meet them?"

It was a cheap—and incredibly effective—way to win an argument.

She'd go, of course. With backup. Which Joe had, since there was no way she'd let him do this alone. That's why Katelyn had worn jeans and a T-shirt and stuffed her hair beneath a Rangers baseball cap. It was as close to a disguise as she could get on such short notice. The plan they'd put together on the drive over was for her to do surveillance from the car and alert him via the communicator if anyone suspicious approached the place.

"What about Fiona's *someone's been following me. I think it might be this sniper* comment?" Katelyn reminded him. "Think it's true?"

"Could be."

And that was all the more reason to stay alert. She didn't want the sniper or anyone else sneaking up on them.

Joe drove slowly past Java Dan's. It wasn't exactly quaint and cozy with the massive floor-to-ceiling windows that fronted the place. Even though there were only about a half dozen customers, with those windows and jammed parking lot, it'd be next to impossible to make sure someone didn't pull out a rifle and start firing right through that glass.

"I'll sit in a booth near the back," Joe commented, obviously addressing her concern before Katelyn could even voice it. Something he did often. It was almost as if they could read each other's minds.

Almost.

The big exception to that was all the personal stuff going on between them. Other than his *the only thing I want is you, Katelyn* comment on the bed, they hadn't talked a lot about, well, their feelings.

She took the blame for that though.

She'd done the majority of the stonewalling, but she wouldn't be able to keep it up. Eventually, they'd be alone. Eventually, the phone wouldn't ring, and they'd get around to having that mind-blowing sex that she'd been fantasizing about. In addition to a thoroughly enjoyable experience, which it would certainly be, it'd create a bond between them that even her surly attitude and devotion to the badge might not be able to break.

Still, that wouldn't stop her.

Whatever was brewing between them wouldn't be put off by her doubts. Or her fears.

Frustrated at her inability to keep her mind on the mission, Katelyn checked the time. Since they'd left not long after Fiona's call, they still had a good fifteen minutes to spare. Well, unless the woman was the always-arrive-early type like Katelyn was. If so, then Ms. Shipley might come walking up at any moment.

She glanced in the vanity mirror to make sure her

too-visible hair hadn't escaped the cap, and while she was tucking and hiding, something occurred to her. "How about this? I'll take one of the booths on the right, facing the window. That way, I can make sure no one comes in unannounced. You take Fiona to a booth on the other side of the shop."

"And what if she recognizes you?" Joe asked.

"That's what outstretched newspapers are for. I'll buy one on my way in. Look," Katelyn added when she saw the hesitancy in his eyes. "This might be the only chance we get to talk to Fiona. She might know something that can help us stop the sniper."

Joe glanced at the coffee shop. At her. And then at those windows. He shook his head. "Don't make me regret this."

Too bad she couldn't promise him that.

Katelyn wished him good luck and got out before he could change his mind. Keeping a vigilant watch and trying to stay inconspicuous, she hurried across the parking lot and into the shop. As planned, she bought a paper and ducked into one of the booths.

And waited.

Joe came in several minutes later, and he took the only booth that was available on the far side of the room. He was visible, but barely. Katelyn had to scrunch herself in the corner to keep him and the windows in sight.

"Equipment check," she whispered into her communicator.

"I hear you," Joe responded.

So the equipment cooperated. Hopefully, everything else would. She hated stakeouts in public places. There were just too many factors she couldn't control.

The door finally swung open, and Fiona walked in. Obviously this was not one of her better appearance days. Dressed all in dark colors, she had her hair pulled back and was wearing a pair of large-lens sunglasses.

"Joe," Fiona greeted.

Katelyn had a nervous moment when the waiter blocked her line of sight, but thankfully Joe and Fiona ordered quickly, and the man moved.

"I guess you know about the other couple who were shot last night?" Katelyn heard Joe ask the woman right away.

Fiona nodded and pulled off her sunglasses. Katelyn carefully examined her expression now that she could see Fiona's eyes. Her attention wasn't on Joe but the windows. Yes. She was definitely watching her back.

"Both survived," Joe continued. "A lot better outcome than the first couple, that's for sure. What were their names? Something like Ralph and Gail?"

"Raul," Fiona corrected. "We dated, briefly."

Joe didn't respond to that right away. He waited until after they had their coffee, and he took a long sip. It was a good strategy. Fiona was obviously uncomfortable with the silence and began to fidget with her sunglasses.

"The police questioned me about the deaths," Joe finally said. "I guess they did the same to you?"

"I've been, uh, unavailable." Fiona glanced out the window again. Katelyn did the same.

A longer pause this time for Joe. "You said something on the phone about being followed?"

"I think it might be the sniper." But then she immediately shook her head. "Or else it's Addison Merrick. That's one of the reasons I agreed to see you. I noticed you've been visiting him a lot—"

"How did you know that?"

A spark of surprise. Followed by more fidgeting. Another glance out the window. A glance that turned into a full stare. Katelyn followed the woman's gaze to see what had captured her attention and saw the black BMW cruise by.

Judas Priest.

"The BMW's back," Katelyn whispered into the communicator. She moved out to the edge of the seat in case she had to use her weapon.

"You were saying something about Addison," Joe prompted Fiona.

She nodded and moistened her lips. "I wondered if he'd said anything to you about me?"

The car turned, circled and came back toward the coffee shop. If it was Donovan, he was either stupid or desperate. But the real question was, what had made him want to follow Fiona?

Or had he actually followed Joe and her?

Of course, there was also the stomach-churning possibility that it wasn't Donovan at all. Maybe Donovan wasn't the only person with access to a black

BMW. Maybe it was Merrick. And maybe Fiona had been right, and it was the sniper following her.

If so, this visit could turn deadly in a hurry.

"Addison's mentioned you a couple of times," Joe told her. Practically a lie, but it seemed to get Fiona's concentration back on him. It also helped her temporary attention deficit when the car darted out of sight again.

"Addison and I started dating after his fiancée broke off their engagement." She moistened her lips again and ran her index finger over her eyebrow. "He was devastated, said he needed me. He even told me that he was in love with me."

"And then what happened?" Joe asked.

She shrugged. "I don't know. I really don't. He changed, said it wasn't right for him to see me since I was a client. He said he didn't want something like that getting back to his father."

Yes. Merrick definitely wouldn't want that. From all accounts, his father wouldn't have approved of anything that might be detrimental to the business.

"Sometimes, I wonder if Addison's the Veiled Sniper," Fiona said softly. "I mean, all three of those grooms were men I once dated."

"Push that button," Katelyn whispered to Joe, knowing he would have probably jumped on it anyway.

But the pushing wasn't even necessary. Fiona continued on her own. "I think Addison needs help."

"Yeah. I've heard he's in therapy with Dr. Kent," Joe answered.

Fiona made a sound. A soft burst of sarcasm that didn't contain any humor. "Now, there's a pair. The sick trying to heal the sick." Her gaze flew to the window again. "I believe Addison's mentally unstable."

The BMW was back, slowly weaving its way through the parking lot like some demon on the prowl. Those tinted windows only made it seem more menacing.

"What makes you say that?" Joe asked, drawing Fiona's attention back to him.

"He threatened to kill me. Just two weeks ago, I went to the icebreaker at Perfect Match, and he ordered me out. He said he was going to hire a security guard and if I came back, he'd have the guard take care of me. Is that unstable enough for you?" Fiona snatched up her purse but left her sunglasses lying on the table. "Excuse me. I need to go to the ladies' room."

Unfortunately, the ladies' room was close to the booth where Katelyn was sitting. While she tried to keep an eye on the car and Fiona, she lifted the newspaper high enough so the woman couldn't see her face. It worked. Maybe because Fiona was in a serious hurry.

"Where's the BMW?" she heard Joe whisper through the communicator.

"Still circling the place. Should I call a cruiser to pull him over?"

"No. There's no law against driving around a parking lot. Plus, I don't want him to think we have any connection to the police.''

Both good points, but it didn't make it any easier to sit there and watch him. ''You think Fiona's opinion of Merrick is an act?''

''Could be. She's wired, and it's not from the coffee. She's either scared of Merrick or of her own shadow.''

''Or maybe she's just jittery about sitting in a booth with the man she's thinks will be her next victim?''

''That, too,'' Joe said calmly. Too calmly for Katelyn's liking. After all, they were talking about a potential plan to murder him. ''We'll tail her when she leaves and see what she's up to.''

The moment Joe said the words, he fired another glance at Katelyn. She understood it without further explanation. ''Keep an eye on the BMW, and I'll check on Fiona.''

''Be careful,'' he warned.

Katelyn kept her head low and her hand on her concealed weapon when she went down the short hallway and eased open the swinging door. The bathroom was small. Just one stall. A sink. And an open window.

The room was empty.

Their murder suspect wasn't anywhere in sight.

Chapter Fifteen

"Anything?" Katelyn called out when she heard Joe end his phone conversation with headquarters.

"Nope. No sign of Fiona."

She groaned, but it was exactly the news she'd expected. After all, Fiona had managed to elude the police most of the week, so it wasn't surprising that she'd been able to slip out of a bathroom window at the coffee shop and go on the run again.

Of course, it would have been nice if Joe and she had anticipated that little maneuver so she could have posted herself outside the window and stopped the woman. Instead, they had to accept the fact that Fiona had provided them with a lot more questions than answers and then lulled them into allowing her to escape.

Since hindsight wasn't doing much to improve her mood, Katelyn moved on to the second point of contention.

The wedding dress.

Or more specifically, her mother's wedding dress.

The metaphorical dead fish wrapped in newspaper.

In the adjoining room she heard Joe open the fridge. Maybe an early dinner would keep him occupied while she tried on the dress. It wasn't really modesty that made her want him to stay on the other side of that wall. She just didn't want him to get the idea that she had stars in her eyes and marriage—a genuine marriage—on her mind.

She didn't.

Really.

But she still found herself mumbling profanity under her breath when she held the dress in front of her and glanced at herself in the mirror.

Katelyn frowned.

What was it about lace and silk that managed to make a woman look great, even when that woman didn't want such cosmetic changes? She was practically glowing, and she wasn't the glowing sort.

Was she?

After dwelling on it for a couple of miserable seconds, she realized the idea was growing on her. Well, growing on her if the glowing part included Joe.

She was definitely in trouble.

Since it was making her depressed and since there was no chance she'd be able to do the dozen silk-covered back buttons by herself, Katelyn put the dress aside and moved on to an important logistics problem.

Her weapons.

Hiking up the satiny floor-length slip to her waist, she planted her bare foot on the bed and strapped on a leg holster. Then a second one on her other leg.

They'd make great backups, but she still needed a primary position with better accessibility. It'd take her too long to work her way through the yards of silk to get to two semiautomatics. Those excess yards could get them killed—a thought she quickly pushed aside.

That thought didn't stay pushed aside, however.

It came back with a vengeance, and every worst-case scenario started racing through her head. The sniper opening fire. Joe in the path of the bullets. Or Joe protecting her by throwing himself in the path. No matter which way it played out, he'd be right there.

Directly in the path.

Of course, she'd almost certainly do the same, which meant they'd be so busy protecting each other that it would increase the risk a hundred times over.

With each image came the inevitable slam of adrenaline. An increase in her heart rate. A tightening of her muscles. Her imagination was a little too good, because her body was reacting as if the danger was right there in the room with her.

Which in a way, it was, she soon realized.

"Lara Croft has nothing on you," Joe commented.

He was standing in the doorway, one hand bracketed on the frame. A beer in his other hand. With his shirt unbuttoned, his hair mussed and that desperado stubble shadowing his sexy chin, he looked like the main player in her darkest fears. Her hottest fantasies.

And like the source of her only sanctuary.

She wasn't sure which one worried her most.

"Maybe you can put your primary in your bouquet?" he suggested.

She heard herself mumble *it's not big enough,* but the truth was his comment barely penetrated her consciousness. Katelyn turned and went to him. Not for sex. It would have been so much easier if it'd been just for that. But she needed to melt into his arms. She needed to feel that all would be right with the world. At the moment, she just wanted those frightening images of snipers and death to go away. Joe could do that for her. He could become her sanctuary.

And he cooperated.

Joe put his beer on the dresser. As if he had all the time in the world, he circled his arm around her. He drew her to him and touched his mouth to hers. Slow and lingering. Tender. A touch that gave her a little too much time to consider exactly what was happening.

Her slip was cut low in the back, and Joe skimmed a finger down her bare skin, tracing her spine all the way down.

The heat rolled through her.

"I won't have to think about this if it's fast," she whispered against his mouth.

"I know."

With that assurance, he didn't speed up. In fact, that single stroking, sliding finger on her back slowed to a trickle. Hardly a touch at all. He handled her like fragile, paper-thin crystal and fueled a lot of flames in the process.

Did he know what this was doing to her?

No doubt.

Katelyn tried to speed things up on her own. She French kissed him. Deep and hungry. And then took those kisses to his ear, and then his neck. A major attention getter, she'd already learned, and his slight rattle of breath let her know she'd gotten his attention in exactly the way she wanted to get it.

She pushed down the slip, stepped out of it, and with his cooperation, she maneuvered them across the room.

The cooperation didn't continue.

Joe stopped them just short of the bed. He leaned down. No hurried motion, either. He brushed a kiss on the top of her right breast. Then on the left. He kept going down. Kissing. Her stomach. Her hip. The lower front of her panties. Until he reached for her ankle.

Finally, she thought. Finally!

This would lead to something wild, hot and fast. A bout of mind-boggling sex that would occupy her mind so she wouldn't worry. But he slid his clever hand up, over her leg. Over her knee. And slowly, leisurely made his way to her thigh.

He was getting closer, but it definitely wasn't where she wanted his hand.

"Joe?" Katelyn whispered, trying to convey the urgency. She got off his shirt, somehow, and had the pleasure of feeling his chest muscles jump beneath her fingers.

"Shh," he answered, his warm breath brushing

against her skin. He unstrapped her holsters, one by one, and laid them on the nightstand. "It's all right."

But was it? Was it really?

The room seemed to be turning. Not quickly, either. Slowly, like his touch. Like some gentle spiral pulling her down into it. She couldn't catch her breath. And why was her heart pounding so hard? It wasn't the only thing pounding, either. Every inch of her ached. Pulsed.

Burned.

This wasn't sex. It couldn't be. This was something leaps and bounds beyond that. Something so intimate, it frightened her almost as much as those other deadly images in her head.

Shaken, Katelyn tried again, pulling Joe onto the bed next to her. She succeeded and even managed to shove down his pants and anchor her leg over his so he wouldn't move away. It didn't stop his slow, methodical hands or mouth. He kissed her. Touched her.

Really touched her.

Those fingers moved over her. Exploring. Discovering. Pleasuring her.

He slipped his hand into her panties. He was definitely getting closer, but what she had in mind was having him inside her. Now.

"I have a condom," she said in between breaths. Just in case that was the issue here. She'd picked up some when Joe had filled up the car at the convenience store and had gotten a strange look from the clerk.

"I have some, too," he informed her right back.

Okay. So if safe sex wasn't the issue, then what the heck was?

With those same slow strokes that matched his incredibly slow kiss, he eased his fingers inside her. Not especially deep. But then, deep wasn't necessary. He got the right spot.

Definitely.

The right pace. That, too.

And he even had the perfect pressure to make her forget all about the speed that she'd thought she wanted.

No.

She wanted this instead.

And Katelyn suddenly didn't care if it took all night for him to get her there.

It occurred to her that she should be pleasuring him as well, but even that thought faded when he turned them until they were face-to-face, and he slid down her body. His hair, his face, his mouth brushed against her skin. Joe kissed her along the way, not missing any available spot, before he rid her of her panties.

In a move that had her wondering what she'd done to deserve this special treatment, or Joe, he replaced those clever fingers with his mouth.

The room didn't just turn. It whirled around. Her breath vanished. Her heart slammed against her chest. And she was lost. Willingly lost.

Katelyn moaned, arched into him and ran her own hand into his hair. Her body sought out everything he was giving her. His mouth and tongue took her higher. Higher. Higher. Until letting go was her only option.

So she did. Katelyn let go. And Joe sent her world spinning out of control.

IT DIDN'T TAKE long before Katelyn came back down to Earth. Mere seconds. Not that Joe had expected her to languish in the aftermath, especially when she realized he'd pulled a fast one on her.

Or rather, a slow one.

That climax obviously had its intended effect—to take off the edge. To lessen some of that raw energy inside her so they could spend a little time—all right, a lot of time—just enjoying each other.

It worked.

She moved almost lazily and smiled the smile of a sated woman—who planned to do some sating of her own.

Katelyn tugged off his boxers while she reached over and took a condom from her purse on the nightstand. She did all the work of putting it on him and made his eyes cross in the process.

When she finished, he caught the back of her neck and pulled her to him. He kissed her. Hot and deep. And did a necessary repositioning of their bodies so that she was on top of him and so that he didn't hurt her arm. He took a moment to savor the sight of her.

All that strength.

All that beauty.

Leaning forward, she slid her hands slowly over his chest, her palms gliding through the sweat that already dampened his skin. "Ready for the ride of your life?" she whispered like a challenge.

"Are you?" he fired back.

She laughed. And he savored that as well, for a moment or two, before he moved just slightly beneath her. The tip of his erection grazed her. And judging from the way her eyelids fluttered and the shudder that went through her body, he'd grazed her in just the right place.

That sent her in search of him. Not that she had to search far, but she shifted. Restlessly. Seeking. Joe did some seeking of his own.

One thrust, and he was inside her.

Oh, man.

It was better than he'd anticipated. A hell of a lot better. And his anticipation had been pretty darn high.

She reared up, her fiery hair like a halo around her face. Bracketing her hands on his chest, she began to move. Joe caught her hips, to guide her, to take them both where they needed to go.

Picking up the pace, she rocked and slid against him. Their bodies creating the friction. The deep, intimate contact. The rhythm. Until she had him close. This wasn't simply to take off the edge, either. She was obviously aiming for something he'd never forget—as if he ever could.

Then, she stopped.

Just stopped.

Joe fought through the haze and stared at her to see why she'd done that.

"What's wrong?" he managed to say.

She hovered above him, staring, and then she reached down and laced her fingers with his. "Are you okay with me being on top?"

It wasn't exactly a question he'd been expecting, and even though just about every inch of him was throbbing for release, he took the time to grasp what she was saying.

And what she was saying was a lot.

He nodded. It was the best he could manage. For some reason, his throat had clamped shut.

Katelyn returned the nod, and there was no apprehension, no hesitancy in her clear green eyes when she lowered her body and lay against him. Her bare breasts against his chest. Her face touching his.

Without fully breaking the intimate contact of their joined bodies, she slowly rolled over. Until their positions were reversed. Until he was looking down at her.

Joe held his breath.

"It's good," she said, sounding not surprised but rather pleased with her decision.

He held his breath a little longer, until she moved. Not a move to get away from him, either. But up. With some not-so-gentle pressure, she dug her heels into the mattress, lifted her hips, then wrapped her legs around him.

And sent him sliding deep inside her.

Now he breathed. Long and rough. He fought to keep a restraint on everything that she'd unleashed inside him, but it was a fight he knew he'd soon lose.

"Am I too heavy for you?" Joe asked. Not easily, but he asked it anyway because it was important.

"No." She repeated it and kissed him. "It's a lot better than I ever thought it would be."

"I know the feeling," he mumbled.

And he was absolutely sure she knew he wasn't just talking about their present position.

He tested the waters and moved inside her. A short, quick, easy stroke. The test was a success.

Man, was it ever.

After a few more of those testing strokes, his body was already pleading with him to take this, and her, to the next level. But then, Katelyn's body was doing the same. Despite her climax only minutes earlier, he felt the aftershocks gain new life before they'd even fully subsided.

Still careful not to make her feel trapped beneath him, Joe gathered her into his arms. He took everything she offered. Everything. And he made sure he gave it right back to her. He moved high against her, hard inside her. Deep. Sliding through the slick, hot moisture of her body.

When she begged him for more, he gave it to her. He went higher still and found a responsive, sensitive spot that made her shudder.

She insisted on more.

He gave it to her.

No longer wary of her response, he pinned her hands to the bed and was pleased when she jerked and twisted beneath him. Not to get away. No, the throaty moan, the half smile, the scorching look in her eyes was the best *welcome home, Joe* he could have ever gotten.

Her legs tightened around him. They matched each other. Move for move. Frantic stroke for frantic stroke. Until the pressure built to an unbearable level. And yet they continued. Somehow. Trying to hang on to every second, every sensation.

They climbed, together.

Drawing on each other.

Feeding each other.

Pleasuring each other.

To get to the only place they wanted to go.

She came in a flash, whispering his name in rhythm to the shudders that ravaged through her. He heard her murmurs over his own heartbeat, over his heavy breath. Over hers. It was her surrender. A sweet, sensual, complete surrender.

Joe buried his face against her neck and surrendered right along with her.

Chapter Sixteen

Naked, Joe eased out of the bed. The room was dark. Pitch black, actually. He'd been so wrapped up in Katelyn that he hadn't even noticed that the sun had set.

She stirred, reaching for him, but he kissed her hand and placed it gently on the pillow. She went back to sleep almost immediately.

He pulled on his pants. Grabbed his cell phone, and went into the living room, shutting the door between Katelyn and him. The A/C was on full-blast and he hoped the hum of the cool air seeping through the vents would create enough white noise that his conversation wouldn't wake her.

This wasn't something he especially wanted her to hear.

After he turned on the lamp, Joe took out his wallet and located the private number for Chief Ryland. It was on a business card tucked behind the only photo he carried. A posed family shot with his parents, his brothers and him. One taken years ago, when his father and he had still been on speaking terms.

He pushed that particular reminder aside, laid his wallet on the end table and pressed in the numbers. Ryland answered the phone.

"Two things," Joe started after they got past the hellos. He sat down even though he figured this might not be an especially long conversation. "There's not even a hint of impropriety or favoritism on Brayden O'Malley's part. He runs a clean department, and I don't want to be part of any witch hunt designed to bring him down."

The chief paused, made a sound to indicate he was thinking about that. "Mind sharing with me how you arrived at this conclusion?"

"I asked questions. A lot of them. In fact, I spent most of Monday and Tuesday doing just that. And I've watched how the man operates. Brayden doesn't need to rely on favoritism and impropriety. He gets the job done the old-fashioned way, through hard work and dedication. You're lucky to have him on your team."

"Pretty frank talk," Ryland grumbled.

"You mean frank talk for a man who's on the brink of a potential promotion?" Joe didn't wait for Ryland to confirm it. "And that brings me to the second thing I want to discuss. After this case, I'll need to be moved from Homicide."

"Say what? I don't think I heard you right, Rico. You want to be moved from a department you fought for months to get into?" Another of those sounds of contemplation. "Does this have anything to do with Katelyn O'Malley?"

"It does," Joe admitted. "I'm personally involved with her, and that means we shouldn't be working together."

"Well, yeah, it happens. Personal involvement, I mean. Work hard, play hard, and all that other crap we do to get us through the night. But that doesn't mean you have to leave Homicide. I can have her moved instead."

"No," Joe quickly answered. "She stays in Homicide. I'm the one requesting the transfer."

"No?" Ryland repeated. "I swear I didn't see anything in your records to indicate you'd let yourself be ruled by *playing hard*. You've been like a bulldozer, Rico, pushing and shoving your way to the top."

"Well, things change." For the first time in his career, there was something more important than the bulldozing, the pushing and the shoving. More important even than his badge.

Katelyn.

Now he had to do everything in his power to prevent her from being killed.

Ryland made Joe wait several seconds before he delivered his verdict. But the verdict wasn't exactly conclusive. "I'll get back to you on these *two things* you just dumped in my lap," Ryland finally snarled. "In the meantime, you and Katelyn O'Malley need to collar this scumhead Veiled Sniper and get the press and the whiny watchdog groups off my back."

"We're doing our best."

"Yeah, well, do better." And with the gruff farewell, the chief hung up.

Joe punched the end call button with his thumb and put the phone on the end table next to him.

"Thin walls," he heard Katelyn say. He also heard the mattress springs groan when she got off the bed. She appeared in the doorway wearing only her panties, slipping on a shirt. His shirt. "Are you sorry you just made that call?"

"No." Joe didn't even have to think about it.

The call was a necessity. But he gave some thought to her. Her hair was all messed up, in a very sexy sort of way with loose, damp strands framing her face.

And then there was her mouth.

Man, her mouth always sucker punched him. Her lips were still swollen from the torrid war they'd waged with his mouth.

"Any idea what you look like standing there?" he asked.

She glanced down at her seminaked torso and smiled. "Are you trying to distract me?"

"Maybe. But if so, your distraction's a heck of a lot better than mine."

"Is that right?" Still smiling, she crossed the room. Instead of climbing onto his lap—something he was fantasizing about—Katelyn pulled the sides of the shirt over her naked breasts and dropped down on the sofa next to him. She linked her fingers with his, brought his hand to her lips and kissed it.

"This morning I asked Brayden to transfer me to another department," she said with her mouth still against his skin. "With the latest round of retirements, I could move to Special Investigations or Vice—"

"No. That's not fair to you. I'm the newcomer. You earned your spot in Homicide."

She climbed onto his lap. Maybe it was to distract him so he couldn't win this argument. He tried not to let her succeed. His resolve faltered a little when her silky leg brushed against his arm as she straddled him. However, instead of doing anything sexual, she kissed his cheek. It was almost chaste.

Almost.

"We are so pathetic." She chuckled. "Brayden and Garrett would have so much fun if they could see this. You and me arguing with each because we're both putting the other first. It's one for the record, Joe."

Because it was peeking out at him, he gave her right nipple a gentle pinch. "Frankly, I'm glad they aren't here to see this. Having an audience would spoil the moment. And they'd probably try to beat me senseless."

She shook her head, and the swish of movement exposed her other breast. No pinch this time. But he leaned forward and nipped the tight bud with his teeth.

Katelyn sucked in her breath, gave his already hardening erection a little nudge, but she stopped him from closing his mouth around her nipple.

"Seriously," she said, pressing her fingers over his lips. "My brothers respect you. And they like you, despite all that posturing and bravado.'' She reached over and picked up the photo that he'd left on the end table.

''What about them?'' she asked.

''I don't think they like me.'' Normally, this would have been the point in the conversation where Joe clammed up, but there was nothing normal about anything anymore. ''My mother died six weeks ago. A drunk driver broadsided her on the way to mass one Sunday morning.''

''Oh. I'm so sorry, Joe.'' It wasn't just lip service, either. Katelyn gathered him in her arms, held him and brushed another kiss on his cheek. When she pulled back, he saw that her eyes were misty with tears.

He almost shrugged, but decided the tough-guy facade wasn't necessary. ''I didn't get to make my peace with her before she died.''

She nodded. ''That explains the personal leave you took right before your transfer. I read your file,'' Katelyn admitted.

Yes. He remembered.

She probably could have offered a sincere condolence or insisted that his dream of being a cop wasn't something for which he should have to make peace. But she didn't. Katelyn sat there and held him.

They stayed that way, wrapped around each other for heaven knows how long. Long enough for Joe to realize that walking away from Katelyn O'Malley wouldn't be just hard.

It would be impossible.

AS INCREDIBLE as Joe's arms were, one glance at the clock, and Katelyn knew it was time to get to work. She lifted her head from his shoulder, kissed him— for slightly longer than she'd planned—and eased off his lap.

"I need to try on the dress," she let him know. "I have to figure out where I can put my weapon."

Groaning as he got to his feet, he followed her into the bedroom and stood in the doorway, watching her. "You said the bouquet was too small to use for cover?"

"Yes." She pointed to the small silk floral arrangement that had been stuffed into the box with the dress. "Baby's breath and miniature pink rosebuds just aren't very effective for hiding Glocks. Go figure."

She put on her bra and long slip first, and then, as if bracing herself for a flu shot, Katelyn grabbed the dress. She eased it on over her head.

The silk whispered over her skin.

A seriously nice sensation she tried to ignore.

"I'll need you to do the buttons," she said, ignoring the mirror, as well. She hitched her thumb to the back of the dress and stepped into the satiny pair of off-white shoes. Heels. Uncomfortable ones that pinched her toes. But they put the finishing touches on the costume.

Joe moved behind her. And then he moved her. He positioned her directly in front of the mirror affixed to the outside of the bathroom door. A wide, full-length mirror.

The very one she'd been trying to avoid.

"We're going to look like those plastic figures that go on top of wedding cakes," she complained as he fastened the buttons.

Not exactly true. The dress was real. Joe was real. And what she felt for him was as real as it got. Still, she'd keep that to herself. With the mission all but closing in around them, this wasn't the time to pour out her heart.

He reached in the closet, extracted his tux shirt and jacket and put them on. Since he was already wearing black pants, the only thing missing was the tie. In true badass form, he threaded it around his collar and left it loose so it dangled against the front of his shirt.

Oh, mercy.

Talk about a surefire way to lose her breath. He simply took it away.

He brushed a kiss on her neck, met her gaze in the mirror, and smiled.

To give her hands something to do, she snatched up the bouquet and the Glock. Somehow, even the sinister-looking gun couldn't kill the moment.

But the doorbell did.

Katelyn groaned when she heard the incredibly annoying sound. Joe went one step better and cursed.

"Just a minute," she called out to the visitor.

She tossed the bouquet on the bed and checked the time again. It was nearly 10:00 p.m. Not good. It was probably Garrett or Brayden, which meant something had gone wrong.

And that put her on immediate alert.

It obviously did the same for Joe. He hurriedly put on his shoes and grabbed his weapon.

The bell rang again. Not a quick jab of sound this time, but a long wail of noise, as if somebody was leaning on the darn thing. When the noise finally stopped, Katelyn heard a barely audible groan.

"Who is it?" she asked.

The person answered, something weak and muffled. It was a man, and the image of her brothers, wounded, flew through her head. She turned to run toward the door, but Joe grabbed her arm.

The feeling of panic and dread was so strong, so overwhelming, that Katelyn nearly pushed him away so she could make sure neither Garrett nor Brayden were hurt.

"Don't do it. It could be a trap," Joe reminded her.

He was right, of course. After all, they were deep in an undercover murder investigation, and someone had already tried to kill them. It was procedure to stay back, to make sure they wouldn't be facing a gun when they opened that door. Still, she had to battle everything inside her to keep from throwing open the door.

And more—she had to trust that Joe was doing the right thing.

"Stay behind me," Joe instructed. He aimed his gun and while staying low, he went into the living room. He reached over and turned off the lamp.

"Please help me," the voice said from outside the door.

She listened for anything recognizable about it, but again it was hardly more than a murmur of pain. If it were a trap, if the person was faking, he was doing an incredibly convincing job. Her heart was racing. Her breath was in her throat. And that buzz was there. That awful buzz in her head that told her all was far from being well.

Her eyes adjusted to the darkness, and soon the illumination from the stove panel allowed her to see the two windows that flanked the door. Not clearly, but at least she could maneuver around and not bump into anything.

Moving slowly, Joe inched away from the lamp toward the window that was closest to him. Katelyn followed. Not easily though. The dress wasn't exactly meant for skulking about, but there was no way she could take the time to undo all those buttons and change into something more maneuverable.

Joe didn't step in front of the window but instead crouched even lower and lifted the blinds just a fraction.

"The security lights in the parking lot are out," he whispered.

Okay. That didn't help. Since they'd been working fine the night before, she had to assume that someone had tampered with them.

"Who's out there?" Joe yelled. He immediately shifted his position so that if it was indeed a trap, the person wouldn't be able to pinpoint his position.

The only response they got was another of those painful groans.

Mercy. She prayed it wasn't one of her brothers.

"Call for backup," Joe said. "But tell them not to approach the building, to stay back and await orders." He tossed her his cell phone.

Katelyn snatched it from the air, flipped it open and would have pressed in the numbers for headquarters if something hadn't distracted her.

Something seeping from beneath the door onto the tiny patch of cream-colored tile.

It was blood.

And lots of it.

Chapter Seventeen

"Joe?" Katelyn whispered.

He glanced at her, and she tipped her head toward the floor. Joe had no trouble whatsoever spotting the dark pool of blood.

Hell.

Whoever was out there was either putting on a very convincing show with fake blood, or else the man was genuinely dying.

"Call for backup," Joe reminded her, and he shouted to the person on the other side of the door. "Who's out there?"

"Bruce," the man finally answered.

Even though Katelyn didn't waiver from calling headquarters, Joe saw the relief flash through her eyes. It wasn't her brothers out there but Bruce Donovan. That realization would help her regain her focus.

Thank God.

Because Joe was a hundred percent sure they'd both need all the focus they could get.

"Someone…shot me," Donovan added. He sounded as if he was getting weaker by the moment.

But the key words were *as if* because there were a lot of as if's about this situation that could get them killed.

"Backup's on the way," Katelyn let him know.

Joe nodded and returned his attention to the pseudo interrogation with his possibly wounded suspect. "Who shot you, Donovan?"

"Uh…I don't know. I didn't see who it was, but the bullet was fired from a gun with a silencer. I didn't hear it until it was too late. Please let me in."

Oh, yeah. Like they were going to do that any time soon. Donovan was their number one murder suspect, and this was exactly the kind of trap a guy like him would try to pull.

"I think it might have been Fiona who shot me," Donovan tried again. "I've been following her." He paused for another of those gasps. "She might be the sniper."

"It's funny you mentioned that. I was thinking the same thing about you."

"Not me." And Donovan repeated it like a mantra. A mantra that got weaker with each word.

Joe glanced at the pool of blood. It was spreading. If by some miracle Donovan was telling the truth, he was bleeding out fast.

"Should I call an ambulance?" Katelyn asked.

He nodded. "But tell them the same thing you told backup. I don't want them to approach the suspect. I want them to wait until they have clearance from either me, you or the backup officers."

"Fiona's crazy enough to do this," Donovan went on, the pitch of his voice wavering wildly. "She has this problem... She, uh, flies off the handle when a man rejects her. She's been stalking Addison."

Joe hadn't needed Donovan to tell him that. "What were you doing here anyway?"

"Watching you and Kate," he readily admitted. "I figured if Fiona wasn't the sniper, then maybe it was...the two of you. I wanted to stop anyone else from dying."

"Playing detective can be dangerous," Joe growled.

He hurried past the door to the other window and peered through the corner of the blinds. There was just enough light from the nearby apartment complex for him to see the shadowy figure lying on the small concrete entry just outside the door. The person was curled up in a fetal position—maybe out of fear. Or maybe Donovan was trying to conceal a weapon.

"Is he armed?" Katelyn whispered. She put the phone on the snack bar and aimed both her guns at the door.

Joe shook his head. "I can't tell."

And that left him with a serious dilemma. If by some miracle what Donovan said was the truth, if Fiona had indeed shot him, then the man needed help. Render assistance, was what Joe had been taught to do. That was training.

Procedure.

But if this was a trap, then the sniper was the one calling the shots. Literally. Because when backup or the ambulance arrived in the next couple of minutes, that would put them in the line of fire, as well.

If it comes down to a situation where someone negates the rules, trust Katelyn, Brayden had said.

All in all, it was damn good advice.

"What does your gut instinct say about this?" Joe asked her in a whisper.

Katelyn blinked, probably surprised that he'd put this on her shoulders, but he was positive her shoulders could handle it.

She glanced at the blood again. "I don't think Donovan's the sniper. He wouldn't have gotten this close because he doesn't trust me not to kill him on the spot. My guess is he's the bait. And I think if we open that door, then someone will open fire on us."

Joe nodded. Everything she said made sense. So he had his answer, and he took it one step further.

Moving back to the window and without touching the blinds, he looked out into the parking lot for any sign of the person who'd likely shot Donovan and was trying to use the man to draw them out.

"See anything?" Katelyn asked.

"No."

Well, nothing other than at least three dozen cars, all jammed into the space that separated the two multistory apartment buildings. But a car probably wouldn't have given the sniper a good view, since their apartment was on the second floor. No. He or she would want to be higher.

Joe's gaze combed over the masonry fence located at the back of the parking lot. It was a possibility and would provide an escape since there was an alley by it and then a street just on the other side.

But the angle was all wrong.

It was the same for the street on the left. A bad angle, and it was way too visible. This guy liked to stand back, aim and fire. He liked hiding.

That left the three-story apartment building directly across from them.

It was a good deduction, he soon realized. Because Joe caught a glint of something. Just a glimmer of movement.

"Get down," he yelled to Katelyn. And he dove for the floor.

Right before the shot came crashing through the window where he'd been standing.

KATELYN HIT the floor, sheltering her face and eyes from the flying glass. Joe did the same, but in their scramble to get away from the gunfire, they ended on opposite sides of the room.

And worse, the gunfire wasn't a single shot.

Another quickly followed and tore its way through what was left of the glass. And another. Just like the night in the alley and that day at the church, it was a barrage.

"Those shots are too high to have come from Donovan," Joe shouted over the blasts.

Katelyn agreed. That meant she'd been right about him not being the sniper.

For all the good it'd done her.

They were still pinned down. Still in danger. But at least the sniper didn't seem to be shooting at Donovan. Now that she knew he might be an innocent player in this, she didn't want another bullet hitting him.

"The bedroom," Joe yelled.

Katelyn kept her weapon in her hands, but she threw open the door so that Donovan could perhaps get inside. He did. Crawling and groaning. And she saw the still-spreading stain of blood on his shoulder and the front of his shirt. No weapon, but even if he'd had one, he was likely too weak to use it.

"The ambulance is on the way," she told Donovan. "Stay down."

With Joe yelling for her to hurry, she crawled toward him. Not easily. The bulky dress got in her way. And even after she got into the bedroom, Katelyn discovered it wasn't much safer than the area they'd just left.

The single window near the head of the bed was taking a pounding as well, and there was glass strewn all over the bedding. She reached over the debris and grabbed their communicators from the nightstand. If they got separated during an escape, they'd need them.

Joe circled an arm around her waist and pushed her into the bathroom. He didn't stop there. He got them into the tiled shower. A temporary safe haven. But only temporary. Only long enough for them to come up with a plan.

The shots continued through the bedroom window and were already gashing holes in the wall. If the sniper kept the firepower pinpointed, then those bullets would eventually come through the tile.

"How about the balcony?" she asked. "It's on the opposite side of the building from those shots."

Joe's gaze met hers, and she knew it was something he had already considered. And he'd also already dismissed it because of the danger.

"Whoever that sniper is, he or she will kill anyone who tries to help us," Katelyn pointed out. "The stray shots—"

"There aren't enough stray shots," Joe insisted.

Somehow, she heard him over the racket and over the pounding of her heartbeat.

He was right.

There weren't many strays. The shots were going through the window with much better than average precision, far more accurate than the gunfire they'd encountered at the church or in the alley. This pattern was more like the first shooting.

The one that had killed Gail and her groom.

Katelyn might have taken longer to consider that inconsistency if a bullet hadn't come through the wall and the tile.

Joe shoved her down with the bits of ceramic and plaster. The deafening noise continued to crash around them.

"We'll go out the balcony," Joe instructed. "We'll climb down the fire escape and circle back around to the edge of the building. I might be able to get a good enough look to pick off the sniper.''

''You think the sniper's on the roof of that apartment building?'' she asked.

''I know he is. I got a glimpse of something before he fired. I'm almost positive he's on the right side of a huge ventilation shaft where no one can see him from the street.''

And it would also allow the gunman refuge since it'd take a while for the cops to block off that street. Then, he could probably escape over that fence into the alley. From there he'd simply fade into the city.

Unless they stopped him first.

''What do you want me do?'' Katelyn asked.

He ducked his head when a shot rammed through another section of the tile. ''After we're on the ground, one of us will need to go to the left of the building.''

For a distraction. A necessary one. If she had the layout of the roof correct in her mind, the left was the sniper's blindside since he was on the right of the ventilation shaft. That meant one of them had to be the diversion while the other delivered the shot that would hopefully take him out.

''You'll be the diversion,'' Joe insisted.

Because it was the safer of two positions. The sniper would have to leave cover to return fire at the person creating the diversion. But if the shooter didn't do that, if the ploy didn't work, then that would leave the person on the right—Joe—in the killer's direct line of fire.

Oh, God.

It wasn't a scenario she even wanted to consider. Katelyn would have much preferred to take the more dangerous route herself. In fact, her heart screamed for her to do just that, to protect him at all cost.

But she couldn't.

She couldn't.

Because it wasn't just their lives at stake. Donovan needed medical attention, fast. The medics couldn't get to him until Joe and she stopped the sniper. If they didn't stop him, now, he'd continue to fire, he'd continue to kill.

And simply put, Joe was the best shot.

She choked back the sob that threatened to make its way past her throat. But she couldn't stop the fear. Nothing could do that. Her hand was trembling when she draped the communicator around his neck and did the same to hers.

Katelyn pressed her mouth to his. Something brief but hopefully it said a lot more than words, because they didn't have time for long explanations.

"Don't you dare fail," she insisted.

His jaw muscles went to war with each other. "You, either."

That was it as for goodbyes.

But it was enough.

"When we get outside, hurry," Joe insisted, swallowing hard. "Use every bit of speed that I know you have because I don't want you out in the open any longer than necessary. Maintain cover and fire a shot or two to get his attention. That's it. Only a shot or two, and only if it's safe.''

She nodded. Took a deep breath. And the moment he said, ''Let's go,'' Katelyn did.

They stayed on the floor, crawling their way to the balcony. There was a pause in the shots. As he'd done at the church, the gunman was probably reloading or trading weapons. Joe and she used that lapse to their advantage. They went out onto the balcony and climbed over the railing to the fire escape.

''Equipment check,'' she said into her communicator.

''I hear you,'' Joe responded.

The shots started up again. Another barrage. Another attempt to kill whoever got in the way.

Adrenaline was like a knife cutting through her lungs. The thick humid air didn't help, either. But she ran, even in the heels and the dress, Katelyn ran as if her very life depended on it. Because it did. And not just her life, but Joe's. If she blew this diversion, then the sniper would go after him.

That couldn't happen.

She slowed down as she neared the corner and checked her surroundings to make sure the angle of the shots hadn't changed. They hadn't. The sniper was still on the roof, even though she couldn't see him. Not even a glimpse.

And that was what she had to remedy. She needed him or her out in the open for at least a second or two.

''I'm in position,'' she relayed to Joe.

"So am I. You go on three. I'll go on four."

"One," they counted in unison.

"Two."

"Three."

Katelyn pulled her breath, darted out from behind the cover of the building. And fired.

So did the sniper.

Right at her.

Chapter Eighteen

It'd happened too fast.

On the count of three Joe had expected to hear Katelyn's shot, and by the four count, he figured the sniper would come out from cover to take aim at her. By five, Joe was supposed to have already fired a deadly shot that would keep Katelyn out of harm's way.

He was wrong.

Things didn't happen as planned.

Katelyn fired. He'd heard that all right. But then, the sniper fired, too. Immediately. Not a second later as he should have done.

A thousand thoughts went through Joe's head. None good. This was what he feared most. Not losing a promotion. Not blowing a case. But losing Katelyn.

He couldn't lose her.

"Say something!" Joe demanded into his communicator. And he held his breath.

"I'm okay."

Those two words were the most welcome two

words he'd ever heard. Joe leaned his shoulder against the building and let it support him.

"He missed," Katelyn added. "I'll try again—"

"No! He'll be looking for you. He aimed right at you, Katelyn, and that means he's not hiding *behind* the ventilation shaft but he's crouched down in front of it."

"Okay," and she repeated it. "So how about this? I strip off the dress and toss it into the parking lot. It's big enough and light-colored enough to make a great distraction. When he fires at it, I'll shoot to draw him out, and then you can do your Robocop thing."

He didn't have enough breath left to ask about that Robocop reference, and from the ragged pauses in her own breathing and the sound of tearing fabric, he could tell she was already getting out of that dress.

Joe moved into position.

"On three," Katelyn said. And she didn't hesitate long enough for him to change his mind.

"One. Two. Three."

Nothing.

Then, something.

A blast of sound. From Katelyn's gun. And once again, the sniper fired right at her without so much as lifting his head. But this time, Joe did see the barrel of the rifle.

"Talk to me, Katelyn," Joe barked.

She didn't.

Not one word.

"Talk to me!" he repeated.

"She dove into some shrubs," Joe heard someone

say through his communicator. Not Katelyn. But Garrett.

"Is she all right?" Joe immediately asked.

"Hard to say."

Not the reassurance Joe needed, especially since she wasn't giving him that reassurance herself. He consoled himself with the possibility her communicator had been damaged in the fall.

"How about you?" Garrett again. "You have a visual on this sniper?"

"If I did, he'd already be dead."

But what Joe did have was the next best thing. He knew the sniper's position. If he aimed just below where he'd seen that rifle, then he could perhaps kill him before he did any more damage.

First though, he had to make sure Katelyn was all right.

"Katelyn?" Joe barked. "If you're there, talk to me."

The next few seconds dragged into an eternity.

"We'll keep monitoring this line, and I'll do some adjusting to see if we can increase reception so we can contact her," Garrett explained. "We're assembling a team to go on the roof, but we're still a good ten, maybe fifteen minutes out."

At the moment, ten or fifteen was a couple of lifetimes. They didn't have lifetimes.

"Make sure that masonry fence is covered," Joe insisted.

"It is. Don't worry. If this guy tries to get down, he won't get far."

Maybe. But it was a risk Joe didn't want to take. He wanted to end it here and now—after he made sure Katelyn was safe.

More seconds. Long ones. And just when Joe was ready to break into a run and check on Katelyn, her voice came through the communicator. "Joe, can you hear me?"

"Loud and clear." Thank God. He was glad he was still leaning against that wall. "I thought I'd lost you."

"No way. My communicator fell off, and I had to find it. Are you okay?"

"I am now. Stay put. I'll get this guy."

"Wait. That sounds scary. I don't want the details though," Katelyn quickly added. "Just please don't do anything… Mercy, I was about to say dangerous, but it will be. It just will be."

She was right, and there was nothing they could do about it. "Remember, stay put."

"Joe, I'm in love with you," she blurted out.

Okay. So he hadn't exactly been expecting her to say that. And she likely didn't know her brother and heaven knows who else was listening in on their conversation. Joe didn't have to inform her of that, or time to respond.

He saw the rifle again, and he automatically zoomed in on it. He took aim. Shut out everything else. His focus pinpointed to that one spot.

And he fired.

Fired.

Fired.

Silence followed.

The sounds of the city and the nearby street slowly began to penetrate his consciousness. He shut them out as well, all the sounds, all the flurries of movement on the street, and Joe concentrated just on that one spot on the roof. A sign of activity, any activity, and he'd fire again.

"I think you got him," Katelyn said into the communicator.

"So do I. Maintain your position just in case."

And if the sniper was indeed dead, then it was all over.

Well, maybe.

"Please tell me you weren't hurt," she demanded.

"I'm fine. You?"

"Just a scratch or two."

Joe cursed. "Our definitions of scratches aren't the same." He'd have a medic check her out ASAP.

She paused and Joe could hear her heavy breath. Or was that his? "It'll either be Fiona or Dr. Kent on that roof," Katelyn said. "Because I think all of this was done to cover up the first shooting, those first two murders."

So Katelyn had come to the same conclusion he had. Not surprising at all. Either Kent had wanted to get back at his ex-wife or else Fiona had wanted to eliminate the happy groom. It explained the reason the first shots had been accurate. Either Fiona or Kent had fired with intent to kill. Everything else had been sloppy, a dangerous facade designed to mask the killer's motive.

Until tonight.

Tonight had been to eliminate Katelyn and him because they'd obviously gotten too close to the truth.

Heck, the sniper had almost succeeded.

"We have a visual of a body on the roof," Garrett said through the communicator.

It was the only green light he needed. Joe turned to find Katelyn.

She found him first.

He'd hardly gotten to the back corner when he almost ran into her. They skidded to a stop. Stared at each other. There was indeed a thin scratch on her chin, but other than that, she was fine.

Katelyn launched herself into his arms. He was right there to catch her.

And kiss her.

It was probably their shortest kiss ever.

"Sergeant Rico?" someone immediately called out. Brayden. He was already on the scene, and after another glance, Joe realized he wasn't the only one. At least a half dozen other officers were there, as well.

With the wedding dress thrown over his shoulder, Brayden approached them and handed it to Katelyn as she eased out of Joe's embrace.

"The press is here," Brayden said.

Which meant there'd likely be pictures. She put on the dress—probably because it beat the alternative of being photographed in her slip.

Her brother gave her arm a gentle squeeze and whispered, "Good job." Brayden said the same to Joe before they were interrupted for an update on

Donovan. The man was alive and would be taken to the hospital.

The routine chaos started. The inevitable aftermath of a violent crime. There was the wail of the ambulance coming for Donovan. Shouts. Orders. The smell of gunfire and leftover adrenaline. It wasn't surprising Joe soon found himself engulfed in it.

A medic pulled Katelyn aside, checking her scratch, while Garrett came over the communicator with an update of his own.

"The sniper's Dr. Allen Kent," he heard Garrett say. "And he's a DOA. Good shooting, Rico."

So it was really over.

Well, except for one not so minor detail. There was Katelyn's comment about being in love with him.

That required Joe to take a deep breath or two.

Now that they weren't in a life-and-death situation, he wanted to get her take on it. Maybe it'd been the adrenaline and fear talking and not...

Hell, he didn't even want to finish that.

Joe turned to find her, but she'd already disappeared into the gathering crowd of officers and medics.

Chapter Nineteen

Katelyn raked her thumb over the volume dial of her clip-on CD player and cranked up the music as loud as she could stand it. Axl Rose did his part, his gritty voice belting out the words to "Sweet Child O'Mine" as her running shoes pounded against the sidewalk.

She ran fast. Much faster than her usual Sunday morning pace from her apartment to her parents' home. She pushed herself hard. Harder. Until her muscles protested. Until her heart pounded.

But it still wasn't fast enough.

The thoughts she'd been trying to keep at bay caught up with her, and no matter how much she kicked up the pace, no matter how high she cranked up the volume, the thoughts just kept coming.

Thoughts of a killer and his victims.

Joe and she had stopped Dr. Allen Kent. A cold-blooded killer who according to his own computer diary had refused to give up the woman he loved, or go to jail for murdering her. He'd been willing to hurt or even kill others to cover that crime, and by Kent's own admission, he'd wanted Joe and her dead after he became suspicious of them.

But in the end, Joe and she had prevented Kent from killing others—including Bruce Donovan. He was alive and recovering in the hospital. Fiona Shipley, Addison Merrick and the other Perfect Match clients were all safe, as well. Heck, even a lot of the paperwork for the case had been finished.

The only thing missing was Joe.

They'd spoken, of course. Briefly. In the halls at headquarters as they were shuffled from one interview to the other. She'd had time to give him back his grandmother's ring and little else since a great deal of the past day and a half had involved hours of separate sessions with Internal Affairs and supervisors. All routine. All part of the checks and balances to make sure deadly force had been warranted.

Not that anyone had ever thought differently. Kent had had to be stopped.

The interviews were just time-consuming square fillers. But now those interviews were done, the squares had been filled, and Joe still hadn't contacted her.

Katelyn ran harder.

The night of the shooting, she'd told him that she loved him—on an open communicator, she'd since learned. Her brothers and probably plenty of other people had heard her, so certainly Joe hadn't missed it. Or maybe he had. Maybe he'd *wanted* to miss it.

And maybe the excessive endorphins from the run were simply making her crazy.

She slowed into a cooldown, hoping it'd cool her thoughts. It didn't. The *I love you* she'd told him kept going through her head. An *I love you* that was real, and yet it hadn't been said to her in return. No amount of running could take the sting out of that. She felt as if her heart were breaking into a million pieces.

How was it possible that she'd lived twenty-eight and a half years without Joe Rico when he now seemed more important than her next breath?

Katelyn did some extra minutes of cooldown to give herself time for a serious attitude adjustment. That didn't work, either. Since she felt on the verge of crying, she cut through the backyard, hoping to sneak into her parents' house and grab a shower before the rest of the O'Malley clan showed up for Sunday brunch. Of course, she didn't hold out much hope that mere soap and water could make her feel better, but at least that way she could cry in private.

"There you are," her father greeted before Katelyn even got through the door.

Not that a greeting in itself was unusual, but her father wasn't cooking. He wasn't even wearing his Kiss The Cook apron, and there wasn't so much as a whiff of waffles and bacon.

Katelyn turned off her music, slipped off her headphones and peered past her father into the sprawling country-style kitchen. Her family was already there. Her brothers, her mother and even Colton. With the exception of Colton, they were all staring at her as if she had the answers to questions that she didn't know had been asked.

"Aunt Kay-lin!" Colton shouted.

"Hey, short stuff." He bolted for her, and Katelyn scooped him up in her arms, giving him a full circle spin around. She planted a sloppy kiss on his cheek. A kiss that earned her a giggle.

"Any idea what's going on?" Katelyn whispered to her nephew. Not that she expected an answer from a two-and-a-half-year-old.

Colton cupped his small hand around his mouth and tried to whisper back. "It's a secret."

That didn't narrow it down much.

"Mom," Katelyn greeted, giving her a kiss on the cheek, as well. There wasn't a strand of her mother's auburn hair out of place, and she'd already applied makeup. Hardly her normal Sunday routine.

Her mom brushed her fingers over the scratch on Katelyn's chin, issued a disapproving grunt, and that's when Katelyn noticed she had no megamug of coffee in her hands. Definitely abnormal. The woman stood shoulder-to-shoulder next to Brayden and appeared to have been waiting for her. Heck, all four of them appeared to be waiting.

"What?" Katelyn asked cautiously. "Did something go wrong with the Kent case?"

"Everything's fine," Brayden said. "The last few ends were tied up when Fiona Shipley volunteered to go back into therapy for her relationship issues."

"Yeah. Therapy with a shrink who doesn't m-u-r-d-e-r people," Garrett added, obviously spelling it out since Colton was listening. "Oh, and Bruce Donovan wanted me to tell you how sorry he was about the incident in the hall at Perfect Match, and he wanted to thank you for saving his life."

Nothing wrong with any of that—which only made Katelyn more suspicious. "So if it's not the Kent case, why are all of you staring at me?" And then it hit her. "Wait, does this have anything to do with the investigation into the favoritism allegations?"

"No," Brayden assured her. "The chief decided to terminate the inquiry for lack of evidence."

In other words, Joe had intervened, and justice had been served. "So if it's not that or the Kent case, then what is it?"

Her brothers exchanged a couple of glances, lifted eyebrows and other assorted facial gestures before Brayden extended his hand to her. "Congratulations, Sergeant O'Malley."

It took several moments for that to sink in. "I got the promotion?" she gasped.

Somehow, amazingly, Katelyn had forgotten all about it.

The hugs started. Ditto for the excited kisses and well wishes from her parents. Katelyn braced herself for the flood of joy, the rush of success. And it happened. Sort of. But it was more of a trickle than a flood.

"What about Joe?" she asked. Colton wriggled out of her grip. "Did he make lieutenant?"

Garrett and Brayden traded another of those ocular

volleys, and this time they included their parents in the raised eyebrow exchanges.

"Told you," Garrett assured them.

"Told them what?" But Katelyn wasn't entirely sure she wanted to hear this.

Garrett shrugged as if the answer were obvious. "That you're in love with Joe Rico."

She huffed, a short burst of air that hopefully was a vague enough reaction so she wouldn't have to out-and-out lie. She didn't want to discuss this with anyone until she'd had time to...heck, she didn't even know what she wanted to do about it. Sulking, maybe even crying, was a distinct possibility.

"Well, are you?" her mother asked, staring at her with eyes that were a genetic copy of her own.

Katelyn went on the offensive. Not with her mother. But she aimed her offensive attention at Brayden. "Did Joe get the promotion or not?"

"He got it. He'll be put in charge of Special Investigations."

But the answer hadn't come from anyone with an O'Malley surname. Katelyn's gaze flew across the room, to the adjoining family room.

And there was Joe.

Sitting on the sofa.

He got up, slid his hands into the pockets of his great-fitting jeans and ambled toward her. "Congratulations, Sergeant."

He smiled.

Just smiled.

Now here was the rush, and the rest of the room faded away. "Congratulations, Lieutenant."

"Joe dropped by to bring back my wedding dress," her mother explained, causing the room to reenter the fringes of Katelyn's consciousness. But even that couldn't get her attention off the hot-looking man walking toward her. "You left it at headquarters the night of the shooting."

"*One* of the reasons I came was to return the dress," Joe clarified. "I'm also here to ask Katelyn something."

From that look, the question wasn't about Kent or a report. Her heart landed in the vicinity of her knees.

"Oh, yeah?" Garrett commented. He nudged Brayden with his elbow.

Joe nodded, without taking his eyes away from her. "I wanted to ask her to marry me."

Okay. Another rush.

Well, more like an avalanche.

Katelyn was sure her family was doing a lot of glance exchanges, elbow nudges and the like, but she didn't care. Joe was going to ask her to marry him.

"And what do you think she'll say?" Garrett, again.

Joe stopped right in front of her. "I'm hoping she'll say yes once she's knows I'm in love with her and that I want to spend the rest of my life with her." He hooked his finger into the waist of her running shorts and pulled her to him. He touched his mouth to Katelyn's.

She felt that simple kiss from head to toe. "I'm positive she'll say yes."

"Positive?" Joe questioned, the corner of his mouth lifting.

"It's a sure thing."

So this was what it was like to be totally in love. Sweet heaven. There was nothing like it. Not the thrill of an arrest, not the promotion. Not even the badge. Just an overwhelming sense that everything was right.

The room went silent. For a moment or two. Until her mother squealed. A second wave of congratulations, hugs and well wishes started, and she found herself in some very loving arms, including Joe's.

"You knew about this?" Katelyn whispered to Garrett, noting that he was grinning as much as the others. "And you approve?"

He shrugged. "Hey, what can I say? Joe makes you happy."

Yes, he did.

And Joe obviously wanted to continue to make her happy in private because after several more minutes of celebrating, he politely asked if he could have just a few moments alone with her. Under her father's direction, the O'Malleys scattered like proverbial flies.

Joe never once let go of her. "Are you upset I chose a public proposal?" he asked.

"Not at all."

"Well, I thought it was only fair after your public announcement on the communicator."

Katelyn winced, but that public announcement would save them some time. Everyone at headquarters probably already knew how she felt about Joe Rico.

"I'd like to invite your family to the wedding," she said while she could still speak. The kiss he gave her seriously put a damper on what was left of that particular ability. "Any objections?"

He shook his head. "None. Knowing you, you'll be able to talk them into coming."

Between her father and her, it was practically guaranteed.

"It'll be a new beginning." Joe took her hand and slipped his grandmother's ring back on her finger. "A new start. A new life. Oh, and lots of great sex."

Katelyn ran her tongue over her bottom lip and felt a nice jolt when she tasted him there. "Great sex, huh?" She smiled. "But you left something out—the happily ever after part."

"I didn't leave it out." Joe laced their fingers together. Drew her against him. "With us, happily ever after is a given."

Yes. It was.

A true perfect match.

And Joe let her know that with a long, lingering kiss.

* * * * *

Juror No.7

MALLORY KANE

Mallory Kane credits her love of books to her mother, a librarian, who taught her that books are a precious resource and should be treated with loving respect. Her father and grandfather were steeped in the southern tradition of oral history, and could hold an audience spellbound for hours with their storytelling skills. Mallory aspires to be as good a storyteller as her father.

She loves romantic suspense with dangerous heroes and dauntless heroines, and often uses her medical background to add an extra dose of intrigue to her books. Another fascination that she enjoys exploring in her reading and writing is the infinite capacity of the brain to adapt and develop higher skills.

Mallory lives in Mississippi with her computer-genius husband, their two fascinating cats, and, at current count, seven computers. She loves to hear from readers. You can write her at mallory @mallorykane.com.

Chapter One

Something was wrong. Lily Raines knew it as soon as the door closed behind her. It was too dark, the only light coming from the streetlamp outside her living room window. Hadn't she left the light on over her sink? She set down her purse and keys and listened.

Nothing.

The light must have burned out. She puffed her cheeks in a weary sigh and shrugged out of her jacket, the rustle of silk echoing in the silence.

Her scalp tingled with that creepy spider-on-your-skin feeling—as if someone were watching her. She'd had it ever since the trial started.

Stress. That's all it was. Goodness knew she had enough reason.

She reached for the living room light switch.

"I wouldn't do that."

Lily shrieked.

A dark figure rose up in front of her.

She tried to scream but her throat seized; tried to turn and run but her legs wouldn't carry her.

Hard hands grabbed her shoulders, twisted her violently and shoved her onto the couch.

Gasping for air, Lily bounced back up and swung her fist at the dark shape. She connected with flesh.

"Ouch! *Maudit!*" The owner of the voice grabbed her and shoved her again, hard. She fell across the arm of the couch and onto the floor, bumping her hip and elbow painfully.

"Hey—"

Different voice. There were two of them. Panic clawed at her throat and she scrambled to regain her footing. She screamed for help and tried to get up but her head hit the end table and she saw stars. She tried to crawl away but there was nowhere to go. They were between her and the door.

"Get her!"

A different pair of hands closed around her upper arms from behind and lifted her with no effort.

"Let go of me!" she cried, kicking backward. The hands turned into steely arms that wrapped around her, immobilizing her. This one was big, tall, solid. His breath sawed in her ear.

She stomped but missed his instep. His hold tightened. She clawed at his forearms, but he squeezed her so fiercely she could barely breathe. She gasped for air.

The first man stepped in front of her and into the faint light from the window. She squinted. He was skinny. Her height, maybe. Shorter than the one who held her. She'd need that information later to tell the police—if they let her live.

Desperately she kicked, using the second man's hold

for leverage. He squeezed her until her ribs ached and whispered something close to her ear. She didn't understand what he said, but the feel of his hot breath on her skin sent terror streaking through her.

The skinny guy laughed as he dodged her kicks. Then his laughter stopped and he grabbed her chin. He stuck his face in front of hers. His breath reeked of garlic. "Calm yo-self, *Lily.*"

He knew her name? She froze, horrified. These men weren't burglars. This was personal.

"Who are y—"

The fingers moved from her chin to her throat. "Good girl. Now you gon' be quiet for me?"

His fingers pushed painfully into her neck as she tried to nod. Tried to stop her brain from imagining what they planned to do to her.

Frantically, she searched her memory. She didn't recognize the voice or the accent. Cajun, maybe. She'd never done anything to anybody.

"What do you want?" she gasped.

The Cajun bared his teeth and his fingers tightened. Her larynx closed up. He was crushing it. He was going to kill her.

"Di'n I tell you be quiet?"

She struggled for air. She didn't want to die. She made a strangled sound and clawed at the arms holding her. Her vision went black.

"Careful," the man who held her rasped. "She can't breathe." The punishing pressure on her chest relaxed slightly.

"You shut your face!" the skinny guy hissed, but he loosened his hold.

She sucked air through her aching throat. From behind her the rock-hard arms loosened a bit more.

Her eyes were beginning to adapt to the darkness, but she still couldn't distinguish features or clothing. There was too little light and she was too afraid. She swallowed, her throat moving against the Cajun's hand.

"Just tell me what you want. I don't have much money—"

He released her throat and snagged a handful of her hair, twisting roughly.

Tears of pain sprang to her eyes.

From somewhere he pulled out a long, thin-bladed knife. He held it up before her eyes, then touched its point just beneath her chin. She automatically lifted her head, cringing away from the deadly blade.

"Come on, *Lily,* don't make me hurt you. I will, and I'll enjoy it."

The man holding her tensed up. His forearms, strapped under her breasts, tightened.

She strained backward as far as she could. The Cajun grinned at her fear. She swallowed and felt the point of the knife prick her skin. Between the hand clutching her hair, the knife and the other man holding her, she was totally helpless. Totally at the mercy of merciless men. They could do anything to her. She was powerless to stop them.

"Understand?"

She nodded jerkily. Tears slid down her cheeks. They were going to kill her and she didn't even know why.

"You're on the jury for Sack Simon's murder case."

She stiffened in surprise. *The trial!* Her pulse thrummed in her ears.

"Aren't you?"

"Yes," she whispered. Her fists clenched automatically and her fingernails dug into the arms holding her.

"My boss, he wants the trial over. He don' want Simon convicted."

Lily stared at the shadows of his face. Sharp chin. Long nose. Eyes that were nothing but black holes.

"I—don't understand." She didn't. The trial was half over. The prosecution had presented ample evidence to put Simon away for life.

"Den I make it simple, *Lily.* The jury can't convict Simon."

The way he kept saying her name terrified her.

"Can't convict—?" she repeated, trying to make sense of what he was saying. Her brain wouldn't work. How could they not convict? "But he's guilty."

The Cajun pressed the knife blade harder, just enough to sting her neck. "Damn it, woman. I know you ain't that stupid. 'Cause if you are, I might as well just kill you now."

Suddenly, she got it. They wanted her to hang the jury. "But I can't—"

He let go of her hair and grabbed her throat again, squeezing.

She coughed.

"Pay attention, Lily. The only thing you can't do is tell anyone we was here. My boss wants to know that *you* will vote not guilty."

"Not guilty? That won't work. There's too much evidence. There's DNA."

"Shut up." He tightened his hold on her throat.

She gagged and lost her footing as the man holding her pulled her away from the little guy's punishing hold.

"Stop choking her," he snapped.

"Hey, *bioque.* You don' give the orders. I do." The skinny Cajun turned his attention back to Lily. He grabbed her jaw again.

"Evidence can be wrong. Do you understand, *Lily?*"

One juror out of twelve. A hung jury. They wanted her to force a mistrial. She nodded.

"Tell me!"

"You want me to vote not guilty." She coughed again, her throat raw and sore.

"You understand why?"

"To deadlock the jury. A mistrial," she croaked.

"Good girl." He patted her cheek. His fingers smelled of garlic and cigarettes—a nauseating, stomach-churning mixture.

By contrast, she had a vague sense of soap and mint from the man behind her. He'd bathed and brushed his teeth before coming here to terrorize her? She almost giggled hysterically.

The garlicky fingers slid down her neck and past the vee of her shirt to touch the top of her breast in an obscene caress.

Lily's stomach turned over. She recoiled, straining backward against the other man. "Please—please don't hurt me."

The man holding her backed up enough to pull her away from the Cajun's probing fingers.

Of the two of them, she'd rather be at the mercy of the bigger man. He seemed to be trying to keep her safe from the little Cajun's pawing.

"Wh-why me?" she stammered, turning her head away from the man's leering gaze.

"My boss, he's a very smart man. He studied the jury. Then he picked you. You the perfect juror."

She didn't have to ask why. She knew. It was because she lived alone and her interior design business was at a virtual standstill since her biggest client had declared bankruptcy. She'd cleared her schedule to design the interior of their high-rise and now she was out of a job.

There were eight men and four women on the jury. The other women had children, husbands, jobs. The attorneys had asked each one about family.

Family.

"Oh, God." Her eyes widened in horror as the real reason she'd been chosen dawned on her. *Her father.* He was in a nursing home, helpless to defend himself. They could hurt him if she didn't cooperate. Her knees buckled. Only the big man's arms kept her from crumpling to the floor.

"There you go. Now you figured it out. I knew you weren't stupid, Lily."

His voice lingered over her name, sending chills down her spine.

"You be hearin' something very soon. Then you'll understand how serious my boss really is."

The Cajun backed toward the door. "Take care of her," he ordered the man holding her.

The tall man released his tight hold and grabbed her wrist. She barely had time for a breath and a fleeting glimpse of his profile before he flipped the afghan from her couch up and over her head.

He spun her around a few times until she stumbled dizzily. Then he lifted her in his arms.

"Don't mess with these people," he whispered. "Do what he said." He knelt and set her gently on the floor, then pushed her. She slid across the hardwood and hit the wall.

Kicking and struggling, she tore at the fuzzy material that blanketed her. Her limbs were weak with fear. She was shaking so badly she couldn't catch hold of the afghan. She sucked in a deep breath, and lint and dust choked her. She coughed, then moaned at the pain in her throat.

Her front door slammed.

Finally she fought her way free of the tangle of knots and yarn. For an instant she crouched there against the wall, hugging the afghan to her chest. Were they really gone?

She held her breath and listened. Silence. She looked around. The apartment was dark. It felt empty.

Barely daring to breathe, she tried to push herself to her feet, but her knees gave way. She collapsed back to the floor, her sore throat contracting around the sobs that erupted from her chest.

She gave up trying to stand and crawled over to her couch, expecting at any moment to be grabbed again. She switched on the lamp with shaky fingers.

Nothing. They were gone.

She huddled in the corner of the couch, hugging her knees to her chest, unable to stop shivering. She was chilled to the bone, although it was September and still summertime-hot in Biloxi, Mississippi.

She didn't know how long she sat there staring at the front door, terrified they'd return. Sick with the knowledge that they knew where she lived.

Still afraid to trust her trembling legs, she crawled over to the door and reached up to throw the dead bolt. The useless gesture was almost funny. They'd gotten into her apartment once. They could do it again. They could come back any time they wanted.

She pulled herself to her feet, her body aching with tension, her head woozy with fear. Leaning against her kitchen counter, she chafed her sore arms. Her throat and jaw hurt. She couldn't stop trembling.

What was she going to do? They'd threatened her. Threatened her father.

Dad! The little Cajun hadn't said anything specific, but his implication sent icy fear surging through her veins. His boss had chosen her because she was alone and vulnerable—and so was her father.

She had to check on him. Carefully she walked over to the couch. Where was the phone? It had been knocked onto the floor when she'd bumped her head on the end table. It was halfway across the room.

She moved unsteadily toward it as pain shot through her shoulders. The man who'd held her had been strong. Thank God he wasn't as cruel as the Cajun.

Just as she touched the handset, it rang.

She jerked away with a startled cry and covered her mouth with both hands to keep from screaming.

It rang again. Her temples throbbed. Her heart raced. She forced herself to pick it up.

"Ms. Raines? This is Mary Bankston, night supervisor at Beachside Manor."

Horror clutched at her chest. *No, please!*

"Ms. Bank—" Her voice wouldn't work. She swallowed painfully and tried again. "Ms. Bankston. What's wrong?"

"Don't worry. Your father is fine. But I need to let you know that there was a small incident a few minutes ago. Somehow, some papers in the trash can in your father's room caught fire. The nurse on duty put them out immediately, and made sure your father wasn't injured. I can't imagine how he managed to get matches or light a fire. But it's all under control now."

Lily's hand cramped around the phone. "You're sure? You're sure he's okay? I can be there in twenty minutes."

"I don't think he even realizes anything happened. You certainly don't need to drive over here—"

"Yes. Yes, I do." She hung up the phone, old, familiar guilt squeezing her chest.

Her father, a cop, had once been so vital, so big and strong, so courageous. But a gunshot to the head during a liquor store robbery had turned him into a bewildered, docile shell of the man who'd raised her.

He'd survived the shooting, but the loving father who had taught her right from wrong, who'd stressed the importance of truth and justice, was gone.

Unable to speak and barely able to understand rudimentary conversation, Joe Raines seemed to look forward to her visits, but the times were fewer and fewer that his brown eyes lit up with recognition.

The intruder's Cajun twang echoed in her ears. *You be hearin' something very soon.*

Bile burned her throat and nausea made her double over. They'd made their point. They'd already gotten to her father.

Suddenly her head spun and acrid saliva filled her mouth. She stumbled into the bathroom, making it just in time.

Collapsing onto the cold tile floor, she bent her head over the toilet, giving in to the spasms. She gagged and coughed until there was nothing left inside her.

Tears streamed down her cheeks as she flopped back against the wall and wiped her face with unsteady fingers. For a few moments she just cried. She was so scared. So tired.

It was amazing how fragile humans were. And how fast hope could turn to despair. In an instant, everything could change.

About the same time as her father was shot, she'd found out her husband was cheating on her. He'd always been controlling, but she believed in marriage, so she'd tried desperately to make hers work.

He'd asked for a divorce and moved out.

Then, because of the time she had to devote to caring for her father, her fledgling interior design business had suffered.

Still, she'd survived. She'd started over, like so many others.

Then, just last week, she'd begun negotiations to design the interior of a new high-rise being built in Biloxi. She'd started feeling hopeful once again. Strong and safe.

But no more. Today, her life and her father's had changed again. Their lives were threatened.

Her dad's beloved, confused face rose in her mind. He was all she had. And she was all he had. She had to get to the nursing home, to see for herself that he was all right.

She struggled to her feet, her muscles stiff from the cold tile, her stomach fighting the nausea that still clung to her. She splashed water on her face.

How would she face her father, knowing what she had to do? *Vote not guilty. Let a murderer go free.*

It went against everything he'd stood for all his life. Everything he'd taught her about justice and truth. To protect him, she would have to betray everything he believed in.

She looked at her pale face in the mirror. How could she do anything else?

BRANDON GALLAGHER TOSSED down a straight shot of Irish whiskey and grimaced. The burn felt good, but it didn't wash the taste of self-disgust from his mouth. He slapped the glass down on the counter and nodded at the bartender, then got up and headed for the bathroom.

He splashed cold water on his face, and when he did, his senses were filled with the scent that clung to his fingers. Vanilla and fresh coconut.

He held out his arms and examined the scratches. A ghost of a smile crossed his face.

He turned on the hot water and scrubbed his hands

with soap, then rinsed his face. Lifting his head he met his eyes in the flaking mirror.

"Can't wash away your own stench with whiskey, nor her perfume with soap, can you, Gallagher?" he muttered. He patted his face and hands dry with a paper towel, then he wet a corner of it and wiped the specks of blood off his forearms. She was a fighter. That was good. She'd need to be.

Foshee had carped at him all the way down the stairs and back to Gio's. *This ain't good cop, bad cop, salaud. You too soft. Mais, yeah, I better tell the boss you can't handle it.*

Brand hadn't reacted, although his insides had clenched with worry. He'd prayed he was reading the little Cajun right. Foshee was merely flexing his non-existent muscles. He wouldn't really go to Castellano.

Feigning unconcern, Brand had just grunted and muttered that there were better things to do with females than rough them up.

To his relief, Foshee had laughed.

You better watch her. Make sure she don' turn tail. You watch her and I watch you. Boss wants to hear how you handle this job. You try something with her, I be waitin' my turn, yeah.

As soon as he'd gotten free of Foshee, Brand had driven back to Lily Raines's apartment. He was surprised to see her car still there. But just about the time he cut his engine, she'd rushed out and taken off in a spray of gravel. He knew where she was going. To Beachside Manor—her father's nursing home.

She'd definitely gotten the message.

Satisfied that she'd understood the threat Foshee had made, and relieved that she hadn't been hurt by his man-handling, Brand had turned his car around and headed straight here, to the neighborhood bar. He sent his reflection a disgusted glance.

The local watering hole. God love it. His dad would have been proud.

Grimacing at that thought, he pushed his hands through his hair, and went back to his seat at the bar.

He faced down the shot glass filled to the brim with pale brown liquid. The sight of it made his mouth water.

No. He rubbed a hand across his face, feeling the day's growth of stubble and smelling the last faint whiff of Lily Raines's perfume.

He'd come too close too many times to sinking into a bottle, just like his old man. Just like his oldest brother. There were better ways to die.

And there'll allus be worse ones. His dad's slurred Irish brogue echoed in his ears.

"Shut up, Dad," he muttered.

As much as he'd like to use a quart of Irish whiskey to drown the look of terror in Lily Raines's eyes and forget the reason he'd been there to see it, he couldn't afford to.

Three years and thousands of hours of undercover work were on the line. And as of tonight, his career probably was, as well.

Because Giovanni Castellano, the King of the Coast, had ordered "Jake Brand," with Armand Foshee to watch over him, to make sure Juror Number Seven held out for acquittal in Theodore "Sack" Simon's murder trial.

With a sigh, Brand threw some cash down on the bar,

turned his back on the brimming shot glass and headed for his car. He maneuvered the dark streets to a private pack-and-mail store that rented post office boxes. The store was closed, but he had a key to the alcove where the boxes were located.

He parked at the entrance and took a moment to roll up the leg of his jeans. Gritting his teeth, he ripped the tape off his ankle and with it the miniature tape recorder that had been a part of him for the last three years.

He massaged his skin where the tape had abraded it, ejected the tiny cassette and inserted a brand new one. He stuck the tape recorder in his shirt pocket. His ankle could use a rest. He'd tape the device back on his leg first thing in the morning.

He pulled his sock up and his cuff down.

Then he wrote the date on the used tape's label and dropped it into an envelope, unlocked the box and shoved it inside, just as he'd done three or four times a week for the past three years. His fingers encountered a note. A single sheet of paper, folded once. He stuck it in his pocket and grabbed the untraceable prepaid cell phone his contact had left in the mail box.

He dialed the only number programmed into it. The cell phone of FBI Special Agent Thomas Pruitt.

"Pruitt. It's Gallagher." He could hear voices in the background. It sounded like a ball game.

"What's up?"

"I got an assignment today from Castellano."

"No kidding? Hang on."

Brand heard Pruitt tell someone he'd be right back. After a few seconds the background noise lessened.

"Sorry. My kid's baseball game. Go ahead. What happened?"

"Castellano put me with a ratty little lowlife named Foshee. We paid a visit to a juror in the Simon case. Leaned on her hard. Foshee threatened her to vote not guilty, to hang the jury, or something would happen to her father."

"Wait a minute. Castellano gave you this assignment himself?"

"Yep. I got called into his inner sanctum—his table at Gio's. Foshee was there, along with a couple of muscle-heads with machine pistols."

"I'll be damned. Finally! We've waited for three years for a break like this. Who is she? The juror?"

"Name's Lily Raines. She's juror number seven."

"Raines. I wonder if she's related to a guy named Raines I used to know. He got shot on the job a couple of years ago."

"That's him. He's in Beachside Manor Nursing Home. Something happened there tonight. Foshee didn't tell me what, but it was enough to send Lily tearing over there about twenty minutes after we left her apartment."

"I'll check on it."

"How do you want me to handle this? You going to let the D.A. know Castellano's tampering with the jury?"

"How'd you handle it tonight?"

Brand made a rude gesture toward the phone. He didn't like Pruitt. "How the hell do you think? I went along. I didn't know any specifics until we got to her apartment." It had sickened him to have to hold her still while Foshee manhandled her and threatened her. "I tried to keep Foshee from being too rough."

"You did right. You've gotta play along. Three of you undercover for three years and this is the closest we've gotten to Castellano. We had a feeling he would try something during the trial, but this is better than we'd hoped. We can't risk any screw-ups at this point."

Brand's gut clenched. His lieutenant, Gary Morrison, who had been his contact for his first year undercover, had stressed the importance of not going outside the law any more than necessary. If an undercover cop was going into a situation where he would be forced to commit a felony, his commanding officer had an obligation to extract him.

Brand and the other two officers working inside Castellano's operation were protected up to a point, but they were required to report any illegal activities in which they were involved.

"Yeah, well, you haven't been working with the damn mob for three years. I don't want any screw-ups, either, but I'd like to know you've got my back once this is all over."

"You do the assignment. I'll protect your back."

Brand blew out a frustrated breath. Pruitt was FBI, and there was no love lost between the Feds and local law enforcement. He wondered if he was being set up to take a fall.

He pulled the microcassette recorder out of his pocket. With his thumb he pressed record and held it near the phone. *Never hurts to have insurance.*

"Gallagher? You there?"

"Yeah. Just thinking. Make sure you understand, Pruitt. I've worked too hard to end up getting my badge yanked for committing a felony."

"Listen to me. The justice department is behind this operation one hundred percent. They've given us carte blanche. Any means necessary. Have you talked to Springer or Carson?"

His fellow officers working undercover. Brand frowned. "Nope. Hardly ever see 'em."

"Well, Carson is working the docks. He's convinced Castellano's moving weapons and explosives in. Springer agrees. Plus, he says they're bringing in illegal aliens."

"Terrorist activities."

"Right. So you're covered on all sides, by justice, homeland security—you know the drill."

Brand did. Job one was to protect his fellow officers. Job two, earn Castellano's trust.

"You think we can get Castellano on terrorist charges?"

"I think so." The excitement in Pruitt's voice was obvious through the phone line. "If we can, he'll go away for a long time and the careers of everybody involved will be assured."

Yeah, Brand thought. You mean *your* career. But he didn't say anything.

"So do what Castellano wants you to do. You'll be protected. We'll have plainclothes watching you and the lowlife, what's his name?"

"Foshee. Armand Foshee."

"Right. Foshee. The task force will step in before the verdict. We'll probably pull Foshee in on some lesser charge. You, too, so your cover isn't blown. The trial will end in a mistrial, but it won't come down on you. Trust me, we've got plenty on Simon. We can pick him up on another murder charge before he sets foot outside the courtroom."

Pruitt made it sound easy. But then he wasn't out in the field. He didn't have to worry about who got hurt.

Brand's thoughts returned to Lily Raines. Terrified, trembling, her soft breasts pressed against his forearms, her dark, shiny hair tickling his nose. He grimaced as his body began to stir. "What about the woman? What about her father?"

"They're not your concern. We'll take care of them."

"The hell they're not. I'm the one leaning on her. I don't like it. I don't like the threats against her father, either. Can't the police give him protection?"

"We don't want to blow your cover or endanger your juror. We can't afford to let Castellano see any change in her father's care. You just do your job."

Damn. He didn't like working with the FBI. They played everything too close to the vest. He rubbed his neck. "Should I call you back to confirm?"

"No. You've got the go-ahead. I'll take care of making it right with the justice department." Pruitt disconnected.

Brand turned off his cell phone and stuck it in his pocket. Then he stopped the tape recorder, ejected the cassette and held it between his thumb and forefinger.

Like he'd told Pruitt, he'd worked like a dog to pull himself out of the chaos of his childhood. He was not going to let anything ruin his career as a police detective. It was all he had.

He tossed the cassette a couple of inches into the air

and caught it in his fist. Insurance. He had Pruitt on tape promising to cover his butt.

As he walked back to his car, he stuck the cassette in his pocket. His fingers encountered the note he'd picked up from the mailbox.

After climbing into the driver's seat, he scanned the note and cursed. He shook his head as he crumpled the note in his fist. His request for two days' leave to go to Alexandria, Louisiana, for his father's funeral had been denied.

He'd expected it. He was in too deep with the Gulf Coast mob to risk disappearing even for, a day or two. Especially now that he had finally penetrated the impenetrable armor surrounding Giovanni Castellano.

His eyelids stung and he blinked rapidly. Pop had been dying for a long time. The alcohol had finally killed him. But his death dredged up memories of another death, that of his oldest brother, Patrick. There was nobody to blame for Pop's death except Pop himself.

But Patrick was another story. Brand's brother had gotten in too deep with gambling and drugs. He owed Castellano more money than he could ever pay, so the mob boss had ordered his execution to make an example. For all Brand knew, Sack Simon had pulled the trigger.

Patrick was the reason Brand had become a cop. The reason he'd volunteered for this particular assignment in the first place.

He sighed. Now to catch Castellano, he had to let the assassin who may have killed his brother go free. God, he hoped Pruitt was telling the truth when he'd said Simon wouldn't walk out of the courthouse before they arrested him again.

He cranked his car and pulled away. He had to be up early tomorrow to go to the courthouse with Foshee.

As he drove back to his apartment, the remembered scent of vanilla and coconut filled his nostrils. He squirmed as his body reacted to the memory of Lily's slender, sturdy body pressed against him.

The justice department had damn sure better protect his badge, because he had no choice but to do this. For more than one reason.

Sure, he was doing it to avenge his brother's death and to protect his fellow undercover officers. But there was a third reason. His body tightened and a thrilling ache throbbed in his loins. He shifted uncomfortably, trying to ease the pressure of the tight denim.

Lily Raines needed him. She had no one else to protect her.

Chapter Two

The empty halls of the courthouse mocked Lily as the click of her heels echoed through the silent corridors. Within an hour, these same halls would be buzzing with activity, and yet she'd still be alone.

She hadn't slept a wink all night. She'd been afraid to turn off the lights, and every noise she heard sent fear slicing through her.

Her father's bland, trusting face haunted her. He was so helpless, and Castellano was ruthless. He'd gotten to her dad inside the nursing home. How could she keep him safe anywhere?

Still, she'd done her best. She'd stalked into the nursing home, indignant and worried, and demanding that whoever had let her father get hold of matches should be let go. She pulled it off with just enough of a touch of frantic daughter that she'd managed to back the head nurse into a corner.

She had agreed to move Lily's dad next to the nurse's station so they could keep an eye on him.

She also promised Lily that she would find out who

had left matches lying around and have them fired. Lily didn't bother to tell her that she wouldn't find anything.

Lily stepped through a set of double doors, and passed one of the assistant district attorneys assigned to the Sack Simon case. The medium-height young man looked smart and capable as he nodded absently at her. Lily wondered what he would do if she told him Castellano had sent thugs to threaten her.

But she kept walking, her hand clenched around her purse strap. The spider-on-your-skin feeling was still with her. She glanced around, expecting to see the little Cajun or his tall partner watching her, but the only person she spotted was a security guard.

She went through the door into the jury room. It was empty. She managed to make a pot of coffee, but spilled a little when she poured herself a cup. Standing at the door, she searched the face of each person who walked by. She recognized some, such as the ADAs, one of the court reporters and a couple of police officers who knew her father.

Every single time someone walked past, her heart sped up and she prayed for the courage to reach out— to ask for help. But each time she gripped her cup more tightly and remained quiet. None of them could protect her against the most powerful man on the Gulf Coast.

How could this happen in this day and age? Years ago, organized crime had been rampant up the eastern seaboard, along the Gulf, even in the Midwest. Back then the mob was into drugs and prostitution, loan-sharking and money-laundering.

Giovanni Castellano was of a totally different breed.

He owned legitimate businesses, paid health insurance for his employees. He was even on the committee for the renovation of the Gulf Coast.

According to defense counsel, Castellano and everyone who worked for him, including Sack Simon, were model citizens.

Whatever illegal activities Castellano was involved in, they were hidden behind a facade of honest business practices. And that meant it would be almost impossible to find anyone who could protect her against him. Who could she trust?

Icy fear crawled up her spine. Even if she could get protection for herself, what about her father? Giovanni Castellano, the King of the Coast, was untouchable.

It was the Gulf Coast's worst kept secret that Castellano's money came from illegal activities such as smuggling and loan-sharking. Yet somehow he'd never been indicted by the police. Her father had always complained that Castellano had a politician in his pocket.

"Lily Raines? Little Lily? Is that you?"

She jumped and almost spilled her coffee again.

A man in an ill-fitting brown suit smiled at her. "Didn't mean to scare you," he said.

Swallowing the urge to back away, she smiled quizzically. "Yes. I'm Lily Raines. Do I know you?"

"Bill Henderson. I used to be on the job. Worked with your dad." The man's florid face lit with a smile as he tugged on his belt, adjusting it over his pot belly.

"Of course, Officer Henderson. It's been a long time."

Henderson's smile faded. "Sure has. Last time I

saw you, you were still in high school. Call me Bill. I heard about your dad. Been meaning to get by to see him, but you know how it is. I'm real sorry. He was one of a kind."

She nodded. She remembered her dad talking about Henderson. *Good people,* her father had called him.

"You're on jury duty?" Henderson asked, raising one gray eyebrow.

"The Sack Simon case."

"Whoa! That rat bastard." Henderson shook his head. "He's guilty as sin. Everybody knows he's Castellano's top hit man. Got at least fifteen notches in his gun."

Lily nodded and glanced up and down the hall. As a juror on the case, she wasn't supposed to talk about it with anyone. "You said you *were* on the job?"

"Yep, I took my twenty-five and retired. I do some private work here and there, when I'm not fishing."

"What brings you to the courthouse?" she asked, her thoughts racing. He knew her dad. He'd been a police officer for twenty-five years. She could trust him.

"Divorce case." He made a face. "I've gotta testify. I took the pictures the wife is using to squeeze a bundle out of her soon-to-be ex-husband."

Lily's pulse thrummed in her ears. Maybe he could help her. If she knew her father was safe, she could vote guilty. Then, as soon as the trial was over, she and her dad could move far away from Castellano's reach.

She glanced around again. "Can I ask you a question, Bill?"

"Sure. Anything for Raines's girl." Henderson laughed. "You need a ticket fixed, I'm your man."

A nervous smile lifted the corners of her mouth. "Not exactly." She took a deep breath just as the double door opened.

It was the bailiff. Lily blew her breath out in frustration. He would reprimand her if he caught her talking in front of the jury room.

Two of her fellow jurors entered behind the bailiff.

As she watched the bailiff approach, Lily decided to go ahead. If she was going to reveal what had happened, what difference did it make if the bailiff overheard? Maybe she could let the court know what had happened to her, and Castellano could be arrested for jury-tampering.

"Bill, what if I told you that—" The door opened again, and when she saw who entered, terror sheared her breath.

Sauntering in behind the jurors was a skinny man with sun-darkened skin and coal-black eyes. He leered at her and bared his teeth.

Just like last night. It was *him*. The Cajun. Lily's throat closed up. She couldn't breathe at all.

Behind him came another man—taller, broad-shouldered and confident. It was the Cajun's tall, menacing partner. His gaze met hers and he frowned. His eyes were a piercing blue, she noticed abstractedly.

He gave a quick, almost imperceptible shake of his head.

She froze, unable to look away from his intense blue gaze. Her fingers tightened reflexively around the ceramic mug in her hands. He was warning her.

She looked from him to the Cajun.

"Lily?" Henderson raised his bushy brows.

She sucked in a long breath and forced herself to face her dad's former colleague. "N-nice to see you," Lily stammered as the bailiff stopped in front of her.

"Good morning, Ms. Raines," the bailiff said.

Lily nodded jerkily.

"I'll let my father know you asked about him," she said to Henderson, stepping backward into the room. Her voice was too loud, but she couldn't help it.

Please don't say anything, she silently begged Henderson.

More people entered the hallway. The Cajun and his partner passed the door. The Cajun's black eyes sparkled and he made an offhand gesture at the level of his neck. Lily read his message loud and clear. She touched her throat where the point of the Cajun's knife had pricked her the night before.

The other man kept his gaze averted, but she felt his presence, his overwhelming attention, and she remembered that he'd stopped the Cajun from hurting her— twice.

She watched the back of his head as he followed the Cajun through the door into the main corridor of the courthouse. Just as he stepped inside, his head angled, as if acknowledging her gaze.

She shuddered, her stomach flipping over. They had to be here checking on her. There was no way she could escape them. They would be there through every minute of the trial. They'd watch her when she went in and out of the jury box. And anytime they wanted to, they could hurt her father.

She ducked inside the jury room, her stomach rebelling at the black coffee she'd swallowed. How would she make it through the day, much less the whole trial?

"WHAT THE HELL'S the matter with her?" Foshee said.

Brand bit back a curse. He knew exactly what Foshee was talking about.

Lily looked as if she might faint and fall right out of her chair. Her face was pale and her eyes had dark circles under them. Her dark hair hung limp and straight around her face, and she clutched the armrest of the jury box chair so hard he could see her whitened knuckles from across the room.

He bent his head and whispered to the shorter man. "She didn't sleep. She's probably so scared she's sick, and I can see the bruise you left on her jaw from here." *You stinking little bully,* he added silently.

"Whassup wi' you, Brand? You sweet on her?" Foshee grinned, showing crooked, stained teeth.

"Nah. Guess I just know better than you how to handle a lady."

"Zat so?" Foshee angled his head. "Mebbe I let you *handle* her after I finish wit' her, eh? 'Cause if she don' straighten up, she get herself kicked off the jury. See how the DA's watching her?"

Brand clenched his fists. He'd already noticed. The Assistant District Attorney in charge of the case had been watching Lily all morning, probably worried about the same thing Brand feared. She was so pale and drawn. Was she about to faint?

It was time for the ADA's summation to the jury. He

looked at Lily again, then whispered to his co-counsel. Brand could imagine what they were saying.

They wouldn't want a sick juror, or one who was terrified, helping to decide the fate of Sack Simon. They had to be sure all the jurors were capable of coherent thought and rational reasoning.

Brand had been there through the jury selection and *voir dire*. There were two very competent alternates waiting in the wings. The ADA could easily replace Lily.

After another few seconds of whispering, the ADA nodded at his colleague and stood. "Your honor, may we approach?"

Brand stiffened. This was about Lily. He knew it. What if the ADA demanded she be excused from the jury? What would Castellano do then?

He wished he could catch her eye, but after last night, anything he did would be interpreted by her as a threat. If he even made eye contact with her, she *would* faint.

The judge and the two attorneys consulted while eleven jurors fidgeted. Lily sat stiff and still, her too-wide eyes watching the lawyers and the judge talk. Every so often, her gaze would flicker toward either him or Foshee.

He saw her throat move as she swallowed nervously. *Get yourself together, Lily,* he begged her silently. *They'll kill you.*

Then the defense attorney glanced their way with a tiny smile.

The lawyers returned to their seats and the judge rapped his gavel. "We'll recess until tomorrow morning at ten o'clock."

Brand let out a deep sigh.

"What's going on?" Foshee asked in surprise as they stood while the judge left the bench.

"We just dodged a bullet. I'm guessing the ADA was asking to excuse juror number seven."

Foshee's black eyes glittered. "We gonna have to pay our girlfriend another visit?"

"No," Brand said quickly. "Look at her. She looks better already. She's exhausted and scared to death. A good night's sleep and she'll be okay. She just needs some time."

"*Mais, oui.* We call her, eh? Tell her good-night?"

Brand shook his head. "Leave her alone, Foshee. You hurt her. You scared her half to death. Trust me, she got the message. Let's give her a day to think about it. She's smart. She'll come around."

They filed out of the courtroom with the rest of the curious onlookers and walked around to the side of the courthouse to stand at the door where the jurors exited. They mingled with the media and the onlookers.

Brand stood beside Foshee, dreading the moment when Lily walked out and saw them waiting for her.

She was the last one through the door. Her face was still pale, and she clutched a tissue as she was escorted to the door by a security guard.

"Sure you're okay, honey?" the uniformed woman asked her.

Lily nodded and smiled faintly. "Thank you. I feel much better. I appreciate the ice water. It's probably just a bug. I'll be fine by tomorrow I'm sure—" Her gaze met Brand's and she faltered.

Brand lifted his chin and sent her a faint nod.

Her gaze flickered from him to Foshee. She brought the hand holding the tissue to her mouth and hurried past them, catching up with a middle-aged man—juror number three, if Brand wasn't mistaken.

"Okay. We gotta check in," Foshee said. "See if the boss wants us to follow her."

"She's not going anywhere. Other than maybe to see her father."

Foshee squinted up at him. "You sure do know a lot for a two-bit bouncer."

Brand glared down at the little man. "Castellano obviously thinks I do. He gave me this job."

"*Mais, non.* He give *me* the job. He give you to me to train. And I guarantee you he ain't gonna like how you're so 'fatiated with our girl."

Brand shrugged. "It's your fault she's too scared to function. Give her a break. She's got a lot of thinking to do."

The Cajun laughed, showing his crooked teeth. "That she does, *brau*. That she does."

BRAND DIDN'T EVEN GLANCE at the neighborhood bar on his way to his cover apartment that night. He licked his lips and ran a hand through his hair. He'd been deep undercover too long. Hanging out with thugs and lowlifes put a bad taste in his mouth, and he knew from his childhood that it couldn't be washed away with whiskey.

As soon as this assignment was over, he was done with the undercover racket. He'd take homicide. Work-

ing with plain old murderers. At least that way he could
feel like a cop, instead of some lowlife.

In his one-bedroom apartment, he turned the radio to
an oldies station and grabbed a bottle of water from the
small refrigerator.

Flopping down on the sagging couch, he glanced at
his watch, took a long drink of the cold water, then
sucked in a dose of courage. He needed to call his
brother, Ryan.

Ryan was four years older than Brand, and he'd often
protected Brand against their father's alcoholic rages.

He picked up his cell phone and dialed. It took
several rings for Ryan to answer.

"Hey, Ry."

"Hey." Ryan's voice was remote.

"How'd it go?" Brand sat forward and propped his
elbows on his knees.

"How do you think it went? It was a funeral. *Dad*
missed you."

The jab hit home. Brand's chest constricted. "Yeah,
well, lift a glass to him from me," he shot back.

Ryan was silent.

"Come on, Ry. You know why I can't be there. I
asked. They turned me down."

"Did you?"

"What do you mean, did I? Hell, yeah, I did."

"Hard to believe they wouldn't let a guy go to his
own father's funeral."

"Cut it out, Ryan." Brand stood and paced, clenching and unclenching his fist. Maybe it was a bad idea to
call him so soon. The funeral had been today.

"You know better than that. I'm undercover, and I just got my first break in the case. I can't afford to blow the operation by disappearing. There are lives at stake."

"Yeah. You're so damn important. Everybody was asking about you. Mom's made you into a hero around here—big bad cop who's too busy to see his own father buried."

"Well, at least I saw Patrick," he threw back.

Damn it. It happened every time they talked. The same old argument. The same old hurts.

Ryan felt guilty because he had been away at school when their oldest brother, Patrick, was murdered. Thirteen-year-old Brand had found him lying across the doorstep of their house, dead from a single bullet to the head, with a dollar bill stuffed in his mouth.

Castellano's calling card.

"Yeah, and you finally got what you wanted. Revenge." Ryan's voice was rough with emotion.

Grief, Brand figured, and guilt, mixed with disapproval of how Brand had chosen to live his life.

"Come on, Ry. I'm not doing this for revenge. I'm doing it because it's the right thing."

"Sure you are. That's why you chose to isolate yourself from your family, and why you went so deep undercover that you're becoming one of them." Ryan took a breath. "I saw Aimee the other day. She's engaged."

"Aimee?" Brand's gut tightened. He'd been thinking about giving her a ring when the undercover assignment had come up. He'd only seen her once in the past three years, and he'd had to pretend he didn't know her.

"Sorry."

"Yeah. Me, too. Is Mom okay?"

"She's making it." Ryan's voice sounded less tense. He'd needed to blow off some steam, just like Brand had.

"I think we might stay for a while. Mom's having a fit over the baby. Cassie can help Mom clean out Dad's stuff, and I might see what kind of contracting jobs are available."

"Stay? In Alexandria?" A pang in Brand's chest made him realize how much he'd miss his brother. Even if they didn't always get along, even if he hadn't been able to see much of him while he'd been undercover, he'd always known Ryan was just across town if he needed him. Ryan had always been there for him. But Alexandria, where his parents had moved once he'd moved out, was almost three hundred miles away.

"What about the house? Cassie's studio?"

"I've got a guy watching the house. And Cassie hasn't used the studio since she got pregnant. Fumes from the oil paint and turpentine. I'm thinking about selling it."

"Right. Tell her I'm sorry I haven't gotten to see the baby. I didn't want to put y'all in danger."

"Sure. We understand."

Brand cleared his throat. "Gotta go, Ry. Tell Mom I'll call her when I get a chance. Tell her I love her."

"Try to stay out of trouble—okay?"

"Always do." Brand disconnected, blinking hard. He didn't know why his dad's dying had affected him. The old man had either been in a rage or passed out drunk during most of Brand's life. Brand had learned early that the best thing to do was stay out of his way.

He finished his water and shot the empty plastic bottle into the trash can like a basketball.

Thoughts of his father led to thoughts of Lily Raines, and the horror in her eyes when she'd realized Foshee was threatening her father. Her obvious love and fear for her dad haunted him. The way she'd frantically rushed to his side as soon as he and Foshee left made Brand feel guilty and somehow deprived.

He'd felt a secret relief when his request to go to his father's funeral had been denied. And that had made him feel even more guilty. But the truth was, he hadn't seen his dad in five years, and as far as he was concerned, that wasn't nearly long enough.

For him, family equaled pain. His childhood memories were those of crying, yelling, fists and rage. He'd spent his boyhood hiding behind Ryan or hanging out with kids from school—kids whose fathers didn't trash the house if dinner wasn't on the table when he got home. Mothers who didn't jump at every little noise, or stare out the window with haunted eyes in the late afternoon. Kids whose parents were normal.

Then there was his oldest brother. Poor Patrick had followed in his father's footsteps, all right. He hadn't even made it to thirty.

He didn't remember ever feeling the way Lily obviously felt about her father. He had no concept of that kind of love. A place inside him ached—hollow, empty. He ran his hand over his face trying to wipe away his maudlin thoughts.

But he couldn't wipe away the vision of Lily with her big, frightened brown eyes and her soft, vulnerable lips.

He couldn't get the smell of vanilla and coconut out of his nostrils.

Damn it, he wished he could warn her how necessary it was for her to be strong and brave. This was life and death. He hoped she knew that.

He longed to tell her he would do anything in his power to keep her safe, but that she *had* to make it through the trial without faltering.

He ached to touch her again, this time to comfort her, rather than scaring her half to death. But if he broke cover, not only would her life and her father's be forfeit, he and two other cops could die.

LILY PULLED INTO her parking lot and glanced at the dashboard clock. She'd intended to be home before dark, but her father had seemed so happy to have her visit she hadn't had the heart to leave early. He'd nodded sagely when she mentioned Bill Henderson. He'd even repeated his name.

She'd told him about Castellano's hit man, and the men who'd threatened her, but he'd just nodded again.

For a moment she sat in her car as her eyes filled with tears of grief. Her dad had once been so strapping and smart.

Ever since her mother had died when she was twelve, she and her dad had depended on each other. She didn't count the months right after her mother's death, when her dad had retreated into his own grief. For the most part, he'd been a great dad. He'd taught her how to defend herself, how to handle a gun, so she'd never be helpless. He'd listened when she'd cried with her first broken heart. And he'd been there to cheer when she'd graduated college with a degree in interior design.

"I need you now, Dad," she whispered. "More than ever. I need to know what to do."

The father who'd raised her would be appalled if he knew she was even considering voting not guilty. Not with the kind of evidence the prosecution had against Simon. He'd have waved away the danger.

I can take care of myself, he'd have told her. *And I can take care of you.*

But there was no way he could do that now. She had to take care of him. And if that meant letting a killer go free—so be it.

Still, the strong, beloved voice she'd listened to all her life echoed in her ears.

It all comes down to what's right, Lilybell. You can't outrun your conscience.

She slapped the steering wheel with her palms, and wiped her eyes. Enough of acting like a baby. She'd find a way to get help. There had to be someone she could trust.

A car's headlights glared in the rearview mirror, causing her heart to leap into her throat. She'd broken one of the basic rules of personal safety. Don't park the car and sit in it. She needed to get inside and put the chain on the door.

Imaginary spiders crawled up the back of her neck as she grabbed her jacket and purse. She shuddered and glanced around. Then she took a deep breath, jumped out of her car and ran up the steps to her second-floor apartment.

As she unlocked her door, her shoulders tightened in awful expectation of the feel of a heavy hand.

She looked over her shoulder. Nothing. She pushed open the door and sighed in relief when she saw her living room bathed in the light from the lamp she'd left on.

The attack came from her left.

A hand clapped over her mouth.

No! Not again! She kicked and bit and tried to scream for help.

The hand pressed tighter and a rock-hard arm pinned hers to her sides. She flung her head backward, trying to head-butt her attacker, but he dodged and pressed the left side of his head against the right side of hers, then pushed her inside and kicked the door shut.

She smelled soap and mint. Alarm sent her heart racing out of control.

"Shh! Lily!" His voice was raspy and soft. "Be still. Shh. Stop struggling."

Desperately, she stomped his instep.

"Ow. Stop it! Listen to me." He lifted her as if she weighed nothing and carried her into the living room.

She was so helpless, so weak. None of the defensive moves her father had taught her worked against this man. She struggled, but he was like a massive tree—immovable, sturdy, unbending.

His hand over her mouth loosened and she took a breath to scream.

"Don't." The hand tightened again, as did the arm across her chest. She could barely breathe.

She went limp, tears of frustration and fear filling her eyes.

"Promise?" his whisper rasped in her ear. His stubble scraped her cheek.

She tried to nod.

"This is serious, Lily. Don't try anything. Don't yell, don't hit, and for heaven's sake, don't bite."

She nodded again. Her chest burned for air. She sucked as much as she could through her nose. It wasn't enough.

His hand on her mouth eased up.

She gasped.

He slid his hand down past her jaw, which was still sore from the Cajun's punishing fingers the night before, to her neck. He didn't grab her, he didn't punish. His thumb touched the minuscule wound left by the Cajun's knife.

In another world, in another time, she might have thought his fingers were gentle, caressing. But here and now, she knew who he was. He'd been here last night. He'd held her—let the Cajun touch her. A quiver of revulsion rippled through her.

He'd threatened her with a searing glare and watched her like a hawk in court.

Lily felt sick. A cold sweat broke out across her face and neck.

He tightened his hold. "Don't faint on me, Lily. I need you to be strong. You have to listen to me." His breath was hot on her ear.

She tried to turn, but he held her in place, tight up against his unyielding body. The heat he gave off burned her to her core.

"You almost got kicked off the jury today. Do you know that?"

She swallowed against his fingers, which still held

her throat in an ominous caress. Any second he could tighten them and choke her.

"Do you?" he snapped.

She nodded jerkily.

"You've got to be brave. You've got to stop looking like a doe facing a rifle."

His low voice sounded earnest, as if he was worried about her. She closed her eyes and fought the urge to give up, to lean against him and stop struggling.

But she knew he couldn't be trusted. He was the enemy. He had hurt her. He'd held her while the Cajun had hurt her.

"That's pretty much what I am," she said shakily.

"You've got to look confident. Can you do that? It's the only way you'll survive."

"Wha-what are you talking about?" she croaked, confused by the urgency in his tone.

His hands slid down over her sleeveless top and tightened on her bare upper arms. He turned her around to face him.

His face was grave, his blue eyes burning with intensity as they searched her face. He lifted one hand and traced the bruise the Cajun had left on her jaw with a surprisingly gentle brush of his fingers.

Conflicting emotions swirled inside her. He'd grabbed her, threatened her. Why was he being so kind? Was it a trick? Was the Cajun waiting outside?

She stiffened, and cut her eyes over to her front door.

"Shh. It's okay. He's not here."

Her gaze shot to his, suspicious. "He sent you?"

"No. I came on my own, to warn you." His left hand

touched her chin. "Listen to me, Lily. Jury summations are tomorrow. They won't take long. The prosecution thinks they've got the case sewn up. Get up in the morning, shower and fix your hair. Put on makeup. Do whatever it is you do to look good."

Tears burned her eyes. She shook her head. "I can't do it. I can't sit there in front of the judge and the lawyers, with the families of people Sack Simon killed watching me with their hopeful eyes. I can't betray them."

"You've got to. You have to walk into the jury box like you own it. Don't give the ADA a reason to kick you off the jury. If you do, your father will die." His face darkened. "You'll die."

She blinked and the tears streamed down her cheeks, down her neck. His thumb moved, rubbing the dampness into her skin, touching her in a way he had no right to. Making her feel safe when she knew she wasn't.

"Don't cry, Lily. Be strong."

She sobbed.

"Shh." He bent his head and put his mouth against her ear. She sniffled and was hit with the scent of him— soap and mint.

He'd brushed his teeth to come threaten her again. A little hiccuping giggle burst up from her chest.

"If you can be strong, if you can hold out, I promise you I'll keep you safe."

"You?" she spat, jerking her head away from his seductive whisper. She hiccuped again and looked him in the eye. "I'd rather die."

He sighed and his eyes went storm-cloud gray. "Then you will."

He turned her around and pulled her back up close against him again. His soft, ominous whisper burned through her. "Think about it, Lily. It's your only chance. It's the only way your dad will survive."

He pushed her toward the couch.

She stumbled and fell onto the cushions. By the time she'd righted herself, he was gone.

The smell of soap and mint lingered in the air.

Chapter Three

When the jurors filed into the jury box, Brand's mouth fell open. He'd told Lily to do whatever she did to look good, but he hadn't expected much.

Whatever she'd done, it had worked. She looked like a different person. Gone was the pale skin, the fearful, darting eyes, the entwined fingers.

Her brown eyes sparkled, her hair was shiny and wavy and her skin glowed under the harsh fluorescent lights of the courtroom.

He frowned, feeling the knots of tension in his neck tighten even more. He'd tossed and turned all night, worrying that his visit had been too much for her, that she wouldn't show up at all this morning.

Her transformation was amazing. *Too amazing.*

A sick dread spread through his gut. She didn't look like this because he'd warned her. He eyed the pugnacious lift of her chin, the determined line of her jaw, and his mouth went dry.

She looked like a new woman because she was. She'd come to a decision.

Beside him, Foshee whistled under his breath. "I reckon you was right about one thing, *brau*. She jus' needed some rest. Looks like a whole new woman."

Too much like a whole new woman. *Ah, Lily, what have you done?*

As the DA got up to make his closing arguments, Brand shifted and cursed under his breath for Foshee's benefit. "Damn it, I gotta take a piss," he muttered.

The little Cajun looked at him sidelong. "Mebbe I better go wit' you."

"Oh yeah? Like girls? I don't think so. I'll be right back."

Brand stood and slipped out of the courtroom, aware of Lily's eyes following him. He didn't dare look at her—he wasn't sure why.

Standing alone on the courthouse steps, out of earshot of anyone who might walk up, he pulled out his cell phone and dialed the preset number.

"Pruitt."

"It's Gallagher."

"Isn't court in session?"

"Yeah. This is important." Brand kept an eye on the courthouse doors. He didn't want to be surprised while talking to his FBI contact. "What's happened?"

There was a pause on the other end of the line. "I don't know what you mean," the FBI agent said finally.

"I think you do. Yesterday Lily Raines was about to fall out of her chair, she was so scared. Today she looks like a new woman."

"Maybe she got some rest."

"Did she talk to someone? Has anyone talked to

her?" Anger blossomed in his chest. "Damn it, Pruitt. If something's up, I need to know."

"I swear, Gallagher, I don't know a thing. She didn't talk to the DA's office, or I'd have heard. Maybe you're overreacting. Take a chill-pill."

Brand commented on what Pruitt could do with his chill-pill. "What about Springer and Carson? Anything going on with them?" He rarely ran into the other two officers who were working undercover with Castellano's operation.

"They're checking in daily. Nothing from their end. Look, I told you I'd protect you, and I will."

"Can you protect her, too?"

"We're on it. We figure it'll take about three days for the jury to figure out she's not going to change her vote to guilty. We'll be there to intercept you and Foshee, and to rearrest Simon. It's all going smooth as silk."

"I hope to hell you're right."

Brand disconnected and headed back inside. He sat down next to Foshee, who sent him a suspicious look.

"What took you so long?" he whispered.

"Got a call." In case Foshee had looked out the courthouse door and seen him on the phone, he needed to stick as close to the truth as possible.

"Yeah?"

"Ex-girlfriend. Wants to hook up."

Foshee grinned. "You could hook me up."

"That would serve her right," he muttered.

Foshee scowled at him.

Brand listened to the DA's monotonous drone. *Crap.* In typical lawyer fashion, he was telling the jury what

he was about to tell them. Then he'd tell them, then he'd
tell them what he'd just told them.

After him, the defense attorney, paid for with Castellano's money, got to put on his own performance.

And Brand was stuck here sitting next to Foshee,
with his garlic breath and his bad teeth.

It was going to be a long day.

THREE DAYS LATER, retired police officer Bill Henderson drove his wife's van toward Beachside Manor
Nursing Home. He'd been surprised to hear from Joe
Raines's girl the other night. Lily had sounded frantic,
scared to death. He'd tried to calm her down, but she'd
begged him to listen to her.

He shook his head, amazed at what Lily had told him
and ashamed at how hard he'd tried to weasel out of
helping her. Especially now.

Like he'd told Lily, he'd done his twenty-five years
on the force. He was looking forward to a lot of years
of sitting out on the water in his little boat, fishing and
drinking beer and just being happy to be alive.

He'd decided not to take any more private jobs. Most
of them were just this side of sleazy. He didn't like spying
on cheating spouses or rounding up deadbeat dads.

His pension was enough, with his wife's income
from teaching, to keep them comfortable.

He turned onto the street that wound back around the
bayous to the grounds of Beachside Manor. Funny name
for a nursing home that was nowhere near the beach.

Lily had asked him to go to the nursing home on
Friday morning and pick up her father for what she'd

termed a "day trip." She said she'd called the nursing home and given her permission. All he had to do was show photo ID.

"Take him somewhere, Bill. Please. I'll pay you. Take him up to Jackson to a hotel. Just for a few days, until this trial is over. Then I'll come get him and we'll be out of your hair. Please. Do it for a fellow officer. You know he'd do it for you."

As soon as she'd said those words, Bill had known he was sunk. So here he was, about to abduct a buddy of his who didn't even know his own name. Like he'd promised Lily, he'd lied to his wife—told her he had to be out of town for a few days on a case.

He'd asked Lily what was going on, but she wouldn't tell him. He had a feeling he knew. Another reason he'd tried his best to refuse. This had something to do with Sack Simon's murder trial. Therefore it had something to do with Giovanni Castellano. He sure as hell didn't want to tangle with Castellano.

The idea made Bill very nervous. He ran a finger under his tight collar and checked his weapon, which he'd stuck in a paddle holster at his back. He rarely carried it anymore, even though he had a permit.

The road to Beachside Manor was asphalt, with a narrow shoulder that quickly dropped off into a swamp. He kept his van toward the middle of the road as he rounded a steep curve.

A car was stopped in the middle of the road, and a woman in a tight skirt and a tighter blouse with the top buttons undone waved both arms at him. She looked hot and harried.

Bill slowed down and pulled up beside her. He lowered his passenger window. "Got car trouble, miss?" he asked.

"I don't know what's wrong. It just stopped, right here in the middle of the road. I'm supposed to be at the nursing home to pick up my mother." She gestured behind her with a hand holding a cigarette.

"Hop in and I'll give you a ride." Bill pressed the button that unlocked the doors. As soon as he did, the driver's door jerked open and a hefty guy stuck a gun into the folds of skin at his neck.

"Wha—?"

"Don't move, Henderson."

Bill didn't move. Sweat popped out on his forehead and under his arms. He should have been prepared for this. Twenty-five years on the force had taught him better than to be caught by the oldest trick in the book.

"What do you want? Money?" Stupid question. It wasn't money. The gunman had called him by name. This was Castellano's doing.

Icy sweat gathered and trickled down his back and under his arms. His mouth went dry as a bone.

"Come on, man, I'm not hurting anyone. I'm just visiting a buddy."

"Too bad you won't get to see him. Did you think we wouldn't have a bug on his daughter's phone? She wouldn't know, but you, Henderson. You're an ex-cop. You should know better."

Bill shook his head as sweat dripped down his face. "Don't, please. I got a wife—"

It was the last thing he ever said.

SEVERAL HOURS LATER, in the confines of the jury room, eleven pairs of eyes stared at Lily in disgust and anger. It was the end of the second day of jury deliberations and they were all hot and tired and sick of each other.

To their surprise, the judge had sequestered them. The trial was too public, he'd said. The media was all over it. He wasn't going to risk a mistrial.

He'd instructed them that they could either have a family member bring them clothing or go to their home accompanied by a court official to pick up their things.

Lily had been given five minutes to gather her makeup, clothes and toiletries. No mail. No newspaper. No laptop.

The foreman stood at the head of the table, waiting. "Well, Ms. Raines? Did you hear me? We still have eleven guilty votes. I trust that now, after you've had several hours to review the evidence, you are prepared to admit that Sack Simon is indeed guilty?" The insurance salesman managed to sound irritable and defeated at the same time.

Lily glanced at her watch. Bill Henderson should have picked up her father hours ago. It was scary as hell not being able to talk with him to be sure everything went as planned.

The slight bulk of her cell phone pressed against her thigh. She'd hidden it in a secret pocket of her handbag, and had stuck it in the pocket of her black suit skirt this morning with the ringer turned off.

She knew she'd be in legal hot water if the bailiff discovered that she had it, but she couldn't afford to be without some means to contact Bill Henderson. She'd given him her number. Of course, she'd had no time alone to call out or check for incoming calls. Even during the two hours she'd requested to go over the evidence again, stalling for time, a security guard had sat with her.

It wasn't that she didn't trust Bill. He was as reliable as they came. He would never let down a fellow officer. Plus, he and her father had been good friends.

By this time he and her father should have arrived in Jackson safe and sound.

As soon as she got out of here, she'd call and be sure everything had gone smoothly. Then she'd run home, pick up her important papers and the small stash of cash she kept hidden in her closet and head north to Jackson.

She'd pick up her dad and keep going north until she got to Memphis or even farther—so far away that Castellano's influence wouldn't reach them. She'd change her name if she had to. She'd started over before. She could do it again.

She looked at each of the jurors in turn, hoping the desperation and uncertainty she felt wasn't reflected on her face.

It all comes down to what's right, Lilybell. You can't outrun your conscience.

I know, Dad. I'm doing it. You'd be proud of me.

"Ms. Raines, please don't make us stay here another night. It would be a travesty of justice if we had to go out there and report that we're deadlocked. Surely even you can't still believe the evidence is inadequate."

Lily took a deep breath, praying that Bill hadn't had any trouble, wishing there was a way she could know for sure. But he had promised her he wouldn't let her down. He was a former police officer. He could take care of himself and her father.

She had to trust him. She wasn't sure she could live with herself or face her father again if she let a killer go free.

She clasped her hands together in her lap and took a deep breath. "I've studied the DNA evidence and the fingerprint, and the testimony," she said, her voice trembling with anxiety. "I vote guilty."

BRAND AND FOSHEE were waiting on the courthouse steps when someone shouted that the jury was back. Foshee dropped his cigarette and stomped on it.

"Let's go. This oughtta be good."

Brand's phone rang. He stiffened.

Foshee turned. "Who's that? Your ex-girlfriend again?"

Brand forced a smile. "Yeah. Go on. I'll catch up."

Foshee's black eyes narrowed. "Nah. I'll wait."

Brand looked at the caller ID and felt his heart rate pick up. It was Pruitt.

"You know I'm busy, *sweetheart,*" he growled, turning the volume on the phone down. Foshee was standing uncomfortably close.

Pruitt laughed shortly. "Okay, I get it. You can't talk. Got a report that an ex-cop buddy of Raines's was shot in his van on Lindon Road earlier. The road to Beachside Manor."

"Damn it!" So that's what Lily had done. She'd tried to get her father away from the nursing home, away from the long reach of Giovanni Castellano.

She was going to vote guilty!

Sweat prickled his scalp and stung the back of his

neck. He racked his brain for a way to give Pruitt a clue. "You know what that means, don't you? Is everything else all right?"

"Yeah. A car came along and interrupted the killers. The driver called 911. The killers took a couple of potshots at the Good Samaritan, but he wasn't injured. He got a partial tag number, too."

"Well, that's good, I guess. So what are you going to do now?"

Foshee's curious black eyes snapped as he did his best to eavesdrop. Brand turned away.

"We'll pick up Raines. Put him in protective custody."

"You'd better hurry."

"I'll take care of it. You lay low."

"I can't—"

Pruitt disconnected.

Brand punched the disconnect button on his phone and burst out with a string of insulting adjectives describing his fictitious ex-girlfriend.

"Come on. We gonna miss the verdict."

Brand pocketed his phone with unsteady hands, his mind racing.

If—no, when—the verdict was read, Lily's life wouldn't be worth a plugged nickel. He had to do something. He couldn't guarantee that he'd gotten that across to Pruitt. Surely if the FBI man had sense enough to put her father under protection, he had a plan for rescuing her.

"Whassa matter wit' your girlfriend?"

Brand looked at the little Cajun, trying to process

what he'd just said. "Girlfriend? Oh. My ex. She let my washing machine overflow."

"So you did hook up." Foshee laughed as they filed into the courtroom.

Brand's neck muscles knotted and his chest grew tight as the jury filed in. Then they all stood while the judge entered and got settled behind the bench.

He asked the defendant to stand.

Theodore "Sack" Simon, nicknamed because of his habit of hiding his gun in a paper bag and shooting through the bag, stood, smoothing his tie and adjusting the sleeves of his custom-made suit. He glanced back over the onlookers, caught Foshee's eye and smiled.

Brand grimaced.

"Jurors, have you reached a verdict?" the judge asked the foreman.

"We have, Your Honor."

Foshee tensed beside him. "What the f—" he whispered.

The bailiff took the verdict from the hands of the foreman and walked it over to the judge.

Brand couldn't tear his gaze away from Lily. She was pale, and her fingers were white-knuckled. Her eyes were clear though, and as he studied her, she met his gaze. A ghost of a smile touched her full lips.

No, Lily! But it was too late.

His pulse hammered in his ears. His fingers tingled. He didn't think he'd ever been as utterly terrified as he was right now, not even when he was seven and his father had broken his mother's nose, sending blood spatter flying, spraying all over him.

The judge read the note and handed it back to the bailiff, who gave it back to the foreman.

Brand's pulse hammered louder and louder. He doubled his left hand into a fist and pushed the knuckles against his lips.

Foshee chewed a dirty fingernail.

Simon nervously picked an invisible speck off his sleeve.

"What say ye?" the judge recited.

"On the single count of murder in the first degree, the jury finds the defendant, Theodore Simon, guilty."

Simon swayed. His lawyer steadied him and whispered in his ear.

The courtroom erupted in noise. The judge's gavel echoed again and again, the sound reverberating inside Brand's skull.

Guilty. Guilty. Guilty.

Foshee let out a little squeak.

Lily's throat moved as she swallowed, but there was a look of pride on her face, a blush of triumph in her cheeks that sent dismay coursing through Brand's veins like blood. He clenched his fists, straining to appear unconcerned, while his stomach clenched and sweat prickled the back of his neck.

She didn't know she was dead.

FORTY MINUTES LATER, by the time Lily walked out the side door, most of the media had already grabbed the other jurors for sound bites. She lowered her gaze and headed straight for her car. As she stepped off the curb into the parking lot, a woman brushed against her and shoved a note into her hands.

She stopped and turned, but the woman quickly disappeared into the crowd.

Lily looked down at the note. The words leaped off the page.

Henderson is dead. Your father is—

"Oh, God, no." She stumbled, reaching out to steady herself against the hood of a car. Her head spun. Her stomach turned over.

Bill Henderson was dead. Was somebody playing a sick joke? She looked at the block printing again then turned the note over. Her father was what?

There was nothing on the back of the note.

"Dad—" she whispered.

Was he dead, too? She covered her mouth, afraid she was going to faint or throw up. Had Bill Henderson been murdered? If so, it was her fault. Her stomach churned and she swallowed hard. She couldn't be sick. She had to get to the nursing home. She had to protect her father.

Papers. Money. She needed to go by her apartment to get the forms necessary to have her father discharged. *No time to waste.* If she delayed it would be too late. She tried to straighten but her head spun.

She heard footsteps behind her. She whirled and found herself staring into a camera lens as a zealous reporter shoved a microphone in her face.

"You were one of the jurors. How do you feel about the verdict?"

Panic clogged her throat. She pushed the mic away and shook her head.

"Ma'am. Why did it take two days to reach a verdict? Were you certain from the beginning that you were going to vote to convict?"

"Please leave me alone," she begged as she searched for her keys in her purse. Finally her fingers closed on them, but her hands were shaking so violently she almost dropped them.

"The viewers would like to hear your statement, Ms.—" The reporter consulted a sheet of paper. "Ms. Raines. You were juror number seven. Tell us what your thoughts were—"

"No!" She pressed the remote and unlocked the driver's side door. "I have to go. Get out of my way."

She climbed in and started the engine as the reporter shot her a venomous glance, then composed his face and turned to the camera.

Lily put the car in gear and pulled away. Her hands were white-knuckled on the steering wheel as she scanned the scattering crowd.

Where were the Cajun and Blue Eyes?

Dear God! They were probably already on their way to the nursing home.

She dug in her pocket for the cell phone she'd smuggled into the jury room. She dialed Beachside Manor. The phone was busy.

Cursing, she tried again and again. How could the line be busy this long?

As soon as she got to her apartment building, she vaulted out of the car and ran for the steps. She rammed the cell phone back into her pocket. She had to get her papers and the small stash of money. Then she'd call the nursing home again.

She'd ordered them not to allow any visitors except for poor Bill Henderson. But Castellano had gotten to him once before, with the fire in the wastebasket. She had no doubt the crime boss could get to him again, no matter what precautions the nursing home took.

As she put one foot on the stairs, she had the ominous sense that there was someone behind her.

Her breath caught. She started to turn. All at once her legs were knocked out from under her. She hit the ground hard, bumping her head, and dropped her keys.

Desperate to find them, she groped blindly along the ground.

"Get up."

She couldn't see. Couldn't stand. Pain and fear doubled her over.

She'd failed. Despair blanketed her.

Dad! She'd tried to protect him, tried to do the right thing. Would God let her death be easier because she'd tried so hard? Would He care for her father because none of this was his fault?

A heavy shoe nudged her in the ribs. "Pick her up, *bioque.*"

The accent sunk in. It was the Cajun with his knife and his stinking, stale breath. Raw fear burned through her. He would enjoy killing her.

Hands lifted her. Blue Eyes's hands. At least he wasn't mean. Maybe he'd keep the Cajun from torturing her.

She let herself be picked up. She didn't have the strength to fight, not even when the Cajun grabbed her bruised jaw in his punishing little fingers.

"You ain't so smart after all, girl. You know what? Your dad, he's already dead."

She didn't react outwardly, although her heart squeezed painfully. Blue Eyes's arms tightened around her in a protective gesture.

"Here, *bioque.*"

One of Blue Eyes's arms loosened as the Cajun handed him something.

"You do it. This'll be your initiation. You'll be blooded. Slit her throat. If you can." The Cajun laughed.

Then he grabbed her hair and twisted her head back and to one side. Lily couldn't hold back a whimper.

He ran a finger across her exposed neck. "Right there."

She felt the cold, sharp edge of a knife against the skin of her neck. Too close. Too sharp. Her skin tightened, as if shrinking away from the deadly blade.

She couldn't even swallow. If she moved, the razor-sharp edge would sink into her skin.

Blue Eyes rested the hand holding the knife against her collarbone. She felt his hand tremble, and a dreadful hope bloomed inside her.

She closed her eyes. He didn't want to kill her. Or maybe he was just nervous about his first murder. The Cajun had said it was his initiation.

"Well?" the Cajun prodded. "You gon' stand there all night?" He jerked on her hair and she felt the blade slice into her skin.

Her breath scraped her throat. *God, please let me die bravely, and please take care of my father.*

BRAND'S VISION TURNED red with rage. Foshee's cruel punishment of Lily had caused Brand's hand to slip. He'd accidentally cut her.

One quick glance and he knew the cut was relatively minor, thank God. But it wouldn't have mattered even if it were nothing but a scratch. Foshee had forced him to hurt her.

He'd had enough.

He knocked Foshee's hand away from Lily's hair with his forearm. At the same time he threw her sideways, out of the way. Then he coldcocked the Cajun with a sharp left.

Foshee dropped to his knees.

Brand held the knife in his fist and pummeled Foshee's face, once, twice, until the slimy rat collapsed, unconscious, in a heap on the ground.

Then he turned to Lily.

She'd risen to her knees, and was struggling to stand.

Brand tossed the knife aside and grabbed her. Whispering an apology that he knew she wouldn't believe, he pulled a Flexicuff out of his back pocket and strapped her wrists together in front of her.

She didn't say anything. She just watched him the way his mother had watched his father. Like a whipped pup watches its master.

The fleeting thought cut Brand to the bone. He met her gaze.

"It's okay," he whispered, but as he'd predicted, she didn't believe him.

Her brown eyes held a heartbreaking resignation. They swam with tears.

The idea that she thought he was going to kill her filled him with self-disgust, but he didn't have time to explain.

He'd already heard a couple of shouts. Above his head an apartment door slammed. There were witnesses. The police were probably already on their way.

He grabbed Lily by her hands and pulled her up, then wrapped an arm around her. He half carried her to his car. As he opened the passenger door, her weight collapsed on his arms. She'd fainted.

He tossed her into the passenger seat, locked the door, rounded the car and climbed in the driver's side. With his heart pumping and his senses on hyper alert, he stomped the gas and took off.

Once he'd cleared the parking lot and hit the main road, he took a second to glance over at her. Blood had run down her neck to stain her white blouse.

Rage and regret choked him. He'd done that. He'd cut her. But at least he'd saved her from death. For now.

He gave a brief thought to Foshee. Would the Cajun get away before the police got there? Brand hoped not. He hoped the perverted lowlife got himself arrested.

It might buy him some time to get Lily to a safe place.

Thinking about Foshee reminded him of Pruitt's promise. What had happened to the officers who were going to pick up him and Foshee after the verdict? For that matter, why hadn't Simon been rearrested?

His anger at Foshee expanded to encompass Special Agent Pruitt. The jerk had lied to him.

LILY'S NECK STUNG. She tried to touch the cut but something was wrong with her hands.

She opened her eyes. She was in a car, a fast car. And her hands were bound.

What had happened?

Then she remembered.

The note. The knife.

"Dad!" She pushed herself up and blinked at the driver. "Oh, my God!" It was Blue Eyes. She whirled, looking for the Cajun.

"Settle down, Lily. Your dad's okay." The man with the blue eyes sent her a worried look. "How's your neck?"

"Where's the Cajun?"

"Back there on the ground."

She remembered Blue Eyes pummeling him. "Dead?"

Blue Eyes shook his head. "No."

She swallowed against nausea. Her throat ached and her mouth grew dry with panic. "Where are you going? What are you going to do with me?"

He glanced over at her. "I'm not sure." He sounded angry.

"Who are you? Did you kill Bill Henderson?" Her voice broke. "Did you kill my father?"

A grimace crossed his face and the muscles of his jaw tightened. "No."

She looked at him narrowly. "You had that woman hand me that note, didn't you? You killed Henderson."

He shook his head. "Not me."

Fear like ice water surged through her veins. She shivered. "I don't believe you."

"You don't have a choice. You have to trust me."

"Trust—" she choked on the word. "You cut my throat. You let him touch me."

He didn't react, unless his chin lifted a fraction. It could have been a trick of the light, though.

"Are you going to kill me?"

His eyes cut over to her, then back to the road. "Probably not."

His calm answers and bland expression frightened her. Maybe more than the Cajun had with his cackling laugh and his disgusting, punishing hands.

She'd thought the Cajun was the bad guy. She'd thought this man's blue eyes were kind, his hands gentle, his provocative minty scent comforting.

A shudder racked her body. "Where are you taking me?"

He didn't answer. His profile was stoic, unmoving as he maneuvered his car quickly through side streets that she didn't recognize.

"Tell me *something*. You're scaring me."

He nodded. "I know." His voice seemed to hold a tinge of regret.

Her lip trembled. Her heart hammered in her chest. "I don't understand. Where's my father? Please talk to me!" She didn't believe his assurance that her father was all right. He'd held her, helped the Cajun threaten her. She couldn't trust him.

How could she go on if her father had died because of what she'd done?

"Okay, Lily. I'll tell you something." His quick, intense look turned her limbs to jelly. In some ways he was more frightening than the Cajun.

"Because of you, one man is already dead. Now, by voting guilty, you may have five other deaths on your conscience, including your own."

Chapter Four

Brand cursed silently. He'd told Lily the truth when he'd said he had no idea what he was doing. He'd acted on the protective instinct he'd felt for her from the first time he'd been forced to restrain her. He hadn't been able to stand by and let her be harmed.

His hand went to his pocket where he felt the weight of his prepaid cell phone. He wanted to call Pruitt and demand to know why he'd reneged on his promise. Nobody had showed up to intercept him and Foshee before the verdict.

Pruitt had lied to him. He should have known better than to trust the FBI. Bureaucratic asses. Pruitt was probably waiting on some damn paperwork, or approval from his bosses or something.

Meanwhile, Foshee had pushed him too far. He'd known Foshee was ready to kill Lily if she voted to convict. Hell, he'd probably been instructed to kill her either way. She knew too much to be allowed to remain alive.

He'd had to save her. Now his cover was blown and

his fellow undercover officers were in danger. When Castellano found out that Brand was a cop working undercover, he'd turn his scrutiny on his other employees. Springer and Carson wouldn't stand a chance.

Brand slammed the heel of his hand against the steering wheel and cursed out loud.

Beside him Lily started, then shrank against the passenger door. Her fear of him infuriated him.

"What the hell were you thinking, voting guilty? You signed your own death certificate, and your father's." He glared at her. Her eyes had little flecks of gold in them, he noticed as they filled with tears.

She blinked and tears spilled over and ran down her cheeks. "So my father's dead?"

Her small, heartbroken voice cut him to the quick. He shook his head, considering what he should say. He wasn't about to tell her he was a cop. Not until he figured out what he was going to do with her.

"I don't think so."

Her face drained of color. "You don't?" She tried to lift one hand, but the Flexicuffs hindered her. More tears dripped down her cheeks.

Brand glanced in the rearview mirror as he turned onto the street that ran behind his apartment house. There was a narrow driveway that led almost up to his back door. He'd never told anyone who worked for Castellano where he lived, but they knew his car, and he was sure they could find his apartment if they wanted to. Hell, somebody could have followed him home to check him out before they hired him.

He didn't dare linger. He'd be there just long enough

to get his gun and badge. Then he had to figure out what to do with Lily.

He didn't have much time. And he didn't have a clue what to do. Castellano would be out for blood. He hoped Springer and Carson were ready for this. He didn't want two fellow officers' blood on his hands.

"Where are we going?" Lily asked, sitting up. "Please. Take me to see my father."

"Please—could you shut up for a minute?" he growled as he backed into the driveway and stopped the car at his back steps. "I need to think."

His apartment was in an old clapboard house that had been divided up by its enterprising owner. The house had escaped the ravages of weather and time, but suffered from the owner's long-term neglect.

Restrained by the Flexicuffs, Lily fumbled with her door handle. Brand quickly rounded the front of the car and opened it for her. He hooked a hand around her arm and lifted her out. She started to struggle, but he squeezed her arm and pulled her close as he shut the door.

"Don't." He scowled at her and felt a grim satisfaction when her throat moved nervously. She stopped trying to get away from him, but her body grew so rigid it felt like she might break. The spark of terror in her eyes told him she still thought he might kill her.

She sucked in a deep breath. He put his fingers gently against her lips to stop her from screaming.

"I said don't. That means don't struggle. Don't scream. Don't do anything except what I tell you to do." He snaked his arm around her and guided her up the concrete steps into the house. The hallway was dark.

She stumbled as they crossed the threshold and a drop of liquid splashed onto his hand.

She was crying. He could imagine the direction her thoughts were taking. For all she knew he was one of Castellano's enforcers. In her mind that would make him no different from Foshee or Sack Simon.

As his fingers twirled his keys, feeling for the one that unlocked his door, he squeezed her shoulders with his other hand. "Don't worry. I'm not going to hurt you."

"You already did," she spat.

He pushed her through the door ahead of him.

Lily lost her footing but caught herself on the kitchen counter, wincing as the plastic thing binding her wrists cut into her skin. Fear bubbled up from her chest, stealing her breath.

Turning, she flung her hair out of her eyes and studied the man who'd abducted her. He tossed his keys on the counter without looking and kicked the door shut behind him with a familiarity that struck her like a blow.

This was his apartment.

Alarm streaked through her. "Who are you? Why did you bring me here?"

He frowned down at her and shook his head slowly. "That's a good question."

She studied him warily. "Then answer it. What do you want from me?"

He walked over to the front window and looked out, then checked his watch. "Believe it or not, I don't want anything from you."

She stared at him, her head swimming with his contradictions. He'd saved her life, but he'd also held her still while the Cajun had groped her. Suddenly her memory flashed on the glint of the knife he'd held against her throat, and the sharp sting as the blade drew blood.

Her hand reached up to touch the wound, but the strip of plastic stopped her.

"Ouch," she uttered softly as she pressed her wrists together to keep the plastic from cutting her skin.

"Here," he said, crossing the tiny living room in two strides. "Let me get those off you." He pulled out a pocket knife and opened it, then hesitated, his blue eyes searching her face. "If you'll promise me you won't run."

"Where am I going to go? I don't even know what street we're on."

"Good. Although I'd have thought your father would have taught you the importance of observing your surroundings."

Her mouth went dry at his mention of her dad. She was so afraid for him. "He did," she snapped. "I was too scared. I let my guard down."

He took her hands and slid the knife blade up under the plastic tether. It popped apart, exposing a pair of matching red marks on her wrists.

A curse hissed through his teeth as he lightly traced the inflamed skin of her wrist with his forefinger. He bent his head. "I don't think the skin is broken, but you're probably going to have bruises. You struggled too much."

She jerked her hand away and resisted the urge to rub her wrists. "When can I see my father? Take me to him. Or at least let me call him."

"No time. We can't stay here." He grabbed her arm. "Come on. I need to take a look at your neck. See how bad it is. Then I've got to—" He stopped, eyeing her sidelong. "There's something I've got to do."

"I need to know whether my father is—whether he's okay."

He flipped an ancient chrome dinette chair around from the table. "Sit."

She lifted her chin and stood firm, fighting to keep her lip from trembling.

"Look, Lily, we don't have much time. Do what I say and I promise I'll check on your father."

"Why?"

His lips flattened into a thin, straight line. "Why what?"

"Why would you do that? Why did you turn on your partner? Why'd you bring me here? What's your name? Tell me *something*."

He sighed. "Brand."

"Brand? That's your name?"

A curt nod was her only answer. "Now sit!" He glowered at her from under lowered brows.

She sat.

Brand watched her as he reached up into the kitchen cabinet for his first-aid kit. He didn't have much, just the essentials: alcohol wipes, antibiotic ointment, bandages and Steri-Strips to use in the place of stitches if necessary.

He pulled out another chair and sat down in front of her. He ripped open an alcohol wipe, then wrapped his right hand around the side of her neck and urged her chin up with his thumb.

She cringed when he touched her, which sent a wave

of self-loathing coursing all the way down to his toes. He clenched his jaw and reminded himself that it was better if she was afraid of him. Better for her, and easier for him.

He pressed his thumb harder against her jaw, forcing her head up a bit more.

Her pale ivory skin was creamy and smooth, and her cheeks matched the blush on a peach's skin. Her dark hair and dark eyes contrasted with her fair skin, giving her an exotic beauty.

The cut on her neck was ugly. It was about an inch and a half long. Luckily for her, it wasn't deep. He touched it with the alcohol wipe.

She flinched.

"Sorry. Hold your breath."

He cleaned the cut as air hissed through her teeth. His gaze followed the tense line of her jaw up to her full lips and petal-soft cheeks. His thumb slid lightly across the curve of her jaw as he berated himself for being an idiot.

As if to punctuate his self-contempt, his body hardened in reaction to the feel of her supple skin and the sight of her small pink tongue as she nervously moistened her lips.

He imagined that tongue touching his, those full, smooth lips pliant and yielding as she responded to his kiss.

Damn it! He jerked his hand away, causing her to flinch. She was terrified of him. Even if he wanted to, he'd never kiss her. A twinge of regret pricked him.

He shook off the dangerous, distracting thoughts.

He needed to get in touch with Pruitt. He had to let

him know what he'd done, and make sure Pruitt took steps to protect Springer and Carson. He also wanted to check on Lily's father, and arrange to get the two of them into a safe house.

Because the minute Foshee woke up, Castellano would know about her jury vote, and her life wouldn't be worth a plugged nickel. She'd defied Giovanni Castellano. Brand knew the King of the Coast wouldn't stop until he'd made her pay.

"Turn your head," he said gruffly. "I need to close the edges of that cut and put a bandage on it."

Lily obeyed. She was confused by the way her captor was acting. He acted like he was angry with her, but just now when he'd touched her neck and jaw, his touch had felt like a caress. A far cry from the obscene groping the little Cajun had subjected her to when he'd slid his filthy hand down her blouse.

Brand's touch was as gentle as a lover's. For a few seconds she'd felt the odd sense of safety and comfort she'd noticed before in his presence. But she couldn't forget that he was the one who had cut her. He'd been almost as brutal as the Cajun in his handling of her.

And she still didn't know what he intended to do with her. Had he saved her from the Cajun's clutches so he could have her for himself?

Fear slithered up her spine and she recoiled, straining away from his hands. When she did, he sat back.

She touched the bandage. It seemed huge. "How bad is it?" she asked.

"Just a scratch." He closed the lid of the first-aid kit. "Wait here. I'll be right back." He picked up his keys and locked the double dead bolt on the back door. With an arch look he pocketed the keys.

"I need to go to the bathroom," she said.

He shook his head. "We've been here too long already. You'll have to wait."

"You'll be sorry."

He cursed. "Go on, then. Hurry. I'll be right outside."

She looked around the efficiency apartment. There were only four doors. The front and back doors, one that was closed and beside it, the bathroom door, which stood ajar.

She went inside and closed the door behind her. As soon as the latch snicked into place, she stepped to the far corner of the room and pulled her phone from her pocket.

Her trembling hands almost dropped it. Gripping it tightly, she hit the preprogrammed button for the nursing home, almost crying with the combination of relief and fear. *Please let him be all right.*

A voice answered. "Beachside Manor, Blue Wing. May I help you?"

"Yes," she whispered. "This is Lily Raines. I need to check on my father, Joe Raines. He's in room 118."

"I'm sorry, ma'am, I can't hear you."

Lily glanced at the door, then bent over the phone and repeated her request.

"Just a moment please."

"No, don't—" The woman had put her on hold.

Lily pressed her clenched fist against her mouth. *Hurry, please,* she whispered silently. With another glance at the door, she turned on the water in the sink.

She was running out of time. She had to make a

choice. As a lump grew in her throat and her eyes stung with tears, she set her jaw and pressed the disconnect button. She had to cover her mouth to keep from crying aloud. She'd cut off contact with her father.

Dear God, please keep my dad safe.

A sharp rapping on the door made her jump. *Brand.*

"Come on, Lily." His voice carried easily over the running water. "You're taking too long. Don't make me come in there."

Standing with her back to the far wall of the bathroom, Lily debated whether she'd made the right choice. Her thumb hovered over the nine.

BRAND HAD RETRIEVED his badge and gun and changed into jeans and running shoes as soon as Lily shut the bathroom door. He'd stuck the weapon in his belt and his badge in his wallet. Then he'd pulled on a long-sleeved shirt, leaving the tail out to hide the bulk of his weapon.

Now he paced back and forth in front of the closed bathroom door, staring in frustration at his cell phone. He knew he ought to call Pruitt, but he couldn't shake the feeling that there was something wrong with the whole operation. The assignment Castellano had given him was too perfect.

He'd worked as a bouncer in Gio's for over a year, and in all that time the crime boss had barely spared him a glance. He'd ingratiated himself with the other bouncers and Castellano's private bodyguards, hoping for a chance to work his way into the boss's good graces.

Then finally, Castellano had sent for him. But the importance of the assignment Castellano had given him seemed too good to be true. Foshee's curious attitude had increased his suspicions.

Finally, Pruitt had lied to him. He'd hung him out to dry.

None of it made sense, and all of it smelled like a setup.

His fingers keyed in a familiar number. His lieutenant's cell phone. He knew he could trust Gary Morrison. They'd worked together for five years, including the first year he was undercover with Castellano. But then the task force had replaced all the local law enforcement with federal officers. Brand was reassigned to Pruitt.

He winced as an annoying tone screeched in his ear.

"We're sorry, but the number you have dialed is not in service at this time."

What the hell? A frisson of alarm skittered through him. He double-checked the number. It was correct.

His pacing took him back to the bathroom door. He stopped and raised a fist, prepared to knock again. Lily was taking far too long.

He heard something. He frowned, listening. She was talking.

"Damn it," he muttered as he shoved the door open.

"—don't know the address—" he heard her say as the door slammed into the wall.

She had a cell phone.

In one swift motion he cornered her and ripped the phone out of her hands. He closed it, disconnecting the call.

"That was not smart. Who'd you call?"

Her face was pale as she shook her head. "Nobody."

"Come on, Lily. Give me some credit. I heard you say you didn't know the address. You called 911, didn't you?"

Her tongue darted out to moisten her lips. She shook her head.

"You're a really bad liar. Let's go. If the cops got a bead on your phone, they'll be here any minute." He took her by the arm and guided her out of the bathroom and back into the kitchen, where he ran water into a bowl and dropped her cell phone into it.

"No! Wait!" she cried, trying to push him aside and reach for the phone.

He caught her hand and stopped her.

"You've ruined it! Oh, God. It had the phone number of the nursing home. I need to check on my father."

"I told you, Lily. He'll be all right."

"Why should I believe you?"

He shrugged. "I can't think of a reason, except maybe that you don't have a choice."

"Will you tell me now what you're going to do? Are you going to kill me, rape me? Hold me for ransom?" She gave a brittle laugh. "Don't waste your time. There's nobody to pay the—"

Brand held up a hand. "Shh."

"What—"

He put his palm against her lips. "Quiet!"

A car had stopped out front. He stood still and listened. Footsteps on concrete, then the sound of the door to the hallway opening. God bless that creaky door.

"They're here. Let's go." He took hold of her arm and pushed her ahead of him toward the back door. He peered out through the window curtains. *Nobody.*

Outside, he closed and locked the back door just as a crash echoed through the apartment. They'd broken in through the front.

Lily heard it, too, because she started and looked over her shoulder.

"That's Castellano's men. We gotta get out of here." Her face drained of color. "Castellano—?" she mouthed.

Nodding, he deposited her in the passenger seat, confident she'd stay put, then skirted the front of the car.

As he opened the car door, a figure rounded the side of the house.

"Here! Out back!" the guy yelled and lifted an automatic pistol.

Brand ducked behind the car door and drew his weapon. "Get down!" he barked at Lily as a spray of bullets exploded from the man's gun.

Brand rose and fired off two quick shots. He saw another man circling the house. At the same time, wood splintered as a third man broke through the back door.

He fired again, several times, and ducked as the thugs unloaded more rounds on them.

Keeping his head down, he climbed into the driver's seat, quickly inserted the key and started the car. Lily shrieked as slugs shattered the rear window. He burned rubber.

"Are you all right?" he shouted to her.

She was crouched down in the passenger seat. Out of the corner of his eye he saw her nod.

Relief spread through him. Over the roar of his engine he heard shouts and a car engine revving.

Glancing in the rearview mirror, he looked down the barrels of two weapons trained on them.

Lily raised her head and turned in her seat to look out the back window.

"Get down!" He reached for her arm. "Down!"

A rain of bullets zinged past them. A metallic thud echoed through the car. Lily cried out and put her hands over her head.

He hoped like hell that wasn't the gas tank. Jerking the steering wheel to the right, he turned onto the street off the alley.

She moved to sit up.

He pressed his palm against the back of her head. "Stay down. They saw which way we went. They'll be right behind us. They may even have the place staked out."

Sure enough, just as he braked at the first stop sign, a car pulled out. He floored the accelerator and ran the stop sign right in front of an oncoming car.

Lily had burrowed into the far corner of the seat. She cowered, her arms wrapped around herself, her hands clenched into fists.

He spared her a glare, but he didn't have a hand to wrestle her back down in the seat. He needed both hands on the wheel and all his attention on the road while he whipped around corners and cut through alleys.

Good thing he knew all the back alleys of Biloxi from his teenage days.

A glance in the rearview mirror told him he'd lost their pursuers for the moment, but he had to make sure they didn't pick up the trail again.

He turned the car toward the Back Bay. They could

hide in an abandoned warehouse where kids used to go parking years ago. He'd been there a few times.

It had been old and creaky way back then. He hoped it hadn't been demolished.

Keeping an eye out for Castellano's thugs, he drove a winding route to the gravel road fronting the warehouse.

Lily watched Brand maneuver the car with expert ease. His hands were steady and competent on the steering wheel. His jaw was set and his blue eyes darted between the road and the rearview mirror.

The past days had played hell with her nerves. Now she was hostage to one of Castellano's musclemen and dodging bullets. She had every right to be terrified.

She was scared all right, but somehow not of the man next to her. For reasons she couldn't begin to fathom, he was risking his life to keep her safe.

When he finally slowed to a normal speed, she sat up warily. "You're sure those were Castellano's men?"

"Pretty damn sure."

"What if they were the police?"

"They weren't."

"How do you know?"

He sent her a hard glare as he turned left onto a gravel road. The noise of rocks crunching under the tires filled the car.

"The police wouldn't open fire without warning," he said shortly.

His biting responses frustrated her. She looked around. The big-city atmosphere of Biloxi had disappeared. The road they were on was deserted. Only a few buildings lined the road and they looked abandoned.

He slowed down just before the road ended at the edge of a bayou. When he turned onto a dirt driveway and drove into a dark, dilapidated warehouse, fear froze her heart.

As the car entered the darkened interior of the building, its headlights snapped on.

"What are you going to do now? Who's here?" she asked as he turned the car around so it faced the open warehouse door.

He stopped the car and cut the engine, still silent.

Lily clenched her fists and sighed in irritation. "I don't understand any of this. I thought you worked for Castellano. What made you beat up your partner and abduct me?"

His face was shadowed but his gaze pierced her. "I'd think you'd have figured that one out by now. I beat up Foshee because he was ready to kill you."

She shivered. "I know that. What I can't figure out is why you turned on him."

He scowled at her. "I thought it'd be damned inconvenient if you bled all over my new jeans."

"Okay fine, Brand. Or is it Mr. Brand?"

"Just Brand."

"Great. Brand. You abducted me to save me from that little dirtbag. So if you're so hot to save me, why aren't we at the police station right now? Wouldn't that make more sense than holing up in some abandoned warehouse?"

He drummed his fingers on the steering wheel, then made a fist and grazed his knuckles with his teeth. After a few seconds, he nodded without looking at her. "Yeah. It would make more sense—if I trusted the police."

She stared at him. He'd run from Castellano's men. And he wouldn't go to the police. His actions and his annoying habit of not answering her questions didn't inspire trust, either. Something was wrong with this picture.

"Are you a fugitive or something?"

He turned his head and sent her a dark look. "You could say that."

His words were ominous. He was a mass of contradiction. He had frightened her out of her wits more than once. He'd threatened her life, and done everything Foshee had told him to do, up until the point where the Cajun had demanded that he kill her.

He'd rescued her from certain death and apparently appointed himself her protector. Or had he? She still couldn't bring herself to completely trust him, no matter how safe his presence made her feel. He was too mysterious, too closedmouthed.

The awful question still hovered in her brain. Had he taken her for himself? Was he a killer or a sexual predator? A deep sense of helplessness engulfed her.

She'd read the horror stories of abductions. Heard neighbors and friends of sex offenders talk about how they'd never have suspected John or Frank or Ralph. Even seen pictures of normal, safe-looking men who'd turned out to be monsters.

Brand could do anything to her. He was a man, and he outweighed her by at least eighty pounds. He could break her in half or assault her with no effort, and there was nothing she could do about it.

She'd heard stories of how people had saved their own lives by talking about themselves, forcing their captor to look at them as a real person and not just an object to be played with.

Lily swallowed hard. She didn't know how to begin. "What did you do?"

Not a great start, Lilybell, her father's voice said in her mind.

Brand forced his breath out in a whoosh. "What did I do? Hell. I've done a lot of things in my life."

"But you ended up working for Castellano."

He nodded. "That's right."

"And you don't trust the police."

"Nope."

"My father was on the job. He'd almost completed his twenty-five when he was shot."

He squeezed his eyes shut for an instant.

"But you already knew that, didn't you? You also knew he was in a nursing home, helpless to defend himself. His condition is one of the reasons Castellano chose me as the juror most likely to cave."

He fidgeted and shrugged his shoulders. "Look, Lily—"

"He responded to a liquor store robbery in progress. Alone. He called for backup, but when he got there, he heard shots so he went in. The kid was sixteen. He shot my father in the head. The doctors thought he was going to die."

Her small, hurt voice embedded itself in his heart like a splinter. He grimaced inwardly. He didn't want to hear her heartbreaking story of her beloved father. He didn't want to listen to her at all.

He had to figure out what he was going to do. He

thought about calling the police station for his lieutenant, but too many people knew him. They'd know his
voice. He couldn't risk it. Not until he was sure whom
he could trust.

By now the news media probably had the full story
of Lily's abduction, complete with their descriptions. He
hadn't seen anyone around the apartment complex when
he and Foshee had grabbed her, but he'd heard that
slamming door, and he'd heard shouts. Somebody
probably saw them tear off in his car.

He was surprised Pruitt hadn't tried to contact him.
Maybe the FBI agent was worried that he'd been
picked up by Castellano's men, and he didn't want to
blow his cover.

Maybe.

"He's been in the nursing home for two years, and
he's only getting worse."

Lily was still talking about her father. Her voice
was small and brittle. Her chin was in the air, emphasizing the curve of her lovely, graceful neck. Her eyes
stared upward and she blinked rapidly, obviously
trying not to cry.

Brand's insides squeezed in sympathy. "I'm sorry
about your father. All I can tell you is he's probably fine."

She rounded on him, her dark eyes snapping. "You
cannot possibly know that. Unless—" She gasped.
"Unless you were the one who was supposed to kill him."

"Lily, think about it. What use is your father now?
You've already voted guilty. Your father's death
wouldn't do them any good. If anything, they'd want to
leave him alive hoping you'd go see him. Castellano

doesn't like to have his orders disobeyed. He'll have men watching the nursing home. Somewhere out there is a bullet with your name on it."

Her brown eyes widened as she absorbed the real horror of what he was saying. Her hand flew to her mouth and a tiny sob escaped her lips. "Bill Henderson is dead and it's my fault," she whispered breathlessly. "I asked him to pick up my father and take him to Jackson and wait for me there."

"So that's how Henderson got involved. What the hell were you thinking?"

"I thought if I got my dad away from Castellano's reach, if I knew he was safe, I could vote guilty. Oh, God, I got Bill Henderson killed, and I still don't know if my father is safe."

"You thought Jackson was far enough to get away from Castellano? That's only two hundred miles."

She nodded miserably. "I didn't know what else to do."

Brand's throat tightened. What would it be like to care that much for someone? To have had a father who cared, who'd been there all the times a kid needed his dad? He silently shook his head. His life had certainly not been like that.

"I believe your father is safe," he said quietly, watching enthralled as her face lit up, her cheeks blushed with rosy color and the tense line of her lips relaxed.

Damn, she had great lips.

"I hope you know what you're talking about. Will you take me to see him?"

He grimaced. "If I can," he said. It wasn't actually a lie. If a miracle occurred and he could safely take her to the nursing home, he would. But miracles were few and far between, especially for a cop on the run.

"So, Brand, is there a bullet with your name on it, too?"

He met her gaze. "I wouldn't doubt it."

"Does that mean we're both fugitives? We're in this together?"

Together. Not likely. In order to save her life, he'd been forced to break the code of the lawman—protect your own. A cop didn't put a fellow cop in danger—ever. But he had left her father vulnerable, unprotected. Lily already feared and mistrusted him. If—no, when—she learned he was a cop, she'd hate him for putting her father's life in danger.

Chapter Five

Lily fidgeted. It was getting late. The sun was about to go down. She could tell from the long shadows around the warehouse. On the far side of the open expanse, Brand leaned against the wall, watching the road from underneath the partially open door. They'd been here at least an hour.

Her imagination had run the gamut of reasons he'd brought her here to this deserted warehouse. Was he waiting for someone? Waiting for dark to kill her and dispose of her body? Hiding from Castellano?

She'd cycled through panic, defeat, anger. Now she was exhausted. She wished that whatever was supposed to happen would happen. It would be better than this ceaseless waiting.

He stuck his hands in the back pockets of his jeans and cocked one hip. Lily let her gaze roam over his body.

She hadn't had much chance to look him over, although she had noticed he was a good-looking man. He was in jeans and a white long-sleeved shirt with the tail hanging out. He'd changed out of his suit while she was in the bathroom, she realized suddenly.

She knew why he wore the shirt. He was hiding his weapon. Lily had been around guns all her life. Her father had taught her how to shoot. He'd taught her to respect deadly weapons. She'd only gotten a glimpse of Brand's weapon, not enough to know what it was. She did know it wasn't a machine pistol, like the men pursuing them had wielded with such deadly intent.

She took in his broad shoulders and sturdy legs, and the casual ease with which he leaned against the wall. He looked perfectly relaxed, but somehow she was certain that every muscle in his body was poised for action.

With the shirt and the snug jeans that hugged his thighs, he didn't look nearly as big as he'd felt when he'd restrained her while Foshee had threatened her. But she'd been afraid for her life, and both of them had seemed like monsters.

Brand didn't look like a monster now. He looked capable, confident. He was tall and lean with well-developed muscles.

She'd already been on the receiving end of his piercing blue eyes. His features were sharp and honed, and faint stubble emphasized the strong line of his jaw.

He didn't look like a mob enforcer. But looks could be deceiving. Lily knew that all too well. Her ex-husband hadn't looked like a controlling, cheating jerk, but that's what he was.

Brand straightened and Lily's pulse quickened. Was someone coming? She clenched her fists in fearful anticipation, but all he did was pull out his cell phone and dial a number. After a few seconds he jabbed a button and shoved the phone back into his pocket with a scowl.

Who was he trying to call? She swallowed against the lump of fear that grew in her throat. Surely it wasn't Castellano, she thought hopefully, or he wouldn't have run from the mob boss's gunmen who broke into his apartment.

She couldn't shake the terror of being alone in the dark with this stranger. He hadn't harmed her yet, but that didn't mean he wouldn't.

He propped himself back against the wall, his attention on the road outside.

She squirmed. She was nervous as a cat. Taking a deep breath, she tried to calm her racing heart and relax her tense muscles. She needed to stop imagining all the bad things that could happen to her and think rationally. She was a cop's daughter, after all.

What would her father do? In his prime he probably could have taken down both abductors and handcuffed them on the spot. A sad smile curved her mouth as she pictured that, quickly followed by a sick fear that twisted her gut and burned her throat. Her father was so vulnerable now. She had no idea if he was safe, despite Brand's assurances.

You'd be disappointed in my detective skills, Dad. She'd been too frightened to notice the location of Brand's apartment. Not even the street name. That was a rookie mistake.

Come on, Lilybell. Think like a cop.

She looked around the interior of Brand's car. It was a Dodge, one of the sporty models. There was nothing stuck above either visor, nothing in the map compartments and no papers or trash littering the floor. In fact, there was nothing personal at all about the spotless interior.

Glancing up at Brand, whose eyes were still on the road, she opened the glove box. The only thing inside was the owner's manual. She took it out and opened it.

Yes! He'd stuck his vehicle registration inside the front cover. The vehicle was registered to Jake Brand, address 114B George Street in Biloxi. She committed the information to memory, flipped through the manual to be sure no other personal papers were inside, then returned it to the glove box.

A movement caught her attention. He was on his cell phone again, apparently with the same results. He couldn't reach whomever he was so desperate to talk to. His expression reflected his annoyance and frustration.

Too antsy to sit still any longer, Lily got out of the car. She wanted to get a good look at the bayou road before the sun went down. There were dozens of these dead end dirt roads along the Coast, snaking around the many bayous. She needed to find a landmark that she'd be able to recognize if—no, *when*—she talked to the police.

As she walked toward the warehouse door, Brand stalked toward her, a disapproving frown marring his even features.

"Where the hell do you think you're going?"

"I needed to stretch my legs. How long are you going to keep me here?" She stepped closer to the door to look out. The bayou stretched out before them, and the tangled, overgrown underbrush at the edge of the murky water was deep green. It looked peaceful. There was a sign nailed to a cypress tree. She couldn't make out the words.

"Get away from the door."

"Why? Why are we here?"

Brand didn't answer.

"Are you waiting to turn me over to someone?"

He sent her an exasperated frown. "Just go back to the car."

Lily lifted her chin. "I can't sit in the car doing nothing. If you're going to kill me, why don't you go ahead and do it? It's cruel to make me sit and wait."

He looked down at his feet then out the warehouse door. "I'm not going to kill you, Lily." He shook his head. "I'm trying to save your life. Now will you listen to me and go back to the car?"

Just as he reached for her arm, the distant rumbling of a car engine echoed along the bayou.

He jerked her away from the open doorway and whirled, shoving her against the wall. He flattened his back against the corrugated metal siding beside her. He overlapped her shoulder with his and angled his arm across her middle. The heat from his body seeped into her skin. His bicep rested against her breast and his forearm pressed against her belly. She felt her abdominal muscles quiver.

"Don't move," he warned her as he slid his handgun from the back of his jeans and cradled it in his left hand.

The car came closer, until the roar of its engine bounced off the metal walls.

Then silence.

Whoever it was, they'd stopped right in front of the warehouse. Lily had never felt so small and helpless in her entire life. She was in the clutches of a dangerous man, and they were being stalked.

Brand pressed Lily back against the wall, her shallow

breathing and rapid heartbeat echoing through him. His own pulse hammered as he glanced toward his car. It was dark maroon, which was good. And he'd had sense enough to back it into the warehouse out of the sunlight. However, the door faced west, and the setting sun illuminated the front fender.

Damn it! He'd screwed up. And now, whoever was out there had spotted the car. He had to act fast. They couldn't be discovered here.

He angled his head and whispered to Lily without taking his eyes off the doorway. "We're going to move toward the back. There's an office on the far wall. If you make a sound, I swear I'll knock you out."

He felt her body stiffen. *Good.* He'd scared her. He hated himself for being so harsh, but it was for her sake, even if she'd never believe it.

He heard two car doors slam. Damn it, there was more than one of them.

He wrapped his arm around Lily's slender waist and guided her through the darkness, praying the rest of the old building was as empty as it had been during his high school days. If they tripped over something, they'd be caught for sure. Brand couldn't let that happen.

They came up against the back wall. Still holding Lily, Brand slid along it until his back rested against a door. His breath whooshed out. He hadn't realized he'd been holding it.

The office. Right where he remembered it. A memory of using the sofa inside for some inept high school groping flashed in his brain. It was gone the next instant, however, as he focused on keeping Lily safe.

He felt for the knob and twisted it without turning around.

Relief tightened his throat as the knob turned without resistance. He slid the door open a fraction.

Heavy shoes crunched on gravel and echoed through the building. Two men in uniforms appeared at the open warehouse door.

Police!

Cursing silently, Brand backed through the door to the office and pulled Lily with him. He eased the door shut.

"They're police officers. They can help us," Lily whispered.

"No. Now shut up."

He held her tightly against him, so close he could feel her rapid heartbeats echoing through her frame.

She took a sharp breath. He squeezed her ribs, afraid she was about to scream. Leaning over, he whispered in her ear. "Do I have to remind you what I said? I will do whatever is necessary to keep you quiet. Do you understand?"

He felt her hair move against his cheek as she nodded. Her entire body trembled.

Loathing leached through him, leaving a bad taste in his mouth. She deserved better than this. In a different world, her delicate beauty and vulnerable mouth would make her just his type.

He even liked her stubborn determination. In fact, he especially liked it—the way she stood up to him, the way her mouth tightened and her chin lifted. The way her brown eyes snapped with irritation.

Brand set his jaw. He couldn't lose himself in

thoughts about his lovely hostage. Any lack of focus on his part could get them both killed.

Through the glass-paned door he watched as the officers carefully approached the building, their hands resting on their holstered weapons, their flashlights held at shoulder level. The high-powered beams crossed and swept like spotlights as they scanned the corners and shadows.

Brand eased Lily toward the far side of the tiny office, where he gestured for her to crouch behind the sofa. He hunkered down beside her, waiting, listening, wondering what he would say—what he would do—if the cops found them.

The officers' footsteps were loud in the empty building as they walked around, checking the car and their surroundings.

The footsteps grew closer and closer.

One aimed his flashlight through the glass in the office door, and Brand cringed and held his breath as the beam passed only inches from his foot. He pressed closer to Lily, and rested his left hand against the back of her neck in silent warning.

Tremors shook her slender frame.

"Don't move a muscle," he mouthed in her ear.

She moved her arm. Just as he was about to grab it, she rested her hand on his leg. His thigh muscle jerked.

He swallowed. She was only steadying herself. It wasn't that she trusted him. She didn't. Even if she hadn't said it, he'd seen it in her eyes every time she'd looked at him.

"Hey, Mike. There's an office over here."

Brand raised his gun. It was a futile effort. He could not shoot another officer, even if it meant exposing Lily to danger.

If the officers found them, all he could do was show them his badge and ask to be taken to his lieutenant.

Not that they would agree. Pruitt almost certainly had issued an APB on him by now, and had faxed his name and picture to every police department on the Gulf Coast. If he was caught by the police, he'd be taken into custody in handcuffs and lose his badge.

"Yeah? There's probably a john, too." The second officer's footsteps came closer.

"We ought to check it out."

"Right. Look, I'm ready to get out of here. This place is creepy."

"Creepy?" the first officer repeated with a laugh. "Whoa, Mike. You scared of ghosts?"

"No. If you gotta know, I don't like spiders and there's probably millions of the little monsters in there."

The first officer laughed harder. He swept the interior of the office with his flashlight one more time, aiming the beam at the couch, at the walls, across the floor.

Once again Brand cringed. He shrank back, making his bulk as small as he possibly could. Lily's fingernails dug into his thigh.

"Come on, man, let's go," Mike said. "There's nobody here. We'll call impound. They'll tow the car. Meanwhile we can run the tag, see who pops up. My guess is it's stolen. Some punk kids hid it here until they can sell it."

"Okay, okay. You got the tag number?"

"Yep."

Their voices faded along with their footsteps.

Brand didn't move a muscle until he heard the car start and back out of the driveway.

Then he flopped down on the dirty floor, stretching out his cramped legs in front of him. His breath hissed out through his clenched teeth.

Lily's fingernails were still clamped to his thigh.

Without thinking, he covered her hand with his, running his thumb along her knuckles.

She stiffened.

"It's okay," he whispered, giving her hand a squeeze. "They're gone."

She sat without moving for a long moment. Then she pulled her hand away. "If they run the tag, they'll know who you are, Jake Brand."

He shot her a harsh glance. "You went through the glove box."

She shrugged. "I was bored."

He laughed at her deadpan comment, although inside he acknowledged her statement with a wince.

Yeah, they'd know exactly who he was. A check on the car's registration would reveal that it was a confiscated vehicle signed out to Brandon Gallagher for use in an undercover operation. And in a very short time they'd also know where he was.

"Come on," he said, rising and holding out his hand to her. "We've got to get out of here. They're sending a wrecker for the car."

Lily took his hand and stood, groaning when her leg

muscles protested. Her feet had gone numb. She'd sat for too long without moving.

Brand steadied her, his hands under her elbows. She gripped his hard biceps.

His strength called to her in a way she'd never experienced before.

She'd never let herself lean on another person. Her father had taught her to take care of herself, and her ex-husband's lies had reinforced her belief that she could depend on no one but herself.

But now, looking up into Brand's eyes, she realized a terrifying truth. She could lose all her perspective around him.

His intensity and focus, and something about the determined look in his eyes, reminded her of her father.

His brow furrowed and his fingers tightened around hers. His expression held concern and something else she couldn't interpret. His gaze played over her mouth, her throat, her hair. Then he bent his head and looked directly into her eyes. "Are you all right?"

She let go of his arms and backed away. "Yes, I'm fine, for someone who's been threatened and kidnapped, and who's spent the last few minutes hiding from the police."

His intense scrutiny morphed into a frown. "Get in the car." He turned away.

She caught his wrist. "You know, if you would turn yourself in and offer information about Castellano, you could probably get a reduced sentence, or maybe even immunity from prosecution."

He looked down at her hand on his arm, then took it in his. His thumb ran lightly across her knuckles, just

like it had when they were hiding. The same odd thrill
sang through her, doubling her heart rate.

What was the matter with her? So he was as sexy and
appealing as any man she'd ever met. So he had a couple
of mannerisms that reminded her of her father. That
didn't mean he was anything like Joe Raines. He was a
criminal, a fugitive, and she was his hostage.

"You don't understand everything that's going on."

She almost laughed. "You're right about that. Although it's not like I haven't asked. I'm ready to listen
if you want to explain everything that's going on to me."

"I can't. Not yet. Just try to believe me when I say
I'm doing my best to keep you safe."

She jerked her hand away. "Big of you, since it's your
fault I'm in danger. If you're so all-fired concerned about
me, why won't you do the one thing I've asked you to do?
Let me call the nursing home and check on my father."

He gazed at her for a long moment. Then he pulled
out his phone. "What's the number?"

Lily's eyes suddenly stung with tears of relief and
joy. "Really? You're going to do it? Oh, my God, I don't
have the number. It was in my cell phone, which you
destroyed." Her voice broke.

"All right," he sighed. "I'll call directory assistance
as soon as we're out of here."

Brand rested his hand at the curve of her hip and carefully eased the office door open. Her heart fluttered like
a butterfly in her chest as he guided her back into the
dark, empty warehouse.

Despite what he'd put her through, despite the fact
that he'd been sent by Castellano to kill her, when he

touched her she felt as if she could trust her life to him. It was frightening to acknowledge that this man could so easily make her put aside all her careful caution.

He opened the car's passenger door. "Get in and stay put. I want to be sure everything's clear."

He walked with loose-limbed grace over to the warehouse door. It had grown dark while they'd been hiding from the police. Lily could barely make out his silhouette as he checked out the surrounding area.

Within a few seconds, he was back. He climbed into the car, started the engine and pulled out.

Lily was glad to be out of that warehouse. The officer had been right. It was creepy.

"Where are we going now?"

"I need to check on something," Brand said shortly.

"What about my father?"

He dug out his cell phone.

Lily reached for it, but he held it away from her.

"I'll do the calling."

He dialed three digits without looking at the buttons. After a few seconds he spoke. "Beachside Manor, Biloxi. Yes, go ahead and dial it."

He listened, then handed her the phone.

"May I help you?" the voice asked.

"The nurses' station on the Blue Wing, please."

"Please hold."

Lily clutched the cell phone like a lifeline.

Dear God, please let Dad be all right. She tried to pay attention to the streets Brand took, but she was too anxious to find out about her father. She couldn't concentrate on anything else.

"Blue wing. Starling." It was the Blue wing's supervisory nurse.

"Ms. Starling. It's Lily Raines." Her pulse raced and fear and anticipation clogged her throat.

"Oh, hi, Ms. Raines. I've been trying to reach you."

Lily's heart seized. "Why? Is everything okay? My father?"

"Oh yes, everything is fine. But I am glad you called. I left a message on your home phone earlier today. We've been concerned about that gentleman who was supposed to pick up your father. The poor man who was mugged and killed on the way here."

"I know. It was awful." She glanced over at Brand, who appeared to be concentrating on his driving.

"I wanted to ask you if you had sent someone else to pick him up."

Panic lodged in Lily's throat. "No!" she rasped. "No! You haven't let anyone see him have you?"

"No, ma'am. A man came by earlier this afternoon. He seemed nice enough at first, but when I explained to him that he couldn't see your father without your permission, he became rude and demanding. I had to call the security guard before he finally gave up and went away."

"Who was it?"

"He wouldn't give his name. That's why I called security."

Lily's hands shook so badly she almost dropped the phone. She thought about the fire in her dad's wastebasket.

Castellano's men had gotten to him once. They could again.

"Please make sure no one gets in to see him. No one but me."

"Of course, Ms. Raines. Will you be coming by soon?"

She looked at Brand. "As soon as I possibly can."

"Ms. Raines, are you all right?"

Lily swallowed and tried to make her voice sound normal. "I'm fine. Thank you for letting me know about the man." She fumbled with the disconnect button, her fingers numb with fear.

Brand gently took the phone from her and pocketed it. "What's the matter? Did someone try to get to your father?"

She glared at him. "You should know. Isn't that the plan, to threaten my father? He was sent by Castellano." She took a shaky breath. "You have to take me there. I have to make sure he's safe."

He knew she was right. If it had been the police who'd shown up at the nursing home, they wouldn't have hesitated to flash their badges.

His fists clenched on the steering wheel, his chest tightening with foreboding. Why hadn't Pruitt picked up her father and put him in protective custody? What the hell was Pruitt's problem? That made it three times the FBI agent had let him down.

He vowed to call him as soon as he could manage it without Lily overhearing. He'd demand to know what was going on. There was no excuse for this much delay.

"Answer me!" Lily shouted.

"I can't take you there. The nursing home is being watched."

"Castellano sent someone to kill my father." Her voice was shrill. She was about to fall apart.

Brand nodded, working to keep his expression bland. *Damn it*. It wouldn't take Castellano long to figure out a way to get to Joe Raines. He'd managed it once already. That fire in the wastebasket hadn't been an accident.

"Please. Dear God, please take me to him."

"No. That's not going to happen." Brand stopped at a stop sign and turned to Lily. He covered her hand where it rested on her knee. She tried to pull away, but he wrapped his fingers around hers and held on tight.

"Listen to me. The police will pick up your father and place him in protective custody. They should do that any time now."

"How do you know?"

He shrugged. "You were a juror on a high-profile murder case. Now you're missing. A former police officer was killed on his way to Beachside Manor. The police aren't dumb. They'll be right on top of Henderson's killing and it won't take them long to put two and two together. As soon as they do, they'll get your father out of there." He squeezed her hand. "He'll be transported to a secure facility. He'll be safe."

A sob escaped her throat. "Safe."

He knew what she was thinking. Her father's safety was the most important thing, but she had no idea if Brand were telling the truth or not. She didn't trust him, and he couldn't blame her.

He'd done little to earn her trust.

He turned his attention back to the road. They were

approaching his lieutenant's street. It worried him that he hadn't been able to get in touch with Morrison.

From the time Brand first joined the force, Morrison had taken him under his wing. He'd been more like a father to him than his own father ever had. Morrison was the one man Brand could trust. The one man who would give him straight answers.

So why was he suddenly unreachable?

As he approached the corner, he saw a car turn onto Morrison's street. His senses went on red alert. The vehicle passed under a streetlight, and he recognized the glint of a portable police light on the dashboard.

What the hell? A glimpse of a broad, florid face inside the car told him the driver wasn't Morrison. Brand slowed and looked down the street. There were at least three unmarked vehicles parked along the curb.

Cops. He knew it in his gut. He cursed under his breath.

Had something happened to Morrison, or were they waiting for him? It was well known around the squad room how much he admired the lieutenant.

He sped up and away. He didn't know if any of the cars had spotted him, but he wasn't taking any chances.

"What's the matter?"

He arched his shoulders to relieve the tension. "Nothing."

"That's not true. You saw something."

He grimaced inwardly. She was perceptive. "Nothing you need to be concerned about."

"I disagree. I'm concerned about everything you do, since you're holding me hostage."

Brand studied her. Then he asked the question that

had been gnawing at his gut. "Why didn't you scream for help when the officers showed up at the warehouse?"

She stared at him in surprise. Her mouth opened, but nothing came out. She pressed her lips together and looked down at her hands. "I'm not sure."

"Could it be that you don't trust the police, either?"

"Of course I trust the police. My father was on the force for over twenty years."

Her wide brown eyes met his, and he saw confusion and wariness in their unfathomable depths.

"So? You could be in police custody now, where you'd feel safe. Why didn't you scream?"

She pressed her lips together and looked down at her hands. "I should have, but—"

"But?" Had she thought he would kill her?

"I was afraid they'd shoot you."

Chapter Six

Her answer stunned him. She was afraid for his life?

Her head was still down and her profile was silhouet-ted against the glow from the streetlights. Her nose turned up slightly, her brows arched delicately over her eyes, and as he watched, that stubborn chin lifted.

"Odd behavior from a cop's daughter."

She angled her head to stare at him. "So you think I should have screamed for the police?"

"No. I'm grateful you didn't." He took a right turn, keeping an eye on the traffic. He had no idea where to go. Maybe he should drive east, toward Pascagoula, and look for a hotel.

"I should have," she repeated.

His cell phone rang. Surprised, he checked the caller ID.

Pruitt. Damn it.

He pulled into a dark side street and stopped. He wasn't about to chance Lily overhearing the FBI agent on the phone. In one motion he turned off the car and opened the door.

"Stay put," he told Lily, then slammed the car door.

"Yeah?" he grated through clenched teeth as he walked a few steps away from the vehicle.

"Gallagher, what the hell are you doing?"

"What am I doing? Don't give me that!" He kept his eye on Lily as he walked farther away. "What the hell are *you* doing? Where were your arresting officers, man? I thought you were going to pick up Foshee and me at the courthouse."

"There's a bigger issue at stake here."

"A bigger issue than Lily Raines's life?"

"Listen to me, Gallagher, and drop the attitude. I got word from Carson there's a very important shipment coming in. He thinks it may be automatic weapons."

"What does that have to do with you hanging me out to dry?"

"We've got to stay under the radar. We don't want anything to jeopardize this shipment. If we had picked up Foshee, Castellano would be alerted, and we'd lose our chance."

"Well, I beat up Foshee to keep him from killing Lily. So what do you think Castellano thinks about me?"

"We're hoping he'll think you're a loose cannon—which you are! Look, Gallagher. If we can nail 'em with the smuggled weapons in their hands, then we can put Castellano away for good. That's all you need to know. Now where the hell are you and what the hell are you doing? I assume you have the juror."

"I can't tell you where I am right now, and I'm about to hang up, so don't even think about triangulating on the cell phone signal. There's something fishy going on.

I can't let anyone know where I am until I figure out what it is."

"I'm giving you a direct order. If you don't come in immediately, I'll suspend you."

"No problem, *boss*. Being suspended is the least of my worries right now." He glanced over his shoulder at the car. Lily's head was angled. She was watching him. He started back toward the vehicle. No sense in giving her a chance to run.

"Why haven't you picked up Joe Raines?"

"The old man? You gonna bring the girl in so we can get her signed permission?"

Brand kept silent.

"That's what I thought. So we have to get a court order to remove him from the nursing home. These things take time."

"Well, rush it. Castellano's already gotten to him once, and he tried again today. Call me when he's safe."

"Gallagher, are you really gonna lose your badge over a girl?"

Brand hung up and headed back to the car. He was certain Pruitt had all available squad cars on the lookout for them. He had to find a place where they could hide. He'd ditch the car as soon as he could.

Lily saw the anger and frustration on Brand's face as he got in and started the engine without speaking.

"What was that about?"

He made a U-turn and pulled out of the side street. "Nothing."

"It didn't look like nothing." She studied his grim face. "I keep trying to figure out what you're planning to do with me. You're waiting for instructions, aren't you? Is it Castellano? Is that who you're supposed to turn me over to?" She swallowed hard. The idea had been growing in her mind ever since he'd rescued her from Foshee.

He sent her a dark look. "I'm not turning you over to Castellano. Haven't you figured that out by now?"

Lily's frustration boiled over. "Well, excuse me. I was abducted and handcuffed and thrown into a stranger's car. Forgive me if I can't quite *keep up* with what you're thinking." She crossed her arms and pushed back in her seat, watching him out of the corner of her eye.

He shot her an amused glance, ramping up her anger. She turned away and looked out the window.

After a few moments of driving in silence, he turned east.

Lily found herself watching him again. His hands were white-knuckled on the steering wheel. His wide, straight mouth was set, and a tiny frown furrowed the space between his brows.

"You don't look like a thug."

His brows shot up and his mouth quirked upward. He was smiling. The lump of fear that had settled under her breastbone loosened.

"Thank you, I reckon," he said wryly.

"I mean it. You're not slimy like the Cajun, nor too slick like Sack Simon. How did you end up working for Castellano?"

"I guess I'm just a lucky guy."

His jaw flexed again and the half smile was gone. Lily clung to her mistrust of him like a starving man holding tight to his last morsel of food. She couldn't afford to be influenced by a pair of kind blue eyes or a strong, determined jaw.

"Come on. Nobody wakes up one morning when they're a kid and says 'I want to be an enforcer for an organized crime boss.'"

"That's true."

He glanced in the rearview mirror, and the furrow appeared between his brows again. He muttered a curse under his breath.

"What is it?"

"I'm not sure. We may have picked up a tail."

Lily turned to look behind her. She saw a couple of cars, but neither one of them were close. "How can you tell?"

"So, Lily. What did you want to be when you grew up?"

"What?" She was surprised. Was he trying to distract her from the vehicle following them? Or was he trying to keep her calm?

"A nurse? A teacher? Miss America?"

Despite her worry, she laughed. "I suppose like any child, I wanted to be just like my father. I wanted to be a cop."

Brand cut his eyes up to the rearview mirror again.

"What about you?" she asked.

His lips pressed together for an instant. "I wanted to be anything *but* just like my dad. Hold on."

He took a sharp left in front of a black SUV.

Lily cried out and grabbed for the armrest as the massive vehicle missed the rear of Brand's car by mere inches. Its horn blared.

She jumped. "What are you doing?"

"Losing the tail I hope." He straightened the vehicle and raced down the side street.

Lily turned around in her seat. "Is it the police?"

"More likely Castellano's men."

"How did they find us?"

"They know my car."

Lily saw the dark car turn onto the street behind them. "There they are. They're following us."

Brand whipped the car to the right, down an alley between two restaurants.

Lily's heart jumped into her throat. "Where are you going?"

"Cutting through to a major street. Trying to lose them."

All at once, a wall of rusted metal loomed in front of them.

"Look out!" she cried, automatically raising her arms to shield her face.

It was a metal garbage Dumpster, and it blocked the alley. Brand slammed on the brakes and whipped the car sideways. The tires screeched. The car halted less than two feet from the dirty metal container.

"Damn it!" He slapped the steering wheel with his palm. The garbage truck had set the Dumpster down right in the middle of the alley. There was no room for a car to pass.

He cut the engine and turned off the lights. Shifting in his seat, he kept watch on the narrow alley through which they'd come. "Go around the Dumpster. There'll be a door on your left. Go straight through the kitchen, find the bathroom and stay there until I come and get you."

Lily grabbed his arm. "What about you?"

"I'm going to get these guys off our tail. Now run."

"Not without you."

He shook his head. "Too dangerous. If I do that I'll be leading them into a restaurant full of people. I've got to stop them out here."

"But what if you can't—"

Brand covered her hand with his. "Then you call the police." He squeezed her hand. "Run."

She got out of the car and ran toward the Dumpster. She slipped around it just as the black car passed the alley. Brand had no time to even breathe before the car backed up and turned into the alley.

Cursing under his breath, he slid out of the driver's seat and crouched behind the car, using it as a shield. With calm efficiency he drew his weapon and checked it, making sure he had a full magazine.

The dark car stopped a few feet away from his rear bumper. Both doors opened and two men jumped out, using the open car doors as shields.

"Hey, *bioque.*" It was Foshee. His voice was more nasal than usual.

Brand trained his weapon on the passenger door, where a narrow strip of white bobbed up and down in the shadows.

"You broke my nose. You gonna pay for that." Foshee let loose a string of nasty curses in French.

Brand laughed without humor. The strip of white was a bandage on Foshee's large nose.

The other man, the driver, yelled at Brand. "Where's the girl?"

"Gone. I don't have her."

"You're a lying pig. You got her there somewhere. Give her up and we'll let you live."

"Yeah. Long enough to deliver me to Castellano."

Foshee's head popped up from behind the car door and a shot zinged past Brand's head.

He fired back, aiming for the window. It shattered. Then he shifted his aim and shot the driver's window out.

"Get out of here, Foshee. I don't want to have to kill you."

The Cajun laughed. "It's two against one, Brand. You got no chance."

Brand eyed the shoes that stuck out beneath the car door. "Sounds like pretty good odds to me."

Foshee fired, and the bullet screeched along the top of Brand's car. He ducked, feeling a sliver of metal prick his cheek. After a couple of seconds he rose and fired off two rounds at Foshee's feet.

The Cajun screamed and dove back into the car.

The driver's side of the car was angled slightly away from his line of sight, so he couldn't get a bead on the driver's feet. He fired anyway, trying to aim through the shattered window.

The last thing he wanted to do was kill someone, but Lily was inside the restaurant waiting for him, depending on him to protect her from Castellano. He'd do what he had to.

The driver fired back. The metallic thud of the bullet hitting the side of the car rang in Brand's ears. Then he heard something else.

Sirens. Getting louder.

Were they responding to the gunshots? Equal parts of relief and apprehension coursed through him.

A muffled groan and shadowy movement in the car's interior told him Foshee was still conscious. Brand fired again at each door, then took careful aim and shot out the vehicle's two front tires.

The police sirens kept coming, getting louder. As a squad car sped past the alley and its brake lights flashed, Brand turned and skirted the Dumpster and burst into the restaurant's kitchen.

The odors of grease, fish and fresh bread wafted around him as he ploughed through the service area, ignoring the shocked looks and exclamations of the staff. He headed for the women's bathroom.

He flung open the door and crossed the lounge in two long strides. As his pulse raced with apprehension, he stuck his head in the bathroom door.

"Lily?"

He heard a muffled sob. The sound froze his heart. With his weapon clutched in both hands, he slipped through the door.

There, at the far end of the tiled room, a man in a dark suit with a fighter's flattened nose held a gun to Lily's head. His other arm was wrapped around her neck.

She stood stiffly, her eyes sparkling with tears as she met Brand's gaze.

"I'm sorry," she whispered.

"Shut up!" The man pushed the gun into her temple and tightened his arm.

She coughed.

"You coward," Brand taunted. "Hiding behind a woman. How the hell did you get in here, anyhow?"

The thug grinned. "When you pulled into this alley, there was only two ways you could go. Through the alley on foot, or into the restaurant. There's a guy at the other end of the alley, too."

Brand wanted to shoot the sneering grin off the man's face. "Let her go. She's got nothing to do with this. Shoot me."

"It ain't you he wants. You I can take care of right here with one shot."

"Yeah? Go ahead. Shoot me, but I'll guarantee I'll drop you before I die."

A muffled cry escaped Lily's lips and tears slipped down her cheeks.

Brand moved closer.

"Don't try it," the thug warned.

But Brand only had one chance, and he was betting it all on Castellano giving orders to have Lily brought to him alive. The thug couldn't kill her, so he had to kill Brand.

He sent Lily a quick look, hoping beyond hope that she could read his intent. She was a cop's daughter. Surely her father had taught her how to defend herself.

She clasped her fingers together in front of her in a pleading gesture. "I'll go with you. Just don't hurt him, please," she begged the man holding her.

Brand's heart skipped a beat.

The thug took his gun away from her temple and aimed it at Brand. "Sorry, sweetheart," he laughed. "But I've got my orders. Besides, I'm going to enjoy this."

Lily used the force of her left hand against her right fist to drive her elbow into his midsection.

"Oof!" He doubled over. His finger reflexively pulled the trigger but his shot went wild. Lily broke away and backed up against the wall.

At the same time, Brand hit the floor and rolled. He knocked the guy's two-hundred-dollar shoes out from under him. The big man collapsed with a loud thud and his gun skidded across the slick tile floor and clanged against the far wall.

Brand came up onto his knees. He aimed his gun right at the guy's heart.

But the thug just groaned and tried to push himself up. A knot was already swelling on his sweaty forehead where he'd hit the floor.

Brand stood and placed a foot on the man's burly neck and pulled a Flexicuff out of his jeans. He cuffed the man's hands behind his back. Then he grabbed a couple of paper towels and stuffed them in his mouth. With one foot, he shoved him under the door of the closest stall.

"Come on."

Lily turned toward him, stopping just short of flinging herself into his arms. Her wide brown eyes were huge in her pale face and the tracks of tears glistened on her cheeks. She quickly gave him the once-over.

"Are you hurt? Did he hit you?" she asked shakily.

He shook his head. "What about you?"

She shook her head. "I'm fine."

But Brand could tell that she wasn't. Her hands were shaking. Her eyes still held a haunted fear.

"That was a good move. Your dad teach you that?"

She nodded jerkily. "I never did it for real before."

"Well, you did good." He gave her a little smile. "You're tougher than you look. Let's get out of here. We don't have much time. It's not going to take long for somebody to figure out that those were gunshots."

"Shouldn't we get his gun?"

Just as she spoke the lounge door opened and an older woman entered. She gasped. "Oh, my word! What is going on here?"

Brand took Lily's arm and squeezed it. "Nothing, ma'am. I was worried about my wife. But she's fine."

He surreptitiously tucked his gun into his belt and guided Lily past the woman and out the door. They turned right, toward the main exit.

Behind them, a scream loud enough to be heard over the music erupted from the women's bathroom.

"Help! There's a dead man in here!"

The door from the kitchen burst open. Lily looked over her shoulder. She went rigid.

"It's the police," she whispered.

Brand's heart hammered. He kept his head down. "Don't look at them. Keep walking."

They were almost at the exit. Another three seconds and they'd be out of there.

"But they could help us." Lily half turned, but Brand held on to her arm as the woman from the bathroom emerged, screaming, "It's them! They're getting away!"

People began to stir and whisper. A waiter started toward them.

"Walk," he commanded.

Once they were outside, he looked up and down the street. "Come on. This way." He headed east.

Lily was forced to half run to keep up with him. "I don't understand. Castellano's men are trying to kill you. Why won't you let the police help?"

"I've seen things that make me worry that some of the police are in Castellano's pocket."

"That can't be true."

Brand stopped. "Whether you believe it or not, it can be true. And if I trust the wrong person, you may not escape Castellano's clutches next time."

Her shoulders hunched and he watched a shiver ripple through her.

He stole a glance back at the restaurant they'd just left. Then he pointed ahead of them. "See the hotel up there? We'll cut through there and grab a cab on the other side, the Carroll Street entrance."

He pulled her with him to the building side of the sidewalk, staying out of the line of sight of the police when they came out of the restaurant.

As they reached the hotel, he risked another glance backward. Sure enough, two police officers ran out of the restaurant, looking up and down the street.

Brand wrapped his arm around Lily's neck like a lover and urged her forward, wincing when a breeze lifted her hair and blew it across his face.

The smell of fresh coconut and vanilla reminded him of how soft and vulnerable her neck had been when he'd bandaged it. How close he'd been to her lips, close enough to see them quiver.

He groaned silently as he followed her through the hotel lobby door.

"Keep walking," he said, pushing her ahead of him and dropping back a few steps. He pulled out his cell phone and dialed a familiar number. When his brother answered, Brand breathed a sigh of relief.

"Ry, it's me. Can I ask a favor of you?"

"I can barely hear you. What is it? I'm on my way to bed."

The impatience in Ryan's voice made Brand sad. He'd always looked up to his older brother, always counted on him. But ever since he'd gone undercover, they'd grown apart.

He put his mouth right against the phone, making sure Lily couldn't hear him. "You said Cassie wasn't using her studio?"

"That's right. Hasn't since she found out she was pregnant. Turpentine, mineral spirits—all that can be bad for the baby."

"Can I borrow it? Just for a day or two."

"What kind of jam have you gotten yourself into this time, kid?"

"I'm, uh—protecting a witness. Come on, Ry. I'm in a hurry. I need a place to hide out where no one would think to look for me."

Ryan sighed. "Does this have to do with Castellano?"

"Kind of."

Ryan cursed. "I don't like it."

"It's just a couple of days. Ry, it's a matter of life and death."

"Get serious, Brand."

"I *am* serious. I've got a witness who can bring Castellano down."

Ryan was silent.

"Thanks, bud. I won't touch a thing. I promise."

"Brand, how much trouble are you in?"

"Not too much."

"Damn it, Brand. How do you let yourself get sucked into these situations?"

Ahead of him, Lily had reached the Carroll Street entrance. She turned and sent him a questioning glance, her face drawn and white. His heart squeezed in sympathy. She was so tired and so scared. No matter how brave she acted, she'd almost died back there, and she knew it.

He hated being the reason her brown eyes were dull and the spark he'd admired was gone. She wouldn't make it much further without rest.

He considered Ryan's question. How had he gotten sucked into this situation? How could he not? He couldn't let Foshee kill her. He turned his attention back to his brother. "I've always had a flair for excitement," he said wryly.

"Yeah, I'd say so. So who's the witness you're protecting?"

"You know I can't tell you that. Is there a key somewhere, so I can get into the studio without having to break in?"

Ryan sighed. "Look in the mailbox. Cassie keeps a spare key there. I've warned her about it, but for some reason she thinks nobody can figure that out."

Brand smiled. "You tell her thanks."

"I'd just as soon not tell her anything. See that you don't mess up the place, okay?"

Brand grunted. Messing up the place was the least of his worries. "Ry, how's Mom?"

"She's doing okay. She's having a ball with the baby."

"That's good. Would you tell her something for me? Tell her I'll see her as soon as I can."

"Yeah. I'll tell her. Take care of yourself, kid."

A pricking behind his eyes surprised him. When did he get so damned sentimental about family?

"I will, Ry. Thanks."

He disconnected and glanced over his shoulder. So far the police hadn't gotten to the hotel.

He guided Lily to the lobby door. "Wait here until I get a taxi."

Lily nodded. As soon as Brand's hand left her back, she reached out to steady herself against the wall. She was so tired she could barely stand and so spooked she couldn't think. She'd never been so close to death. She could still feel the cold steel of the gun's barrel pressed into her temple, still smell the cigarette smoke on the man's breath.

Suddenly, her stomach churned. Now that it was all over, she couldn't believe she'd had sense enough to use her elbow like her father had taught her. She couldn't believe the move had worked. All she could do was shake her head in wonder. She'd helped, but Brand had saved her again.

He'd saved her. She had no idea who he was, no clue what his motives were. But his strong arms around her made her feel as if nothing bad could happen to her. His intense blue eyes promised her safety. And if she looked closely enough, she could imagine that they promised something else. Something baser, sweeter than security.

An electric spark of desire ignited deep within her. She gasped quietly, then blew air out through her pursed lips. She couldn't think that way. She couldn't *feel* that way.

She wasn't thinking clearly, that was all. She hadn't had a decent night's sleep since Brand and the Cajun had threatened her and her father the first time, and today she'd been close to death three times. She felt numb and terrified at the same time—an odd combination.

Brand spoke quickly with the doorman, who made a call on his cell phone. Then he stepped back inside the door, filling her senses with the aura of confidence and strong sexiness that surrounded him.

"The taxi will be here in a few minutes," he said. "Stay back, away from the door. It's too bright here in the entryway."

She nodded jerkily. She hadn't forgotten how dangerous their situation was.

"Are you all right?" he asked, taking her arm.

"Sure. I'm fine."

"We'll be somewhere safe in ten minutes."

"Somewhere safe?" Dear God, if she could only believe that. A laugh that felt faintly hysterical bubbled up from her chest. "Are you kidding me? The only safe place I can think of is the one place you won't go." She put up a shaky hand to tuck her hair behind her ear.

"The police? I told you I can't afford to do that. Not yet."

Helpless frustration swept through her, along with

apprehension. What if Brand was playing her for a fool until he could get her to Castellano? What if she were blinded by the kindness she glimpsed in his eyes when he looked at her?

To her dismay, her eyes filled with tears. "Well, when then? How many times do we have to be chased and shot at before you turn yourself in?"

The taxi appeared.

"Turn myself in?" His voice held a hard edge.

"You're running from Castellano and running from the law. That tells me you've done something really bad."

"Does it?" He scowled at her, his expression hard. "Our ride's here. Let's go."

The doorman held the door and Brand guided her quickly to the vehicle. He deposited her in the backseat then climbed in after her.

"Three eleven Woodmont," he told the driver. "In Pass Christian."

The taxi pulled out and made a U-turn.

Lily sat back in the seat and sighed. She longed to close her burning eyes, but she found herself watching Brand.

He scanned the sidewalks and the oncoming traffic as well as the cars behind them. His hand rested lightly on her knee, and his shoulder pressed against hers.

She should scoot away from him. She shouldn't allow him to touch her. She didn't trust him, so how could the weight of his hand wrap her in feelings of warmth and safety?

There she went again. Apparently the fact that it was a false sense of security didn't matter to her exhausted brain.

She shook her head, trying to dislodge the dangerous notion that he wasn't a threat. She was beginning to think of him as some sort of hero. She'd be hallucinating in a minute.

Still, she couldn't shake the notion that there was something innately honorable about this man who'd taken her hostage. In many ways, he reminded her of her father, compassionate but ruthless when he had to be. And like her father, he exuded strength and integrity.

She tilted her head and examined his profile. She knew appearances could be deceiving. Knew better than to trust someone just because they looked like a nice person. She'd trusted her ex-husband and look where that had gotten her.

He'd cheated on her and tried to exert a measure of control over her that had bordered on emotional abuse.

But all her careful caution and her meager experience with men didn't stop her from trusting Brand. She trusted him even though she knew how dangerous that could be. Because he had to be one of two things—an enforcer for Castellano, or some kind of vigilante.

A third possibility tickled the edge of her mind. She rejected it immediately. There was no way he was a cop. Not with his obvious disdain for the police. Unless—

Her pulse sped up and her mouth went dry as she realized his attitude could have another root cause. And if that was the case, she was in a lot more trouble than she'd first thought.

Her father had always said that there was nothing more dangerous than a rogue cop.

Chapter Seven

The place where Brand had brought them was an old building, subdivided into offices. As he retrieved a key from the mailbox, Lily tried to read the name on the box's label. It looked like *Galloway* or *Gallagher*—she couldn't quite tell. She only got a brief glimpse.

They went up to the second floor and Brand unlocked the door to what appeared to be a small studio. The first thing that hit Lily was the smell of turpentine. She stepped inside, around a roll of canvas and a box of paint tubes.

An easel stood near the window, with a stool in front of it. An artist's palette, covered with globs of bright paint, lay on the stool. There were canvases stacked everywhere—against the walls and on the floor. On her left a bedraggled daybed was piled high with sketches and books.

"Whose studio is this?"

Brand turned from locking the dead bolt. "I can't answer that."

"Of course not." Lily sighed. "I don't understand

why you don't trust me." She flung her arms out. "Who am I going to tell?"

"You're safer not knowing anything. Then you won't have to lie."

"Lie? Why would I lie?"

"Don't worry about it. It doesn't matter anyhow." He pocketed the keys and stepped past her, his shoulder brushing hers. That ridiculous spark of yearning streaked through her again, weakening her knees and shocking her senses. How was she going to fight this absurd attraction to the man who had taken her hostage?

The man who'd saved her.

Her heart sped up in a staccato rhythm as she tried to deny the sudden thrill that flowed from her loins all the way out to her fingers and toes.

She was *not* attracted to him, she told herself sternly. She couldn't be. He wasn't one of the good guys.

Her reaction came from fear and helplessness, she reasoned. Of course. That had to be it. He was her best hope in a dangerous situation, so naturally she was drawn to his strength, his competence and the sense of safety she felt with him.

He crossed the tiny room and peered through the edge of the closed blinds. "We can see the street from here. That's good. As long as we keep watch, nobody can sneak up on us."

He surveyed the room. "That door leads to the bathroom. There's a window in there, but I wouldn't advise climbing out. It's a long drop to the ground."

Lily smiled grimly. "No problem. But if you don't mind—" She gestured toward the door.

"Go ahead." Brand stepped aside.

Lily eased past him and slipped into the minuscule bathroom. Closing the door behind her, she leaned against it for a few seconds as tears stung her eyes and a sob escaped her lips.

It was all too much. Had it really been just this afternoon that she'd sat in the courtroom with eleven other jurors and returned a guilty verdict? Had it been no more than a few hours ago that Brand had held her at knifepoint, then turned the tables and rescued her from Foshee?

She peered in the tiny mirror and fingered the awkward bandage on her neck. Peeling off the tape, she tilted her head to look at the cut. It wasn't deep but it was almost two inches long. Two inches. That's how close she'd come to dying.

She turned on the water and splashed it on her face. The cool liquid soothed her burning eyes and helped to clear her head.

A couple of towels were folded on the back of the toilet and a bottle of floral-scented hand soap sat next to the sink. At least she'd figured out one thing. The owner of the studio was a woman. She quickly splashed her face one more time, then used one of the towels to dry off.

When she opened the bathroom door, Brand was gathering up a stack of sketches from the daybed.

He had to move out of the way before the door would open fully. Lily slipped past him and went over to the easel. "She's good."

"Who?"

"Whoever painted these. Is it your girlfriend?" She

picked up one of the canvases stacked against the wall and held it up. It was a portrait of a child, done in a soft, impressionistic style.

He looked up from turning down the covers. "No. Leave them alone."

She set the portrait down and turned another canvas around. It depicted a bowl of apples sitting on the windowsill. "They're really lovely."

"Come away from the window," he said irritably. "You can sleep here. I'll keep watch."

"All night? You can't do that."

"Just try to sleep."

Lily slipped out of her heels and her suit jacket and lay down. She relaxed into the too-soft mattress of the daybed. Her shoulders and neck ached, her feet hurt, and she didn't think she'd ever been so tired in her life.

Brand turned out the lights, but a glaring yellow glow from a gas station across the street filtered through the blinds, casting long, striped shadows on the floor.

He stood beside the window, peered out through the edge of the blinds and started unbuttoning his shirt.

Lily watched him in stunned silence. She could hardly breathe as he shrugged out of the dress shirt.

He tossed it on a stack of canvases. The white T-shirt underneath stretched over his broad shoulders and across his tight middle. His arms were corded with long, sleek muscles.

The light from the window threw him into silhouette, emphasizing the clean planes of his face and body. With his arms bare, he looked less bulky, less formidable, though not a bit less sexy.

He pulled his weapon out of his waistband and checked it thoroughly before placing it on top of his shirt. Then he went back to keeping watch.

Lily fought the desire that arrowed through her. Despite her efforts, her thighs tightened and her pulse pounded. She decided Brand was the sexiest man she'd ever known.

Her eyes traced the strong curve of his back, the sleek line of his shoulders. His profile was classic, marred only by a slightly crooked nose. His mouth was straight, his jaw strong. He looked like a warrior silhouetted against the night sky.

Her pulse pounded and a strange ache began in the region of her heart. What would it be like to be loved by him? To make love with someone that intense, someone that strong?

She clenched her fists. She had to stop thinking about him in that way. She had to concentrate on getting to the police.

"Do you think they'll find us?"

He angled his head without taking his gaze from the street outside. "Not unless—" He stopped. "No."

Lily sat up and hugged a throw pillow. "Not unless what?"

"Nothing. Go to sleep."

"What are you waiting for? Are you supposed to hear from somebody? Is that who you keep trying to call?"

He didn't answer.

"You could just drop me off at police headquarters. I know a lot of the officers. They'll protect me. I promise I wouldn't say anything about you."

"You promise?" He laughed. "That makes me feel better."

"So you're holding me to protect yourself? It doesn't look like it's working very well. I'd think you'd do better without me."

"Listen to me, Lily. Whether you choose to believe me or not, your life is in danger. And trust me, going to the police is no guarantee of safety."

"Why do you keep saying that?" His dogged certainty planted a seed of doubt in her breast. She did her best to ignore it. "I grew up around the police. My father was a police officer. His fellow officers, his friends, will take care of me. That's what police officers do. They take care of their own. They'll put me in protective custody until Castellano is caught."

"Yeah? And what if one of those officers you think you know so well is actually working for Castellano? What then?"

"That won't happen."

"It already has."

"You know that for a fact?"

He nodded. "I just don't know who."

His cell phone rang, startling her.

Brand dug the phone out of his pocket and looked at the caller ID. It was Pruitt again. He pressed the disconnect button, rejecting the call.

Lily turned onto her side. Her eyes glittered in the faint light from the blinds. "I'm really tired."

"I know," he said softly. "Why don't you get some sleep?"

"I'm not sure I can. It's been a rough day."

"Yeah."

"Talk to me," she murmured.

Brand's gaze followed the sleek line of her neck, the curve of her hip, her long, shapely legs. "About what?" he asked, hearing the rasp of yearning in his voice.

"Anything, I don't care. Just talk."

He thought about her growing up with a police officer for a father. How reassuring that must have been for a child to know that her dad was a good man.

"Was your dad always a cop?"

She nodded. "Ever since I can remember. He was the strongest, most honest man I've ever known."

Brand's heart ached. The closest he'd ever had to a father like that was his older brother. But Ryan had never approved of him becoming a cop. Then when Brand had taken the undercover assignment to bring down Castellano, Ryan had accused him of seeking revenge for Patrick's murder.

Brand had never admitted to Ryan that revenge on Castellano was always in the back of his mind. Revenge wasn't a heroic purpose. But then he'd never claimed to be a hero. Still, he'd like to think he was bringing Castellano down because it was the right thing to do. The crime boss had hurt too many people, including Lily.

He looked up to find her sleepy gaze on him.

"What about your mother?" he asked her.

"She died when I was twelve. My dad reared me on his own."

"No brothers and sisters?"

"No. Just me and my dad."

"Is your ex-husband a cop?"

"No. He's a prominent real-estate lawyer. I can't even remember why I married him. And trust me, I will never forget why I divorced him."

"Why did you?"

She sighed. "The usual reason I suppose. He cheated on me." Her shoulders moved in a slight shrug. "And he hated that I had my own career. He tried to stop me from working, tried to control every aspect of my life."

Brand knew the type. He'd worked his share of domestic disturbances. But he'd never understand that kind of cruel bastard. How could anyone married to a woman like Lily mistreat or cheat on her? His heart squeezed painfully. She was beautiful, kind, gutsy. And sexy as hell. Everything a man could want in a woman.

Impotent anger at the jerk who'd treated her badly swelled inside him. If she'd stayed in the marriage, she could have ended up hurt or dead. A sudden urge overwhelmed him. He wanted to gather her into his arms and show her what a man who didn't hate women could give her.

Quickly, he changed the direction of his thoughts.

"So what do you do, Lily?"

"I'm an interior designer. But what about you, Jake Brand? Are you married?"

He laughed shortly. She'd turned the tables on him. He should have seen that coming. He shook his head. "Not even close."

"What about your parents? Brothers and sisters?"

"My father just died."

"I'm sorry."

"Don't be. He was an alcoholic. Made my mother's life a living hell."

"Your poor mother. That's so sad. Is that why you said you'd rather be anything other than like your father?"

Brand didn't answer. Couldn't. He never talked about his family to anyone. It surprised the hell out of him that he'd said so much to Lily.

"You were going to tell me how you ended up working for Castellano."

"Was I?"

She smiled. "I need to know."

"No, you don't. Like I told you, the less you know, the safer you'll be."

"You actually believe the police are the bad guys, don't you?"

He looked out the window. "Not all of them. Just certain ones."

"You shouldn't judge everyone based on what one person did to you."

He grimaced at her words. He'd lived his life believing all families were as dysfunctional as his. That all fathers drank and yelled and hit. That everyone's mother cried and cowered in the corner.

In his experience family and what passed for love was inextricably bound in pain and fear.

Lily would never understand how his life had been shaped by what his father had done to his mother, to his brothers and him. She'd had a good father and a decent, loving family.

She yawned. "I can't stay awake."

"You don't have to. I'm here. I'll take care of you."

He sat still, listening to her quiet breaths until they turned soft and even. She was asleep.

Brand walked over and pulled the covers up to her shoulders.

She smiled and said something he didn't catch.

"Sleep tight, Lily," he whispered. An impulse he couldn't explain made him lean over and kiss her cheek. Her soft scent enveloped him and her hair tickled his nose.

He pulled back and studied her face, her hair, the red scratch on her neck where he'd cut her. He frowned and reached out a hand, but stopped short of touching her.

He wasn't quite sure what made her so appealing. She was pretty, with dark brown eyes and hair and a fair complexion. Her slim body was nice enough.

She was pleasant to look at, but nothing special. Except that when all of it came together—when her eyes snapped with interest or irritation and her teeth scraped gently across her vulnerable lower lip, he had to struggle to maintain control of his body.

Ever since the first time he'd seen her, while he'd held her for Foshee to threaten, he'd been attracted to her. As much as he fought it, he couldn't deny that she turned him on like no one he'd ever dated.

He touched her hair. "I'm sorry you got mixed up in this, Lily. I'm doing my best to protect you."

Turning away, he searched in the dark until he found Cassie's phone book in a desk drawer. He looked up his lieutenant's home phone number and punched it into his cell phone. Then he unlocked the dead bolt and slipped out into the hall.

He pressed the call button. The phone rang and rang.

"Damn it, Morrison." Brand scowled. What was going on? Had something happened to the lieutenant?

Finally someone picked up. "Yeah?" a gruff voice said.

"Morrison? It's Gallagher."

He heard a low groan and the sharp creak of bed-springs. "Hang on," Morrison whispered.

Brand paced back and forth, grazing his knuckles with his teeth. Through the phone he heard rustling and the sound of a door closing softly.

Then the lieutenant was back. "Brand. Where the hell are you? What's the matter with you? I've got unmarked cars up and down my street, waiting for you to show up."

"I know. I couldn't reach you on your cell phone, so I drove by."

"My kid broke the damn phone. I had to get a new one. New number."

"What have you heard about the missing juror in the Simon case?"

"I heard you abducted her and you've been hiding from the police. Pruitt's bringing you up on charges of disobeying a superior officer and going AWOL."

Brand rubbed his temple. "Yeah, no doubt. What do you think about Pruitt?"

"You know what I think. He horned in and took over our operation, right when we were close to breaking into Castellano's inner circle. I think he's a jerk."

"But is he honest? Would he sell out?"

"He's FBI and he's a control freak. I don't think he'd do anything to jeopardize his career." Morrison paused. "Why? What's the problem?"

"Something's not right about this whole thing. He promised to pick up me and Foshee, and said he'd protect Lily Raines. He didn't do any of that. He left us swinging in the wind."

"Yeah. He said he couldn't afford to take the chance of tipping off Castellano. Apparently there's some big breakthrough in the works at one of his shipyards."

"So he sacrificed an innocent woman and a police officer for the sake of the operation?"

"He had to make a choice."

"That's total BS, Morrison. It would be okay if it were just me. But Lily Raines is completely innocent. If I hadn't stopped him, Foshee would have killed her."

"Why don't you come in? We can protect her, and maybe you won't lose your career."

"I can't and you know it. There's more. I don't think Castellano chose me for that assignment based on my excellent track record. He'd never even looked me in the eye before the day he gave me the assignment. To him I was nothing but a bouncer."

Brand stopped. His heart pounded. He was about to tell his former boss the real reason he couldn't bring Lily in.

"Somebody set me up. I think Castellano knew I was a cop. He knew I wouldn't kill Lily. Foshee was there to be sure my prints were on the knife. He was going to make sure Lily was dead and take me back to Castellano to force me to give up the other undercover officers. When I foiled his plan, he sent thugs to my apartment. I never told anyone where I lived."

"That's quite a theory, Brand. Don't underestimate

Castellano. He's a powerful man. He'd have no trouble finding out your address."

Brand frowned. "What's going on, Morrison? Since when don't you believe me?"

"I believe you, Brand. Why don't you come on in and I'll help you get this sorted out?"

"Not until I'm sure Lily's safe." He glanced at his watch. "Right now I don't know who to trust. Got to go, Lieu, before someone has a chance to trace this call."

"Brand, wait. I was going to call you. I need to meet with you. I've got some information you can use."

"What is it? Tell me now."

"I can't."

"Then I'll call you back. What's your new cell number?"

Morrison gave it to him. "Brand. I can get your girl to a safe place. Just let me know where you are."

"Sorry, Lieu. I'll call you back about a place to meet. You convince me you can keep Lily safe and I'll gladly turn her over to you. The longer she's with me, the more dangerous it gets for her."

"I'm glad you realize that."

"I realize a lot of things."

"Brand, let me pick you two up. I'll see that you get to tell your side of the story."

"Nope. I'll be in touch." He disconnected with a heavy sigh. Why the hell couldn't Morrison tell him his information over the phone? Had Pruitt gotten to him? They must have put a monitor on his phone, or Pruitt had threatened him with losing his job if he helped Brand.

Damn. He slipped back into the studio and locked the

dead bolt, then pocketed the key. Was he being paranoid? Was he reading too much into what could be a series of random events?

He glanced at Lily. Her lips were slightly parted and her breaths were even and soothing in the darkness.

In Castellano's world, killing Lily would be a trial by fire—proof that a prospective member of his elite team could be trusted. Maybe it hadn't been a setup to expose Brand as a ringer.

Morrison was right about one thing though. Even though Brand's apartment wasn't in his real name, even though he took a different route home every day and kept an eye out for suspicious vehicles, Castellano probably had connections in enough places that he wouldn't have any trouble finding out where Brand lived.

But what if one of those connections was a dirty cop?

Brand couldn't take that chance. Until he could be certain Lily was beyond Castellano's reach, he couldn't let her out of his sight.

He had no one to trust to keep her safe, except himself.

Chapter Eight

Lily opened her eyes. Where was she? The room was dark, except for a sliver of light slanting across the hardwood floor. A resinous smell filled her nostrils as she blinked and sat up.

She was stiff and sore, and she'd fallen asleep in her clothes.

A disturbance of shadows near the window startled her. She tensed and grabbed a pillow. Her brain screamed *danger* as her mind conjured visions of the Cajun's terrifying smile.

Then she remembered.

It was Brand. She was with Brand. And the smells were oil paint and turpentine.

He sat up straight and looked over at her, rubbing his face with both hands. "Sorry," he said, his voice hoarse with exhaustion. "I didn't mean to wake you."

"You didn't. I dreamed someone had a knife to my throat. I dreamed they killed my father and—" She stopped as the rest of her dream came rushing into her consciousness.

"And I dreamed they killed you." Her voice broke. She shrank back against the wall and hugged the pillow.

The worst part of her dream was that it was no more of a nightmare than the reality she was living.

"I can't stand this any longer," she said in a small voice. Her stomach churned with nauseating fear. Her head swam with exhaustion. Her hands were shaking and to her utter shame, she started crying.

"Damn it," she sobbed, swiping angrily at the tears. "I need to be doing something. I need to see my father, be sure he's safe. Instead I'm stuck here with a total stranger, waiting for something to happen and I don't even know what. I can't do anything to protect him."

Brand stood and walked toward her.

She watched him approach, not knowing if the flutter of her heart was because she was glad to have him close, or because she was afraid of what he might do. Her feelings were in turmoil.

The pale light filtering through the blinds sent shadows and highlights along his neck, shoulders and lean waist. He looked strong, competent.

He sat beside her on the daybed.

She didn't move. She wasn't sure she could.

"I know you're scared," he said. "You never should have been involved in this. Don't worry, first thing in the morning, we'll check on your father. I feel sure the police have moved him to a secure facility. Now you need to sleep. You're going to need all your strength in the next couple of days."

Without thinking about the consequences, Lily scooted closer to his comforting yet disturbing presence.

She needed to touch him, to draw on his strength to help bolster her own.

It didn't make any sense that she trusted this man who'd taken her hostage, but she did. That thought triggered another—something she'd read about kidnap victims and their captors. *Stockholm syndrome.* Was she nothing more than a pathetic kidnap victim who'd come to see her captor as her protector—the only one who could keep her safe?

God, she hoped she wasn't that gullible.

To her surprise, Brand lifted his arm and draped it around her shoulders. She stiffened automatically.

"Just relax. Go to sleep."

His soft, gravelly voice rumbled through her, feeding a flame deep inside her heart—a flame that had been growing ever since he'd saved her from the Cajun's lethal knife.

She leaned her head against the hollow of his shoulder and closed her eyes, but suddenly she wasn't sleepy at all. She was wide-awake and hyperaware of his hard, warm body pressed against hers.

"Promise me you're one of the good guys," she said softly.

He went totally still.

Lily waited, not breathing. A tremor of apprehension slid through her.

Finally, to her relief, he spoke, but his words were not comforting.

"I can't promise you that. I don't feel like a good guy. I feel like a heel, allowing you to get so deeply involved. I should have been able to do something to help you."

"You saved my life." Tentatively, she put a hand on his flat abdomen and felt the muscles quiver at her touch, felt him sigh in frustration.

"For now. There's going to be more danger. And there's nothing I can do to avoid it."

"I know. Because you don't know who to trust."

He nodded. "If I choose the wrong person, you could be facing a gun."

Lily raised her head and looked into his intense blue eyes. "But I can trust you, right?"

"Yes, you can trust me." He touched her cheek and ran his thumb lightly across her lower lip. "I *can* promise you that I'll protect you with my life."

She bent her head and grasped his forearm, wanting to hold on to the feelings he stirred inside her. Her fingers encountered laddered marks—scratches.

She sat up. "What happened to your arm?" She slid her fingertips lightly across the angry red stripes. "That was me. I scratched you."

"It's nothing. You were fighting for your life." His thumb caressed her lower lip.

Lily swallowed and let her gaze dip to his mouth. It wasn't grim or compressed now. It was relaxed. The furrow between his brows had smoothed out. He seemed more at ease than he had been the whole day.

The amazing thing was, so was she.

A deep, visceral thrill shimmered through her as he cradled the side of her face in his palm. She gasped quietly, pressing her cheek against his warm, hard fingers, never taking her eyes off him.

He searched her gaze, his blue eyes soft, questioning. Then he dipped his head and touched his lips to hers. It might have been nothing more than a breath, but Lily felt it all the way down to her deepest core.

She tightened her thighs, trying to relieve the unslaked desire that suddenly sang through her. She lifted her head and offered her mouth to him.

His lips moved over hers, kissing her softly, tenderly. It was the sweetest kiss she'd ever experienced. And it wasn't nearly enough.

She bunched her fist in his T-shirt and pulled him closer, seeking more, craving the taste of him, the feel of his hard body pressed against hers. She strained upward, reaching for his mouth.

He pulled back, studying her intently. "Don't do this, Lily," he muttered. "You don't know what you're doing."

"Yes, I do," she lied. She had no idea what she was doing. Seeking a promise of safety from this stranger? No, she was holding fast to the only person who'd ever risked his life for hers. She needed proof of life in this dark, surreal world in which she found herself.

Whatever the reason, she was certain that if she could brand him with her body, he couldn't possibly betray her. She shuddered with erotic yearning. She ached to feel his strength surrounding her, filling her, chasing away the dark.

Wrapping her hand around his neck, she sought his mouth again.

"You don't know me." His breath whispered across her lips, stirring her more. But his words stopped her.

He was right. She didn't. But did it matter right now? When all she wanted was to feel?

"I don't need to know you," she said, even as her brain taunted her with all the things she wished she could ask him.

But there was one thing she had to know before she could go any further. The one thing that would tell her if she really could trust him.

She took a deep breath, trying to calm her racing heart. Then she looked up into his clear blue eyes. "Are you married?" *Are you a lying, cheating ass like my ex-husband?*

His brows lifted in surprise for an instant. He shook his head solemnly. "No. Not even dating."

He was telling the truth. They were too close for her to miss even the slightest flicker of hesitation.

"Me, neither," she whispered.

With a low moan, Brand pulled her to him and covered her mouth with his. He slid his fingers through her hair as he kissed her deeply, fiercely.

He lifted his head. "Be sure, Lily. Because it's been too long," he rasped, his breath hot against her mouth. "I might not be able to stop."

"I'm not asking you to stop."

An unsteady breath escaped his lips as he cradled her head and kissed her with searing promise.

She turned to him, offering herself, craving his touch.

He took her mouth totally, probing rhythmically with his tongue in an erotic imitation of lovemaking.

Overcome by desire, helpless under his sensual assault, Lily went boneless.

He leaned forward, cradling the back of her head. She let him lay her down on the daybed. He pressed his palm to her flat belly as his mouth trailed soft kisses across her cheeks and down her jaw to her neck.

"I'm so sorry I hurt you," he whispered as his lips grazed the knife cut marring her creamy skin. He gently kissed each millimeter of the wound.

"It wasn't your fault," she whispered. "I know that now."

He sought her mouth again as he slid his hand up her thigh, pushing her skirt up.

A deep sexual hunger engulfed her as he moved closer and closer to the apex of her thighs. Then she felt a featherlight touch. He slid his fingers across the crotch of her panties. Her back arched and her breath caught as his teasing strokes stirred her to a sensual frenzy she'd never before experienced.

He caressed her lightly, persistently, through the thin silk, until liquid pooled deep within her and moisture gathered. She squirmed with embarrassment and need.

He went still. "Do you want to stop? Tell me, before—"

He uttered a strangled moan as she reached for the buttons on his jeans.

He brushed her hand aside and quickly undid them himself. He sat up to peel them down his legs and off. Cool air fanned across her heated skin. She shivered.

His arousal sprang free, throbbing and pulsing against her thigh as he turned his whole attention back to her. His fingers slid beneath the damp silk of her panties and for the first time, he touched her with no barrier between his questing fingers and her most intimate flesh. Lily cried out in shock and pleasure.

Then she touched him. His thick, velvety hardness pulsed against her palm. His quiet moan and sharp intake of breath told her how turned on he was. He was hovering as close to the edge as she was.

He slid his hand up her belly to her waist and unbuttoned her blouse. The lace of the bra she wore enhanced rather than inhibited the exquisite pleasure that engulfed her as he took her nipple in his mouth and gently suckled and tongued it through the thin material.

She arched toward his mouth, caught up in sensation. She'd always been shy, and sex with her ex-husband had never been completely satisfying. But suddenly she wanted to do things she'd never done before.

Her fingers closed around him boldly. She caressed him, driving him to even greater hardness.

His breath sawed in and out as he undid the clasp on the front of her bra and drew her bare nipple into his mouth. He grazed the sensitized tip with his teeth, then soothed it with his tongue.

When she thought she couldn't stand another second of his exhilarating torture, he sat up and pulled her across his lap.

Apprehension and shyness threatened to quash her desire. "I don't know how—"

"Shh. Let me do the work."

He wrapped his fingers around her waist and lifted her. She opened her legs as he held her poised above him. To her surprise, her inhibitions and awkwardness fled as she gave herself to him.

He held her poised above him, the muscles of his arms

and chest bulging, as his gaze roamed over her breasts, her belly, her spread thighs, and he whispered, "Beautiful."

Her senses thrilled. Nobody had ever called her beautiful before.

She grabbed his forearms, readying herself.

He slowly lowered her onto him. When he penetrated her damp flesh, she threw her head back and nearly screamed with pleasure.

His eyes were soft and dark, like the deep blue depths of the ocean. His neck corded with strain and his cheeks turned pink as he arched upward, pressing deeper, filling her, each thrust pushing her closer to fulfillment.

Her body welcomed him. He lifted her, then lowered, then lifted her again until Lily was poised on the very edge of climax. Then he leaned forward and nuzzled her breasts, teasing first one then the other.

Her body spiraled out of control and she gasped. "Brand, please. I can't stand it."

"Come on, Lily," he growled. "Just a little more." He thrust deeply, sinking himself to the hilt inside her.

That was all it took.

Stars burst in front of Lily's eyes as she reached the pinnacle of sensation. Brand groaned and bucked, thrusting into her again and again as her climax shook him. She surrendered herself to the waves of sensation rocking her.

"That's right, Lily. Give in. Feel it," Brand whispered raggedly.

Finally, as Lily's spasms faded into tiny aftershocks, he collapsed. His quivering arms lowered her on top of him.

Lily lay against his chest, her sensitive nipples puckering at the rough, sensuous feel of his chest hair. She buried her nose in his neck and breathed deeply of the scent that was uniquely his.

He fanned his fingertips lightly over the bumps of her spine as he planted kisses on her ear, her forehead, her eyelids.

Then he turned his head and sought her mouth. His kiss was gentle, featherlike, sweet.

Lily sighed as his hand cradled her head. His body thrummed with power as his arousal slowly softened.

She felt safe. Safe and loved.

BRAND OPENED HIS EYES. Dawn had broken and the pale early morning sun crept in around the closed blinds.

He looked at Lily, asleep beside him. Her hair spread across the pillow in waves, her lips were slightly parted as she breathed softly and rhythmically. He lay still for a long time, watching her sleep. She was so lovely she made his heart ache and his eyes sting.

It astounded him that he'd actually let down his guard enough to make love to her. Equally stunning was the fact that she'd allowed him to touch her, was even eager for him.

A spear of desire shot through him at the memory of her beautiful, slender body on top of him, open to him as he let her set the pace of their joining. Watching her face as his thrusts brought her to the pinnacle of pleasure had fed his desire, until he hadn't been able to restrain himself.

He'd poured into her everything he had.

It had been three years since he'd touched a woman. He hadn't dated since he started on the undercover assignment. If he had, it wouldn't have been much of a

relationship, and it certainly wouldn't have been fair to
the woman. He'd decided it was too risky. Even though
he'd missed sex like it was a drug, he'd followed his instincts and steered clear of entanglements. But now—

He pushed a strand of dark hair back from Lily's face,
his fingers trailing tenderly along her cheek.

He'd taken an even greater risk. Although his body
hardened from merely touching her, he knew Lily
wasn't just a casual one-nighter, nor was this merely a
coming together of two strangers trying to forget for a
moment that their lives were in jeopardy.

Ever since he'd first seen her, he'd recognized the
threat she posed to his heart. If he wasn't careful, he
could fall for her.

The thought pierced his soul with fear. That couldn't
happen. He had to stay focused. His goal was to keep
her alive. Emotions couldn't enter into it.

Lying there, holding her in his arms, he vowed not to
go near her again. Still, even as he told himself to get
up, get dressed and forget this ever happened, he knew
that tearing himself away from her supple warmth, from
her innocent trust, was going to be the hardest thing
he'd ever done.

He didn't move. He endured the torture of her soft,
naked body pressed against his. He shivered at the remembered feel of sinking into her.

His hand hovered over her pink cheek. He ached to
touch her. But he took a deep breath and slowly closed
his fist. He had no right.

He'd broken one of the cardinal rules of law enforcement. Never get involved with anyone connected to a case.

Of all the things he'd done that went against his oath and his training, this was the worst. He shook his head in disbelief.

What had happened to him? He'd always prided himself on his logical approach and his restraint.

A wave of self-loathing burned through him. Right now, he didn't like himself very much. He'd taken advantage of a frightened, vulnerable crime victim. He'd betrayed Lily's trust—sweet, brave Lily.

He'd tried so hard not to lie to her, but hiding the whole truth from her was also a lie. It didn't matter at this moment that he'd done it for her sake. He'd lied. And when she found out who he really was, she'd hate him.

Although he'd told her the truth about one thing. He'd never really contemplated the question she'd asked. *Was he one of the good guys?*

Had he become a cop because he'd wanted to take the unhappy world he'd grown up in and turn it on its ear? Make it happy? Make it safe? Or had he done it because it was the furthest he could get from his old man?

On the other hand, maybe Ryan had it right. Maybe he'd really become a cop to wreak vengeance on the person responsible for Patrick's death—Giovanni Castellano. God knew he'd wanted to, ever since he was thirteen and had found his brother's body.

Lily's question echoed in his ears. He'd like to think he was one of the good guys, but deep down, he knew he wasn't. He'd betrayed her trust, and when she woke up she'd realize that.

He'd promised to protect her—to keep her safe from

the people who were trying to harm her. But instead he'd taken advantage of her fear and vulnerability. He'd used her to satiate his own needs.

He was despicable.

Lily murmured his name in her sleep.

Berating himself for a weak, lonely idiot, he slid off the daybed and pulled on his clothes. He stepped over to the window.

He pushed the slats aside. It was dawn, that quiet in-between time when the world existed in muted tones of gray and blue. In the east he saw a faint pink glow.

Another day. Maybe today was the day he could finally get Lily to safety, even reunite her with her father.

He had to meet with Morrison, to see what information he had for him. He should have agreed to meet him last night, but Brand was much more comfortable in the light of day. That way he could watch his back.

A car pulling into the gas station across the street put his senses on full alert. The station was closed. What was that car doing?

He glanced over his shoulder at Lily, then at the door, gauging how fast he could get them out of the room.

When he peeked out the window again, the driver had gotten out and retrieved a stack of papers from his trunk. He hefted them over to a newspaper stand.

The guy was delivering today's paper. Brand's pulse quickened as he breathed a sigh of relief. He waited impatiently for the car to pull away. He needed to get a paper so he could find out what the media had to say about the missing juror number seven.

Keeping an eye on Lily to be sure she was still asleep,

he shrugged into his long-sleeved shirt, tucked his weapon into his waistband and unlocked the double dead bolt on the studio door.

After easing it shut, he locked it behind him, then bounded down the stairs and across the street. He'd seen vending machines near the newspaper stand. At the thought of food—even stale vending machine food—his stomach rumbled. Damn, he hoped they weren't empty.

He bought a couple of sodas, some cheese-flavored crackers and a paper.

He looked around cautiously, but the colorless dawn didn't expose any lurking figures. The street was deserted. Quickly, he crossed to the office building and hurried back upstairs.

He unlocked the door, slipped inside and relocked it. When he looked up, the daybed was empty. Alarm sent his pulse pounding.

Then he realized that the bathroom door was closed. Relief burned through him. Rationality told him nothing could have happened to her in the few minutes he'd been gone, but his reaction wasn't logical, it was emotional.

The door opened and Lily came out, finger-combing her hair. She smiled. "Good morning."

"Morning. Sorry if I woke you," he said. "I got us some food and a newspaper."

"Great, thanks. I'm starving."

He couldn't take his eyes off her pink cheeks. His stubble had rubbed her skin. He ran his hand along his jaw. "While you eat I'll clean up." Setting down the newspaper and the snacks, he headed into the bathroom.

As the door closed, Lily sat on the edge of the daybed

and ripped open a package of cheese crackers. She wolfed them down with one of the sodas. She left the rest for Brand. Her hunger assuaged, she lay back and closed her eyes.

A thrill of desire arrowed through her as she recalled Brand's strong body enveloping hers, and the exquisite feel of him sinking into her.

She heard the water running in the bathroom. Opening her eyes, she sat up. It was the first time she'd had even a few minutes alone. She ought to make the most of them.

She glanced toward the door to the hall, but the double dead bolt was locked, and Brand had the key in his pocket. She didn't know what she'd do if she escaped, anyway. She had to admit she was safer with Brand than on her own.

So she surveyed the tiny studio and her gaze lit on the canvases stacked against the wall. He hadn't wanted her to go through them. He'd said he wanted her away from the window, but what if he'd had another reason not to want her snooping around?

Glancing at the closed bathroom door, she rose from the bed. There were a dozen or more canvases turned face to the wall. She flipped one around, then another and another. Then she saw it. The painting he hadn't wanted her to find.

BRAND RUBBED HIS newly shaven cheeks. He'd found a package of disposable razors under the sink. He'd had to use flower-scented soap to shave and wash up, but he felt much better.

When he exited the bathroom, Lily was sitting on the stool in front of Cassie's easel.

"Did you eat?" he asked.

She didn't answer.

"Lily?"

She sat as still as a statue, her face a pale orb, her eyes wide and filled with hurt.

What was wrong? What could have happened in the few minutes he'd left her alone?

"Lily," he said again. "What's the matter?"

She was staring at something. He turned to look at whatever held her attention.

What he saw nearly stopped his heart.

She was looking at an unframed oil painting propped against the wall.

He'd forgotten that Cassie had painted him in his police academy dress uniform. He'd liked the painting, but she'd wanted to work on it some more. She wasn't satisfied with the look in his eye. His expression was too serious, too stiff, she'd said.

He faced Lily, a hollow regret sinking deep into his chest. She'd hate him now. Worse than that, she'd never trust him again.

And if she didn't trust him, he couldn't keep her safe.

Lily had heard Brand's questions, but she couldn't answer him. She couldn't take her eyes off the portrait.

Her senses had gone numb. Her perception of reality had faded into yet another nightmare, and her father's voice rang in her ears.

Nobody's more dangerous than a rogue cop.

Slowly, her brain began to make sense out of what she was seeing.

She knew the stiff, proud figure in the painting was

Brand. In a police uniform. The artist had caught his intensity and dogged determination in the expression on his face. It was a wonderful portrait.

Lily's fingers and toes tingled like waking limbs. Her heart had lodged itself somewhere in the back of her throat, and suddenly she realized she was angrier and more frightened than she'd ever been in her life.

Not even Foshee's terrifying threats nor the gun held to her head in the restaurant had sent cutting shards of panic through her the way discovering this painting had. Her body quaked with fury. Her heart broke with betrayal.

"Lily, let me explain—"

She quelled him with a glance. The face in the painting was younger, less lined than the one looking at her in faint horror now. In the painting, Brand's cheeks still held the blush of youthful pride he must have felt the day he graduated from the police academy.

The academy. The man standing before her—the man to whom she'd given herself in the night—was a cop. *A cop gone bad.*

What else could explain his refusal to take her to the police? Still, he'd saved her from Castellano. He'd helped the Cajun follow and threaten her, but he'd held her and made love to her and kept her safe. Her brain whirled with conflicting thoughts and emotions.

"Lily—"

"Don't talk to me," she said coldly. "Unlock the door. I'm getting out of here." She'd already straightened her clothes and slipped on her shoes.

"No. You can't. We don't know who might be out there, waiting."

"Oh. Do you think whoever is out there will be worse than who's standing here in front of me, lying to me?" She crossed her arms and lifted her chin. "How can I believe anything you say? You're a police officer. And yet you let me be set up to be killed. Worse—you left my father vulnerable. He was on the job for over twenty years. You had to know who he was. How could you do that to a fellow police officer?"

"There's a lot you don't know. You have to trust me."

"I can never trust you." Her face grew warm as she thought about how safe and right she'd felt in his arms. Apparently his body could lie as easily as his mouth. "You lied to me."

"No, I didn't."

"Well, I don't know how you define lying, but you sure as hell didn't tell me the truth. I don't feel like arguing over semantics, if you don't mind. Now are you going to let me out of here or not?"

"No, I'm not. You've got to listen to me." He reached for her but she recoiled, her hands up in a don't-you-dare-touch-me gesture.

"I will not listen to any more of your lies."

He backed off and stood there, his hands out. "I'll tell you what I can. I've been undercover for three years, working to bring down Castellano. I couldn't blow the operation by refusing to do the job Castellano himself assigned to me. There are other lives at stake. Two other undercover officers."

He spread his hands in supplication. "From the moment I saw you—" He stopped and took a deep breath. "I had to go along, or I'd be placing your life and the lives of others in danger. If Castellano suspected I was a cop, Springer and Carson's lives would be over."

"The other undercover officers? What about them? Are they on the run, too?"

He shook his head. "As far as I know, they're still working on the docks. I'm the one who got the assignment. I'm the one who was set up to kill you. Once everything went sour, I had no choice but to grab you and run. I didn't know who to trust. I still don't."

Lily took a step toward him. "Well, since you're being so *honest,* explain that to me. You're a cop. How can you not trust your fellow officers?"

"My contact, the FBI agent in charge of the task force, hung me out to dry. He promised he'd have Foshee and me picked up before we left the courtroom. Nobody showed up, so I had to go with Foshee to your apartment. He was determined to kill you. I had to improvise."

Lily's head swam. He was a cop, yet he was running from both Castellano and the police. He'd lied to her. And he'd denied being a police officer—hadn't he?

She glanced at the daybed and a splinter of remembered desire lodged painfully in her heart. What a fool she'd been. She'd believed in him.

I had to improvise.

Hurt arrowed through her middle. It felt like heartache, like betrayal. "I suppose you were improvising last night, too?"

A shadow of pain crossed his face and he opened his mouth. "Lily, I'm sorry. I never should have—"

"Don't." She held up a hand. "Don't bother lying to me any more. Just move out of the way and let me leave."

In utter desperation she pushed past him. He caught her upper arms.

"You're not going anywhere. Not until I can be sure you're safe." His blue eyes were intense.

She shrugged free. "Don't touch me. The farther I can get from you, the safer I'll be." She rattled the doorknob. "Unlock the damn door!"

"Lily. Stop. You need to calm down."

"Calm down? Are you kidding me?" She stared at him wide-eyed. "You're holding me hostage. For all I know you betrayed your fellow officers like you betrayed my father and me. If you don't let me go, I'll start screaming."

Brand turned her to face him. "You try that and I'll be forced to gag and bind you. Understand?"

She winced at the look on his face. How had she ever thought his blue eyes were kind? Right now they were as opaque and hard as lapis lazuli.

His fingers squeezed her arm. "Do you?" he snapped.

She tried to kick him, but he dodged her and pulled her up tightly against him, holding her so she couldn't move.

She felt the hardness of his body against hers, and an echo of the safety and comfort that he exuded washed over her senses. She shook her head violently. They weren't true—these signals her body received from his. He wasn't safe. Not in any sense of the word.

Brand's hand cradled the back of her head while his other arm held her tight. His breath was hot against her ear. "Do you understand?"

"Yes," she said through gritted teeth. "I understand."

"Are you going to be quiet and still?"

She nodded, trying not to breathe in his evocative male scent. She would never again be able to smell Ivory soap or mint mouthwash without thinking of him. He'd branded her body and soul with his fierce, passionate lovemaking, and now she could barely distinguish danger from safety.

She had to guard against him now more than ever, because he'd slipped beneath her defenses. She hadn't known she was so vulnerable.

"I'm going to arrange to see my lieutenant today. If he's willing to help us, I can probably get you into a safe house before the end of the day."

She frowned. "Really?" She heard the hope in her voice, felt it flutter in her chest. Maybe once she was under the protection of the police, she could see her father. And maybe, once she was away from Brand, she could get rid of the potent attraction she felt for him. She wrenched away from his grip.

"Well, that's good, Brand, or whoever you really are, because I'm not staying around you one minute longer than I have to. Now leave me alone."

Chapter Nine

Brand told the taxi driver to stop in front of the Island Bay Hotel and Casino. He'd arranged this meeting with Morrison only fifteen minutes ago, so that his lieutenant would have to rush to make it.

"I won't wait, Lieu," Brand had warned him. "If you're not there, I'm leaving."

Morrison had sworn he'd be there—alone.

Brand couldn't figure out what Morrison had for him that he couldn't say over the phone. He didn't like the way Morrison was acting. Not one bit. It felt wrong, just like the whole operation.

Before yesterday, he'd have sworn Morrison was the last person on the planet who'd betray him. But today he didn't trust him. He couldn't afford to trust anyone.

He got out of the car with Lily at his side and paid the fare, careful to keep his face averted from the driver. He knew from his experience as a detective that all the cabs in the area had been given his and Lily's descriptions. He could only hope this cabbie was as unconcerned about the two of them as he appeared to be.

As he rounded the back of the car and stepped onto the sidewalk, Lily's eyes snapped with suspicion.

"I thought you told your lieutenant to meet us at the Biloxi Belle."

Brand nodded and grabbed her hand. "The Belle's parking garage backs up to this one. Come on. I don't want to be recognized. We'll cut through."

He'd debated leaving her locked inside the studio. But the idea of letting her out of his sight for any length of time was as abhorrent as the thought of leaving her alone and defenseless, trapped in a locked room.

He wasn't planning to be gone more than a half hour, but still, anything could happen.

It wasn't beyond the realm of possibility that either Castellano or the police would search for family in their efforts to find him. It wouldn't be a huge leap to connect a studio rented in the name of Cassandra Gallagher to Brand Gallagher.

If his cover was blown with Castellano, he had no doubt the crime boss knew his real name.

Brand led Lily through the opulent lobby of the Island Bay Hotel and Casino, until they got to the elevators. He punched the button labeled Parking.

"You aren't going to do it, are you?"

Brand watched the numbers light up on the elevator sign. "Do what?"

"Turn me over to your lieutenant."

"I'm going to see what he has to say."

"I thought you trusted him."

"I did, once. Now I'm not so sure."

"Why?"

The bell rang and the elevator doors opened. He wrapped his arm around her, feeling her instantly go rigid. He pulled her inside with him. An older woman with a plastic cup full of quarters looked at the button he punched.

"So you two have been here all night, too? Did you have good luck?" she asked. "I did."

Lily started to speak, but Brand squeezed her hand and cut his eyes at her. She clamped her mouth shut, fury radiating from her like heat.

Brand smiled at the woman. "We did all right."

The elevator bell rang. As the doors slid open, the cacophony caused by the people and the machines on the casino floor swelled to deafening proportions.

The woman stepped off the elevator, turned and said something, but the clang of winning bells, the din of coins crashing into metal trays and the sound effects coming from hundreds of flashing, brightly lit slot machines drowned out her words.

Brand smiled and nodded as the doors slid shut.

Lily jerked her hand away from his and shook it. "Ouch! What did you think I was going to do? Beg her to save me? Steal her quarters and run?" She stuck her chin out and frowned up at him.

"Listen to me. We can't afford to draw any attention to ourselves. Law enforcement all along the Coast have orders to watch for us."

She started to speak, but he raised his hand to stop her. "We're fugitives. Our descriptions are everywhere. Today's paper carried a small feature about the missing juror. They didn't identify you, except to name you as Juror Number Seven, but they did have a picture, probably taken after the verdict. You're standing by your car."

"So why isn't that reason enough to turn ourselves over to the police and ask for their protection?"

Brand ignored her biting comment. An ominous thought had occurred to him. "Look at you. You're still in the outfit you wore in court. You look exactly like that picture." The blouse was wrinkled, but she still looked like she'd be comfortable walking on a fashion runway.

She certainly didn't look like she belonged with him in his worn jeans, once-white T-shirt and wrinkled, un-buttoned dress shirt. But his attire didn't matter.

"We've got to get you some new clothes."

"What about you?"

He glanced at the mirror that covered one wall of the elevator. "I look pretty damned generic."

"Not really."

What did she mean by that? He frowned at their re-flections. Did they look like gamblers that had been up all night, or desperate fugitives on the run? He couldn't decide.

The bell rang and the light on the parking level button went out.

"Let's go," he said, sliding his arm around Lily's waist.

She stiffened. "Where are we meeting him?"

"On Parking Level Four, near the elevators."

He led her through the glass-enclosed parking lobby and into the concrete parking garage.

"The elevators are over there," Lily pointed out.

"We're taking the stairs," Brand snapped. "Now be

quiet. If there's anyone on the stairs I want to know before we run into them."

He pushed open the door marked Fire Stairs and started climbing. He kept hold of Lily's hand, making sure she stayed close behind him. He moved his weapon to the front of his jeans and rested his right hand on it.

They went up, past the doors marked Two and Three. He paused at the door that read Four. Through the tiny pane of wire-reinforced glass, he surveyed the area. He could see the elevators across the way, but he didn't see the lieutenant anywhere.

Damn. He'd warned him that he wouldn't wait. Still, he had to check the area. Morrison was a careful guy. Maybe he was staying out of sight until he was sure Brand hadn't been followed.

Easing open the level four door, Brand took in the space around him with one swift glance. He didn't see anyone. He'd known the parking garage would be shadowy, but as he'd hoped, the top level was essentially empty. There were only a couple of cars.

He didn't recognize either one, but that didn't mean anything. Morrison could have brought his wife's car, or even borrowed one from police impound.

Behind him Lily tugged against his tight grip. He let go of her hand and pulled his weapon.

Looking her in the eye, he mouthed, "Stay with me. Walk where I walk, and if you hear anything, duck. This is life or death. Understand?"

Her face turned pale and her gaze flickered from one part of the garage to another then back to him. She nodded.

Brand didn't know if she would obey him or not. But

her brown eyes were clear, and when he moved she obediently followed right in his footsteps. Maybe she trusted him enough to believe that she was safest with him.

He could only hope.

He edged along the wall with Lily right behind him. He paused, listening. He had to step into the open in order to examine the two cars.

Just as he moved away from the relative safety of the solid wall, the elevator bell rang.

Someone was coming.

As the heavy doors creaked open, Brand wrapped his left arm around Lily's waist, both to protect her and to use her body to hide the gun in his hand.

Lily's breath caught.

"Shh," he hissed in her ear. "Pretend we snuck up here for a quick grope."

Her body trembled, but she gamely wrapped her arms around his neck and pressed her cheek to his. "Don't get any ideas. I still don't trust you."

"You've made that abundantly clear," he whispered back, watching out of the corner of his eye as a couple exited the elevator. The young woman stopped short when she saw them, but her companion urged her on.

"Come on. Don't worry about them. They're not thinking about mugging anybody," Brand heard the man mutter.

Lily clung to Brand's neck, tortured by his closeness and struck by the absurdity of their situation. His muscled arm around her waist held her protectively and provocatively molded against his body, yet in his other hand he clutched a deadly weapon.

They were sneaking around the casino's parking garage as if they were crooks, but one quick glance had convinced the couple that she and Brand weren't dangerous.

Brand was alert and jittery, expecting an ambush at every corner, an enemy in every shadow. He was so paranoid, so certain that one of his fellows was a traitor. It was absurd that she felt so safe in his arms.

He was a mass of contradiction and she was a mass of frayed nerves.

She stood on tiptoes and watched over his shoulder as the man and woman walked toward their car.

"Where's your lieutenant?" she whispered in his ear.

He drew in a quick breath. "He'll be here."

Lily heard the doubt in his voice. He was afraid he'd been betrayed again. Despite her apprehension, her heart went out to him.

"What are the man and woman doing?"

"They're just about to reach the first car."

Brand's hand holding the gun pressed into her side. He kissed her cheek. His fingers spread over the small of her back. "Good. They'll be gone soon. Morrison's probably waiting for them to leave."

Just as he spoke, the woman grabbed her companion's arm and screamed.

Brand whirled and in one motion, pushed Lily behind him and pointed his weapon.

The woman screamed again. The man grabbed her. "Oh, my God!" he gasped.

Brand moved toward them, his gun still at the ready. "Hold it!" he shouted. "I'm a police officer."

Lily followed him. As they approached the dark

sedan, she caught a glimpse of what had made the woman scream. A man lay beside the car with blood pooling on the concrete beneath his shoulders.

Lily's stomach turned over. She covered her mouth. "Oh, dear God, no!"

Brand gestured toward the couple with the barrel of his weapon. "Move away from the vehicle," he said. "Do it now! Is this your car?"

The man put out his hand to shield his wife. "No. Ours is th-that one." He pointed to a light blue car several parking spaces away.

The woman whimpered and clutched at his sleeve. "Don't hurt us, please. We have children."

"Get out of here!" Brand lowered his gun.

Lily felt the tension radiating from him. The barrel of his gun was unsteady. He never stopped looking around, never left his back unguarded.

"What? Why?" the man said. "What about the man? We should call someone—"

"Get in your car and get out of here. After you exit the parking garage, call 911."

The man hesitated, glancing toward the body.

"Go!"

The two turned and ran up the hill to their car. After a few seconds its engine roared to life and they sped away with a screech of tires.

Brand bent over the man. "Morrison! Gary!" His voice cracked. He felt the man's neck for a pulse.

Lily held her breath.

"He's alive."

"What—what happened to him?"

Brand quickly examined him. "He has a bulletproof vest on, but he's been shot in the neck. Hang in there, Lieu. Help is coming."

"Brand," the man whispered.

"Morrison, you're going to be okay." Brand's voice shook. "What the hell happened?"

"—followed."

An ominous gurgle bubbled up from the injured man's throat. Lily's entire body went cold. This was Morrison. Brand's lieutenant. The only man he trusted.

"Who followed you? Where are they now?" Brand leaned close.

"I spotted 'em. Drew my weapon. They—didn't play by the rules." Morrison's pinched mouth turned up slightly. "Shot me above the—vest."

"We've got an ambulance on its way. You're going to be fine."

Lily heard a noise from the stairwell. "Brand, someone's coming."

Brand straightened, listening.

"Go. Get out of here," Morrison gasped.

Lily tugged on Brand's shoulder. "That couple called 911. It might be the police."

Brand hesitated.

"Brand—get her out of here. You were right." Morrison sucked in a rattling breath. "They found out—I was meeting—you. Pruitt wouldn't—"

The sound Lily had heard turned into footsteps— more than one set.

The bleat of a siren split the air.

"Pruitt wouldn't what? Lieutenant!"

Morrison coughed and blood spewed from his mouth.

Brand pulled up Morrison's pant leg and retrieved the backup service revolver from his ankle holster. He put it into his lieutenant's trembling hands and leaned close to his ear. "Police are on their way, Lieu. Shoot first. I'll cover you as long as I can."

Then he rose and grabbed Lily's waist.

"Behind the post," he said, pushing her ahead of him. He trained his gun on the fire stairs.

Lily ran for the concrete pillar.

Brand was right behind her. He stuck his head out and jerked it back. "Damn it! It's Castellano's men," he whispered. "And they're armed."

He nodded toward the ramp leading down to level three. "Run, Lily. Don't stop until you reach the street. Then call the police."

"But that couple already did—"

"Maybe, maybe not. Remember, you don't know who to trust."

Lily peered at the fire stair door, at the ramp to level three, then at Brand's lieutenant, fighting for his life on the concrete floor. "What about you? What about him?"

"We'll be all right."

She saw something shiny under the back fender of the lieutenant's car. It was a gun.

The stair door crashed open. Lily had only a split second to make a decision.

There was only one thing she could do. She couldn't leave Brand here to face the killers alone.

She dove across the open space and reached under the car. Her fingers barely closed around the lieutenant's service revolver just as two men burst through the stairway door, weapons in hand.

She crouched behind the lieutenant's car and quickly ejected the magazine. There were several rounds left. She slapped it back into place.

"Lily!" Brand shouted.

She nodded at him, earning her a glare before he turned his attention back to the men.

One guy saw her. "Hey! There she is!" He fired, barely missing her cheek.

She ducked, then braced herself to shoot.

Brand got off two shots before the other man started shooting at him.

Lily's hands shook. Her father had taught her how to shoot a 9mm a long time ago. She knew her way around a gun. But she'd never shot at anything alive before—not even a rabbit or a squirrel.

She held her breath, aimed and squeezed the trigger. One of the men yelped and grabbed his shoulder.

Her heart jumped into her throat. She'd hit him!

Brand fired two more quick rounds, then ducked back behind the pillar.

He gestured with his head. She read his signal loud and clear.

Get over here.

She peered over the car's back, looking for the men. The man she'd shot held his arm. The other was braced to shoot. As she watched, he fired three times at Brand. Concrete shards flew as bullets ricocheted off the pillar.

She shot at him but missed.

Brand sent her a telling look, nodded and leaned out, firing off several quick rounds.

He was giving her cover. She took a deep breath and dashed for the pillar, shooting wildly. She gritted her teeth, expecting to feel the bite of a bullet in her side at any second.

She made it without being hit. It was a miracle, with all the bullets flying.

Brand stopped her headlong flight with one hard arm, pulling her into his side. Setting her back against the pillar, he held her while he shot again, then ducked to safety as the two men launched a volley of slugs at them.

"What the hell were you thinking?" he snapped.

Lily's breath rasped through her fear-clogged throat. She held Morrison's gun in both shaking hands, its cold steel pressed between her abdomen and Brand's.

His breaths were harsh in her ear, his chest rose and fell rapidly against hers. His heart pounded.

"I saw the gun," she panted. "Figured we needed it."

He pulled his head back to look down at her. "You shoot like a pro."

"My father taught me." Lily heard more sirens. She clutched Brand's shirt. "I hear police sirens. That couple must have called 911."

He angled around the pillar, shot and pulled back. "Run up the ramp to five," he commanded. "I'll cover you."

"What about you?"

"I'll be right behind you."

The sirens got louder. She heard the screech of tires as a vehicle roared up the ramp on the level below. The hollow echo inside the parking garage distorted the sounds. What was it? An ambulance? A police car?

She took a deep breath, made herself let go of Brand's shirt and ran.

The pop-pop of gunfire followed her. She heard the zing of a ricocheting bullet after it hit the garage floor next to her foot.

She reached the ramp and darted up it as fast as she could, turning and firing a couple of times, taking care to give Brand's pillar a wide berth. When she reached the top, she hid behind the concrete guardrail and fired two more rounds, giving Brand the cover he'd given her.

He vaulted up the ramp just as an ambulance roared up beside Morrison's unmoving form.

The two gunmen took one look at the ambulance and stopped shooting. They turned tail and ducked back through the stairwell door.

"Let's go!" Brand took Lily's hand and sprinted across the open expanse of the parking lot toward a glass door at the far end. If they were lucky, it would lead to a crosswalk from the parking lot to the hotel.

"What about your lieutenant?" Lily asked.

"The paramedics will take care of him."

"But who shot him?"

Brand didn't stop to consider Lily's question. He heard the stairwell door behind them creak open and his heart slammed against his chest.

The gunmen had taken the stairs to the fifth level.

"Go!" He pushed Lily toward the doors and turned back to face their pursuers.

For the first time, he had a split second to look at their

faces. He recognized them. They were two of Castellano's favorite musclemen.

The one Lily had winged held his gun awkwardly in his left hand, but his partner looked perfectly healthy and capable of killing.

"Give it up, Brand. Mr. Castellano wants to see you." The man raised his weapon. "I'd suggest you come with us. We'll send someone to pick up your girlfriend."

In answer, Brand dove behind the concrete guardrail and fired off several rounds.

The air around him exploded with gunfire as he ducked down and checked his magazine. Only six rounds left.

Damn it. He gauged the distance to the glass doors. With any luck at all, he'd make it.

He raised up and shot four times, just as a piercing wail announced the approach of a police car.

Brand sprinted across the open space and through the doors.

Lily was waiting for him inside the glass-enclosed corridor, holding a mop in her hands. As Brand watched in amazement she shoved the handle of the mop through the door latches.

She turned to him. "Maybe it'll slow them down."

"Good job." He grinned. "Learn that from your dad?"

"No. From TV."

"Hah! We've got a chance to lose them. Come on. Let's get out of here."

"What should I do with the gun?" She held it clutched tightly in her fingers. She shrugged. "No pockets."

Brand assessed her. Her hair was tangled, her eyes

were huge and frightened in her pale face and her hands trembled. But as he studied her, she raised her chin and looked him straight in the eye.

He reached for her, wincing in hollow regret when she flinched.

"It's okay," he said. "Stick it in your waistband." He tugged on her blouse.

She recoiled, and pulled the tail of her blouse out of her skirt herself. Then she sucked in a deep breath and slid the pistol into place. She shivered as the cool metal touched her skin.

They walked through the glass crosswalk toward another set of double doors.

Two men pushed through. They were engrossed in an argument about a poker tournament and didn't even spare Brand or Lily a glance.

Inside, they found themselves on a mezzanine overlooking the main floor of the Biloxi Belle Casino. The din was deafening.

Brand searched the corners of the vast room, looking for a gift shop or boutique. Didn't all these fancy casino hotels have shopping facilities?

He spotted a sign in the far corner of the floor. He pointed. "We need to get over there."

Lily looked where he'd pointed. "Why? What's that?"

"I'm hoping it's a shopping court."

He put his hand in the small of her back and guided her to the escalator. He never let down his guard, not even for a second. He was taking a deadly risk, possibly endangering innocent lives. But he had to hope the police had slowed down Castellano's men.

As the escalator took them down to the casino floor, Brand checked out the exits. The closest one was on the south side. But the easiest to navigate was on the west, near their destination.

A familiar blue uniform caught his eye. A police officer had just entered the casino through the south doors and was sweeping the room with his gaze.

Brand quickly propelled Lily toward the shopping court. His number one priority was to get her safely away.

Now that someone had shot Morrison, he was even more convinced that he couldn't trust anyone—not even the police.

Chapter Ten

By the time they returned to the studio, Lily was shivering with a combination of exhaustion and reaction to the gun fight. They'd run the twenty or so blocks from the casino. It was a good thing Brand had bought her new clothes at the hotel's exclusive boutique.

The acid-washed jeans, designer T-shirt and slip-on tennis shoes were a lot easier to run in than her tight skirt and pumps, but their price tags had shocked her.

She'd been surprised when Brand pulled out a credit card, but he'd assured her the police already knew they'd been in at least one of the two casinos, because of Morrison. It wouldn't matter if a credit card charge came in. The bigger problem would be the store's record of what they'd bought. If detectives obtained that information, they'd have an updated description of what Lily was wearing.

Brand unlocked the door to the studio.

"Wait here. I want to make sure everything's okay." He entered with his gun drawn. A few seconds later he gestured for her. "All clear."

She headed straight for the bathroom. With shaky fingers she pulled the lieutenant's gun out of her waistband and gingerly set it on the counter.

Tremors spread up her arms and through her entire body as she stared at the weapon, then at her hands.

She'd shot a man. Her eyes stung and her throat closed up. Granted she'd nearly missed him, and the wound had barely slowed him down, but that wasn't the point.

The point was she'd shot him. And with hardly any hesitation. Of course, he'd been shooting at her and Brand, so her shot was self-defense.

That didn't make her feel one bit better.

She studied her reflection in the mirror. She was white as a ghost. Her eyes were rimmed with dark circles and her lips were tight and white at the corners.

All at once her knees buckled, her stomach lurched and she dropped to the floor. She pulled herself up enough to hang her head over the toilet as heaving spasms wracked her.

By the time her stomach was empty and the spasms had finally stopped, Brand was at her side with a warm, wet cloth.

She took it gratefully and covered her face, relishing the warmth as she waited to see if her stomach was going to rebel again. After a few seconds she sat back against the door and lifted her hair to run the cloth around the back of her neck.

When she finally opened her eyes, Brand was watching her, a thoughtful expression on his face. "You okay?" he asked.

She shook her head. "I shot a man." Her mouth filled with acrid saliva. She pressed the cloth to her cheeks.

"A man who was going to kill you."

"Somehow, knowing that doesn't make me feel a whole lot better."

"I know. But you should be proud. You did a great job out there. As good as any cop—especially considering you're a rookie." He sent her a reassuring smile and dropped to the floor beside her.

She didn't feel like smiling back at him or allowing him to get any closer. She felt like crying. She was so tired. So scared and so damned confused.

She lowered the cloth. The question that had nagged at her from the moment they'd seen Morrison rose in her mind.

"Who shot your lieutenant?"

Brand frowned. She'd asked the same question when they were running from Castellano's gunmen. Then he hadn't had the luxury of time to consider the answer. Now—

"I don't know. But I doubt it was the two goons who chased us. Why would they shoot him then stick around waiting to see if we showed up?"

"They wouldn't. Unless they knew we were coming to meet him. But if that were the case, why shoot him first? Why not take out all of us at once?" As soon as Lily said the words, what little color remained in her face drained away.

Brand's heart squeezed in compassion. The danger she'd been exposed to in the last few days was foreign to her. It didn't matter that her father had been on the job for over twenty years. As much as he'd taught her, he'd obviously shielded her from the worst aspects of his work.

"There were two of them," he said. "If they'd waited, they would have been facing three of us, not two."

"Or they didn't want to take the chance that Morrison would tell you what he knew."

Brand nodded. "That makes sense. But how did they know we were meeting him? Or where we would be?"

"Someone in the police department is feeding information to Castellano."

"That's what I've thought all along." Brand nodded. "But no one knew Morrison was meeting us."

"You don't think it's him?"

"No. I've known Morrison for years. He was my lieutenant for four years and my contact for the first year I was undercover."

"But what did he have to tell you that he couldn't say over the phone?"

"I don't know. He didn't say much. Said he'd been followed. He said something about Pruitt."

"Pruitt?"

"My contact for the past two years. He's with the FBI."

Lily must have heard the suspicion in his voice, because she sent him a sidelong glance. "You don't trust him."

"Not much."

"What did Morrison say?"

He shook his head. "All I got was 'Pruitt wouldn't.'"

Lily pushed herself up, but slipped back to the floor with a moan. Brand stood and offered his hand. She took it. When she stood upright, she swayed.

"Hey," he said, putting his arm around her. "Be careful. You're exhausted and you have nothing in your stomach."

She leaned close.

He gave in to a dangerous urge and buried his nose in her hair. The faint smell of coconut stirred his desire. He pulled her closer and cradled the back of her head in his palm.

He felt a shaky sigh ripple through her. Her breath warmed the skin of his neck. He slid his fingers beneath her hair and massaged the knotted muscles in her neck and shoulders.

"Brand?" Her voice was small and hesitant, and the question in it shot straight to his loins. The foreign urge he'd been fighting from the first moment he laid eyes on her slipped beneath his careful reserve—the urge to care for her, to protect her, to love her.

As if she sensed the change in him, she pulled away, avoiding his gaze. "Do you think there's any toothpaste in here?" she asked tightly.

He reluctantly let her go. "There's mouthwash." He opened the cabinet behind the mirror and pulled out a bottle of green liquid.

"Thanks." She grabbed the bottle and clutched it in front of her like a shield.

She wanted him to leave.

He exited the bathroom and went over to the window, sucking in a deep breath to calm his racing heart. He reminded himself of his vow not to touch her. She didn't want *him*. She just wanted her life back.

If he had the power, he'd give her what she wanted. He'd planned on turning her over to Morrison. But

whoever had betrayed him and the entire police force
had made that impossible.

Lifting the edge of the blinds, he checked the street
below. He was certain they hadn't been followed, but
what if whoever was leaking information to Castellano
knew about Cassie's studio?

The snitch could be anyone on the force. Before he'd
been given the undercover assignment, Brand had
shared a few tidbits about his life with some of his
fellow officers. If he had been a bit more reticent than
most, it was because he hadn't wanted to get into the
melodrama of growing up in an alcoholic household.

Still, there was no one he could eliminate. Not even the
lieutenant or his fellow undercover officers. Certainly not
Pruitt. Not only did he not trust the FBI agent, he had no
idea what information Pruitt had been given about him.

For the first time, Brand faced the raw truth—
Morrison had been his last hope. There was literally no
one he could trust now.

On a visceral level he had known it, but he'd never
admitted to himself that even his closest peers could be
working for Castellano. It was an abhorrent thought
that a cop would turn on his fellow officers, but it had
happened before. And it would happen again.

If the traitor knew about his brother's wife's studio,
he and Lily were sitting ducks. He had to be extra
vigilant until he could figure out another place for them
to hide. How much longer could he keep Lily safe
against the monsters who wanted to kill her?

He had to get her to someplace safe. But where?

His cell phone rang. It was Pruitt. For an instant,

Brand considered turning off the phone, but the displayed number flashed, mocking him. He pressed the answer key.

"Are you happy now, Gallagher? You got Morrison shot."

"Did he tell you he was meeting me?"

Pruitt cursed. "Hell, no. If he had, he wouldn't be in surgery now."

Brand went cold. "How is he?"

"It's touch and go. He had on a vest, but slugs caught him in the shoulder and the neck."

"Where is he? Which hospital?"

"I'm not answering any more questions. I'm asking them," Pruitt growled. "Where are you?"

"What did Morrison have to tell me?"

"Gallagher, I'm warning you—"

"No, *I'm* warning you! If you would be up-front with me just once, I might be persuaded to trust you. But you keep lying to me."

He heard a heavy sigh on the other end of the line. "There's a leak."

Brand spat a curse. "You're just now figuring that out?" Was Pruitt baiting him with information he already knew, hoping to lure him in? "I thought it was you," he snapped.

The FBI agent snorted. "You think I'd risk jeopardizing this operation? This is a once-in-a-lifetime opportunity for me. If I can bring down Castellano, I can write my own ticket. If I knew who's leaking intel to Castellano, I'd kill him myself."

"What about Springer and Carson?"

"They're still undercover. I've been in touch with them on a daily basis. We're almost ready to blow Castellano's arms-smuggling operation right out of the water." Pruitt paused. "I think the leak is someone closer to the administration. I think Morrison knows."

"You think that's what he wanted to tell me? Who the leak is? That's interesting, because the last thing he said was your name."

"You talked to him? I thought he was unconscious."

"So, Special Agent Pruitt, if the lieutenant had vital information to give, why didn't he share it with you?"

"Because he didn't want me to get all the glory."

Wrong answer. Brand shook his head. Pruitt had just given himself away. "You don't really believe that. You're not that dumb." The FBI agent had to be running on ego. "Morrison suspects you, doesn't he? That's why he wanted to talk to me."

"You're on awfully thin ice, Gallagher."

"I've been on thin ice before. Where is he? County General?"

"You're AWOL. There's no way I'm giving you that information."

"I'll find out on my own if you won't tell me."

"You go right ahead. We'll be waiting for you."

"Yeah? Fine. You spend your time and energy waiting for me. What about Lily's dad?"

"I told you we have that covered."

"Covered? Does that mean he's been picked up and placed in protective custody?"

"We're on it. You get in here and maybe I'll answer that question for you."

Brand angrily punched the disconnect button. "Son of a—"

The bathroom door opened and Lily came out. Her face was clean and shiny, her hair was slightly damp, and she looked if not a hundred percent better, at least seventy percent. The small T-shirt with its sequined logo clung to her slim figure, outlining her enticing curves that were emphasized by the low-cut jeans. A sliver of her flat, smooth belly showed between the bottom of the T-shirt and the low-riding waistband of the jeans.

Her wide eyes sent him a message he'd give anything to avoid. That despite her I-can-take-care-of-myself attitude, she looked to him to protect her. He saw trust in her gaze, and it terrified him.

Who was he kidding? He couldn't risk her life any longer. He had to take her to the police. He was being selfish and arrogant, keeping her here with him. Although he still believed there was an element of danger in putting her in police custody, it didn't make sense to do anything else.

She sat down on the daybed and clasped her hands.

Brand looked at her more closely. Her eyes were red. She'd been crying. His heart twisted in compassion and guilt.

"I need to check on my father," she said quietly without looking at him.

"Okay."

Her gaze snapped to his. "Okay?"

He nodded and dug his phone out of his pocket. He tossed it to her. "It's the third phone number in the queue."

He hoped like hell that Pruitt was just baiting him.

Surely the task force had transported Joe Raines to a secure facility by now.

Lily grasped the cell phone like a lifeline. "You're going to let me dial it?"

He shrugged. "One of us has got to trust the other."

She raised her brows, then nodded as she searched for the number and punched the call button.

An unfamiliar voice answered. "Blue Wing, may I help you?"

"Yes, this is Lily Raines. I want to check on my father."

"Who's your father?" the woman asked.

Lily frowned. She didn't recognize the voice. "Joe Raines. Who is this?"

"I'm the ward clerk."

The sound of papers rustling crackled through the phone.

"Joe Raines? Would he be under another name?"

Gritting her teeth, Lily answered as calmly as she could. "Try Joseph Raines. Room 118."

"One-eighteen? Nah, that's Mrs. Brown's room."

Lily's heart flip-flopped in her chest. "What? For how long?"

Brand stepped over beside her, concern obvious on his face.

"I'd have to look that up."

"Where is my father?"

"Ma'am, don't raise your voice at me."

Lily gritted her teeth. "I want to know where my father is. Let me speak to the nurse, right now!"

The clerk sighed loudly. "All the nurses are in report. I can have one of them call you."

"I don't want one of them to call me. I want to talk to a nurse, right now."

"If you'll give me your number I'll have them give you a call."

"And you can't tell me anything about Joe Raines? What about his chart?"

"I don't see a chart with that name on it, ma'am. I'm filling in on Blue Wing tonight. I usually work on the Orange Wing."

Her hands shaking so much she could hardly hold the phone, Lily turned to Brand. "What's this number?"

He recited it for her and she gave it to the clerk, then pressed the disconnect button and threw the phone aside. Her eyes burned with the need to cry, but she was too tired, too upset, too frightened.

Brand retrieved the cell phone and pocketed it, then sat beside her. He took her hand. "Pruitt told me he was working on getting your dad to a secure location. I'm sure they picked him up."

"Are you?" she said archly. "Are you sure? How do you know you can trust him? You didn't trust him earlier today."

"Okay. I can't be sure. But Pruitt told me yesterday he was getting a court order. What did the nurse say?"

"All the nurses were in report. I couldn't talk to any of them. The ward clerk *said* she'd have them call me back."

Lily flopped down on the daybed and rubbed her temples, lifted her hair off her neck. "What am I going to do now?" she asked. "My father has disappeared. What if Castellano has him?"

Brand kneeled down beside her and tucked her hand

into his. "First thing in the morning, I'll take you to the police. I promise. Then you can see for yourself that your father is safe."

She looked up, startled. "You'd do that? But what about you?"

"I've still got to find out who's been feeding information to Castellano."

"You're convinced someone is."

"Hell, yeah. He knew where I lived. He followed us to the restaurant. And he knew we were meeting Morrison at the casino."

"What about all your issues with the police?"

Brand scowled and rose.

His powerful denim-clad thighs were in Lily's line of sight.

"My issues don't enter into this. Not now. Your safety and your father's is the most important thing. And you're sure as hell not safe with me. The longer this goes on, the more dangerous it's going to get for you."

He retrieved his gun, ejected the magazine and pulled a full one from his pocket. He slapped it into place.

"Where's your weapon?" he asked.

Lily moved to stand. "On the bathroom counter."

"I'll get it." He retrieved the standard issue Glock 9mm and examined its magazine. It only had two rounds left. He quickly took the last four bullets from his used magazine and inserted them into hers, then slapped it back into place. "Just in case."

He tossed the pistol onto the daybed beside her. "Keep it with you. Now try to get some sleep."

Lily studied him. Strong thighs aside, he was tired,

too. He was looking ragged around the edges. The hollows in his cheeks were deeper, as were the lines around his mouth. His blue eyes were dull. "What about you? You're exhausted."

He shook his head. "I'll keep watch."

"The door's locked. We're not going to do more than nap, anyway. We might as well get as much rest as we can."

He searched her face. "I'll sit over here." He held up a hand when she opened her mouth. "And try to nap."

Her gaze traced the tense curve of his shoulders and back that spoke to his exhaustion. He rubbed his face.

Damn, he was stubborn. She sat up and glared at him. "Whatever line you're reluctant to cross, I think we crossed it last night and left it far behind. It won't hurt anything if we lie together just to *sleep*. It's not like we haven't been here before."

His jaw clenched as he stared at her. After a few seconds he pushed a hand through his hair and stood up. "I don't have the strength to do anything but sleep."

"Neither do I. And I feel selfish taking the only bed when you so obviously need rest."

Lily slid toward the wall as he sat down on the bed. He set his gun on the floor within easy reach, then stretched out carefully on the small daybed.

He took up so much space! It was the same as with the tiny studio—he overpowered it with his masculine presence.

He shut his eyes, his long lashes resting against his cheeks. She let herself absorb the sensations created by his closeness. The easy rise and fall of his chest, the hard comfort of his shoulder and bicep against her side, and his long legs.

He turned over with his back to her. Following an impulse she wasn't sure she completely understood, Lily spooned herself against him.

He tensed as she slipped her arm around his waist, but when she didn't do anything else, he relaxed back against her with a sigh.

She closed her eyes and prayed for a few hours of safety.

THEY WERE AFTER HER. They had her father and they were chasing her. She ran as fast as she could, but her legs were like lead weights. She could barely lift them.

Where was Brand? He'd promised to keep her safe, but he was nowhere around. Why had he abandoned her and her father?

She'd thought he was trustworthy. She'd thought he was one of the good guys.

She screamed his name!

"Lily."

The men chasing her dissolved, melted into the hot asphalt beneath her feet.

A strong, protective arm held her tight.

"Lily, wake up. You're having a bad dream."

She opened her eyes and arched her back, prepared to fight.

It was Brand. The yellow light streaming in through the ancient blinds planed his face in eerie shadows.

"Where were you?" she whispered frantically.

"I'm right here. You were dreaming."

"No, they were right behind me. They were catching up. They almost—"

His warm hands framed her face, his thumbs lightly tracing her lips. "Shh. It's okay. It was only a dream."

She closed her eyes. "They had my dad—"

"Shh. Your father's safe, remember? He's in police custody."

The haze of sleep finally left her. She was in the little studio with Brand. Fully awake and achingly aware of Brand's hard body pressed close to hers, Lily nodded carefully. "We don't know that for sure, do we?"

"No, but we will first thing in the morning. Try not to worry. I'm sure he's safe."

She remembered his earlier words. *One of us has to trust the other.* "Okay. I'm sorry." She rested her head against his shoulder.

Brand pressed his lips to her forehead, trying desperately to think of her as nothing more than an innocent citizen in need of his protection. Unfortunately, his body wasn't having any of it.

His arousal pressed painfully against the seam of his jeans. He carefully slid away from her on the narrow bed. He didn't want to frighten her with his desperate, obvious need.

And truthfully, he didn't relish being rebuffed.

She clutched at his T-shirt. "Are you getting up?" she asked in a small voice.

Brand brushed his thumbs across her damp cheeks and turned her face up to his. "I'll be right here," he said, working to keep his voice calm.

She didn't let go of his shirt. "Will you hold me? Please?"

Wincing internally, he nodded and slipped his arm under her. She curled into his side, her head lying in the hollow of his shoulder. Her sweet scent tortured him. Her innocent trust humbled and shamed him. He wasn't worthy. He'd hurt her and put her in danger.

Some protector he was.

He put his hand over hers and gently pried her fingers from the material of his T-shirt. "You're wound tighter than a spring. Look how stiff your fingers are. Relax. Try to sleep."

"I'm afraid I'll have another nightmare."

"Think good thoughts. Concentrate on something pleasant."

She snuggled a bit closer. She was quiet for so long he thought she'd gone to sleep.

"Why did you become a cop?"

Her question came out of nowhere. It surprised him. He took a deep breath of her intoxicating scent, then opened his mouth to give her the pat answer. *To do something good, something meaningful with my life.*

But the canned words wouldn't come.

She was beginning to trust him. Maybe she had a right to know exactly why he'd started on the path that had brought them together in this place and time.

"All my life my pop was a drunk. He was also a carpenter—a good one, when he wasn't drinking. When he was drinking he was a bastard." He heard the bitterness that scraped across his throat.

Lily's fingers entwined with his. Her touch was comforting, caring.

"I had two big brothers. Patrick was eleven years older than me. He went into business with Pop. He wanted to be just like him." He paused and sighed. "He was."

"Patrick drinks?"

He nodded. "He did. And gambled."

"What about your other brother?"

"Ryan? He's four years older. He always took care of me when I was little. Many nights he stood between me and Pop. He tried to stand between Mom and Pop, too, but—" The old memories were still so vivid, the wounds raw and biting.

Lily stayed quiet. He pressed her hand to his chest and turned his head to breathe in her erotic scent.

"You told me earlier that your father just died."

"Last week. He had cirrhosis of the liver, a bad heart, emphysema—you name it."

"I'm really sorry. You said you didn't want to be like him. So did you become a cop to get away from him? From that life?"

He shook his head. If he was going to be honest, he might as well tell her the whole truth. "I became a cop because of Patrick. When I was thirteen and Ryan was away at school, I found Patrick on our doorstep. He'd been shot in the head."

Shock registered on Lily's face. "Oh no! Brand! What happened? Who—"

Her voice gave out and she raised a hand to her mouth.

He watched her expression change to horror as the truth dawned. "Castellano?" she whispered.

"Patrick had a dollar bill stuffed in his mouth. Castellano's trademark."

"But why?"

"He owed Castellano a lot of money. Gambling. Castellano knew he'd never be able to pay up, so he made an example out of him."

Lily looked at him quizzically. "And that's why you became a police officer? To avenge your brother's murder?"

He heard the faint note of censure in her voice. Did she realize she was disappointed in him? Maybe not, but he did.

"What did you expect me to say, that I wanted to make the world a better place? Make it safe? Or that I felt I should repay society for my brother and my father's mistakes by doing good deeds?"

Lily looked stunned. She shook her head. "No, I—"

"Come on, Lily. Admit it. You think I'm tarnishing the badge, don't you? I tried to tell you. Your father may have been one of the good guys, but there aren't that many of them left. Did you really expect me to be one?"

She swiped her fingers across her cheeks. "I'm so sorry about your brother and your father, and the things you had to endure."

Brand sat up, pushing her away. "Don't be. I'm not. What's the saying? *What doesn't kill me makes me strong?* Well, what I lived with made me very strong. Made me sure of what I wanted to do with my life. Kept me from sinking into a bottle like my old man."

"So you sank into bitterness instead?"

He forced a laugh through his tight throat. "I'm not

bitter. Just realistic. My family was a far cry from your idealistic childhood—" He stopped when she went rigid and fury turned her eyes black.

He'd gone too far. He didn't want to destroy her memories. He just wanted her to realize how different they were from his.

"Idealistic? You think my life was idealistic? You think I've forgotten how devastated I was when my mother died? How much I needed my father? But he wasn't there for me. He took a leave of absence. For months he sat in the dark day after day because he didn't know how to deal with losing her. You think I don't remember that he wouldn't even look at me because I reminded him of her?"

"Lily, I didn't mean to—"

"You think I wouldn't rather remember my father as the big, strong man who took care of me and my mother, rather than the way he is now? Some days he thinks I'm one of the nurses. He tells me the same things every time I see him, as if I haven't just been there the day before."

Her lower lip trembled and her eyes sparkled with unshed tears.

He wrapped his arm around her again.

She didn't pull away. "We have the ability to choose our memories, to choose what we bring from the life we were born into," she said, sitting up.

He thought she was going to get up, but instead she leaned over and placed her hand in the middle of his chest. She kissed his cheek.

"Your memories are what you make them," she whispered against his ear.

He pressed his forehead to hers, his chest tight with emotion. "I suppose we can always make new memories."

Lily smiled. "I suppose."

He lay down and pulled her with him, nuzzling the soft skin under her chin, running his hand over her shoulders and down her arms, then around her waist and up, to cup her small, firm breasts. His thumb teased the peaks that were clearly outlined under her cotton T-shirt.

With a quiet gasp she sought his mouth.

He rose and held himself above her. Then he smiled and kissed her deeply, intimately, as his arousal sprang to full hardness. He couldn't hide what she did to him.

She opened herself to him, arching upward. As he slipped one hand between them to undo her jeans, she reached for his. Quickly they disposed of their clothing and lay skin to skin.

Lily ran her hands over his steely biceps, his smooth, sculpted chest, his flat, hard belly. He was so totally, deliciously male. Then, as her body readied itself for his penetration, she touched him, guided him.

He pushed into her, at first slowly, then with growing intensity. She threw her head back with a soft cry.

Fiercely, urgently, he thrust again and again, driving her into a frenzy of sensation. Nothing had ever felt so good. No one had ever coaxed such a primal, wanton response from her body.

She bit his shoulder to keep from screaming as she came. His guttural moan and straining hips told her he was right there with her.

He thrust one final time, shuddering, and lay carefully against her as her body tightened around him in the aftershocks of orgasm.

He rested his head on her shoulder, his quick, sharp breaths warming her skin. She slid her fingers along the nape of his neck, ruffling his hair, breathing in his clean soap-and-mint scent.

Brand's eyes stung. He felt like a schoolboy experiencing the agonies of first love. For the first time in his life he felt a real connection with another person—something far beyond the simple physical couplings that had been his previous experience.

This was different. Lily was different.

During their enforced closeness, she'd learned more about him than he'd ever told anyone. She saw him as he really was. That scared the crap out of him.

He lifted his head and looked down at her. "How're you doing?" he whispered, touching her cheek.

She nodded and kissed him lightly. Her eyes drifted shut. She sighed through parted lips.

He lay beside her and watched her, wondering what he was going to do, now that he'd allowed himself to care for her.

He closed his eyes and drifted to the edge of sleep, feeling more content, more relaxed than he remembered ever feeling before in his life.

The sound of metal sliding against metal shocked him awake.

Someone was trying to unlock the door!

Chapter Eleven

Brand rolled out of bed in one swift motion and grabbed his jeans, pulling them on quickly, then picked up his weapon.

He glanced at his watch. Who would come to an empty studio at two o'clock in the morning?

As he started for the door, he heard Lily stir. He turned, his finger at his lips, warning her to stay quiet. "Get into the bathroom," he whispered.

She stared at him wide-eyed.

"Do it!" he said through gritted teeth.

She grabbed up her jeans and T-shirt and looked around.

Brand jerked his head toward the bathroom.

She reached across to an end table and picked up the Glock he'd reloaded for her. Then she rushed into the tiny bathroom.

Brand flattened himself against the wall beside the door, his weapon ready. He heard the jangle of keys.

Could it be a housekeeper? His racing pulse slowed a bit. Did Cassie's building have a cleaning service?

He didn't have time to ponder the answer. The scrape of metal against metal told him whoever was out there had slipped a key into the lock.

He stepped in front of the door, pointing his gun through the wood toward the person on the other side of the panels.

"Who's there?" he yelled gruffly.

He heard a surprised squeal and a jangling crash as a ring of keys hit the floor.

"Who's in there?" a shaky female voice responded. "Nobody's supposed to be in Mrs. Gallagher's studio." The footsteps retreated.

"Wait!" he shouted. It was Housekeeping. He had to make a decision—fast. He sure didn't want the woman calling the police and reporting a break-in.

He unlocked the door and peered out. A young woman with tired eyes stood behind a cleaning cart. She had the keys in one hand and her cell phone in the other, and she was backing away from the door.

"Hi," Brand said, hiding his gun behind the wooden door. He wiped his face and forced a yawn. "I'm Mrs. Gallagher's brother-in-law. I'm staying here for a couple of days while I'm in town."

The young woman eyed him suspiciously, her thumb poised over the phone's buttons.

"I can show you my driver's license, or I could give you her number. You could check with her." He nodded at her cell phone and smiled. "Although it's pretty late."

The young woman wasn't impressed. Her thumb twitched nervously. "What's your name?"

"Brand. Brand Gallagher. My brother is Ryan Gal-

lagher. This studio belongs to my sister-in-law, Cassie."
He ran a hand through his hair and smothered another
yawn. "She just had a baby."

She looked past him, then met his gaze again. "I'm
supposed to clean twice a week."

"Could you skip tonight? I've got an early meeting
tomorrow. Need to get some sleep."

She frowned and opened her mouth.

Brand dug in his pocket. "I'd be glad to reimburse
you for any trouble." He found a crumpled twenty and
offered it.

She squeezed her cell phone in her fist and reached for
the bill. "I'll be back on Wednesday. You will be gone?"

"I'll be out of here by then. Thanks." He pushed the
door shut and locked it.

She'd agreed easily enough, but his gut told him
she hadn't bought his story about the early meeting.
He didn't blame her. He wouldn't have bought it,
either. He wasn't even sure she believed he was
Cassie's brother-in-law.

Would she call the police? She'd hadn't hesitated to
yank the twenty out of his fingers. Maybe he should
have given her more.

The bathroom door opened with a soft creak.

"So *Brand Gallagher,* who was that? The cleaning
service?"

"You heard."

She nodded. "Were you ever going to tell me your
real name?"

"My real name is Brand."

"You know what I'm talking about."

He shrugged. "There never seemed to be a good time."

"Right." She'd dressed and pulled her hair back into a ponytail. It made her look like a teenager. "Do you think she's going to call somebody?"

He didn't know. "I don't think so. She's got a lot of offices to clean, and she's already tired."

Lily nodded, not looking at him. "What are we going to do now?"

She was acting like a skittish colt. She'd been lulled, as he had, into a false sense of security in the quiet, cozy studio. In reality Castellano's men were still after her, and he still didn't know who to trust.

"Like I told you, first thing in the morning I'm going to take you to the police. That's the best thing. You can see your father and the police will protect you until Castellano's put away."

"You've gone to as much trouble to keep me away from the police as you have to keep me away from Castellano. What makes you suddenly so certain that I'll be safer with the police than with you?"

He spread his hands. "I haven't done such a good job so far. Obviously, I can't keep you safe. As long as you're out here with me, you're exposed. The police can hide you, guard you."

"They could have done that two days ago. Why now? Why are you suddenly eager to get rid of me?"

Damn it, she was stubborn. "Because you're too much of a distraction," he said.

She blinked, then propped her fists on her hips. "So you're going to turn me over to the people you don't trust just to get me out of the way?"

"If that's how you want to look at it."

"You'll be putting me into a virtual prison. I guess I'm supposed to just sit there and wait? While you do what?"

"Keep looking for answers. Try to stop the people who're determined to kill you." He shook his head in regret. "I should have taken you in a long time ago."

Lily assessed the man who'd been her enemy and turned into her rescuer—and much more.

His blue eyes were clouded with doubt. Two deep lines furrowed his brow. She read the worry and regret in his face.

She nodded. "But you didn't."

His gaze faltered. "I'm sorry. I did what I thought was best at the time."

She bit her lip. "I know," she said gently.

Everything he'd done had been to protect her. It was an unfamiliar feeling, having someone else worry about her. It gave her a sense of security she hadn't felt in a very long time.

"What now?"

"I need to check on my lieutenant." He pulled out his cell phone, looked at it and cursed. "There's not much battery power left."

To her surprise, he tossed the phone to her. Then he retrieved the phone book from his sister-in-law's desk.

"Call County General and ask if Gary Morrison is able to talk. Here's the number." He read off a series of numbers and Lily punched them into the phone.

"Tell them you're his sister."

She pressed the call button and spoke to the hospital's switchboard.

"I'm sorry, ma'am. I have no information on a Mr. Morrison."

Lily met Brand's gaze. "But I'm his sister. I just got word he's been injured. Please. I need to speak to him. I have to know if he's all right."

The operator hesitated. "I'm sorry, ma'am. I'm not authorized to give out any information. You should speak with your brother's family."

She disconnected.

"What did they say?"

"The operator finally said she wasn't authorized to give out information. So my guess is he's there, but either the police have him under guard, or—"

"Or he didn't survive."

"Don't think that way."

"I've got to see him. I think Pruitt's right. Morrison knows or suspects who's leaking information to Castellano."

"What are you going to do?"

"Go to the hospital."

"But the police will be waiting for you."

He nodded as he reached for his T-shirt. "Most likely."

"What will they do?"

"Pruitt's already told me he'll have my badge."

"But that's not fair. None of this is your fault."

Brand smiled without humor. "I admire your sudden faith in me, but the brass won't see it that way."

Lily thought about Brand walking into County General and being picked up, possibly even put under arrest, by his fellow officers. "I'll go."

He pulled his T-shirt over his head and smoothed it

down over his ribs. "You? No, you won't. The only place you're going is to Pruitt's office to be placed in protective custody."

"No, I can do it. I can walk into the hospital without being noticed. If your lieutenant is there, he'll be guarded, right? I can find out where he is, maybe even talk to his family. I can get them to let you see him."

"That's a great plan, Lily. But it won't work."

"Why not?"

"First of all, if the police are guarding him, it's not going to be his family's choice who gets in to see him. And as you say, as soon as I'm spotted, they'll take me into custody."

"Then I'll get in to see him myself and ask him what he wanted to tell you."

Brand shook his head. "All this is based on the assumption that Morrison is there and able to talk."

"Well, what's *your* plan based on?"

He sent her a sidelong glance as he checked his weapon and slid it into the waistband of his jeans. "Same thing."

She propped her fists on her hips. "Okay then. My way makes more sense."

He shrugged into his shirt, leaving the tail out to hide his gun. "No, it doesn't."

"Yes, it does. Besides, we need to hurry. It will be better if we go during the midnight shift." Lily picked up her gun and slipped it into a zippered tote bag that she picked up off the desk by the door.

He nodded. "Okay."

"Okay?" Lily's heart thumped in surprise. "You're agreeing with me?"

He shrugged as he opened the door a crack to peer out. "It's as good a plan as any."

He gestured for her to precede him through the door. "Let's go. Like you said, it'll be easier on the midnight shift."

Lily glanced around the studio, her gaze lingering on the tangled sheets on the daybed. Then she slipped through the door.

"Stay behind me," Brand whispered as he locked the studio and pocketed the keys.

"How are we getting to the hospital?"

"It's only about three miles. We'll walk, or hail a cab."

"Brand." Lily caught his wrist as he stepped in front of her.

He patted her hand. "It'll be okay. Don't worry. You'll be in protective custody by morning. You'll get to see your father."

She hesitated, then nodded. It was probably better that he hadn't given her the chance to say what she'd started to say. There was no need to complicate the situation by bringing emotions into it.

Better that he think she was worried about herself and her father.

She followed him down the fire stairs. At the door to the street, he paused.

"Wait here while I check out the area. Watch through the reinforced glass. I'll signal you when it's safe for you to come out."

Lily nodded. "Who do you think—"

"I don't know. Maybe nobody. But it never hurts to be careful."

Brand pushed through the fire door into the parking lot. It had rained earlier, and the streetlights were haloed by the damp mist that hung in the freshly washed air. He breathed in the smells of cool rain and hot asphalt. It was unseasonably warm, and wisps of steam rose from the street.

The gas station across the street from the office building was deserted. Its ugly yellow sign barely penetrated the damp air.

He studied the dark street for a few moments, but nothing moved. Everything was quiet. Not even a breeze was blowing.

Taking a deep breath of the still night air, he turned and gestured to Lily.

She slipped through the fire door and hurried to his side.

"Let's get away from here. It's too dark. Too isolated. We'll follow Highway 90. Stick close."

He stepped out onto the street, his hand poised near the handle of his weapon.

He heard the ricochet of the bullet before he heard the report.

Whirling, he threw himself on top of Lily. They hit the ground together, his arm cradling her head.

"What—oof!"

"Shh!" He raised his head and drew his gun. Where had the shot come from?

The answer came in a volley of gunfire. Brand cringed and tried to spread himself more completely over Lily as bullets sent bits of asphalt shooting into the air and zinged past their ears.

The shots were coming from the direction of the gas

station. He should have checked the area more closely. He'd been too anxious to get to the hospital. His carelessness had exposed them—they were sitting ducks.

Brand cast about for shelter. About twenty feet in front of them was a garbage bin. He got his feet under him and hovered in a crouch.

"See the metal bin? Run for it," he said to Lily. "I'll cover you."

The mist was growing heavier. Brand could barely make out dark shapes moving toward them under the garish yellow light.

He lifted Lily and pushed her toward the Dumpster. Her breaths sobbed and caught and her tennis shoes crunched on gravel as she sprinted across the open space.

He was right behind her. He got off a couple of shots in the general direction of the building.

More gunfire erupted all around them. Several rounds ricocheted off the garbage bin and thudded into the asphalt.

A bullet caught the edge of his hip as he dove and rolled.

"Ouch! Crap!" He touched the torn denim and felt the scraped skin. The bullet had barely skimmed his flesh.

"Are you hurt?" Lily cried.

"No. It's nothing. Get down!"

He heard a car engine start up. "They're coming. Can you shoot?"

"Yes!"

Lily was breathless, but her head was high and her jaw was set. She crawled to the side of the Dumpster and crouched, her gun trained in the direction of the car's engine.

"I can't see!"

Brand saw a shadow moving toward them. Two shadows. "Watch the shadows! Here they come. Try to wound them. We don't know whether they're police or Castellano's men."

He was almost certain it wasn't the police. They wouldn't sneak up in dark clothes, taking potshots at them without identifying themselves as law enforcement.

Had Castellano's connections led him to Brand's sister-in-law's studio? Or had someone on the force betrayed him again?

He shot off several rounds, aiming low. He didn't want to kill anyone if he didn't have to.

"Shoot at their feet!" he shouted to Lily.

Helpless fury raged through him. Once again he'd put Lily in danger. He should have turned her over to the police when he had the chance. Now they were trapped.

Castellano wanted her dead, and Brand had delivered her right into the mob boss's hands.

He aimed at a shadow. In the distance he heard a car engine turn over. A black sedan appeared from the darkness behind the gas station. It approached slowly.

He swung his gun, aiming at the vehicle's windshield, although it was probably a waste of a bullet. If the car belonged to Castellano, it probably had bulletproof glass.

Just as he was about to squeeze the trigger, his ears picked up another sound—sirens wailing in the distance. Someone had heard the gunfire and called the police.

Automatic weapons fire sprayed the garbage bin with dozens of rounds.

"Lily! Stay down," he shouted, cringing backward. A quick glance told him her back was pressed against the dirty metal, and she held her gun in both hands, prepared to shoot. She was on the balls of her feet, poised to whirl and fire off several rounds as soon as the volley stopped. Her expression was intense, focused.

Her bravery in the face of possible death awed him.

The sound of a second car engine split the air. He angled his head to steal a quick glance. A pair of watery headlights sped toward them through the mist. He trained his weapon on the windshield of the new arrival.

More gunfire filled the air. His pulse pounded and his breath rasped in his throat as he struggled to sort out the sounds.

The new car was firing *at* the other vehicle. He heard a startled shout from one of the gunmen.

Who was it? The police in an unmarked car? He wiped mist from his face and aimed his weapon at the newcomer as it screeched to a halt in front of the Dumpster.

Brand pointed his weapon at the passenger window and tightened his finger on the trigger.

The passenger door swung open.

"Brand!"

He blinked at the familiar voice. It was Springer. How had Springer found them?

"Get the hell in here." Springer's driver's window was down. He took potshots at the moving shadows.

Brand heard the dark car's engine rev.

"They're moving in. Let's go!" Springer's voice was shrill with reaction. He ducked as a bullet ricocheted off the top of his car. "Damn it, hurry!"

Brand grabbed Lily's arm. "Come on. Let's go."

"Who—"

He yanked the passenger seat forward and climbed into the back, then pulled the front seat back into position. Lily dove in. Before she even got the door closed Springer gunned the engine and roared away.

Automatic weapons fire pinged the rear of Springer's car. The undercover officer's hands were white-knuckled on the steering wheel.

"That was close. How the hell are you?" Springer flashed a toothy grin.

"Where did you come from?" Brand shouted. "How'd you know where we were?"

Springer was too busy to answer. He careered around a corner, wheels screeching, then raced up a side street before finally slowing to a more normal pace.

Lily held on as tightly as she could. She hadn't even had a chance to put on her seat belt. Once Springer slowed down, she turned in her seat.

"Are you all right?" she asked Brand. "You got hit, didn't you? Where?"

He frowned. "It's nothing. Caught the edge of my hip."

Her weapon pressed against her side. She pulled it out, ejected the magazine and held it up. "I'm out of ammunition."

"That's okay," he said. "I've got several rounds left."

Springer glanced over at Lily. "You must be the missing juror," he said conversationally. "So you got yourself one who can shoot, Gallagher?"

Lily stared at the undercover cop for a few seconds. He was a chunky guy, maybe midforties, with a receding hairline and an expanding waist. He had a barrel chest and hefty biceps. She remembered Brand saying that the other two undercover cops worked on the docks. This guy looked as if he could hold his own among longshoremen.

"So are you okay, Ms. Raines?" He waggled his eyebrows at her, then gave a sharp chuckle and glanced in the rearview mirror. "Your juror don't talk much," he tossed back over his shoulder.

He knew who she was? Lily supposed she shouldn't be surprised. Brand had said her picture was plastered all over the papers and the television. But the newspaper had withheld her name.

She supposed Springer had her name because he was a police officer.

Still, she turned and sent Brand a questioning look. "Springer—"

"Okay. Okay. I overheard a couple of Castellano's goons talking about how you'd screwed him over. They said you roughed up Foshee and ran off with the juror. Gio ain't happy. I can tell you that."

"No kidding. He didn't make me as a cop though, did he?"

"Well, I got the idea he figured you weren't just a bouncer." Springer leered at Lily. "Maybe he thinks you went wacko over the chick."

Brand glanced behind him.

Lily followed his gaze, but the damp street was deserted.

"So when I heard them saying they were on their way to check your sister-in-law's place I figured I'd better see if I could intercept you. Looks like I got there just in time."

"How did they know about Cassie's studio?"

Springer shook his head. "Hell if I know. I just work the docks. Castellano don't confide in me."

"I can't wait to find out who ratted me out."

Springer looked at Brand in the rearview mirror. "Yep. That ain't just your problem, either. If Castellano knows you're a cop, it's only a matter of time before he tumbles to Carson and me. I probably screwed myself, anyhow, coming after you."

A police car passed them going in the opposite direction. Springer turned right onto a side street.

"You don't think whoever betrayed me ratted you two out, too?"

Springer shrugged his massive shoulders. "I don't think so. From what I heard, you were set up to take the fall. Foshee was supposed to kill you after he took out the girl."

Lily stared at him. His bald statement brought home to her how close she'd come to being killed.

How many times could she cheat death? First the Cajun with his lethal knife. Then the pug-nosed gunman in the restaurant. Not to mention the bullets she'd been dodging in the casino garage and in the street just now.

Icy fear crawled up her spine as it occurred to her that her luck might run out at any second. The next attack could be fatal.

Springer glanced at her, and apparently read her mind. "Sorry, Sugar, but it's the truth."

Brand grunted. "That doesn't make sense. Why

wouldn't he bring me in, force me to tell him more about the operation before killing me?"

Lily listened in stunned awe, her pulse hammering in her ears. She couldn't believe how nonchalantly they were talking about being tortured and killed. Was this the life her father had led?

Springer just shrugged his shoulders.

"Unless—" Brand paused. "Unless he already knew everything he needed to know."

Springer turned right again. Lily squinted, trying to read the street signs. She wasn't sure where they were, but it felt like they were headed back the way they'd come.

As if picking up on her thoughts, Brand asked, "Where are we going?"

Springer nodded in the general direction of the road ahead. "There's a place down near the docks where we can hide out until morning."

"Why don't we go on in to police headquarters? I need to talk to Pruitt as soon as possible, and I want to see Morrison. You heard he got shot?"

Springer nodded. "How's he doing?"

"I don't know. That's where we were headed, to check on him, when we were ambushed. I think Morrison knows who the leak is."

"Oh yeah? Pruitt didn't tell me that."

Lily noticed an easing of the tension that radiated from Brand. She let herself relax a little, sitting back in her seat. She took a deep, shaky breath, her limbs trembling in a delayed reaction. She'd been so scared.

But now Brand and Springer seemed to have everything under control.

Springer made another turn. They were nearing the shipyards.

"I wonder if Morrison is right."

"About the leak?" Brand shrugged. "I don't know. He's pretty smart."

"Yeah." Springer shifted in his seat and took his right hand off the steering wheel.

He bent over and reached under his seat. Lily glanced down. To her surprise, he pulled out a large Glock 9mm without taking his eyes off the road.

"What is it?" she asked. "What's wrong?"

Behind her, Brand sat up. He must have heard the note of alarm in her voice. "What's the matter, Lily?"

Her mouth went dry. All she could do was shake her head.

Springer wrapped his hand around the gun without taking his eyes off the road. "We're almost there."

"Where?" Brand snapped. "This looks like Castellano's place."

Springer pressed the barrel of the gun into Lily's thigh. "You got good eyes, Gallagher. It's the alley behind Gio's. Now listen to me and listen good. You so much as breathe wrong and your girlfriend here loses her leg."

Chapter Twelve

Lily stifled a scream as the gun barrel dug painfully into her flesh.

Brand's fellow officer had betrayed them. She read the shock and fury on his face in the split second it took him to realize what Springer was doing.

He reached for his weapon.

"Hands up, Gallagher!" Springer snapped. The car jerked as his hand tightened on the steering wheel. "Let me see 'em. I'll shoot her leg off, I swear."

Brand grimaced and raised his empty hands. His gaze met hers briefly, warning her not to move. "What the hell's the matter with you, Springer?"

"Don't give me that. Where's your gun? Don't move a muscle. Just tell me."

"It's stuck in the waistband of my jeans. In the middle of my back."

"Then you keep your hands where I can see 'em."

Brand stuck his empty hands up in the air. "I don't get it. What happened to you? You're a good cop. A good man. What about your family?"

Springer laughed. "My family?" he spat. "You want to know what happened to my family? Come on, man. Didn't you notice what happened when you took this job? You were engaged, right? Where's your pretty little fiancée now?"

Brand blinked. "What's that got to do with this?"

Fiancée? The word cut through Lily like a saber. The sharpness of the pain surprised her. Brand had told her he wasn't in a relationship. He'd said it was because of his undercover assignment. She'd believed him. In fact, she hadn't even considered that he might have a past. That showed how naive she was.

Springer was talking. "I had a wife and two kids. I got nothing now. She left me, took the kids back to Dallas, where she grew up. You know why?"

Lily heard the anger and grief in Springer's voice. He was desperate. His chest heaved as the barrel of his gun pushed into her thigh muscle, causing it to cramp.

She cringed and took a deep, shaky breath.

"Do—you—know—why?" Springer yelled.

Brand sat up a little straighter. "Because you were never home?"

"Because even when I was there I wasn't there. That's what *she* said."

Lily looked down at his hand. He was squeezing the gun's handle so hard the barrel shook.

"Now I got nothing. I can't even see my kids. And I'm doing Castellano's dirty work."

"Man, I'm sorry—"

"Shut up! I've got to think." He turned the steering wheel one-handed into the parking lot of Gio's.

The upscale nightclub was located on a side street down near the docks. Its fame had spread by word of mouth over the past twenty years. These days, with the casinos pulling in the Vegas crowds, Gio's was still *the* place for A-list celebrities to relax and party.

Lily had never been there, but like everyone else, she'd heard the stories—the major star who'd died on the dance floor, the shooting one night that left an intern to a famous politician paralyzed.

"So that's how Castellano kept finding us. You've been feeding him information. You knew my brother's name, knew about my sister-in-law's studio."

Springer stopped the car and reached across with his left hand to turn off the key. He moved the gun from Lily's thigh to her ribs. "Tell him where the gun's pointing now, Sugar."

She cringed as he dug the weapon into her side. "It's pointed at my heart."

"That's right, Gallagher. And I'm watching you. Keep those hands up."

"Why did it take so long to ambush us there? Why didn't you move in on us the first night?"

Without bothering to answer him, Springer pulled a cell phone from his shirt pocket and pressed a pre-recorded number. "Yo, Foshee. It's Springer. I've got 'em. Hell, yeah. I told you I would. Come out here and give me a hand."

He half turned toward Brand. "Nah, not yet," he said into the phone.

He paused and Lily heard the Cajun's nasal twang

through the phone, although she couldn't understand what he was saying.

"Because Castellano wants to see 'em first. Don't worry, you'll get your chance."

Lily saw the back door of Gio's open. The little Cajun came swaggering out, toying with his knife. A big gun was visible under his jacket and he had a strip bandage across the bridge of his nose.

As he drew closer, she saw that he had a black eye and a cut, swollen lip, too. Brand had done that. She swallowed nervously. The Cajun was going to be out for revenge.

Springer lowered the driver's side window.

"Foshee, watch Gallagher. He's got a gun stuck in his pants."

Foshee walked around to the passenger door. He closed his knife with one hand and drew his gun before opening the car door.

Lily didn't move as the Cajun stuck his head in and grinned at her. "Hello, Lily. You didn't pay attention to me. Dat was a bad mistake. Now you and your boyfriend gotta pay."

He pointed his gun at Brand and grabbed her arm with his left hand. He leaned closer, until his garlicky breath was hot against her cheek. "You try anything and my buddy Brand gets his head blown off. Understand?"

She nodded. Terror stole her breath and paralyzed her limbs. She couldn't move. She was certain of it.

"Come on, Lily." He jerked on her arm, never taking his eyes off Brand.

She tried to rise, but her knees gave out.

Foshee jerked harder, twisting her arm.

She bit her lip against the pain and tried to think, tried to come up with a plan to disarm the Cajun, but her brain wouldn't work. All she could think of was his big gun aimed right at Brand's head. There was nothing she could do.

She swung her quivering legs out of the car and stood, certain she was going to crumple. Her hand went to the door to steady herself.

Foshee shoved her away from the door, hanging on to her arm and keeping Brand covered.

He knew who the real threat was. Lily felt helpless, impotent against Foshee and Springer and their guns. Even if she tried to create a diversion, she knew Foshee would make good on his threat. He'd shoot Brand first.

"Get out," he snarled at Brand. "And keep your hands up. If you drop 'em, I drop you. Springer, watch his back."

Brand placed both hands on the seat back, pushed it forward and climbed out of Springer's car. He kept his hands in full sight of both men at all times.

Lily met his gaze as he straightened, his hands still held up in front of him. He gave a quick shake of his head. She knew exactly what he was saying.

Don't try anything.

Springer rounded the car and shoved Brand up against it.

"Spread 'em." He took Brand's gun, then patted him down.

Brand's fists clenched against the car's metal roof.

"Let's go," Foshee said as Springer finished his search. "Mr. Castellano wants to see you both."

As soon as Springer let him move, Brand glanced over at Lily. She looked small and terrified, with Foshee's skinny arm wrapped around her and his big 9mm pointed at the back of her neck.

Springer nudged him with his gun. "Get a move on, Gallagher. Walk to the back door. Keep those hands up. You heard Foshee. Make a wrong move and his itchy trigger finger will jerk."

"Oops!" Foshee said, then cackled.

Brand cringed.

"It almost jerked right then, just looking at your lying face, *bioque.*"

Brand sent the Cajun a lethal glare, then turned toward the back door to Giovanni Castellano's exclusive club.

He had no clue how to get out of this. More importantly, he had no idea how to get Lily out of it. He should have realized the leak was one of his fellow undercover officers. It made perfect sense. They had access to the kind of information that was being leaked.

But he'd trusted them because they were on the side of the good guys. They'd taken the same oaths as he had. They'd become cops for the same reason he had. To right the wrongs in the world. Or at least that's what he'd assumed.

"How did you know we were meeting with Morrison?" he asked Springer.

The cop nudged him in the back with his gun barrel. "Move it."

Brand walked faster.

At the door, Springer stopped. "You always were his pet. We figured you'd try to contact him, so we kept an eye on him. Pruitt had the same idea, because Morrison's street was crawling with unmarked cars. When he headed to the casinos, it was pretty obvious he was going to meet you. Morrison's no gambler. So we had him followed."

"So it *was* Castellano's men who shot him."

"Sure. I don't know what he'd found out, but we couldn't take the chance. We had to take him out, so he couldn't tip you off. Then we waited for you two to show up."

He pushed the gun barrel into Brand's side. "Open the door."

Brand knew Castellano was never surprised. The door, which led into the kitchen, would be covered by armed guards. Castellano was very careful about safety—particularly his own.

Sure enough, standing inside the kitchen were two men in dark suits holding automatic weapons under their arms. They looked nonchalant, harmless, but Brand knew they were anything but.

Behind him Lily made a small, hurt noise. He turned but Springer dug the gun barrel into his side.

"Don't get worried about your girlfriend, Gallagher. Foshee is taking good care of her."

Brand's whole body tensed in fury. If the Cajun laid one hand on her, Brand would make him pay. Even if it cost Brand his own life.

They passed through the kitchen, which smelled like tomato sauce and freshly baked bread, and entered the dimly lit main rooms of the restaurant.

Over in the far corner, away from the bandstand and close to the exit to his offices, at the table that was always kept reserved for him, Castellano sat. He was surrounded by two of his bodyguards and kept company by two beautiful women.

They were all in evening attire, although it had to be five o'clock in the morning. Brand figured they hadn't gone to bed yet.

Castellano had a glass half filled with amber liquid in front of him. As Springer and Foshee pushed them toward his table, he lifted the glass. His eyes were puffy and heavy-lidded with lost sleep, but he grinned broadly.

"Ah, my trusted employee, Jake Brand. How nice to see you." Castellano saluted him with his drink, then turned it up. "And Ms. Raines. Such a lovely, disobedient little juror. Please, take a seat. I want to try and understand why you couldn't follow simple instructions."

Lily didn't move. Her fists were clenched at her sides and her face was a pale oval in the dim light.

"I said have a seat," Castellano repeated harshly.

Foshee shoved her roughly into a leather chair and stood behind it, his gun pointed at the back of her neck.

Brand's muscles contracted in impotent rage. Castellano was going to toy with her and then, with a nod of his head, her fate would be sealed. She would die, and her death wouldn't be easy.

"Brand, you, too. Come now. We're civilized here."

Springer's gun dug into his ribs. Brand sat in the chair next to Lily. She didn't look up.

His heart ached with searing regret and a lump

clogged his throat. He saw in her eyes that she knew he couldn't save her. He longed to touch her, to reassure her, but he didn't have any reassurance for her.

How could he have trusted Springer? He'd been so careful up until that point. But Castellano's gunmen were closing in on them, and Springer was a cop, after all.

Lily's question echoed in his memory. *How can you not trust your fellow officers?*

Too late, he realized that was his fatal flaw.

As cautious and suspicious as he'd been, when it came down to it, he didn't hesitate to trust Springer. Deep down, he did believe the police were the good guys.

"Ms. Raines." Castellano's voice was harsh.

Lily jumped, and Foshee put his hand on her shoulder. She cringed.

"Aren't you going to answer me?"

Lily lifted her chin. "Wh-what was the question?"

Brand hid a smile. She was terrified, yet she refused to give the crime boss the satisfaction of hearing her plead for her life.

While Castellano's attention was on Lily, Brand let his gaze roam over the room, taking in everything and everyone around them, searching for a way out. Their table was equidistant from the front and rear doors of the restaurant.

Behind and to the left was a door that Brand knew led to a private office. He'd never been in there, so he had no idea if there was an exit, but judging by the care Castellano took for his own safety, Brand was sure the King of the Coast wouldn't let himself be trapped in his own office. There had to be an exit.

Brand gauged the distance to the door as Castellano questioned Lily.

"Why did you vote to convict my dear friend Theodore Simon?"

Lily moistened her lips as she deliberately relaxed her hands and flexed her fingers. "He was guilty, Mr. Castellano."

Despite the gravity of their predicament, Brand's heart swelled in admiration and pride. Lily was gutsy, there was no doubt about that.

Castellano's face turned red. "That's entirely beside the point. I asked you to do me a simple favor and vote not guilty. The jury wouldn't have had a unanimous verdict, a mistrial would have been declared and my friend would have been freed. It was a fine plan."

"Fine for you, maybe. Not for me." Lily's voice quavered slightly. "As soon as the jury was dismissed, you planned to kill me."

Castellano waved his hand. "Why in the world would I do that?"

Lily didn't bother answering.

He laughed. "I like you, Ms. Raines. You've got moxie. It took a lot of courage to do what you did—to vote to convict even though by doing so you caused the death of an innocent man."

Brand saw Castellano's words find their target in Lily's heart. He knew how much Bill Henderson's death weighed on her conscience.

"It's a shame you can't work for me."

"I suppose it is."

At the sound of the door from the kitchen swinging

227227227

shut, Castellano looked up. "Ah, here's the rest of our party."

It was Carson, the other member of their undercover team. He was led in at gunpoint by a muscle-necked goon. He looked confused and frightened.

"Mr. Carson, welcome to our little party."

Carson looked at Springer, at Brand, then at Castellano. "I don't understand."

The mob boss took a sip of his drink. "No, of course you don't. But you will." He caught Springer's eye and nodded.

"Get up." Springer nudged Brand in the back of his neck with the gun barrel. At the same time, Foshee grabbed Lily's arm and jerked her out of her seat.

Brand met Carson's gaze.

Carson looked at the gun Springer held. "Springer, what the hell—?"

"Mr. Carson, I regret to inform you that your little undercover operation is over. Your trusted friend Mr. Springer has decided to work for me."

"Springer? Why you dirty—" Carson's face turned red and he lunged toward Springer, but the man guarding him coldcocked him with the barrel of his gun.

Carson dropped to the floor with a grunt, then dragged himself to his hands and knees.

The guard nudged him with his foot. "Get up!" He grabbed the back of Carson's shirt and hauled him to his feet.

Lily watched the brutality in horrified amazement. She glanced at Brand and saw anger, frustration and fear cross his face. Her heart sank. She knew what he was thinking. They were hopelessly outnumbered. They were all going to die here.

She longed to reach out and take his hand, to feel his strength, his caring, once more before she died. But even as the thought entered her mind, Foshee dragged her farther away from him.

"Take them away," Castellano said. "You know what to do. Just make sure you dispose of them far enough out in the Gulf that they'll never be found."

Brand's gaze caught Lily's. In that split second, she saw the secrets of his heart reflected in his clear blue eyes. He loved her. Her heart soared.

But then his jaw tightened and her insides clenched with fear. He was going to make a move.

Because he loved her, he would sacrifice his life for her.

No! she wanted to shout. *Please don't make me watch you die.*

Springer's weapon was aimed directly at Brand's head. No matter what he tried, he'd be too slow. Springer would kill him.

Lily stared at Brand then slowly, deliberately, she rolled her eyes back in her head and collapsed, boneless, to the floor.

All hell broke loose.

Foshee jerked on her arm.

Brand dove over the table toward Castellano.

Springer took aim at Brand but hesitated, probably because Castellano was in his line of fire.

Carson head-butted his guard, whose gun went off.

Lily cringed at the report, but the bullet didn't hit her, and she didn't hear anyone cry out in pain. All she heard were the screams of the two young women who had been sitting with Castellano.

The table splintered under the weight of Brand and Springer as they struggled for Springer's gun. Castellano shrieked.

Foshee let go of Lily's arm and moved to help Springer with Brand. Lily grabbed his leg, but he kicked her away.

She saw two more dark-suited men heading their way. The armed guards from the kitchen. There was no way they'd get out of this alive.

Then suddenly doors crashed open. Light streamed in.

"Stop! Police!"

Lily's heart crashed against her chest.

"Hold it! Nobody move!"

"Drop that gun!"

"Get on the floor! On the floor! Now!"

Lily plastered herself against the carpeted floor. Her pulse pounded in her ears. Her whole body burned with terror. She figured her best bet was not to move.

She heard several shots and more shouts.

Somebody fell on top of her. Was it Foshee? She felt the sticky warmth of blood seeping through the back of her T-shirt.

Then another body crashed down next to her. She lifted her head. It was Springer. His face was frozen in a mask of horror. Was he dead?

It seemed like dozens of pairs of shoes scrambled around her. She closed her eyes and put her hands over her head.

Suddenly, beefy arms wrapped around her and dragged her along the floor.

Kicking and thrashing, she struggled to get away, but the man who held her was too strong. He dragged her through a doorway and kicked it shut behind him.

Lily swung her arms wildly, straining to draw enough breath into her lungs to scream.

"Shut up or I'll shoot you now!"

It was Springer. Blood streamed down the side of his face, the dark red emphasizing the traitor cop's paleness.

She looked down the dark barrel of his massive gun.

"Get up. *Get up!*"

Lily was disoriented. She didn't know where they were. It was a dark, stuffy corridor that smelled like whiskey.

As she tried to get her feet under her, Springer grabbed her by the waist and dragged her across the carpeted floor. He wrapped his arm under hers as he shoved a door open with his shoulder and pulled her outside.

Dawn was just breaking, turning everything a faint purple, Lily noticed as Springer yanked her up against his body. He pressed the gun barrel to the back of her head.

She closed her eyes and held her breath, waiting for the shot she knew she wouldn't hear.

BRAND LAUNCHED HIMSELF across the splintered table and grabbed Castellano.

"My leg!" The mob boss screamed. "My leg's broken. Get off me."

Brand had no sympathy for him. His neck stung. He was pretty sure a bullet had dug a furrow into his flesh, but he hadn't had a chance to check it. He'd been too busy scuffling with Springer and too anxious to get his hands on Castellano.

He wasn't quite sure what had happened, but the place was swarming with FBI Task Force jackets. Someone had tipped them off, and none too soon.

He wondered who.

Suddenly, everything went quiet. The gunfire stopped. The lawmen seemed to have everything under control.

"Gallagher!"

It was Pruitt.

Brand sat up, still holding Castellano in a headlock.

"You—Dawson," Pruitt yelled at an officer. "Take Mr. Castellano into custody."

Pruitt knelt next to Brand. "You can let go now, Gallagher. Dawson has him."

Brand relaxed and looked at Pruitt. "Nice of you to come," he said hoarsely. "You got a pair of cuffs for me?"

Pruitt shook his head. "Not today. Morrison woke up. He told me he suspected Springer of turning. Said Springer had come to him a few weeks ago. Asked him to intervene—get him extracted. Said his wife was going to leave him."

Brand nodded. It made sense. "Springer worked under Morrison about the same time I did. Morrison was like a father to us both. What did the lieutenant tell him?"

"What he should have. To see me."

"But Springer didn't. So Morrison was trying to warn me that Springer might be the leak."

Pruitt nodded. "I wish he'd come to me first."

Brand didn't respond to Pruitt's comment. "How'd you and the cavalry get here just in time?"

"I put a tail on Springer as soon as Morrison told me

what he suspected. The tail hung back during the gunfight, waiting to see what Springer was going to do. Then when Springer picked up you two, he followed you here and called for backup."

The FBI agent sighed. "Look, Gallagher. I know you and Morrison had your doubts about me, but I had to look at the big picture."

Brand didn't want to hear about Pruitt's big picture. He needed to find Lily.

His gaze swept the room. Where was she? He didn't see her anywhere. Concern ripped through him like a stray bullet. He straightened, ignoring the blood that trickled down his neck. "Where's Lily?"

"I don't know. One of the officers may have taken her outside to be checked by the paramedics."

Brand pushed himself to his feet. He swayed, feeling light-headed. "Lily!"

The restaurant was still swarming with police and FBI agents. But he didn't see a little sparkly white T-shirt anywhere.

"Damn it. Where is she? Lily!" he shouted.

"We'll find her. You need to let the paramedics look at that neck."

"Later. Give me a gun." He grabbed the nearest officer and held out his hand. "Your weapon—now!"

The officer looked at Pruitt, who nodded.

Weapon in hand, Brand turned and pushed through the door in back of Castellano's table. He found himself in a dimly lit corridor with several closed doors leading off it.

The door at the end of the corridor was ajar. He rushed toward it and slammed it open. He was in the parking lot of Gio's. And directly in his line of sight stood Springer, holding Lily with a gun to her head.

Brand's heart jumped into his throat. He could barely get breath enough to speak.

"Springer! Don't do it!" He aimed his gun at Springer's head. He felt his arm muscle quiver. God, he hoped he didn't have to shoot. He was so shook up that he was afraid he might hit Lily.

"Get out of here, Gallagher. I don't want to shoot you."

"You don't want to shoot anybody." Brand's heart pounded. His blood ran cold in his veins. He prayed he could stop Springer. How would he live if Lily died?

He caught her eye.

She was terrified. Her face was white and pinched. She gripped Springer's arm with both hands. Her paleness told Brand she was about to collapse.

Hang in there, Lily.

He turned his attention back to the desperate cop. "You haven't killed anybody yet, have you?"

"What the hell difference does that make? I might as well have. There's nothing left for me."

The defeated tone in Springer's voice worried Brand. It sounded like he'd already given up. If that was true, then Lily's life was in the hands of a man who had nothing to live for.

Brand's pulse thrummed rapidly and his gun barrel wavered. "Let her go. We'll talk. I'll testify for you. Tell 'em you didn't have a choice."

Springer shook his head. "That won't change anything. I'm screwed. Got nothing to go back to. My family's gone. I've lost my pension."

He tightened his grip on Lily. Her brown eyes flashed with fear.

"Don't add murder to it. Don't take an innocent life." He heard his voice quaver. If Lily died—

"Come on. Give me the gun." Brand held out his hand and took a step closer without lowering his gun.

Springer stiffened. His eyes darted back and forth.

Brand went still. "Okay." He raised his outstretched hand in a show of surrender. "Okay. Here's what we'll do. You let Lily go, and I'll stay out here with you. We'll figure something out. How's that?"

Springer's gaze wavered. His arm loosened a bit.

Lily swallowed and stared at Brand.

"Yeah. That's right. Let Lily go. Then you and me, we'll go to Pruitt and talk. Figure out what we can do."

Springer squeezed his eyes shut for an instant, then turned the gun from Lily's head to point at Brand.

"What we can do? There's nothing you or anybody else can do. I'm a dead man."

Brand's mouth went dry. He wasn't going to let her go.

"Come on, man. You don't want to die. We've got Castellano. You'll get consideration for the job you did undercover."

Lily hadn't taken her eyes off Brand. They burned into his skin, but he couldn't risk even a glance at her. He had to watch Springer every second.

She took a shaky breath.

Springer's gun hand shook. He took a long, shuddering breath. "I can't, Gallagher. It's too late."

His arm tightened and Lily gasped.

Brand aimed at Springer's head.

Suddenly, Springer loosened his hold on Lily and pushed her toward Brand, still aiming his gun at Brand's chest.

"There!" he shouted. "Take her. You're blowing smoke. She's all you really want, isn't she? You'd promise me anything in exchange for her life."

Brand did his best to hold his gun hand steady as he reached out and snagged Lily by the waist. "Springer, let's talk. I've got Lily now and I still want to help you."

Springer put his other hand on his gun. "I can't—"

A shot rang out.

Lily's whole body spasmed.

Shock slashed through Brand with the suddenness of heat lightning. Had Lily been shot?

Chapter Thirteen

"Lily!" God, no! Brand pulled her closer, praying she was all right.

Springer's face registered surprise as he stared at a point over Brand's shoulder. Then his eyes glazed over, the gun dropped from his hand and he crumpled to the ground.

Brand stared at the fallen cop, his brain slowly realizing that it was Springer who'd been shot, not Lily. She'd collapsed in shock and fear.

Holding her close against him, he looked over his shoulder in time to see Pruitt lower his weapon.

"Pruitt! My God!" His whole body tingled with shock and outrage. He loosened his hold on Lily. "Can you stand?" he asked her.

She was white as a sheet, but she nodded.

"Stay here."

Rushing over, he knelt beside Springer's body. "Pruitt. You shot him!"

"He was going to shoot you."

"You don't know that! He'd let Lily go." He turned the fallen cop over. Springer's eyes fluttered.

"Hang in there, buddy. The paramedics are here."

"He had his weapon pointed right at you."

"Get the paramedics!" Brand yelled.

As if they'd heard him, two EMTs ran around the corner of the restaurant. They bent over Springer.

"Step back, sir."

"We've got him. Please give us some room to work."

Brand stood and moved away.

Lily walked up beside him.

"Come on. You two need to be looked at, too." Pruitt barely glanced at Springer as he guided Brand and Lily around to where the squad cars were parked.

He instructed one of his officers to find an EMT to examine them. When the med-tech came rushing over, Brand held up a hand.

"Lily, you go. I need to talk to Pruitt about something."

She sent him a questioning look. "But your neck. You're bleeding."

He nodded encouragingly. "Go ahead. I'll be there in a couple of minutes."

Lily let the EMT lead her toward one of the ambulances.

Brand turned to Pruitt. "What about her father?"

Pruitt sent him a disgusted look. "I told you I'd take care of it."

"Well, did you? Where is he? I hope to hell you picked him up, because he's not at the nursing home."

"Give me some credit, Gallagher. Of course we picked him up. As soon as we got the court order. He's in a guarded room at County General."

Brand breathed a sigh of relief. "Thanks. When we

called the nursing home, the ward clerk had no clue what had happened to him." He turned toward the ambulance.

"Gallagher."

He stopped and turned halfway around. "Yeah?"

"It was a good shoot. Springer was about to pull the trigger."

Brand shook his head. "No shooting is good."

Pruitt had the grace to grimace and nod.

"Anyhow, good job. Thanks to you and Juror Number Seven, we should be able to put Castellano away for a long time."

Brand angled his head and eyed Pruitt with suspicion. He still didn't like the guy, but he trusted him more than he had at first. He sent the FBI agent a short nod, then headed for the ambulance.

The EMT bandaged Brand's neck. He'd already determined that Lily had no injuries.

"All this blood is the Cajun's," she told him. "He fell on me when he was shot."

Brand didn't protest when the EMT put them in the backseat of a squad car to await transport to the central task force location to give their statements.

He sat there for a minute, trying to wipe the image of Lily with a gun to her head out of his mind. But it wouldn't disappear. Nor could he rid himself of the sight of Springer collapsed on the ground, blood blossoming from the wound in his chest.

Lily sighed.

He roused himself. "Pruitt told me they picked up your father."

A muffled sob escaped from her throat. "Oh! I'm so glad. Where is he?"

"At County General, in a guarded room. If you want, I'll take you to see him later today, when we finish giving our statements."

"Thank you. That would be wonderful."

Brand nodded.

They fell silent.

He stared at the flashing blue lights as his brain picked over everything that had happened in the past twenty-four hours.

He tried desperately to figure out how and when he could have handled things differently, but every scenario played out the same way. Either Lily died, or someone else did.

Where had he gone wrong?

LILY FELT THE TURMOIL inside Brand. She wanted to take his hand and comfort him. She longed to reassure him that he'd done everything he could, and that Springer's shooting wasn't his fault.

Two men came around the side of the building carrying a stretcher. The figure on the stretcher was encased in a body bag.

Brand watched until the stretcher was loaded into an ambulance and the doors were closed, then he looked down at his hands.

"It wasn't your fault."

He didn't say anything or move, but she felt him withdraw.

"You did everything you could. You saved my life."

He shook his head.

"You did. You are the bravest, most honorable man I've ever known. You've been rescuing me and keeping me safe ever since that first night."

Lily's heart felt torn in two. She knew Brand didn't trust love. It had been a long time since she had. But the past few days had reminded her of how unselfish, how generous love was supposed to be.

And how fulfilling.

Brand was afraid of giving his heart, and he had ample reason. Yet she'd seen over and over the proof of his enormous capacity for love. His loyalty to his family, his concern for her and her dad. Even his heartache at the death of the fellow officer who had betrayed him.

She'd felt it in his kiss and in his gentle yet fierce lovemaking.

He hadn't been capable of hiding his goodness and integrity, not even behind a bad-guy facade.

She'd come to know him well in the brief time they'd been forced to rely on each other. She knew he was one of the good guys.

But she also knew that if she let him go tonight, she would never see him again. He might never be able to make the first move. He'd had too much hurt in his life.

Hesitating, she reached for his hand and squeezed his fingers with hers.

"Brand, tell me how you feel. Please." She heard her voice break.

For a moment he sat stiff, rigid. Then he slipped his hand out of her grasp and reached for the car door.

Her heart shattered. He couldn't do it. He couldn't open up.

She swallowed. "Don't go."

He pulled up on the door handle until it clicked open.

A huge lump grew in Lily's throat, making it hard for her to breathe. She bit her lip in an effort to keep tears from gathering.

He tensed, and she waited for him to push the door open and get out of the car. She steeled herself to watch him walk away.

After what seemed like an eternity, he let go of the handle and without raising his head he held out his hand.

She took it.

"I don't understand love," he said quietly. "Why people want it. It hurts. It bleeds. It destroys." He took a breath. "Look at Springer. He loved his wife and children, but she left him and took his kids away, and it ended up killing him."

His fingers tightened. "Look at my family. We're champions at hurting each other. Always have been." He stopped.

"It doesn't have to be like that."

His head jerked as if in response to a blow. "How the hell would you know? Your husband betrayed you in the worst way."

"I don't believe everyone is like him. I believe there are genuinely good people in the world. People worthy of great love. I believe true love can be wonderful."

He was silent for a moment, but he didn't let go of her hand. "What I've found out these last few days is that trying not to love hurts even more." His head bent over their clasped hands.

Lily tried not to rejoice at his words. She had no idea what he was going to say.

She gazed at his dark, tousled hair, at his vulnerable nape, at the trickle of blood drying on his neck. His silky hair and the fine shape of his head made her throat hurt.

It was a moment before he spoke again. "You've been very brave. But I've got to know. Just how brave are you, Lily Raines?" He raised his head. "Are you brave enough to try life with a man who knows nothing about love?"

Lily couldn't move. She was stunned. Had she really heard right? Was he asking her for a lifetime commitment?

Slowly, her mouth stretched in a huge smile. She leaned over and placed her palm against his cheek and turned his head until he looked into her eyes.

"I don't think there's a woman on the planet who's that brave. But thank goodness I don't have to worry about that. The man I love and want to live my life with knows all about love."

Brand's blue eyes sparkled. "You think so?" he asked hoarsely.

She kissed him gently on the lips. "I know so. But if he doesn't mind, I sure would like to hear him say it."

His eyes softened and he smiled. "Say what?"

"I love you."

"Oh, that. I love you, Lily Raines."

He loved her. Her heart soared with joy. "I love you, too, Brand Gallagher—if that *is* your real name."

Brand laughed and lifted her hand to his lips.

"Brandon Christopher Gallagher. That's all of it." He kissed each knuckle then turned her hand over and kissed the palm.

"I don't know why you love me, Lily, but I'm grateful that you do."

"You don't know why?" She looked deep into his blue eyes. "I'd have thought you'd figured that one out by now," she said. "It's obvious, Brandon Christopher Gallagher. You're one of the good guys."

* * * * *

Special Offers

Every month we put together collections and longer reads written by your favourite authors.

Here are some of next month's highlights—and don't miss our fabulous discount online!

On sale 18th January

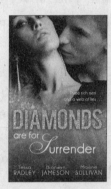

On sale 1st February

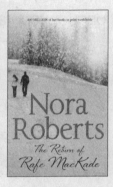

On sale 1st February

Save 20% on all Special Releases

Find out more at
www.millsandboon.co.uk/specialreleases

Visit us Online

0213/ST/MB399

The World of Mills & Boon®

There's a Mills & Boon® series that's perfect for you. We publish ten series and, with new titles every month, you never have to wait long for your favourite to come along.

Blaze.
Scorching hot, sexy reads
4 new stories every month

By Request
Relive the romance with the best of the best
9 new stories every month

Cherish™
Romance to melt the heart every time
12 new stories every month

Desire™
Passionate and dramatic love stories
8 new stories every month

 # *Have Your Say*

You've just finished your book. So what did you think?

We'd love to hear your thoughts on our 'Have your say' online panel
www.millsandboon.co.uk/haveyoursay

- 🌹 Easy to use
- 🌹 Short questionnaire
- 🌹 Chance to win Mills & Boon® goodies